"STAY AWAY FROM ME, JENNIFER,"

Devlin said.

"Why?" Her breasts still trembled from his touch. Dropping his hands from her bodice, he turned away roughly.

"Because eventually I'll take that luscious body of yours. I'll forget that you're the boss's daughter. . . ."

She scurried off the blanket, and when he looked up again she had mounted her horse and was riding toward him. Jennifer pulled the horse to a halt.

"Is this where I'm supposed to take fright and flee, grateful to have escaped the beast McShane? Why is it that I don't scare that easily anymore?"

He grabbed the bridle, genuinely angry now.

"I'll not offer you marriage." His free hand slid up her thigh, and a mocking grin twisted his handsome features. "But if you insist, I'll guarantee satisfaction for services rendered."

Montana Skies

Jan McKee

PUBLISHED BY POCKET BOOKS NEW YORK

This book is dedicated to:
Ron—The very wind beneath my sails
Mike and Mark—The sunshine in my life
Pop—The navigator, keeping the course straight
and
Iverne—The guiding star, shining brightly all
along the journey

An *Original* publication of POCKET BOOKS

POCKET BOOKS, a division of Simon & Schuster, Inc., 1230 Avenue of the Americas, New York, N.Y. 10020

ISBN: 0-671-50835-0

First Pocket Books Printing March, 1986

10 9 8 7 6 5 4 3 2 1

POCKET and colophon are registered trademarks of Simon & Schuster, Inc.

Printed in the U.S.A.

PART I

Chapter One

James Douglas gravitated toward the window, seeking relief from the stifling heat. A coal-burning stove had turned the small office into a bakehouse, and he jerked at the knot of his tie, loosening the high-collared shirt with an impatient gesture that mirrored his mood. It was time—past time—to go home.

He attempted to shut out the nasal whine coming from the attorney seated behind him, only to find the noises of the city outside even more grating. Below this third-story window, the denizens of New York City went about the business of living with a passionate and raucous intensity that no longer had the power to fascinate the rancher from Montana. During the day hawkers called out as they sold their wares at nearly every corner. Freight wagons, many fitted out with jangling bells, maneuvered through the heavy traffic, their drivers often hurling obscene curses at pedestrians and carriages blocking the perpetually crowded streets. And at night . . .

Fatigue tightened the band of pain encircling his brow while Arthur Grayburn snorted and sniffed, his sermon temporarily interrupted by the sinus condition for which there appeared to be no cure. James managed a rueful smile as he watched the gaunt little man toss more coal into the red-hot stove. He had only his own folly to blame for the current discomfort, and the homesickness that had grown to almost unbearable proportions over the last week.

3

For a time the activity and noise of civilization had been what he'd needed. His father's death, quickly followed by heavy November snows, had trapped James with his grief through the seemingly endless winter. At the first sign of thaw he risked the trek to Cheyenne and the train that would carry him east. But never had he dreamed this particular aspect of his business would tie him to New York weeks longer than he intended.

"James, have you heard a single word I've said?"

With a heavy sigh, James turned smoky gray eyes on his attorney. "If you've been summarizing the waste of a morning, Arthur, don't bother."

Grayburn could only shake his head and roll watery blue eyes. "Good heavens, man. Did you expect finding a governess for the child would be easy? Most of the women we interviewed this morning come from sheltered environments; some have never journeyed outside this city. You're asking them to travel more than halfway across the continent to an uncivilized wilderness. Be reasonable, James. Why, it was only three short years ago that our newspapers were reporting the grisly details of General Custer's inglorious defeat."

Grayburn didn't add that by his appearance alone, James did not meet the criteria for an enviable employer. With his full black beard and unfashionably long hair, the man looked like a pirate. And although he was just slightly above medium height, his wide-shouldered frame and barrel chest made a formidable impression. Three of the five women interviewed this morning barely survived the introduction. The remaining two had completely missed the gentle eyes and true nature of this rugged rancher, intimidated as they were by blunt questions and unmasked irritation over their responses.

"Hell," James scoffed, "Indians are the last thing they need to worry about. A single blast of Montana air would see any one of those lily-livered females flat on their . . . backsides. It was a fool idea, Arthur. Jennifer would be better off continuing her lessons with me. Maggie can see to her manners."

Arthur Grayburn's eyebrows shot upward with alarm. "You'd turn over your daughter's upbringing to an unlettered Irish kitchen maid? Have you forgotten Jennifer's heritage? She's a Baxter. Wilfred would spin in his grave at the thought of his granddaughter being reared with indifference to her position in society."

With a lift of his hand, James effectively silenced the mortified attorney. Grayburn was a snob. A well-intentioned one, but a snob nonetheless. Jenny's society consisted of cowhands and cattle; maybe an occasional visit from another rancher with a pedigree no more impressive than his own. And at the age of nine, his daughter had little interest in bloodlines except as they applied to horseflesh. Still, James couldn't completely ignore Grayburn's concern, not to mention his own strong determination to provide Jennifer with every advantage.

"And what of Louise, James?" the lawyer continued, knowing this particular argument would be more effective. "Surely you realize Louise would have wanted her child taught the proper decorum suitable for a young lady."

James Douglas's dark features twisted with pain. The attorney's words thrust deep into a wound yet unhealed after nine lonely years. Grayburn's expression softened when James hid his grief by turning back to the window.

In 1867, James had first appeared in this very office, his pockets filled with Montana gold and his head filled with dreams of a great cattle empire. It was twelve years ago, and there had been no beard to cover the young man's handsome features. The dark gray eyes had been so clearly unworldly that Wilfred Baxter, Grayburn's late partner, had taken pity on the naive young stranger. In return for his kindness, James had captured the heart of Baxter's lovely daughter. With hurricane force the romance swept aside a dismayed father's objections. Louise Baxter took this uncultured cowboy as husband, leaving everything familiar behind. To his credit, James had made Louise sublimely happy in their short time together. That his grief over her loss was still so raw gave testimony to the deep love they'd shared. Some men might have held a grudge against the child whose

5

birth had robbed them of such joy. But it was not in James Douglas's nature to harbor ill feelings. He was devoted to his daughter.

"Patience, James. I'm sure someone suitable will be found."

"Two weeks, Arthur. I'm leaving in two weeks. With or without that teacher."

As he stepped out onto the busy street, James nearly collided with a woman rushing by, her arms loaded with packages. He mumbled an apology and filled his lungs with the crisp March air. The sun glared blindingly off the whitewashed buildings, causing him to crash into several other shoppers before his eyes began to adjust. The narrow walkway and the throngs of people intensified the closed-in feeling that had begun in his lawyer's office, and his teeth clenched involuntarily as a man's elbow jabbed into his midsection. By the time he had walked three blocks he was dangerously close to taking out his bad temper on the next man or woman who trod on his foot or forced him into the side of a building by refusing to step aside.

He didn't see the thin figure that crashed into him as he rounded the corner. Losing his footing, he instinctively reached out and dragged his attacker down with him so that they both lay sprawled on the sidewalk, arms and legs entangled. Finally, an enraged James hauled the offender up and held him against the wall. He had been warned against pickpockets and their manner of relieving a man of his possessions.

So intent was he on making sure his wallet was safe, he didn't look at his quarry until the thin body went limp and sagged against him. Thinking this another trick, James automatically balled his hand into a fist as he shoved his dirty burden back against the wall. His eyes widened in shock at the sight before him, then he looked in disgust at the hand that had been prepared to strike this pitiful specimen of humanity. He was sickened by the boy's face. The right side was swollen and distended with bruises in shades varying from yellow to purple. The eye on that side was swollen completely shut and dried blood crusted the lips and chin.

The youngster's body slumped in defeat as James surveyed his appearance. Blondish hair was matted together and hung nearly to his shoulders. His clothes were tattered and much too small for the long-legged frame. He was so thin that James could feel the ribs protruding from the fleshless body as his chest heaved, the ragged breathing hinting he had run a long distance. Something about this poor creature tugged at James's heart and he relaxed the hand that held the boy so firmly against the wall. The boy's knees buckled and James's arms shot out to give him support.

Suddenly the lifeless body came to life. The youngster straightened to his full height, his one good eye defiant and amazingly clear as he challenged the man who held him.

"I'm sorry I knocked ye down, sir. Let me go and I'll be on me way." There was a kind of wild dignity in his manner.

James blocked the boy's retreat. The pure, deep blue of the boy's good eye turned almost black with fear before becoming nearly violet with rage. The boy lunged, futilely trying to push James aside as he struggled in the strong man's grasp. James was startled by the intensity and wondered if he had cornered a wildcat.

"Who are you running from?" James demanded as he once again pinned the struggling body against the wall.

"Please!" the youngster wailed, his voice rising toward hysteria.

The cruelly battered face and the frantic tone of the plea brought out all the fatherly instincts in James. Whoever he was, wherever he was from, no human being deserved this kind of treatment. James relaxed his hold on the boy and stepped away. If the boy's face was a mirror of the kind of life he had led, he deserved at least a chance to make a better one.

"God bless ye, sir," the boy whispered hoarsely as he hurriedly bent to retrieve a bundle that had fallen from his hands when he collided with James.

James was reaching in his pocket to offer the boy some

money when he was violently pushed aside. A villainous-looking man grabbed the boy and began to beat him about the head and upper shoulders with his closed fist.

Shaking off his momentary shock, James gave an enraged roar and grabbed the man from behind, flinging him away from the terrorized child. He didn't see the flash of steel in the man's hand until the boy cried out a warning. He was able to avoid the first thrust of the knife and move quickly, imprisoning the man's wrist and cracking it over his knee. He felt the large bone snap as the knife clattered harmlessly to the street. The man screamed his agony and his face went white as he grabbed his broken wrist and backed away from the savage fury that advanced upon him.

James watched as the man seemed to disappear into the crowd of onlookers that had gathered. His smoky gaze swept the crowd in disgust. Not one of them would have lifted a hand to help either himself or the boy, not even to summon a policeman.

"The show is over—be on your way!" he shouted as he turned back to the boy sprawled on the sidewalk, his arms thrown over his head in an instinctive gesture of self-protection. James gently turned the boy and examined a fresh cut bleeding profusely above the good eye. He picked up the fallen bundle and, placing his arm around the youngster, lifted him gently. The boy groaned.

"Can you walk on your own, son?" James queried.

The boy slowly raised his head and gave James a blank stare, then nodded, leaning heavily against his rescuer as they made their way down the crowded street. Soon the effort of putting one foot in front of the other became too much and his knees buckled beneath him.

James lifted the boy and carried him toward a hansom cab parked about a block away. After placing the boy inside the vehicle, he looked around for the driver.

A little man scurried out of a building nearby, his face anxious and his smile apologetic. "Sorry, sir, this cab is already spoken for. I'm to wait on a gentleman who will return shortly."

The man trembled at the ferocity of James's gaze. "I have

an injured child inside this cab. Now you can either get your ass up on your perch or I'll drive the damn thing myself!"

When the cab pulled up in front of the hotel, James threw a wad of bills at the driver and carried the ragged creature into the lobby. He shouted at the manager as he proceeded to the stairway. The manager rushed from behind his desk and stared dumbly at James.

"Didn't you hear me, man? Summon a physician!" James bellowed from the bottom stair. "And be quick about it!"

The expression on the hotel manager's face changed to outrage. "You don't really intend to bring that filthy thing in here, do you, Mr. Douglas?" he challenged.

James released his hold on the boy's legs and grabbed the man by the collar of his shirt. "If you don't have a doctor here within the hour, I give you my oath you won't look much better."

When the man's face began to redden, James released his hold. He said in disgust, "My God, man, he's only a boy, not an animal. Have you no fellow feeling?"

He ignored the man's continued bleating and made his way up the long staircase to his room, stumbling several times under the weight of his burden.

In his room, he gently placed the boy in the middle of the bed. The child was listless, and he drifted in and out of a dazed sort of sleep. He did not protest when James began removing the filthy, tattered clothing. The older man gasped in horror at the scarred back and the freshly raised welts and oozing wounds. He swallowed the bile that rose in his throat at the sight of those deep furrows and the smell of unwashed flesh.

Less than an hour later the doctor arrived and quickly, efficiently examined the boy. He muttered to himself as he cleansed the wounds and applied healing ointments. Although the poor creature moaned from time to time, he appeared locked in a fitful sleep. His task complete, the doctor furiously placed the tools of his trade in his bag and snapped it shut before turning to James.

"Besides his obvious injuries the child is suffering from

malnutrition. He needs rest, food, and decent care. Are you prepared to provide such?"

In spite of the caustic tone in the doctor's voice, James could see compassion in the man's eyes and quickly assured him that the child's needs would be met. He paid the fee the doctor stated and walked with the man to the door.

At the door the physician paused. "He's a wild thing from the streets and will probably rob you blind the minute he's on his feet."

"He's a child," James insisted, angered at the man's assumption.

The doctor lifted one eyebrow. "Is he? And what difference does that make? Call me again should he grow worse."

The boy was floating on a soft cloud. There were no fears in this beautiful place. He was warm again, and his father was wiping his brow and speaking to him softly. It was all a bad dream, and he would soon awaken in his own bed in Ireland. There was a soft smile on his lips as he heard his mother's singing and his father's booming laughter as he bounced little Sean on his knee.

The smile was still on his face as he opened his eyes, saying a silent prayer that the nightmare had ended. His eyes widened and then squeezed tightly shut again. The unfamiliar surroundings bespoke neither his waking dream nor his living nightmare. He began to tremble violently in the cold grip of terror. At the touch of a hand on his brow his eyes fluttered open. He jerked his head away from that gentle hand, sending daggers of pain through his temples. He could not prevent the strangled cry that escaped his lips. He hated himself for this show of weakness yet was unable to stop the tremors that shook his body or the tears that burned in his eyes.

"Settle down, son," a voice crooned. "I mean you no harm."

The boy heard the gentleness in the man's voice and searched the face for verification of the words. He found no cruelty in the dark gray eyes, and as his mind cleared, he recognized the man and remembered their encounter.

10

"Jake?" the boy croaked in a hoarse whisper.

"If you're asking about that miserable excuse for a man who attacked you, I can give you my oath he won't be bothering you again."

The boy had no reason to trust this stranger, but he did. He sighed and once again escaped into the void.

For three days the boy drifted within a nightmare haze while he fought the demons that pursued him. Only the soothing voice of the man who continually assured him of safety as he bathed his hot body prevailed upon his instinct for survival. And then, all at once, consciousness was thrust upon him and he could no longer retreat to his dreaming world. He opened his eyes with difficulty, finding them crusted with pus, and gazed up at the man sleeping upright in the chair beside the bed. In slumber, the harsh lines of the man's face were softened, the wintry gray eyes hidden. The boy cautiously moved his body, wincing as aching muscles protested the activity. Struggling into a sitting position, he surveyed the magnificence of the room—velvets and silks, rich mahogany tables, and above his head a canopy of the finest lace—before his trembling arms gave way and he fell back against the pillow.

At the sound of movement from the bed, James's eyes flew open. He breathed a sigh of relief to find that the deep blue eyes were clear and unclouded with fever, though it tore at his heart to see the wild panic in those startling eyes. He compared it to the look of the wild things he had trapped in his snares as a youth. He watched, in silence, the rapid rise and fall of the boy's chest as he fought to conquer his anxiety. He moved quietly, cautiously, to the boy's side, feeling the frail body stiffen as he placed his hand on the cool brow. The blue eyes closed, and there was one more convulsive shudder before they opened again to stare in defiance.

"Careful, or you'll work yourself up into another fever," James cautioned kindly. "You are safe here with me."

The word *safe* brought back vague memories of gentle hands bathing his fevered body as a soft, deep voice spoke that word over and over again. An ache welled up within his chest, and he bit the inside of his mouth till it bled to prevent the tears that threatened to spill. Would he ever feel safe again?

Pity and anger warred within James. Pity that any child should have to suffer the agony this one clearly had, and anger at the truth he knew lay behind the nightmarish ravings he had heard these last three days. James was possessed as he had never been before with the urge to kill. This child's tormentor deserved a fate no less brutal than the one he had visited upon his victim.

He pulled on the bell rope beside the bed, then turned to the boy. "I've ordered some food, so you will have to let me help you into a sitting position."

There was no argument from the bed and as soon as the pillows rested behind the boy's back, James went to the wardrobe to pull out a clean shirt. When he turned back, the boy was studying him in watchful silence, the fear gone from his eyes. James buttoned his shirt and casually stuffed it inside his trousers. Every movement was designed to convey normalcy and security.

"What's your name, son?"

The boy's head snapped up, and James was pleased to see a spark of pride in that battered face and hear a voice that was clear and strong, its heavy brogue signaling his origins. "Devlin McShane, sir."

James's smile was as wide as the Yellowstone as he returned to the bed and took the boy's hand from the coverlet to clasp it tightly. "My name is Douglas, James Douglas. What part of Ireland do you hail from?"

"Near Dublin," came the faltering reply.

"Well, Devlin McShane from near Dublin, I'm from Montana and, to folks in these parts, that makes us both foreigners."

Further conversation was halted by a knock on the door. James took the tray from the man who stood in the doorway craning his neck to peek at the subject of the hotel's gossip. He shut the door in the man's face and set the tray on the table beside the bed. After he spread a napkin across Devlin's chest, he picked up the spoon to begin ladling the warm broth into the boy's mouth, but the spoon was jerked rudely from his hand as the broth dripped down Devlin's chin.

"I think I'm capable of doing for myself. Besides, yer wastin' most of it."

James laughed outright and plunged into his own breakfast with zeal. He seriously doubted those trembling hands would be any more adept than his own, but was pleased to see the show of spirit.

As soon as the breakfast tray had been removed and James was dressed for the day, he turned to the boy and explained that he had an appointment with his attorney. He didn't miss the gleam in the boy's eyes and was quick to quell the thoughts he easily recognized there. "When I return I will order you a bath and a barber. Don't even think about trying to leave, because your legs wouldn't carry you across the room. I don't think you've had much reason to trust anyone lately, Devlin McShane, but right now you don't have much choice either."

Devlin closed his eyes at the soft closing of the door, cursing his weakness. Safety, trust—just words that people mouthed without meaning. He threw back the cover and, clutching the sheet, tried to rise from the bed. After only a few moments of struggle he fell back exhausted. At least the man told one truth. He didn't have the strength to chart his own destiny right now; he couldn't even get out of bed.

When James reached Arthur Grayburn's office, he was introduced to a Miss Hastings, a tall, severe woman who looked down on him from her superior height. She seemed an unlikely prospect for the position of governess to Jennifer, but James politely questioned the woman about her qualifications, making clear his requirements.

Before he was halfway through his recital the woman brusquely interrupted him. "Mr. Douglas, Mr. Grayburn has already given me these facts. I would waste neither your time nor mine if I were not seriously considering the post. First, let me state my terms, and then you can decide if you will be able to meet my requirements.

"My parents died a year ago and my brother has managed to ruin the family's business and reputation. Except for the house, which they wisely left to me, I have nothing. I am twenty-seven years old and, as you can see, my prospects for matrimony are nonexistent. The one advantage I do possess is a fine education.

"If you accept my terms, I propose to tutor your child for no more than five years. At the end of that period I will move farther westward, most likely to San Francisco, where I intend to open an academy for young women. The salary you offer is more than generous and I assume my living expenses will be few when I am in your employ. I intend to sell my home and expect the proceeds from that and the money I save from my salary to cover the cost of establishing my school."

James suppressed the urge to laugh. She had said her prospects for matrimony were nonexistent, and he felt a twinge of guilt for his amusement at this woman's expense. To call her plain was to understate the case. Her face was birdlike with the narrow hooked nose and pinched features, but James admired her straightforward manner and was prepared to hire her on the spot.

"I have no objection to your plans, Miss Hastings; they are, in fact, admirable. But have you considered how lonely it might be on a ranch in the middle of Montana with only a child and one other woman for company?"

Miss Hastings weighed his words thoughtfully and when she spoke, it was with the same forthrightness. "I assume that this other woman does not perform wifely duties that might influence the child's morals."

James nearly strangled on his words. "Maggie is my housekeeper and has cared for Jennifer since her birth. You suggest something of that nature to her and you, madame, will be eating what is left of your teeth for a week."

Miss Hastings nodded and gave him a weak apologetic smile. "I'm sure this Maggie and I will be able to find some common ground to keep one another company. As for the child, I have a fondness for most children. One little girl should not be difficult to handle."

James leaned forward in his chair, a thought springing to his mind unbidden. "And if there were two children?"

The woman didn't hesitate with her response. "Well, then, I would simply increase my fee."

Arthur Grayburn looked at James in dismay, his eyebrows almost reaching his hairline, but he didn't voice his question when he caught James's quelling glance.

When she had gone, the two men sat together, snifters of brandy in their hands. James looked quite pleased with himself, and Arthur Grayburn was dying to ask the meaning of James's last question to Miss Hastings.

"Before you have a fit of apoplexy, Arthur," James said with a smirk, "I do not have an illegitimate child stashed away somewhere. I'm not even sure why I asked the question, but I'm damned glad to know the answer to it."

"I can assure you, James, Annabelle Hastings is quite qualified."

"Annabelle?" James choked on his brandy. "Annabelle? My God, how could anyone name that woman Annabelle? She proposes to travel across most of the United States alone, shows me a revolver big enough to lay out a buffalo, and gives departure and arrival dates like a general. Annabelle?"

Fearing James had lost his reason, Arthur clapped him soundly on the back as the man continued to choke out his laughter. "Are you going to give her the position?"

"Hell, yes!" James shouted as he wiped his eyes with the back of his sleeve. "I wouldn't miss seeing that woman spar with Maggie and Sam for anything. Besides, a bit of her spunk couldn't help but do my little Jennifer good. She's far too quiet."

Devlin lay back in the big tub and allowed the hot soapy water to soak the soreness out of his aching body. The water stung the lacerations on his back, but the smell of clean skin and freshly washed hair was worth the discomfort.

He lifted his broad, long-fingered hand from the water and admired the neatly trimmed nails, now free of grime.

Such luxury for the son of Patrick McShane. The big copper tub was huge compared to the barrel he had barely been able to squeeze into at home on the few occasions a full bath had been allowed. This must be the life of ease Patrick had dreamed of when he set his sights on America.

He avoided looking at the mirror that was placed in a corner of this room used strictly for bathing. The sight of his thin, long-legged frame with its covering of bruises and welts made him want to retch. He closed his eyes, remembering a strapping young boy running across lush green fields, his face splitting in a wide grin. For his mother's sake, he said a small prayer for the lost soul of that child who had begun to die on a ship in the Atlantic and who had ceased to exist on the streets of New York.

He was too tired to protest when James entered to help him from the tub. Silently he endured the touch of the man who dried his body and reapplied the soothing ointments to his wounds. If the man's intent was to abuse him there was nothing he could do about it now. But God help the man later, for he would never be abused again without exacting his measure of revenge.

As he pulled one of his own nightshirts over the boy's head, James asked, "How old are you, Devlin?"

"Past thirteen," the boy answered weakly, his eyes heavy with fatigue.

"You're tall for your age," James observed. "Do you have family that might be worrying about you?"

He shook his dark blond head and leaned heavily on James as they made their way toward the big four-poster bed.

"What about in Ireland?" James pressed.

The blue eyes closed in exhaustion, and James barely heard the whispered reply. "No . . . nowhere in this world."

Each day the boy's strength grew. Whenever James left the room he would pull his body from the bed. At first he managed only a few steps, but now he was able to make it to the window and back without his legs threatening to fold under him.

He was standing at the window when James returned from a shopping expedition. Devlin hid a smile at the sight of the man's arms weighted down with packages. Now he would be forced to listen, in detail, to the reason for each purchase and the person the gift was intended for.

"Up and about, I see," James commented as he pulled off his overcoat and slung it on the chair.

Devlin took a deep breath, gathering courage. "I'll be needing my clothes," he stated bluntly.

"Threw the filthy rags out," James replied calmly, ignoring the imperious tone.

"Threw them out?" Devlin said incredulously. "And just who gave you the authority to be throwing out me only possessions?"

"The critters they were infested with," James replied, pleased at his own wit. "Sorry, didn't know you were so attached to the little varmints."

Angry at being an object of sport, the boy flashed darkened eyes at James. "And did you also see fit to throw out me bundle with the only money I had to make my own way?"

Humor fled at the boy's attitude, and James's next words were anything but gentle. "Don't get snappish with me, Devlin McShane. You'll find your things in the drawer of the table beside the bed."

James watched sadly, his momentary anger fading, as the boy inventoried his personal possessions. If he expected to see a display of emotion, he was disappointed. When Devlin returned the small Bible, silver chain, and gold coins to the drawer, he turned back to James. His eyes were dry and his face was set in its usual impassive expression.

James untied the last package and tossed its contents at the boy. "Here. I think this will make up for the loss of your rags."

Devlin caught the garments easily, stifling the impulse to throw the soft cotton shirt and the stiff trousers back into

17

the man's face. Something in James's eyes prevented him from this ungracious act, and he stepped into the underwear before pulling the unyielding trousers over his thin legs.

"I'll be strong enough to fend for myself in a day or two. If ye'll tell me where to send it, I'll see that you get repaid for all your kindness."

James advanced across the room, grabbing the boy by his shoulders and giving him a none too gentle shake. "A simple 'thank you very kindly, Mr. Douglas' would suffice for now."

Seeing the hurt mixed with anger in James's eyes, Devlin lowered his head in shame. "A McShane pays his debts."

James tightened his grip on the boy's shoulders. He *must* break through that hard shell. If he didn't, he knew it would be more merciful to open the window and toss the boy out onto the street.

"A *man* pays his debts, McShane, and you don't yet qualify for that title. A man also knows when to put pride aside and accept the kindness of others. If the situations were reversed, and I had been the one bleeding on the street, would you have left me lying there?"

Devlin considered his answer carefully before he gave the man a level look. "Aye, at the time I'd have left ye swimming in your own blood."

"Never give an inch, do you, boy?" James said ruefully. While he admired the honesty of the reply, he couldn't help being disappointed by it.

Later the same day James received a message that two Hereford bulls he had arranged to purchase from a man in New Hampshire had been received at the stockyards along with the other breeding stock he'd bought in the East. James grabbed Devlin and danced about the room. "I can quit this city and go home now. Tonight I'll order us the best damned dinner this hotel can provide. I feel like celebrating!"

James rushed out to check on his new stock, leaving Devlin to contemplate the reality of his future. Not since his father's death had he been able to feel anything for another human being, but he had developed a real fondness for this burly, bearded man. He winced at the thought of being separated from James.

He paced the room like a cat in a gilded cage. He had said too many good-byes in his life; he wouldn't do it again if he could help it. He walked to the bedside table and removed his possessions, leaving two gold coins on the table. He had his hand on the doorknob before the fact of his bare feet made him pause. The laughter that emerged from his throat was humorless. "You're a big, hulking fool, McShane, to think that new clothes and a haircut will find you decent work. All a man would have to do is look down at your bare toes and hear your pretty Irish brogue and, before nightfall, ye'd be right back on the streets again."

James was pleasantly surprised to find the boy in high spirits when he returned. He found Devlin to be a good listener as he outlined his plans and hopes for the future of the Douglas ranch. He gave such vivid descriptions of Sam, Maggie, and his beloved Jennifer that Devlin could almost picture the scenes he had never seen. James was the actor, playing all the roles and eliciting an occasional smile and guarded chuckle from his rapt audience of one.

When he had finished with his tales and his supper, James leaned back in his chair and drew a cigar from his pocket. While the smoke curled about him, he studied the face across the table with renewed interest. The swelling had receded and only faint discoloration remained. With a little more meat on it, the youthful face might be called handsome with its strong bone structure, the high, proud brow, the stubborn chin, and the firm, well-molded lips. But it was the eyes that drew attention: a deep pure blue set off by long spiky lashes. If his hands and feet were any indication, someday he'd be of a size that a man would think twice before laying another rod to his back.

"I've been hoping you'd volunteer to tell me about yourself, Dev, but so far you haven't said a word about your family. I don't believe for one minute that you just sprang from the streets of New York City. I know you can read because I've seen you with the newspaper. Your table manners are more than passable. You have, or had, a family somewhere, people who cared enough about you to teach you the things a boy should know."

Devlin jumped up from his chair, startled by the assault on his carefully guarded privacy, but before he could escape, James shoved him down.

"I almost took a knife in my gut for you, boy. I've bathed your fevered body and clothed and fed you for more than three weeks. I'm not prying because of some freakish curiosity, but because I genuinely want to know. It's fine you want to pay me with the few coins in your pocket, but what you owe me has nothing to do with money."

Devlin pleaded with his eyes. To tell this man would open wounds far deeper than the scars on his back.

"Tell me," James ordered. Then he folded his arms and waited.

Chapter Two

It was a long time before the boy spoke, and when he did, his words were halting, the memories they pictured as distant and bittersweet as the land he came from. He began with his father, Patrick McShane, who had been the head groom on a large estate in Ireland owned by a family named Bozworth. Generations of McShanes had lived on that land, long before the English or the Bozworths. All the men were tall, broad shouldered, and handsome. Patrick McShane had been no less so.

Proud without being arrogant, he never lamented that he had been born in the wrong century, a servant rather than a master. He accepted his lot with dignity. During the famine thousands had died, but the McShanes survived because they were hardy and strong, and because they were willing to serve men like Lord Bozworth.

All Patrick really cared about in this world was his wife, Maureen, his sons, and the horses. For them he would cheerfully endure servitude. If he felt differently inside, he never let it show.

"A man is only as good or as bad as he believes himself to be," he would often tell his son. "He is not what others would call him."

For an Englishman, Lord Bozworth was a good master. The McShanes had their own cottage not far from the stables, and Maureen was proud of her home, her children, and the garden she tended daily. Some Nordic ancestor had willed her his wheat-blond hair, and Patrick McShane

21

thought her the most beautiful woman ever born. That she was Irish no one who had felt the lash of her tongue would deny. Her blood flowed with the untamed spirit of her race, tempered by the love of her husband and the two strong sons she had borne him.

Devlin worked in the stable with his father for half the day and then returned to the cottage to look after his baby brother while his mother did the wash and tended her garden. This was a special time for him, for Maureen McShane, who had been to parish school as a child, would read the most marvelous stories, slowly teaching Devlin the letters so he could in turn read to little Sean. Sometimes she just talked as she worked, telling her son the history of their people and recounting the legends or the heroes of Ireland.

The only time Devlin had heard harsh words between his parents had been over his learning to read. "An education is a blight on the Irish!" yelled Patrick. "He'll be gettin' ideas above his station and soon be marchin' off to fight the tyranny."

"Don't you be wantin' a better life for your son, Patrick?" Maureen countered, her eyes flashing blue flame. "Do you forever want him cleaning stables and being less than he can be?"

"I want him alive!" Patrick shouted back. "There's no future in Ireland for the likes of us. Why do you think I'm saving every shilling I can? Someday I'll send him to America where he can be his own master. Someday we might all go."

Devlin listened quietly as they argued his fate. Each was as stubborn as the other. Privately he agreed with his mother, but such was the love he had for his father that he kept his silence.

When Sean was three, Lord Harry, old Bozworth's only son and the devil incarnate, came home from Cambridge. He had been sent down in disgrace from the university, and his father had washed his hands of the young man.

Patrick cursed the way the young master misused the fine-blooded animals he rode, but he had no hint of his darker nature. He made nothing of the fact that the path

Harry always rode went past their little cottage, nor did he think to question when Lord Harry ordered Devlin, now close to twelve years, to spend most of his days tending the horses with his Da.

Only Devlin noticed the trepidation in Maureen's face when Lord Harry rode by on his prancing stallion. He took to sneaking home several times a day just to see that all was well.

One day he had heard his mother's voice cry out in rage and pain as he leapt the stone fence that surrounded the cottage. He hit the door with such force that he nearly fell to the floor as the wood crashed against the wall. He would never forget the sight of Lord Harry straddling his mother and fumbling at his trousers at the same time he tried to subdue the fiercely struggling Maureen.

Seeing her son, Maureen had struggled all the more and screamed, "Get your father!"

Devlin raced across the fields to his father. Seeing the look on Devlin's face, Patrick instantly became alert. "What is it, son?"

Out of breath, Dev could only manage a whispered "Mother" before racing out of the stable, his father close at his heels. Patrick's long legs soon outdistanced his son's, and when Devlin reached the house he found Patrick with his big hands around Lord Harry's throat, the man's face beginning to blacken. Maureen pulled desperately at her husband's arms, begging him to stop.

"Pat, please . . . I'm not hurt. You got here in time. Oh, sweet Jesus, please stop!"

Knowing what the penalty would be if his father succeeded in killing this man, Devlin joined his mother, and soon Patrick's hold slackened as Lord Harry dropped to the floor. He had escaped punishment for his deeds once again. As the son of a high-ranking lord, he could rob, abuse, rape, and murder the servants on his land. No English law would convict him. But Patrick might hang yet for daring to defend his wife, his home, and his honor.

Patrick pulled together the tattered remains of his wife's blouse to cover her heaving breasts and, turning to his son, said, "Bring Lord Bozworth to me. If I'm to spend the rest of my life in some English prison for this scum of humanity, I at least want his father to know why."

Devlin raced toward the manor, not stopping when the footman tried to block his path to the old lord's library. "My father says to come and see what your son has done!"

Lord Bozworth only lifted an eyebrow at the audacity of this youngster. "Just what, pray tell, has Harry done that Patrick McShane should order me to do his bidding?"

Devlin fairly screamed at the old man, "He attacked my mother and tore her clothes. My father almost killed him."

Lord Bozworth immediately rose from his chair, calling for his horse. Minutes later, he stood at the doorway of McShane's cottage, his eyes scanning the interior. He noted the black rage in Patrick's eyes and the disheveled Maureen. His brown eyes blazed contempt at his son, who sat rubbing his aching, bruised throat.

"Pat, I give you my oath that this will never happen again. I'll shoot the whelp myself before he can force himself on an innocent, good woman such as your wife."

Lord Bozworth was as good as his word. He banished Harry from the estate, sending him to an uncle in the Indies. Once again there was peace, although Patrick could not forget his vulnerable position. He continued to save his meager wages in the hope that someday they would all be able to escape.

His dreams might have been realized had not the plague struck that summer. It didn't discriminate between rich and poor, and the old lord died along with half the people on the estate.

Little Sean had been the first to sicken and die, followed shortly afterward by Maureen. Devlin had been too ill himself to remember any part of their passing, but when the fever broke he found Patrick by his bedside, his usually bright eyes devoid of light. Patrick had taken his son in his arms and wept. It was the son who gave his father comfort as the wracking sobs shook the strong body. The strangled cries told Devlin what he most feared, but tears would not come to bring him relief. His grief cemented itself inside, laying hard and heavy on his heart.

Before Sean and Maureen's bodies were cold in the earth, Lord Harry returned and ordered Patrick and Devlin off his land. Patrick had little hope of finding solid employment, and most of his savings had gone to provide a decent burial for his wife and son. What little was left was barely enough to keep them alive.

They made their way to Dublin, taking odd jobs as they went. Devlin couldn't know that his father often gave his son his own share of their small ration of food and spent long nights in worry about their future. When they reached Dublin, Patrick's tall, proud frame had dwindled to a mere shadow. He still had to fold his six-feet-plus to go through doorways, and few men would dare challenge him, but his son saw the tremor in the hands and the gauntness of the face.

They slept in alleys and foraged food from garbage until Patrick finally found a job. A tavern keeper with little care about a man's background or origins had use for a man to keep the riffraff and brawlers out of his place. Bolstered with regular meals, Patrick would serve his purpose well. He even managed to put Devlin to work mopping up. Devlin learned to clean spit and puke from the floors without gagging and accustomed himself to falling asleep against a wall, the mop still in his hand.

It was in this tavern that Patrick regained some of his former spirit, though it tore at his heart to see his bleary-eyed son moving about like a drudge. He began to make friends with the sailors in port from all parts of the world, and it was here that the dream of America was rekindled. Long into the night he would talk, keeping Devlin awake with the stories he had heard and his own tales of the bright future that lay ahead of them.

Finally news came of a ship sorely in need of men. Patrick convinced one of his new friends to speak to his captain. Before Devlin knew it, he was on board a scurvy-looking cargo ship and assigned to kitchen duty. His father was hired on as a common seaman although he knew nothing of the job and had never been aboard a ship in his life.

The roll of the seas took its toll on Devlin's insides. The first few days out of port were hell until he finally found his sea legs and his color returned to normal. He did not see his father the few times he was allowed up on the deck, and as the weeks passed, his anxiety grew. Finally he hailed the sailor they knew from the tavern.

A hush fell among the group of men on deck as the sailor drew him aside. "Your father is being punished for a liar. I warned him the captain was a hard man who'd not countenance a green sailor, but Patrick McShane thought he could charm his way across this ocean. Can't very well hide a man who is heavin' his guts over the side of the ship, nor protect him when he neglects his duties. He'll spend the rest of this journey in chains and, should he live, the captain will see that he regrets that, too."

The look on Devlin's face gave the man warning. He clamped a firm hold about the boy's waist before Devlin could dash toward the captain's cabin. "Ye be mindin' your own self, lad. Joinin' your father down in that hole won't help him any. I promise to look after him if I can. When we dock in New York, we'll think on a way to get him out of this mess. Now be about your business afore the captain turns his attention your way."

Three weeks later Devlin stood on the deck of the *Pelican,* dry eyed, while the body of Patrick McShane was dumped into the churning sea. Not once had he been allowed to see his father, not even when Patrick lay dying and calling for him.

His thirteenth birthday passed unnoticed in the middle of the Atlantic. Only thirteen, yet already he had experienced more grief than most know in a lifetime.

When the ship docked in New York, no one attempted to stall his departure. And when a total stranger stepped forward to post the bond for entry into this new land, Devlin didn't question, following Jake Gill to his rat-infested slum dwelling like a sick dog, too weak in spirit and body to even care where he rested his head. Jake Gill gave him shelter and food. Nothing else mattered anymore.

Devlin lapsed into silence, seemingly unaware that his fingers were raking across the rough fabric of his trousers. His eyes stared sightlessly while involuntary shudders quaked his thin body.

"And?" James prompted softly, alarmed by the boy's high level of anxiety. "What then?"

Slowly Devlin's eyes lost their glassy appearance and focused upon the man offering understanding and compassion. But it wasn't possible to ease the weight of guilt upon his soul. He could not find justification—or forgiveness—for things he had done in the name of survival. The deep lacerations on his back were nothing compared to the everlasting shame of his existence with Jake Gill. He'd do anything, even lie, to keep James's good opinion.

"It's enough to say Jake was a man of foul disposition. I ran away from him, and that's the end of it."

The boy's lips thinned, and the firm jaw jutted stubbornly. The subject was closed, and the protective barrier seemed more impenetrable than before. Whatever Devlin suffered—and James sensed it was horrible—it would be revealed only in life's own good time. Reaching for those hands that had never quite stilled, James gave silent comfort for a time. When he spoke, the words were carefully measured and firm.

"I'm leaving in three days. You're coming home with me."

The expression on the boy's face was incredulous. "Why?" he croaked.

"Does there have to be a reason? Just say I can't toss you out into the streets again. If you're willing to work, there'll be a job until you want to move on—or for the rest of your life if ranching suits you."

Devlin wanted to throw himself at James and weep like a child. But pride, and the experiences of his recent past, kept him in rigid control. He wanted to trust, desperately wanted to accept a kindness without caution. Instead he became defensive.

"No. I'd be nothin' but a mouth to feed with no skills to offer for payin' me own way. It's charity . . . plain and simple."

James's large fist hit the table with such force that the glasses tumbled over and the plates almost jumped off the table. "Damn that foolish pride of yours! One of these days you're going to choke on it!" he yelled as he leapt to his feet, his hands clenched in tight fists. "Do I make it sound easy, boy? Well, ranching is damned hard work. You fry in the summer and freeze your ass off in the winter. There's work to be done from sunup to sundown, and at the end of the day you'll fall in your bunk with every muscle in your body aching. That's the good part. You can get caught in a blizzard, or bushwhacked by rustlers. Only a strong man can survive on the range. You've proved to me that you're a survivor, and I'm offering you an honest job for an honest wage. I thought you had the kind of guts and character it takes . . . guess I was wrong!"

James stormed out of the room, slamming the door behind him so hard the walls shook.

Devlin remained frozen, his head hung in shame. He studied his bare feet once again before walking to the window to watch the light dusting of a late March snow. He would have to swallow his pride and apologize. His only other choice lay out on that cold dark street, and he knew well what awaited him there. If he had to he would beg James to forgive his impulsive words and his arrogant pride. More than anything in this world he wanted to go home with the man from Montana.

Tears coursed down his face, and he made no attempt to wipe them away or still the sobs that shook his body. If James would give him another chance he would pledge him the rest of his life. For the first time since before his mother died, Devlin McShane prayed.

James strolled the streets outside his hotel whistling softly to himself. His self-satisfied features wore not even a hint of the rage he had displayed earlier. He grinned ruefully and spoke softly to himself. "As you would say, Sam old friend, there's more than one way to skin a cat." He was determined to take that boy home with him even if he had to rope and hogtie him. It would be better if Devlin thought it was his own idea, but he was going nonetheless.

It was nearly midnight when James returned to the room to find Devlin sitting in front of the fire, struggling to stay awake. He rose quickly as James approached, and the look on his face confirmed the words James heard.

"If ye'll be givin' me another chance and will forgive my wicked tongue, I'll be going to Montana with you. I've been thinkin' it's the only way to pay me debt, and I promise ye won't be sorry ye picked Devlin Michael McShane up out of the gutter."

James smiled and tousled the boy's hair. "You'll earn your keep, never fear. My foreman will see to it that my charitable nature isn't wasted. Someday you may curse my kindness."

"Never" was the vehement reply.

Chapter Three

The child's eyes were fixed on the tall pines as she made her way up the slippery incline. The drifts were still deep in some areas, and her woolen trousers were soaked to the knees when she reached her destination.

Her mittened hand reverently brushed the snow from the partially buried wooden markers so that the inscriptions carved there were visible. There had been no marker for her grandfather's grave when she was here late last fall. Sometime since, Sam had carved the wooden slab and placed it lovingly in the frozen Montana earth. Another man would have waited for the spring thaw, but Sam would not leave his friend without a marker on his final resting place.

Jennifer stuck her cold, wet hands deep into the pockets of her heavy fleece-lined coat and drew it close about her body. From here she could survey her home and the vastness beyond the fenced enclosure of the ranch. The big white house looked foreign amidst the rough-hewn wooden structures scattered inside the split-rail fence. Steady streams of gray smoke emerged from the chimneys of the main house, the bunkhouse, and the log cabin that not long ago had housed her family. The smoke seemed to blend with the gray of the March sky as pellets of icy snow began to fall, looking like stars on the midnight blackness of her braided hair.

The weather fit her low spirits as she sat down on an old tree stump and pulled her cold knees up under her coat, grateful for its excess of material. The tears she had been unable to shed last November, when Sam carried her grandpa's broken body back to the ranch, fell as she lowered her head to her knees. She was only nine, but years spent in the company of adults made her seem more mature. The only playmate she had ever known had been her grandfather, and now he lay beneath the frozen ground.

When the healing tears passed, she rubbed her face against the woolen fabric of her coat and raised her head to read the names on the markers.

LOUISE BAXTER DOUGLAS
MARCH 16, 1851
TO
JUNE 1, 1870

The mother she had never known had died on the day of her birth. All Jenny had of her mother were some hair ribbons and a small daguerreotype of a pretty woman in a white satin dress. She had learned very early that questions about this woman, who had looked so happy, brought only silence from her father and pain to his eyes. Loving him, she had not pressed her questions and consequently knew little about the woman whose life had been exchanged for her own. The other marker was for the grandfather she had worshiped.

ROBERT IAN DOUGLAS
AUGUST 2, 1817
TO
NOVEMBER 10, 1878

She looked out over the rolling, endless landscape and remembered the times Grandpa had set her in front of him on his big roan stallion as they rode together over the kingdom he had created. She could hear Grandpa Douglas's voice in her ear and, if she closed her eyes tightly, could feel her slight body pressed tightly against his broad chest, her short legs straining as she straddled the huge horse. The memory was so vivid that Jenny could almost smell the summer-scented air as she and her grandfather sat beneath the grove of pines and scrub oaks beside the little stream that had become their special place. His deep, gravelly voice was ingrained in her subconscious and she remembered almost every word of the last talk they had. Much of it had been far too complicated for her young mind to absorb, but she remembered the words and knew in her heart that the man had told her everything there was to tell that last long summer afternoon.

"You got more questions than you got years, Princess," he had said with a laugh. "How on earth am I supposed to cover nearly twenty years of my life in one short summer afternoon?"

"Please, Grandpa," she had cajoled, her silver eyes sparkling as she wrapped her arms around his neck, "tell me again. I want to hear all about the wagon train from Kansas, the soldiers at the fort, and all about the gold."

"Ain't you forgettin' the Indians?" he had reminded her with a tolerant chuckle.

Jenny had leaned forward and put her mouth close to his ear to whisper conspiratorially, "Daddy told me there weren't any Indians. You made that part up."

"Well, now," Robert had mused, "that ain't exactly right either. There were plenty of Indians in these parts back then, but the soldiers kept them too busy to fool with the likes of us. Almost felt sorry for the poor devils when they got chased up into Canada. Can't say I blame them for wanting to hold on to this land, but at least they got their moment of glory with that fool Custer before the whole damned cavalry ran them out."

Robert had gently pulled the girl's arms from around his neck and hauled her playfully over his shoulder before sitting her between his legs on the grass.

"If we're gonna spend the whole afternoon, you best stop your fidgeting about and sit still."

Jennifer had relaxed against the older man and smiled

32

smugly. He hadn't missed her self-satisfied grin and had swatted her playfully on the leg. "You ain't gonna think you're so smart when your ears are aching. I'm gonna tell it all, child. Every last bit so you'll stop plaguing me with questions. Now listen up good, 'cause I don't aim to repeat it again."

Jennifer shivered as the ice started pelting her cheeks. She drew the coat even tighter around her, forcing herself to remember the words he had spoken that day.

"I got a lot to be proud of and a lot to be shamed for. A man don't live as long as I, nor do what I've done, without the good and the bad of life. I ain't gonna spare myself none and I ain't gonna apologize. God will judge me soon enough, and when you're older you can decide if I was right or wrong.

"I was just a kid of eighteen when Santa Anna's army decided to march. My older brother, Darren, and I had gone into the tradin' post to get supplies when a stray company of Mexicans rode onto our place. From what we could see when we got back, Ma and Pa must have put up one hell of a fight 'cause things were pretty well tore up and the house nearly burned to the ground. Darren and I buried what little was left of our folks and started looking for whatever stray stock we could find.

"We found one dead cow out of a whole herd, and when we finally went home Darren didn't say nothin' for almost three days but just walked around with big tears fallin' down his face. I wanted to cry, too, but for some reason I held it all in. On the fourth day he drug me out of the shell of our house and we stood beside our ma and pa's graves. He wasn't cryin' no more, but his look was fierce and I remember how his hands just kept openin' and closin'. I ain't never in my life seen a look like that, before or since, nor will I ever forget the hollow sound of his voice. 'I got to get my pound of flesh, little brother. Now you keep yourself well and healthy 'cause you just might be the last of our family. Make a name for yourself, Robbie. Get out of this cursed land and find a place where the grass grows green and tall and a man can breathe somethin' besides dust.'

"He rode out the next mornin' and nothin' I said or could have said would have stopped him.

"I hung around for a while, hopin' to get word from him, but a buddy he made finally looked me up and told me Darren had been killed at San Jacinto.

"I remembered what he said and started makin' my way north, workin' every kind of job I could find from cow-punchin' to chopping wood. Bummed around in Missouri for a few years and when I was workin' at a place outside Westport, a fella offered me a full-time job as a bronc peeler over in Lawrence, Kansas. He had the finest place you ever did see with a big brick house and a rose garden.

"I don't think I'd been there a month or more before I saw your grandma in town at the general store. I just knew the minute I saw her that she was the one for me, and then I fussed and fretted for weeks until I could get enough information about her to find out if she was married or not. She was the town's only schoolteacher, and they were real protective toward her. I don't think any man before me had guts enough to take them all on, but when I see somethin' I want, there ain't a man alive that can persuade me to change my mind.

"I just kept hangin' around until she finally got tired of trying to avoid me and we started talkin'. Just sort of drifted to the church from that point on. Think she kind of surprised herself.

"Anyway, we bought a little place about fifteen miles outside town, and I went to being a farmer. Seventeen years I worked that useless land. Seventeen years of my life plowed into nothin'. Let me tell you somethin', child: ain't nothin' more miserable than doin' something you hate. I wasn't meant to be no farmer, and as the years went by, I got colder and meaner. It eats a man alive until there's nothin' worthwhile left in him. That's what happened to Anna too. One day I threw down my hoe and looked out over that flat arid land and said 'Enough.' When I walked into the house and saw my wife sittin' at the table, her head over a book with our son beside her, I realized what I had done to her. I had been selfish, lovin' her like I did, not to see that I had taken her away from what she had been destined to do. Love don't always make everythin' right. We were strangers livin' in the same house, and I didn't know my son any better than I knew my wife.

"I told her that very day we was movin' on. She didn't say a word, just gave me one of her cold stares and went right back to James's lessons. When we left Kansas and joined the wagon train, I had to pack up all them damned books. She'd leave half her furniture and most of her clothes, but she wouldn't budge one inch without them books.

"I saw my son turn into a man on the Oregon Trail. He didn't have much time for readin' anymore and spent most of his spare time with the wagon master. His skin lost its pasty whiteness and his gray eyes fair gleamed with excitement. Anna never forgave me for takin' her son away from her.

"When we finally reached Fort Laramie in the Wyoming territory, Anna was ailin' pretty bad. There was no way we could go on with the wagon train to California, so we wintered there. I barely had time to put us up a shelter before the snows hit. God, I'll never forget that first winter. I didn't think any of us would make it, and I know Anna wouldn't have if it hadn't been for the boy. We had to learn to hunt and trap wild game the hard way. James was better at it than I was, even though I could see it hurt him to kill the small animals he would have liked to make pets of.

"Somehow we made it, but when the spring thaw came we were all too weak to move on. Even if we had had the strength, there weren't any big wagon trains to hook up with that year. The country was preparing for war, and most folks were still tryin' to decide just which side they was on. A whole lot of that had been goin' on in Kansas before we left. Neighbors up in arms against neighbors over whether Kansas would be a free state or slave state. That madman John Brown stirrin' everybody up so you didn't know your friends from your enemies.

"So there we were—stuck in the middle of nowhere, with no money and no way to make a living for ourselves. When news came in '62 of a gold strike in the Montana territory the fort was swamped with men heading up there from Colorado and even as far away as California. Guess I got gold fever right along with them. Sort of went crazy for a while. First thing I knew I had bought myself a pick and shovel and was headed north along with the rest of them on the Bozeman Trail. Didn't even look back over my shoulder to say good-bye to my wife or son. I saw a way out for us, and all I could think of was gettin' enough of a stake together to make a decent life for ourselves. I didn't bother to consider how they might survive without me. Just left the woman and an eighteen-year-old boy to fend for themselves.

"Two years I was gone. Two years of breakin' my back and freezin' my butt. I know James thinks I had a grand adventure, but I can tell you, it was miserable cold and I ain't never worked harder any time in my life. But I was one of the lucky ones and when I made my way back to Fort Laramie, I had close to ten thousand dollars in gold in my saddlebags. Must have had an angel on my shoulder all that time. Never even thought that some fella might just love to split my skull for the gold in them bags. Went right through Indian country without even seein' a redskin. By then I was burnin' with a fever inside so strong that I don't think anything could have kept me from my purpose. All that land up there in Montana. It was just sittin' there with its tall green grass. I remembered what my brother had said and felt like I owed it to him to get me a big piece of that grass. With more people movin' into the territory every day, I knew beef would be worth a lot more than the gold in my bags soon.

"I had my speech all planned out for Anna, but I never got to say the words. When I got there she was buried beside that drafty cabin, and I was met by a son who had little need for a father.

"That next winter me and your daddy had to get to know each other all over again. Any other son might have kicked

36

my behind all the way to China after what I done, but he took me in without a word and fed me all winter long. He even listened to my tales and dreams. Sometimes I would catch him lookin' at me with his soul in his eyes, but I never saw any anger—only pity.

"When spring came we started hangin' out around the fort, drinkin' with the men passing through and keepin' our eyes and ears open. Everybody thought I came home busted. James even sold some of our stuff to people passin' through so we could buy the supplies we needed. Your daddy's a real smart man. When I would have been shootin' my mouth off, he was already plannin' and workin' to make my dreams come true.

"One night a group of Texans came in fresh off the trail. They'd brought a herd of beef right up through both Confederate and Union lines and the stories they had to tell made it worth the price of buyin' a few rounds. I was so spellbound that I didn't notice James for a while, but when I did, I got damned nervous. There was a full bottle of whiskey on the table in front of him and he was bent over his glass talkin' to a fellow like he'd known him most of his life. I noticed that the man kept refillin' Jamie's glass and decided to find out just what was so special about this stranger to get my son's tongue so loose.

"I just casually walked over to their table and sat down. James was real quick to make the introductions. 'Pa, this is Sam Smith. He's been telling me about the cattle business in Texas.'

"I remember there bein' somethin' about the man that made me trust him. I noticed that he wasn't as young as I had first thought—must have been close to forty. His hair was almost all white even then. I always considered myself a fair judge of a man's character, and my gut was telling me we could trust this man. Just to bring Jamie out of his shell and cause him to jabber like a magpie was somethin' I'd never seen another man or woman do.

"Before long I was drinkin' and talkin' right along with them. Even went so far as to tell the man about the little valley I had picked out in Montana. He must have thought I was the biggest fool ever born, 'cause he sure put me in my place fast enough. I'll never forget the smirk on his face or his words.

"'Where are you gonna get all those cattle you plan on startin' a big herd with? And if you do find enough good beef around here, what are you gonna do—drive them into your valley and pitch a tent?'

"No man likes his dreams stepped on, and I made an even bigger fool of myself tryin' to defend my position. But Sam just smiled and shook his head like he was talkin' to an infant. 'Need more than just two men to put up buildings and survive in Indian territory.'

"Sam tipped back in his chair and began to study the ceilin' as if he was ponderin' the fate of the world, and when he finally looked back at us, his ice-blue eyes were hard. 'You got land picked out but no stock to put on it and no buildings to quarter yourselves or the men you'll need. On top of that you have the Sioux to worry about. Far as I can see, you don't even have the capital to take yourselves across the room. Now just what the hell gives you the idea that you're gonna have a big spread of cattle and a fine ranch someday?'

"I thought I was gonna have to knock Jamie down to keep him from flying at the man. I don't think I've ever seen him get so fired up. Sam didn't even look as if the boy bothered him at all, and I got the impression he would swat him like a fly if he so much as made a move toward him. He just kept grinnin' at us, but his grin wasn't hateful.

"I strong-armed the boy out of the place and then we sat up half the night talkin' about what the man had said. It ain't easy to admit another man is smarter than you are, but facts is facts. The next morning we went looking for Mr. Sam Smith, and I swear he was just waitin' for us in that bar. Hadn't even moved from the table, far as I could tell.

"Seems like now we'd just been waitin' for Sam to get us off our butts and stop talkin' and start doin'. Funny thing about Sam, he don't push or give orders. He just sort of gives you the fact of a thing and then expects you to take it from there.

"By spring we had a cabin, a bunkhouse, and had picked up Bob Tucker. While Bob and I built the corral and I planned the house in my mind, Sam and James took off for California after our beef. You should have seen those mangy animals they brought back with them. Didn't look like they would last a week, let alone one of our winters, but it was a start.

"Your daddy got real thoughtful 'round about then and spent a lot of time readin' and figurin'. I could almost see the wheels turnin' in his head.

"'Pa, I've been thinkin',' he told me finally. 'This is a real chancy thing we're tryin' to do. We don't really know for sure if cattle can survive out there on the range when the big snows come. Seems to me like we have all our eggs in one basket.'

"I reminded him about the gold, but your daddy always has an answer for just about everythin'. 'Pa, we don't even know just how much of it is left or what it's worth. If we make a go of it out here we are going to have to gamble big. The gold isn't worth anything to us like it is, and we're being cheated every time we part with a little of it here and there. It's worth a great deal more back east where prices aren't so inflated. If I could get to Boston or New York, we could turn it into cash and put it in one of those big banks. And if we invested it in something like steel or railroads we might be able to double, even triple, its value.'

"Arguin' with James was like talkin' to a brick wall. He's more like me than I gave him credit for.

"He was gone more than a year, and you could have blown me over when he came drivin' that wagon carryin' two women and loaded down with furniture into the yard. He'd got himself a pretty little wife, your ma, and saddled the rest of us with that shrew-tongued, red-haired Maggie. Louise was sweet and gentle. Lovin' her was easy. But that other one started right off givin' us orders and makin' sure that house of mine got built so your mama had a decent place to live. Your Grandpa Baxter was an important man in New York, and Maggie just couldn't rest until Louise had a fine house to put her things in.

"Only person I ever knew of who could back that red-haired woman down is Sam. Those two locked horns from the first day, and there were times when the fur just flew. Personally, I think Sam could have found other ways to keep a fine-lookin' woman like that occupied. First time I ever knew him not to get the straight of a thing."

Robert's voice had trailed off and he had lapsed into silence. He hadn't felt the pull of the little girl's hand on his shoulder until her persistent voice tugged him away from his memories.

"Grandpa, tell me more about my mama."

Robert had sighed. "Nothing more to tell, Princess. She was sweet and pretty. A real lady from a good family back east. Your daddy loved her too much, and when she died, a whole lot of him died with her. Maybe he'll find another woman someday to give him the son this place needs, but I doubt it."

"I don't need a brother," the girl had stated emphatically. "I'm the princess."

Robert had swung her up in his arms, his heart swelling with pride and love. "That you are. And don't you ever let anybody tell you different. I ain't countin' on your daddy ever marryin' again, so you just mind what I tell you. You're the firstborn on this land and you have a big responsibility. It would be easier if you was a boy, but you're the princess 'cause I named you that. You're special."

Special. The word kept echoing itself in the girl's mind. It had been the last time she and her grandfather had been together.

The snow was falling heavily when she returned to the present. Sensing that she was not alone, she looked up into sad blue eyes and launched herself into the man's warm embrace.

Sam held her tightly, his voice husky. "I miss him, too, Princess," he said as he took out his handkerchief and wiped the fresh tears off her face. His weathered skin looked like old leather, and a shock of white hair peeped out from beneath the wide brim of his dirty hat.

As Sam carried the child back toward the warm haven of the house, his thoughts were in New York with James. He loved James like a son, but there were times he thought him pigheaded and blind. Too often he treated his only child like a little doll, something to pet and pamper, rather than as the real person she was. The child needed her daddy more than some old-maid teacher right now. Sam intended to tell him so when he got back.

Chapter Four

Devlin stood alone on the platform of the Cheyenne station, nervously twisting his new Stetson in his hands, his heart beating with a strangely mixed pattern of anxiety and excitement.

The platform had cleared of people quickly, and James, not seeing the men who were to meet them, went in search of them. Standing there alone, Devlin once again doubted the wisdom of his decision to come west with James. Nothing in his past experience had prepared him for the sights he saw on the journey that had just ended: miles and miles of unpopulated land, and on the rare occasions when he did see men and women, their faces reflected the harshness of their lives. Yet within those tired eyes and weather-roughened faces, Devlin sensed a fierce independence and pride.

He spotted James making his way across the street with a tall, thin, white-haired man at his side. Both men seemed unconcerned as they trudged through the muddy street, their boots and pants legs blackened by the grime. Devlin wondered why wooden planks hadn't been laid down across the slime. He picked up his new carpetbag and made his way slowly, painfully across the platform. The rough fabric of his trousers chafed against the inside of his thighs, and the stiff new boots punished his feet. James had bought the boots a size large and had forced Devlin into three pairs of heavy woolen socks.

Sam watched as the boy approached, noting the pained look on his face and the stiff way he moved. He had been given a brief sketch of the boy's history and had expected a younger child, an orphan without hope, home, or family. There was nothing in this tall, blond-haired boy with the impassive face that remotely resembled the pitiful orphan James had described. Sam's eyes narrowed as he observed the proud stance and the challenge in the deep blue eyes. There was even a kind of grace in the boy's agonized gait.

Devlin stopped before the two men, his face devoid of expression as the stranger surveyed him from the top of his head to his sore, booted feet. He recognized the man immediately from James's description, but saw nothing of the kindness James had so often mentioned. All he saw were granite features in a face the color of the leather leggings that covered his trousers. The child in him wanted to reach out to James for reassurance, but the adolescent refused to fold under that ice-blue stare.

Sam's expression softened as a momentary flicker of fear blazed out of the boy's unusual eyes. At closer range, Sam could see that the boy was younger than he had first appeared. He grudgingly admired the stiff, straight posture and the refusal to give in to the uncertainty that must be working to overwhelm him. He nudged James in the ribs with a silent plea to break the tension.

James gave Sam a questioning look, totally unaware of the disquiet surrounding him. Sam groaned aloud and rolled his eyes skyward. As usual, it would be up to him.

"Sam Smith," he introduced himself, extending his hand to the youngster, pleased to find that the boy's grip was firm, his palm cool and dry.

The three of them moved off the platform and made their way down the street toward the hotel. Sam watched as the boy moved ahead and saw how carefully he kept his legs apart. Once again he cursed James's stupidity. Didn't he see that the new denim trousers were galling the boy's tender skin? There wasn't a cowhand alive who would wear new denim before it had been washed several times in scalding water and rolled and beaten until the stiffness was out. Obviously James was unaware of how many hours Maggie spent softening his own trousers before he wore them. Far too many people on the ranch pampered this gentle man, and Sam knew he headed the list.

The sun was already beginning to dip beyond the horizon as they entered the hotel. Devlin was introduced to the two men who had accompanied their foreman to Cheyenne to handle the cattle on the way back to the ranch. Bob Tucker was, without doubt, the homeliest man Devlin had ever seen. He had a squat body and a large bulbous nose, but his eyes were kind and he greeted Devlin warmly and without hesitation. The other man, Davie Garrett, was much younger, barely more than twenty. He had the lean build of a horseman, and his green eyes sparkled with mischief as he quickly surveyed the boy before him. Devlin instantly bristled at this unspoken challenge and drew himself up to his full height, which was already greater than Davie's. As he shook hands with both men he couldn't help noticing how pale his skin was in comparison to theirs. He was a pasty-faced lad next to these toughened veterans, and he felt as green and foolish as he looked.

Sam almost felt sorry for the boy. These two would give him hell the next few weeks on the trail. He was tempted to tell them to back off and leave him be, but knew that if Devlin were ever to be accepted he would have to prove himself. Bob and Davie were two of James's best, and if the newcomer couldn't gain the respect of these two, he might just as well hightail it back to wherever he came from. Bob had been with them since the beginning, but Davie had come to them when he wasn't much older than Devlin. The men had put him through a tough time at first, but his cheerful disposition and his bulldog determination had soon won their acceptance. Had James warned the boy of the hazing he could expect? Sam doubted it.

The next morning Devlin was rudely awakened just as the sun was beginning to make an appearance on the horizon. He sat up and rubbed his bleary eyes, blinking twice before he recognized the man who stood beside his bed in the dim light.

"Better get over wanting to sleep the day away, boy. We get up before the sun does," Sam informed him as he tossed something on the bed. "Put those on . . . and here's some ointment for those galled legs of yours."

Sam watched as Devlin silently pulled on the oversize trousers. "Might be a bit big on you, but a hell of a lot more comfortable. Maggie will soften up your new duds so they don't skin you alive."

Devlin responded to the gruff warmth in Sam's voice by dressing quickly and following him out to the street below. Already the ointment and soft trousers were soothing the stinging flesh of his legs.

Except for James the other men were waiting, already mounted on their big horses, impatient to leave and irritated at being forced to wait. But they greeted him civilly, and Davie held out two biscuits and a leathery-looking strip of meat he called jerky. Devlin didn't miss the low chuckle of amusement as he tried to bite the meat, but refused to allow them to see how distasteful he found this food to be.

Soon James joined them, leading a mare whose scurvy looks contrasted with the magnificent roan stallion on which he was mounted. Devlin hesitated as Sam ordered him to mount up. He had seen it done many times, but had never himself been on a horse in his life. He had curried them, fed them, and cleaned out their stalls, but never had he sat upon one's back.

He mounted the gray mare easily, but once on her back, he foolishly pulled the reins and tore at the tender mouth of the animal. The horse reared, almost tossing him off her back. He had the good sense to cling to the animal's neck to keep from being flung to the muddy street.

"Ain't you ever been on the back of a horse before?" Sam spat.

"No, sir," Devlin admitted, knowing it would be sheer stupidity to say otherwise.

"Shit!" Sam cursed as he made his way to Devlin's side. "Boy, your butt is going to have blisters on top of blisters."

Angered by Sam's caustic tone and shamed in front of the others, Devlin's mouth ran away with him. "Just be showin' me the way of it. I'll be mindin' me own butt; see that you look to yours."

Devlin heard the hoots of laughter from the men and felt very pleased with himself until a strong hand bit into the flesh of his upper thigh. "Just see you don't fall off and break your cheeky Irish neck."

Maggie stopped peeling potatoes for a moment, a secret smile lifting the corners of her full mouth, her eyes staring vacantly while her mind created its lovely images. Suddenly the knife slipped. Shoving the dream aside, the woman thrust the injured finger into her mouth.

"Cut your fool finger off one of these days," she scolded herself before standing to remove the apron and rub the small ache at the base of her spine.

There was a feeling of expectation in the air this morning. Maggie opened the kitchen door and stepped out into the yard, her gaze falling on Sam's empty cabin. A few weeks ago there had been snow up to the back stairs, but now the sun shone brightly and the grass was beginning to turn a deep shade of green. It would be an early spring for these parts and, most likely, a sweltering summer.

She walked over to the small patch of ground that she claimed for her flower garden and examined the recent sproutings. Soon daffodils, lilies, and roses would give her something beautiful to look at from the kitchen window as she prepared the meals.

Out of the corner of her eye she saw the two riders at the top of the hill. Squinting, she placed her hand over her brow. James's roan stallion was immediately recognizable, but she couldn't tell who the other rider was from this distance.

She gave a whoop of delight and rushed back into the house, yelling as she went through the downstairs rooms. "Jenny . . . Jenny! Your father's home!"

In the long hallway she could hear the sound of a child's

feet and hear tinkling laughter as doors were slammed. Then the feet were on the stairs and the little girl rushed past and out onto the porch.

Maggie started to follow, but hesitated in the hallway, checking her appearance in the big mirror that hung above a table. She frowned at the dowdy dress and quickly smoothed the material over her full bust. Her red hair had escaped from its tight bun, and she impatiently tucked the slightly graying strands back into the knot. As she gazed at her appearance a disapproving sound issued from her lips. Honest to a fault, Maggie had never carried illusions about herself. She looked very much what she was: a woman slightly past forty, her youth behind her. She was a spinster, so her buxom figure had not lost its firmness through years of childbearing, but her once creamy complexion was now covered with freckles. She chose to ignore the tiny lines around her bright green eyes. She wasn't exactly plain, but no one with eyes in his head could ever call her pretty.

She heard the exuberant yell from the man outside and hurried to the window to watch the reunion of father and child. She smiled as the man leapt from his horse and swung the girl up into his arms, tossing her into the air before enfolding her in his warm embrace.

A tear slipped from Maggie's eyes, and she furiously wiped it away, wrenching her gaze from James and Jennifer to the lone rider sitting motionless on the hill just outside the fence. She didn't recognize horse or rider.

The front door opened, and James entered with Jennifer perched on his shoulder; he ducked so the girl's head wouldn't strike the doorframe. When he put Jennifer down, Maggie received a warm hug.

"Has my girl been behaving herself?"

"You know she's always good as gold, James." Maggie gave the only answer this man wanted or expected to hear. "Where's Sam and the rest of the boys?"

"Putting the new stock to pasture."

Walking back to the window, Maggie narrowed her eyes and pointed. "Well, then, who's that out there?"

James joined her at the window. "That, Maggie girl, is your new project. Another lost sheep to mother. A boy I found in New York who needs you like the rest of us do—maybe more."

Maggie blushed at his implied praise. "All I do is run the house. Any other woman could do as well."

James smiled and put his arm around the woman's shoulders, giving her a playful shake. "Run the house, run us . . . don't be so modest, Maggie. It doesn't suit you."

Devlin remained outside the fenced enclosure for quite some time. He had watched the reunion between the man and the child, his heart constricting with envy at the loving warmth he witnessed.

If the truth were told, it was more than just shyness that kept him outside the gates of the ranch. The incline wasn't particularly steep, but he dreaded forcing the horse one more step. His whole body was a mass of screaming, aching muscles.

The first day out of Cheyenne he had sworn he might die of it. Only the jeers and teasing from Bob and Davie made him remount this cursed animal day after day, seriously doubting that he would ever walk normally again. But somehow he had managed to stay on the horse's back. Somehow he had mastered the pain and the jolts. But it was the cold, hard ground where he slept that had almost finished him. There had been no reprieve on the trail, and he had stubbornly refused to ask for any. The fact that the men ceased to taunt him, included him in their storytelling, and even smiled with genuine liking, did very little to ease the torment of his body.

He surveyed his new home with bewilderment. From the way James had lived in New York, the fine clothing he had worn, Devlin had expected to find a palace. The rough log and wooden structures that were enclosed within the fence looked primitive, and the big house, which James had boasted was the finest in the territory, was merely a large two-story structure that wore a fresh coat of white paint.

There was nothing stately or elegant in its architecture. It was all straight lines except for the ornately carved posts holding up a porch that ran across the front of the house and down both sides.

He had visualized a large estate, much like the one he had left in Ireland, and the folly of his expectations made him laugh at himself. "Whenever are ye gonna learn, Devlin McShane, this is not Ireland . . . thank the Lord."

He clenched his teeth, and a grunt of pain exploded from within as he urged his mount down the incline toward the house.

There was no one in the yard to show him where he should go, so he stopped the animal in front of the house. He heard the creaking of a door, and his eyes followed the sound. A little girl stepped out onto the porch to gaze at him in silent wonderment.

Devlin was unaware that he had stopped breathing at the sight of the beautiful child. Never before had he seen hair so black that it glistened with blue lights, even in the dimness of the porch. Never had he seen eyes the color of liquid silver or a mouth so perfectly formed. He felt slightly dizzy, and as his breathing slowly returned to normal, he realized he had been staring openmouthed at the girl before him. Feeling more foolish than he had felt in his entire life, he clamped his mouth shut and tightened his jaw. The girl's lips quirked in a smile, producing a small dimple in one velvet cheek.

With as much dignity as he could muster, he began to dismount. But his foot caught in the stirrup and he found himself flat on his back in the dust. He heard the bell-like laughter behind him. He was unable to prevent the flush of embarrassment that brought color to his pale face, and his blue eyes were almost black with anger and humiliation.

The girl met his ferocious stare without flinching as she continued to giggle. Something deep inside began to melt, and soon Devlin found himself seeing the scene through her eyes. His own mouth began to twitch in the beginnings of a smile.

His face was transformed with that smile. His body began to shake with laughter. It had been so long since he had laughed that he felt light-headed.

Still laughing, the girl skipped down the stairs to study this wonderful thing her father had brought home. She stared into the handsome face before reaching out to grasp his hand with both of her own. Tugging, she helped him to his feet and led the way up the stairs and into the house.

PART II

Chapter Five

The muscles in his arms and shoulders knotted painfully, and he could feel the blisters break inside the leather gloves he wore, the open wounds on his sweaty palms stinging like fire. He blocked the pain from his mind as he swung the heavy sledgehammer over his head to pound the wooden post into the hard spring ground. Day after day, week after week, they scarred the land with the ugly posts and accursed wire. The pain mixed with angry resignation on the sun-bronzed face matched that of his companion.

"Is she there again?" Devlin spat through clenched teeth, refusing to look behind him and acknowledge the young woman who pursued them throughout their joyless labors.

Davie Garrett merely shifted his eyes, still holding the wooden post, his hands tingling with the vibrations Devlin was sending through the wood. "Yeah, she's there," he replied under his breath. "Damn! Makes me as nervous as a whore in church to look up every mile and see her just sittin' there. It's almost like she thinks this is all our doin'."

"Not ours—mine," Devlin growled as the force of his blows increased with the anger that welled up within him. He threw down the hammer and picked up the shovel while Davie stood and flexed his fingers before moving to the spool of wire.

"I'd say something to James if I was you. She ain't got no business out here day after day on her own, and I'm damned tired of having my back pierced with those silver-dagger eyes of hers."

"If I thought it would do some good I might," Devlin responded tiredly, "but since Miss Hastings left she's been allowed to run wild."

Davie took the shovel from the younger man's hands and began digging the hole for the next post. Getting involved in the discipline of an almost sixteen-year-old girl was definitely not his business, but if she was his kid he'd bust her butt until she couldn't sit on that horse of hers.

He watched Devlin closely as he worked. Closest to Devlin in age, he had always maintained an easy friendship with him. It never occurred to him to resent the young man who was being groomed to eventually replace Sam. He was a natural leader who carried his responsibilities with a maturity rare in many men twice his age. He never took advantage of his privileged position in the Douglas household, but worked as hard as any cowhand, often taking on the more unpleasant chores, such as this one, without complaint. Increasingly the men deferred to his orders as Sam quietly loosened his hold on the reigns of authority.

Davie had never seen the twenty-one-year-old man lose his temper, even when most men would have been provoked to violence. A simple look from those imperturbable blue eyes, backed up by the presence of the solid, muscular six-foot-three-inch frame, was usually enough to control even the most troublesome cowhand.

Watching Devlin now, a small shiver of apprehension coursed up his spine. There was something about the firm set of the lips, the thrust of the jaw, and a burning light in the deep blue eyes that warned of a crack in that solid armor. Something about the girl got under Devlin's skin, and Davie sensed that he was precariously close to losing some of that practiced control. Secretly he hoped he would be around when those two finally clashed. It would be a battle worth watching.

"Why don't you just send her home?" Davie goaded.

Devlin dropped the shovel and turned to glare at the girl,

who sat on the pinto eighty or so yards away. From this distance she could pass for a boy with her waist-length hair stuffed under the dirty wide-brimmed hat, her young woman's body in oversize faded denims and someone's cast-off flannel shirt. Only the delicate bone structure of the face, the full lips, and the gentle swell of breast belied the image. He could almost feel her hate encompass him as their eyes met. Rightful heir to this land, she took exception to the miles and miles of barbed wire that were being stretched across it, and, for reasons known only to herself, she singled him out for her rage.

An almost alien feeling of regret formed a hard knot in his stomach as he remembered the child who had welcomed him into her home. The laughter, the soft hand that would unhesitatingly slip into his, the silver eyes filled with adoration as they shared their lessons in the small library, were things of the past. Often she had purposely made mistakes or played outrageous pranks to divert the imperious Miss Hastings from her tireless harangue against what she called his hateful use of the English language. She clearly disliked him, as she did all males. In time, the rich brogue faded under Miss Hastings's constant drilling until only a soft lilt remained to hint of his origins. Still and all, he treasured the education James had thrust upon him. The fine library provided hours of escape into worlds he could never know. What the prim-faced governess had not taught him, he had learned on his own, often reading into the early morning hours.

When he left the classroom his association with the child diminished until she was no more to him than an object to be faced across the dinner table. The five-year difference in their ages seemed to widen as he grew into manhood and the bond between himself and James Douglas deepened. He had barely been aware of her these past few years; this child-woman who shadowed his movements and repudiated him was a stranger.

Davie started to repeat his plea for Devlin to send the girl home when the young man turned back to him. The look in Devlin's eyes silenced his tongue. Devlin had two choices—

he could deal with the girl or ignore her. He had made his choice.

Jennifer flinched at each stroke of the sledgehammer. It felt as if Devlin were driving those posts through her heart.

"Oh, Grandpa," she cried. "How could they so defile the land!"

This was her punishment for the dual crimes of her birth—the death of her father's beloved and the failure to be his male heir—and she gave herself daily doses of the bitter medicine. Having been born female prevented her from taking part in the decisions that shaped the land and, with it, her destiny. The men—her father no less than the others—closed themselves up in the library for hours, rejecting her opinions as those of one too simpleminded to understand the changes that the last three years had wrought.

Still, she had made it her business to find out why the cattle could no longer graze upon open range. Unable to get even simple answers from her father or Sam, she had done her own detective work. She devoured the newspapers, searched through her father's desk, and stealthily followed them to numerous meetings in Billings.

Hot tears of shame burned her eyes as she remembered the cattlemen's meeting at the tavern in Billings last summer. Pride had welled within as she watched her father shout down the angry mob of ranchers, but then the meaning of his words had hit her like a blow to her midsection. Standing with him, Sam and Devlin remained silent. A silence that seemed to testify to their support as James begged for a reasonable acceptance of what he called inevitable change, but she sensed that Sam at least felt as she did even if he would never publicly speak against James. She had run from her post outside the door, tears coursing down her face. That was, she was certain, the lowest point of her life.

She stiffened her knees and rose up in the saddle to look out beyond the fences to the vast grassy range. Soon the land would be dotted with farms, the tall grass plowed up, the rich soil planted. The cattlemen would hide behind their barbed wire, deluding themselves that another year, another winter, would see these interlopers gone from the land. Foolish musings of cowardly men. Only force would stop the invasion, and few wanted the blood of men, women, and children on their hands. She could not justify this line of defense any more than the men who had made the decision against it.

Unable to sit quietly any longer, she urged her horse forward with gentle pressure of her knees in his flanks. Eyes glinting, she moved the little stallion onward until he pushed between the two laboring men. A slow smile of satisfaction spread across her features as she heard a low growl emerge from Devlin's throat and saw the anger flashing in his eyes. As he turned his back on her she pushed Dusty closer, enjoying her brief moment of mastery. The well-trained horse gave the man a hearty push, and Jennifer laughed heartily as Devlin struggled to remain on his feet, instinctively grabbing for the horse's bridle.

Suddenly she found herself flying backward through the air as Dusty reared. Her breath left her body as she hit the ground hard, and she was helpless to protest as strong hands examined her for injury while a deep lilting voice rained curses on her head.

"Damn foolish girl! You could have broken your neck. . . . Davie, get the canteen off my saddle!"

Taking deep gasps of air, Jennifer struggled to get to her feet only to find herself pinned to the ground by strong hands that refused to allow her to rise, and a sharp voice commanding, "Stay put!"

Devlin drenched the kerchief and his mouth quirked as she sputtered and choked on the water he dripped on her face. The moment he released her, she sprang to her feet with fists flying, but he easily sidestepped her impotent blows.

Davie stood back and watched, a broad grin on his face. The princess was in a fine temper, and he was secretly pleased that this stupid game she had been playing was about to come to a climax. He watched as Devlin reached out and captured her wrists, backing away to protect himself from her kicking feet. Only a little over five feet, she looked like a child next to the tall, strongly muscled man. Her long black hair, no longer concealed under the dirty hat, flew about her face, blinding her to the laughing expression of her captor. The minute she stopped for breath, Devlin was on her; lifting her up in his arms and throwing her none too gently onto Dusty's back. When Devlin motioned for the girl's hat, Davie handed it to him without hesitation.

Devlin slammed the hat down hard on Jennifer's head and handed her the reigns, still holding firmly to the bridle. "You take your little rear end and head for home or else I'm going to wallop the daylights out of you." He spoke the words through gritted teeth, but Davie thought he heard laughter in the voice. "Next time I look up and see you sitting there, I'm going to turn you over my knee."

Jennifer did not lack courage. "You can't order me around, and you had better never lay a hand on me!"

Devlin's grin was wide in the bronzed face when he spoke this time. "Never dare an Irishman unless you're bigger than he is. Go home, Jenny."

Jennifer pointed her index finger at his face. "I'm not a child to be pushed around anymore. I have more right than you to ride wherever I please."

"If you're not a child, you had better start acting like the adult you claim to be."

He swatted the little pinto's rump hard, and the horse leapt forward. As he watched horse and rider retreat he heard her petulant retort: "I'll be back!"

Davie shook his head in surprise at the way Devlin had manhandled the girl. It wasn't like him to use physical force, and the light in his eyes threatened more of the same should the girl cross his path again. Few men would dare defy him, but Davie had no doubts the girl would try time and time again.

"You ain't really gonna wallop her?" Davie questioned fearfully.

Devlin merely shrugged his shoulders and walked back to position the heavy post in the ground.

In most ways he empathized with the girl's feelings. If this were his land he would be shaking his own fist at the sky.

The last three years had crippled the cattle industry in Montana and Wyoming. It had begun with the worst winter in memory. Thousands of cattle had frozen where they stood, unable to forage for food beneath the layers of ice and snow. In the spring, instead of rounding up the herd and watching the birth of calves, they had dug deep trenches for frozen carcasses. And then came the hot dry summer with its blistering winds that dried up streams and ponds and turned the rich grass brown. The cattle, weakened by the hard winter, dropped like flies. And again they buried the stinking, rotten carcasses. They drove what was left to market only to find that there was no market. As the price of beef continued to fall, only the larger ranchers were able to wait it out. Of the ten ranches that had once ruled the area, only the Walters and Davis families had survived along with them.

It seemed as if the laws of man and nature conspired against them. Suddenly land agents from Washington swarmed in, demanding that each rancher account for actual land owned. Right behind them came the farmers, the homesteaders, and the merchants to carve up the land and claim it as their own. And Billings, once a cattle town that had been built by the railroads, became a thriving community with all the trappings of civilization: churches, schools, shops, and even a bank.

At Devlin's insistence, James began buying up the land and the sickly herds of cattle from neighbors who were moving on. They patiently outwaited the market, surviving in the meantime on the fruitful investments he had made in his youth. That money had bought the wire and the posts to keep out the farmers. That money had paid for the fields that were now planted with hay and barley.

Bewildered by his rapidly changing world, James had leaned on the young man he had rescued so many years ago, and Devlin felt that finally he had begun, in some small measure, to repay the man to whom he owed his life. For James he would work until his hands bled, until his muscles screamed their agony and his tired body threatened to drop where it stood.

He paused in his chores and removed his hat, wiping his brow with the still-damp kerchief. A broad smile lit his face as he remembered the outraged sputtering of the girl. He had openly declared war this day, and something deep inside looked forward to the battles ahead.

The yard was empty as Jennifer dismounted and led Dusty into the dark, smelly barn. She loosened the cinch and bridle, grunting as she heaved the heavy saddle off his back. Suddenly she was confronted by a pair of ice-blue eyes topped by all-white brows.

"Looks as if you tangled with a wildcat," Sam observed as he took the saddle from her.

"More like a snake!" she spat through clenched teeth, picking up the brush and furiously wiping the foam from Dusty's coat.

Sam lifted an eyebrow. He didn't need names—this was a long-running battle. "Many a wise man would think twice before tanglin' with Dev. Your being a girl don't guarantee you protection."

"Oh, for God's sake!" Jennifer screamed as she threw down the brush. "I'm so sick of listening to the glories of Devlin McShane I could puke. You'd think he were some kind of orphaned prince instead of just an Irish nobody Daddy took under his wing. I just wish he'd go back where he belongs and leave me in peace!" Her body trembled with the anger and hurt that had been bottled up too long.

"Where does Dev belong?" Sam questioned softly. "Does he have a daddy who adores him, or a home that keeps him warm and secure? Does he have a family he can turn to in times of trouble?"

Tears strangled Jennifer's reply. "Yes!" she insisted as she clenched her fists. "He has my home, my family, and *my* father."

Sam stopped her as she tried to push past him, refusing to

allow her to escape. He could not deny there was some truth in her charges, but he wanted her to see the other side. "Let me tell you what I see, Princess. I see a man who lives off the crumbs of other people's lives. I see someone who works harder, labors longer, and asks for no reward. He would lay down his life for your daddy, and you, too, if need be. It's only your jealousy that blinds you to the real man."

Jennifer raised her head, and Sam could see the despair in her eyes. "He'll have it *all* someday. Just wait and see."

Sam watched her as she ran across the yard and stormed into the house. James was doing wrong by the girl, and up till now he had kept quiet. Someday soon he would have to butt in and straighten out this mess before it went too damned far. He picked up the brush from the floor and finished the job Jennifer had started.

As Jennifer stormed into the house, she saw that the door to her father's library was open. James sat behind the massive oak desk, his head bent over the open ledgers. At the sound of a slamming door he looked up to see the wild, unkempt creature he called daughter.

"Jenny," he called softly, and was pleased as she entered the room and sat herself down on the arm of his chair. He wrinkled his nose at the smell of horse and sweat but put his arm around her and gave her a gentle hug.

"Things are looking up, Princess," he said more to himself than to her. "If I follow Dev's long-range plans and *if* we can convince that Thomas woman to sell out, the ranch might be self-supporting again before the year is out."

Jennifer balked at the sound of Devlin's name, but it was so rare that her father confided in her she was loath to ruin the moment. "If we get the Thomas farm that will give us a lot more grazing land, won't it?"

"Stupid, stubborn woman," James responded. "With her husband dead, she can't possibly hope to make a go of that farm. I'm sure she will come to her senses soon."

"Maybe she doesn't consider herself to be stupid or stubborn. Maybe she just wants to hold on to what is hers by right."

James removed his arm from his daughter's waist, dismissal in his voice. "You don't know anything about it, love."

In her room Jennifer removed her clothing, dumping the dirty garments in a heap in the middle of the floor. In only her camisole and cotton drawers, her firm, youthful body no longer appeared boyish. Slowly she stripped the remaining garments from her body, studying her naked reflection in the large oval mirror. There was no denying the firm, jutting breasts and the rounded buttocks. She despised each feminine line and contour. If it weren't for this, she could be the son her father needed, and Devlin McShane could go to the devil.

Devlin McShane was the enemy. So cool, so remote—always in control. She wanted to pick at that granite surface, see him bleed as she was bleeding. At first he had seemed like a welcome friend to a lonely little girl, but as the years passed she began to resent his presence. Resentment grew to outrage as she felt herself being swept aside, much as a bothersome insect. She fought bitterly against it, but thus far had been defeated.

Her chin began to tremble and she pulled on the soft velvet robe before giving way to her tears. She hated crying. Only women cried.

She didn't hear the sound of the door opening through her sobs, but soon she was wrapped in warm, comforting arms while Maggie crooned in her ear.

"There, there. Hush now. Nothing is so bad that it can't be fixed. Tell Maggie what's hurting my baby."

In spite of the sputtering and the sobs, Maggie got the drift of Jennifer's despair. "Silly child," she scolded as she hauled Jennifer to the mirror and forced her to look at the reflection in the glass. "There's your weapon. It's the only one a woman has, but it's a powerful one. Many a kingdom has fallen and many a man has been ruined or made strong by the love of a woman. Don't misunderstand me, child; I'm not hinting that you should use your beauty for evil, but you can make it work for you. Accept what the good Lord blessed you with and turn it to your advantage."

"I don't understand." Jennifer sniffed.

"Well, then, listen. I'm no expert, but I think I've learned a few things in my time . . . mostly from my own mistakes."

Devlin stopped to remove his mud-caked boots before entering the house. The sudden spring shower had soaked him to the skin and he shuddered as a piercing blast of rain-dampened air penetrated the layers of his clothing. The bright sun and hard physical labor had made the early April temperatures seem mild, but the dark clouds and the north wind that brought the rain reminded him that summer was still months away.

Inside the door he set his boots down on the throw rug placed there for that purpose and found himself drawn to the bright glow of the fire in the empty parlor. The huge stone hearth dominated the room. He threw on another log and stoked the fire into brilliance as heat flushed his face and hands, chasing the damp chill from his bones. He longed to throw his tired body into one of the big stuffed chairs that faced the fire, but would have to content himself with only the warmth until he had washed and changed his wet clothes.

This room was the heartbeat of the house and Maggie's pride and joy. Crocheted doilies covered the rich pine tables, lace curtains hung gracefully at the two big windows overlooking the porch, an oriental carpet adorned the hardwood floor. The room was a strange marriage of modest comfort and lavish opulence.

He could hear Maggie's tuneless singing in the kitchen beyond, from which issued the rich smell of freshly baked bread, causing his empty stomach to growl. He leaned heavily against the mantel and closed his eyes, letting the warmth, the smells, the sounds of home, soothe his weary mind and body.

For a time he drifted within this hazy void until the awareness that he was not alone slowly penetrated his consciousness. He opened his eyes warily. Thinking that he still must be dreaming he closed, then opened them again. The vision remained. Only the dangerous glint in the silver eyes hinted of the hoyden he had evicted from the range this morning. Her usually unruly hair had been brushed to a lustrous sheen and pulled back from her forehead with a pink velvet ribbon. He let his gaze roam over her face, taking note, for the first time, of the delicate arching brows, the wide-set, heavily lashed eyes, the pert upturned nose, and the beautifully formed mouth with its full lower lip. He was so hypnotized by the face before him that he didn't see the ruffled pink dress, with its pearl buttons straining against the fullness of her young woman's body.

The penetrating gaze paralyzed Jennifer as she stood at the entrance to the room. Her trembling hands were clasped together, and her eyes dared him to laugh at her ridiculous transformation. The dress was at least a size too small, fitting much too snugly in the bodice with material to spare at the waist. She had kept her promise to Maggie and had donned this ludicrous costume, all the while cursing the moment of weakness that had elicited the pledge. She wanted to run from the room, wanted to hide from those probing eyes, but she stood her ground, waiting for the laughter that would surely come.

Suddenly the loose-limbed pose changed as Devlin moved away from the hearth, almost brushing against her as he silently left the room.

Jennifer didn't understand the tightness in her chest that greeted his indifference. Slowly she turned and made her way back up the stairs to her room. Stopping at the door, she looked across the hall to Devlin's room.

Inside her room, she ripped open the bodice of her dress, the pearl buttons flying. Stripped down to her underwear, she surveyed the childish decor that surrounded her and again felt like an alien in her own home. She sat down in the rocker and stared out the window until twilight disappeared and darkness descended.

A soft tapping at the door interrupted her reverie. "Princess, are you coming down for dinner? It's on the table."

Jennifer didn't move from her chair, but called out loudly

enough to be heard, "Tell Maggie I'm feeling a bit sick. I think I'd just like to rest."

"Let me in," James demanded. "If you're ill you shouldn't be alone."

"I'll be fine, Daddy. It's just a female kind of sickness."

She smiled at her father's embarrassed cough. Once in a while being a woman had its advantages.

As his footsteps echoed in the hall, Jennifer walked to her wardrobe and pulled out the velvet robe and snuggled within its warmth. She stared in disgust at the piles of discarded, childish little-girl dresses that littered the room. Without hesitation she gathered them up and tossed them into the fire blazing in her hearth. She stared for a few minutes at her dirty denims and threadbare flannel shirt lying on her bed, then picked them up and threw them in the fire too. The stench was enough to drive her from the room, so she opened the window and let the chilling, fresh night air cleanse the room of the smell.

Moving about the room slowly, she picked up treasures of her childhood—a porcelain doll, a gilded music box, the tiny figure of a horse on wheels—caressing them lovingly before packing them away in the bottom drawer of the wardrobe.

If she even understood the motivation behind her drastic actions, she felt neither regret nor exhilaration when she returned to the rocker to stare out at the night. Eventually she moved toward the little writing desk in the corner of her room and methodically made a list of items to replace those that were now mere ashes in the hearth. A faint smile produced the small dimple in her cheek as she read the last two items on the list: one pair of denims and a chambray shirt. She would try Maggie's way, but just in case . . .

In the gray dawn, James and Devlin rode the fences together in silence. What they saw weighed heavily on James's conscience. Good friends, acquaintances of long standing, had followed his urging and subsequently had lost everything they held dear. It mattered little that he had purchased their land at a fair price, that he had bought what was left of their sickly herds for twice the market value. What mattered was that men had followed his leadership, and years of hard work and dreams were destroyed as a result.

At the distant sound of a bawling calf, Devlin spurred his horse and moved ahead of his companion. James watched appreciatively as Devlin leaned over his tall chestnut until man and beast seemed one. Again he thanked the fates that had placed this exceptional young man into his care. At a time when he had been almost paralyzed by the decisions that faced him, Devlin had gently pushed and prodded, refusing to allow him to retreat. The education that James had forced upon the child bore fruit as the man shrewdly dealt with the ranchers and land agents. He had been fair—James could not fault him—but he would not let James overpay nor buy where it was not necessary. He had saved the land for future generations of Douglas offspring. It was a restricted land now, enclosed by miles of wire, but the little graveyard remained protected and, from there, the ugly wire was not visible.

James urged his mount to a faster pace and soon joined Devlin, struggling with a calf who had unwisely thrust his head through the spaces between the wire to graze on the forbidden grass beyond. It took both men to free the frightened animal, and they were both sweaty from the labor when the liberated calf scampered to join the rest of the herd grazing nearby.

"Do you think those damned stupid animals will ever learn to stay clear of these fences?" James asked as he pulled the kerchief from his pocket and mopped his brow.

Devlin did not respond to a question that only time could answer, but removed the hat from his head and ran his fingers through his thick hair. The bright sunlight reflected off the pallor of James's skin. Too many hours spent alone in the library had faded the dark bronze to a yellowish hue. There were new streaks of gray in the raven hair and beard. The last few years had changed them all, but James the most. Devlin's heart constricted to see his friend so diminished.

There were days when Devlin was tempted to mount his horse and ride, and keep on riding until he put this land and the people on it far behind him. Then he would look into James's eyes and all thoughts of escape would fade. Patrick McShane had had more freedom under the yoke of English rule than his son had in this land of liberty. The elder McShane had been bound to his master's land only because he knew no other way of life; the constant murmurings of Irish rebellion and the ever-present lure of American shores gave hope. For Devlin escape was impossible. His chains were forged by love and loyalty to this man and his land. Only when James Douglas rested on the little hillside between his wife and father would Devlin truly be free.

Suddenly the wind picked up, and both men looked up at the dark clouds gathering on the horizon. "Let's go home," James said as he remounted his horse.

Home? Devlin had a place to sleep, eat, and pass the years. Never a home. Perhaps he should feel gratitude for the comfortable little room with its braided rug and handmade quilts. How could James know that in taking him into the main house he had isolated the young man from the camaraderie of the bunkhouse. He vividly remembered the bitter argument when he had turned eighteen and had attempted to move his belongings out. James had roared, Maggie had scolded, Jennifer had cheered. Sorrowfully Jennifer's opinion had not been heard, except by himself.

When Jennifer did not come down to breakfast, Maggie demanded entrance to the locked room. "If you don't open that door, my girl, I'll go find Sam and he'll break it down."

Maggie's nose wrinkled at the stench that greeted her when the door opened. "My God, what have you been burning?" she said as she examined the ashes in the hearth. Seeing the scraps of charred cloth, she whirled on Jennifer, her eyes blazing with anger. "If you think you're too old for me to get out that old wooden spoon, think again!"

Jennifer merely shrugged. "Nothing fit," she said calmly as she reached for the paper on the desk. "This is what I need to replace what I burned last night. Since I don't have anything to wear into town, I'll just have to rely on your judgment to get the things I need. Until then, I'll stay in my room."

Maggie took the paper from the girl's hand and read the list in angry silence. Then the hint of a smile appeared at the corners of her mouth. "I see you've thought of just about everything a well-dressed young lady should have in her wardrobe." She folded the paper neatly and slipped it into her apron pocket. "Who are you buying the trousers and the shirt for?"

Jennifer ran to Maggie and wrapped her arms tightly around the woman's waist, resting her head against her full bosom. "I'm going to try, Maggie. But please don't expect too much too soon."

"Oh, love," Maggie said wistfully, "I'm not yet so old that I don't remember how hard it is growin' up. I just wish your mama was here to help you through this. You're surrounded by nothing but men, and I'm too rough-cut to show you an easy way of it."

"Miss Hastings was a lady," Jennifer said, more to herself than to Maggie.

"That skinny bag of bones?" Maggie scoffed. "That woman had no sex. Hated men like they was poison and filled your pretty head with all kinds of nonsense. Now get into your robe and down to breakfast. I'll sweet-talk Sam into taking me into town later."

Chapter Six

James was alone in the library contemplating another way to coax Lottie Thomas off her land when the front door slammed and small, booted feet pounded on the stairs. He frowned slightly as he glimpsed slim hips encased in snug denim passing by the partially open door. The second time the door slammed, his head flew up. Sam threw open the library door with such force, it banged against the wall. His lined face was red with fury, and the ice-blue eyes bored into James as the older man advanced into the room.

"Enough is enough, and I ain't gonna mollycoddle you anymore. You got a responsibility to that girl, and it's time you started acting like a father instead of hermiting yourself in this room and ignoring what's going on around you!"

James opened his mouth to speak, but Sam didn't let him get a word out.

"Just you shut up and listen! That girl is gonna get herself into trouble soon, and I ain't gonna carry the responsibility for her anymore."

James could see that Sam was enraged beyond reason and tried to interject a little sense into what the man was yelling about. "Settle down, Sam. What could the child have done to get you so riled up?"

"Child?" Sam responded incredulously. "You still see a child? Damn, but you're worse off than I thought. Open your eyes, man . . . that girl's almost a woman and a fine-lookin' one at that. She's got just about every man on the place wantin' a turn in the hayloft, and you still see just a child?"

"Who would dare touch her?" James rose from his chair, his eyes turning to smoke as Sam's words penetrated.

Sensing he had almost said too much, Sam sat down in the chair and motioned for James to resume his seat, his voice more controlled. "James, a man is a man. Not one of the men who have been with you long would lay a finger on her, but we had a couple of new fellows who didn't know the rules."

"And?" James prompted as his fingers drummed on the desk.

"And nothing this time 'cause Dev put a quick stop to their filthy mouths with his fists and sent them packing. But it ain't just the men. The girl just flat out asks for it in her tight jeans and those shirts that"—he nearly blushed—"well, you know what I mean?"

"I think I'm beginning to," James said, surprised at Sam's embarrassment. He didn't know Sam *could* blush. "Thank Dev for me. I'll have Maggie talk to her."

Sam looked toward the heavens and gave a roar of impotent rage. "Do you think I'd be stickin' my nose into this if a few words from Maggie would solve the problem? Hell, I could do that myself. You wouldn't be taking this so lightly if you'd seen her out there in the east pasture with that young fella you hired last month. Hank's a good boy and only just seventeen, but he's old enough to get our girl into a pack of trouble."

"He molested her?" James demanded.

"Hell, no . . . but it ain't 'cause she wasn't askin' for it. She's just lucky I happened to be riding that way and saw what was going on. There she stood, bold as brass, with her butt pressed up tight against him while she coaxed him to show her how to use a rifle."

James thought a long time before he responded. "Perhaps you misinterpreted the situation. It sounds innocent enough to me, and I'm sure Jenny has no idea how that could inflame a man."

"Maybe you don't know it," Sam growled, "since you got your head stuffed up your ass most of the time, but that girl has known how to shoot since she was fourteen and is damned good at it. Should be, I taught her myself."

It was true. Ever since Jenny had begun to feel the first stirrings of an unwelcome womanhood, and with it the terrible confusion about where she stood in relation to her father and the surrogate son he had dropped into her life, it was Sam, and Sam alone, who seemed to understand the turmoil within her. He had taken extra time to be with her and extra care to include her in things: He let her tag along as he supervised the ranch, and he taught her how to use firearms—how to load a rifle and a pistol, and how to hit a target dead center every time. He had been a patient teacher and she a star pupil. James might be willing to play father to an orphaned waif, but not, goddamn it, by shucking his real daughter off on Sam!

"What should I do?" James whispered, pleading with his eyes for the words of wisdom he had always been able to count on from this man.

"How the hell should I know? *You're* her father," his old friend replied as he stormed from the room.

James followed Sam out of the library. He stopped at the bottom of the stairway and looked up to see his daughter standing at the top, her face filled with contempt, her eyes shooting daggers at her old friend.

Sam turned back to James and waited for him to see for himself the reasons for the discomfort among the men on the ranch.

She stood defiant, her slim legs spread wide, her hands on her hips, her hair tumbling about her shoulders. James was dumbstruck at the sight of pointed breasts thrusting against the soft cotton shirt. Even with his limited experience he could see plainly that she wore no camisole beneath that shirt.

"Come downstairs, young lady. I think it's time you and I had a long talk."

Her unrestrained breasts jiggled provocatively as she

bounced down the stairs, and by the time the library door closed, Sam saw storm clouds gathering in James's eyes.

Maggie rushed into the hallway at the roar that emerged from the library. She looked in bewilderment at Sam, who leaned against the parlor doorframe, his arms crossed at his chest, a self-satisfied smile on his face.

"What the devil is going on in there? I haven't heard such a ruckus out of a Douglas since old Robert died."

Sam put his arm around the woman and led her toward the kitchen. "Only the inevitable, Maggie love, and about time. Fix me some coffee and tempt me with pie and I'll tell all."

Devlin watched the horse and rider as they crested the hill. He had heard about the altercation between father and child and had silently cheered. Knocking down good men and losing good help over some chit of a girl irked him. She had started dressing like a lady and no longer rode about in pants so tight they drove the men wild, but he was not convinced any real change had occurred.

He hid himself from view as she rode into a little glade and flopped down on her back in the grass. He sat there long enough to assure himself she would remain alone, before he silently rode away. If she discovered that she had been followed he would have felt the bite of her tongue.

Weary of her glacial stares and her barbed words, and not wanting to drag James into their battle, he had removed his belongings from the room he had occupied since age thirteen and moved in with Sam. This time he had not been swayed by James's protests. But Devlin would remember for a long time the smug expression on Jennifer's face while she held the door for him as he carried out the last of his belongings.

James stood on the front porch mesmerized by the brilliant pink sunrise. He took a deep breath of clean, sweet-scented spring air, and a warm contentment flowed through his body. He felt renewed vigor in his veins and he welcomed the labors that spring had brought. The cattle market wasn't what it had been before the crisis of '86, but a profit could be made. He had given Arthur Grayburn free reign over his investments back east, and reports indicated that he was becoming wealthy beyond his wildest imaginings.

With Devlin out of the house he discovered a daughter he had barely known. He hadn't realized that she possessed a quick mind and opinions worth considering. He had even listened tolerantly to her readings of Miss Anthony's views on women's rights. Jennifer pleaded her case brilliantly, and he had laughingly acknowledged that he would have steered her toward a career in law if she had been born a man. He still didn't understand why she had stormed from the room at that remark, refusing to speak to him for the next several days.

James lit a cigar and enjoyed the fragrant smoke as activity began within the yard. Seeing the tall young man cross over to the barn, he was reminded of the new project they were faced with. Today he would send Devlin to Lottie Thomas's place to make a final offer on her farm.

Outside the barbed-wire enclosure of the Douglas ranch, small farms were springing up everywhere. It was inevitable as death, and James accepted it with more grace and tolerance than the other ranchers in the area. The fact that Loren Thomas had settled his wife and two boys on a farm that butted right up to the south pasture had been hard to take with grace, but James had been generous, refusing to listen to Sam when he accused them of purposely asking for trouble. As long as they minded their own business and kept to themselves, James was content to live and let live. He had even sent Maggie over last winter when Loren Thomas was ailing. She had come home shaking her head and clucking her tongue. "That poor woman. That man is near old enough to be her father and isn't gonna last much longer. I don't know what she's going to do with them two little boys and that farm when he's gone."

James had attended the funeral of the man he had never met, his heart going out to the widow and her two feisty boys. He admired the way she kept her head high as she held tightly to the hands of her two children. Her brown eyes had been clear and determined when he offered his condolences and help. He should have known she was stubborn by the set of her chin and her words.

"I thank you for your neighborly concern, Mr. Douglas, and I appreciate you and Miss McGee coming today, but my problems are my own and I will work them out for myself."

She was equally determined several months later when he offered to buy the land for twice what it was worth. Sam had gone to make the first offer, returning with a grim expression. "Stubborn woman," he had muttered, refusing to try again.

Today James would send Devlin. He hoped the younger man would be more persuasive. Women seemed to respond to Devlin's youth and his exceptional good looks . . . all women but Jennifer, that is. She could barely tolerate the sight of him. Open warfare had ceased when Devlin moved out of the house, but the tension between them could still be felt. It disturbed James that Jennifer despised him so, but he refused to dwell on it. She would have to accept Devlin someday. The fact that Devlin did not have to accept her, that he could move on, never occurred to James.

Whistling softly to himself, James returned to the house, beckoned by the smell of bacon drifting from the kitchen. He had complete confidence that he would soon own some good pastureland that was sorely needed.

James had underestimated Lottie Thomas. She had listened politely to Devlin's offer before ordering him off her land.

"You go back and tell your boss that I ain't selling, and if he sends one more of his lackeys, I'll blast them to hell."

"James," Devlin reported, amusement in his voice, "she means it. I guess we could sneak over there some night and throw a sack over her head and carry her out, but she won't sell."

James drummed his fingers on the arm of his chair as his eyes scanned the occupants of the parlor. Maggie had her head bent over her sewing, but her mouth was firmly set. Sam's face looked impassive, but James saw the flicker of irritation in his eyes. James didn't have to ask Jennifer's opinion. If he tried force, his daughter would most likely meet him at the Thomases' doorstep, championing women's rights.

He heaved himself out of his chair and paced the room, feeling all eyes upon him. "Well . . . I can see you all have your own opinions on this. Let's hear them."

The next morning James rode to the Thomas farm with Maggie at his side. He was surprised when Lottie Thomas welcomed them warmly and served them coffee and pie in the immaculate kitchen while her freshly scrubbed children watched in silence.

He made the offer they had agreed upon and saw the relief in the woman's face as she quickly agreed to his terms. With the tension gone from her features, he noted that she was much younger—she appeared to be in her late twenties —and much prettier than he had originally thought.

He offered to send a man over three days a week to help clear the land and do the heavy chores. Once the planting was done, that man would stop by to help one day a week. During harvest she could have him until the crop was ready for market. All this was on the condition that she would raise grain to feed the Douglas herd. This would free up some of his own land for pasture and give the woman a solid start. A contract was signed, but when Lottie Thomas threw her arms around his neck, James knew that no paper was necessary between them: she would keep her part of the bargain.

It hadn't occurred to James that his cowhands might refuse to put their backs to a plow.

"Hell, Mr. Douglas," young Hank had protested, "that's why I left home back in Iowa."

Even Davie, who seemed to enjoy helping Maggie in her garden, had refused. "James, I'd help out, but that woman and I don't see eye to eye. She's too damned bossy, and I'd likely throttle her within a week." James wondered when Davie had gotten acquainted with the woman, but kept his questions to himself. You didn't ask questions like that if you wanted to keep a good man working for you.

Just as James was prepared to swallow his pride and hitch himself to a plow, Devlin came to his rescue. He sighed with relief as the young man rode out in the early light of dawn for his first lesson in farming.

Chapter Seven

Never had Devlin been so hot as he stood to relieve the ache in his back and wipe the sweat from his brow with the back of his hand. He looked over at the pile of boulders he had cleared from the little patch of dirt and ground, his teeth grinding in frustration.

"If you'd take that hot hat and shirt off you'd be more comfortable," Lottie suggested as she held out a bucket of water and a dipper.

Devlin merely grunted his thanks as he drank thirstily. He'd never taken his shirt off in front of anyone, let alone a woman, but he did hand her his hat.

At one time he had thought no work could be more physically draining than ranching, but this past week had changed his opinion forever. The ground had to be cleared of rocks and stumps before it could be plowed, and he had already piled up enough rock to build a small house.

He heard the thud of a rock hitting ground behind him and looked up to see Lottie lugging a heavy boulder over to the pile.

"Here now," he protested, "I can handle this."

"It's my land, Mr. McShane, and my stubbornness that's the cause of your aching back. It's my right to work alongside of you as I would have my husband. I'm no stranger to hard work so don't you fret none."

Devlin's protests fell on deaf ears. Soon they fell into an easy pattern. He would arrive as the sun peeped over the horizon and she would be waiting, a cup of hot coffee for him in her hand. They would work ceaselessly, breaking only for lunch, until daylight was almost gone. The little boys helped when they could, fetching fresh water from the well.

During the weeks that followed, a friendship grew between the young man and the older woman. He admired her determination and hard work. Knowing nothing about farming, he followed her instructions closely as they cleared and plowed the ground. Devlin soon forgot his shame about baring his scarred back. It wasn't long before the sun, scorching the skin on his bare chest and back, turned it a deep bronze.

Often, Devlin and Lottie would sit in the shade of a tree to eat their lunch, and he surprised himself by telling her about his homeland and the family he so rarely spoke of. Lottie sensed the bottled-up anger and pain in this man as she listened quietly, occasionally prompting him to unburden himself of those old hurts. They would laugh over the antics of her two small sons, and she warmed as she watched the horseplay between Devlin and the boys. She doubted very much if this serious young man let down his guard often, and his easy laughter and gentle handling of her children brought joy to her heart.

Like a child waiting for Christmas, she looked forward to the days he came. At first she didn't realize that it was the woman in her who anticipated his presence, but awareness slowly dawned as she watched the rippling muscles in his broad bare chest and felt a warmth in her loins and a blush on her cheeks. Sometimes she would awaken in the night, blood pounding in her ears and flushed from vivid dreams she could not control.

She had married Loren Thomas to escape the poverty of the little farm her family lived on in southern Missouri. He had been twenty-five years her senior, but she had been honored that a man with far-seeing dreams had offered for her. Her ma and pa wouldn't miss the extra mouth at the table, and her four brothers and three sisters would probably fight over the little she had claimed for her own. Without a backward glance she married the older man and moved into his big cabin. The gratitude she felt more than made up for the lack of love, and she took pride in the fact that her body could give him pleasure and that she could give him the children he adored. At first their lovemaking had been awkward, but Lottie was a giving woman by nature and soon her body began to crave the physical release of the marital bed.

She had been saddened when his desire for her seemed to be replaced by a consuming desire to move west. With the opening of the Montana territory, they packed their belongings and headed toward his dreams.

They had made love for the last time the night before they left Missouri. After that Loren was too tired or too preoccupied, or too ill. But Lottie still felt cravings, and the needs of her body did not die with her husband.

Devlin wasn't sure when he became aware of Lottie as a woman. One day he noticed how her chestnut hair glistened with red lights in the afternoon sun, refusing to be confined by her hairpins. He couldn't help but see that though her hands and face were browned by the sun the valley between her breasts, exposed by the open buttons at her bodice, gleamed milky white. He loved to watch her with her children as she hugged them tenderly, her warm brown eyes filled with love. He began to observe her as she worked, enjoying the little tunes she hummed and the way her hips swayed as she made her way gingerly between the plowed and furrowed rows of cleared land.

At times their eyes would meet and he would feel as if he were on fire inside. Not even a frigid dunking under the pump seemed to curb the desire that began to rage within him. Still he held a tight rein on his need.

Lottie sat on a large boulder, watching as Devlin wielded a pick to break up the hard soil. She knew she should be in the house fixing lunch, but she couldn't tear her eyes away from that strong back or the way the light glinted off his sun-streaked hair. His hips were lean and his legs long and muscular. His chest was nearly as bronzed as his back with only a light furring of dark blond hair running down to the corded muscles of his stomach and disappearing beneath his belt. A magnificent male animal, and she felt like a harlot as she watched him.

Devlin threw down the pick and wiped the sweat from his brow with his kerchief. He turned to Lottie, intending to ask about lunch, but the words froze in his throat as he saw the naked hunger on her face. Their eyes locked for what seemed to be an eternity, both caught within their own doubts, their own desires.

Then Devlin moved toward her, but Lottie jumped up and covered her flaming face with her hands as she ran toward the house.

"Shame, shame," she whispered to herself as she slung pots and pans around the kitchen. She shooed the boys outside, not wanting them to see their mother's turmoil.

Devlin entered the kitchen quietly and sat down at the table. He refused to acknowledge what he had seen on her face. Too inexperienced to understand a woman's desires, he chalked it all up to his own frustrated needs.

Neither Lottie nor Devlin spoke during lunch, not even seeming to hear the constant chatter of the children. Afterward Devlin left the kitchen without a word, taking out his anger at himself on the hard ground.

Lottie awoke with a start as the sun streamed in the window of her small bedroom. Throwing back the covers, she leapt from bed and hastily pulled her thin cotton robe over her nightdress. The last two nights she had been through hell, tossing and turning, avoiding sleep and the dreams that mortified her. Exhaustion had finally overcome her, and she had fallen into a dreamless slumber, from which she now awakened far later than normal. By this time she was usually up, dressed, and had the coffee perking.

She ran her fingers through the tangled locks of her hair and rushed out to the pump, grabbing the coffeepot as she passed through the kitchen. The water had barely begun to trickle into the pot when Devlin rode into the yard. She pumped the handle furiously, almost dousing herself as it gushed forth.

She murmured her greeting and held the door open for him as he followed her into the house.

"Sorry," she said breathlessly. "I overslept this morning. Can't remember the last time I did that. I'll have the coffee going in a jiffy."

"No matter" came the slightly hoarse reply. Devlin's gaze wandered over her shapely back in the old cotton robe and the wild disarray of her magnificent hair. Her movements were jerky as she lit the old stove and filled the pot with fresh-ground coffee. He remained by the door, refusing the chair she offered as she pulled the mugs from the cabinet. His breath caught in his throat as she reached above her head, lifting her full breasts in a way that accented their roundness.

The pot on the stove bubbled and boiled as the rich aroma of coffee filled the kitchen. She watched it impatiently, her bare foot tapping the cold wooden floor. "A watched pot never boils, they say." She laughed nervously as she filled one of the mugs and handed it to him.

Her eyes were still languid from sleep, her full mouth soft and warm. Devlin's hands trembled as he took the mug, forcing him to grab it with both hands to keep it from tumbling to the floor.

Lottie could see the desire in his eyes. Suddenly all the recriminations of the past days ceased to matter. Her eyes lowered to the bulge of his manhood as it strained against the tight confines of his denims. Her breathing quickened and, almost with a will of its own, her hand reached out to touch that urgent desire.

Devlin closed his eyes and shuddered, causing scalding coffee to splash onto his hands. But he felt no pain as he quickly set the mug on the floor and drew her into his arms, nearly crushing her as he molded her firmly against him.

As his lips met hers, Lottie sensed his inexperience, and it was she who coaxed the hard mouth to soften. It was her tongue that traced delightful patterns against his lips until her apt and eager pupil met her kiss for kiss, until the tingles began to move up her spine and her legs weakened, until he grew bolder and more self-assured.

Suddenly he pushed away from her, holding her at arm's length as he studied her flushed face. "Lottie, are you sure?"

She threw herself back into his arms and whispered her reply against his broad chest. "It's wrong. I know that, but I need you so."

She sensed the battle within him and knew he would leave her if only she said the word. But she had her own demons to fight; and the feel of his desire against her thigh, the strength in the arms that held her, and the wonderful scent of him sent a fire raging through her body.

Taking a firm hold of his arm, she led the way toward her bedroom, glancing up at the loft where her children still slept soundly. Inside, she closed and latched the door before turning to him. Taking a deep breath for courage, she shrugged out of the robe and hurriedly pulled her old, frayed nightgown over her head.

She stood before him proudly, magnificent in her nakedness. His eyes roamed the length of her; from the full, heavy breasts with their hardened peaks to the slim waist curving outward to wide hips and lusciously contoured thighs. It was the ripe body of a woman who had borne children, yet hard work had kept it firm and supple. His hands ached to touch her.

Lottie trembled under this intense scrutiny, but when she dared meet his eyes she found only tender wonderment. His hand reached out to her, and she quickly closed the distance between them, going into his arms like an eager young girl.

His fingers explored the soft skin of her back before threading themselves through her hair. She lifted her face for his kiss, and their lips touched once again. There was no urgency in this kiss but a slow, tender exploration that soon left them both breathless.

Her hands left his shoulders and her fingers worked the buttons on his shirt, slowly stripping it away as she kissed each newly exposed area of skin. He allowed her to slip the shirt from his shoulders, and his skin tingled as her fingers ran lovingly down the powerful arms. But when her hands went to the buckle of his belt, he stopped her.

The confusion was evident in her face, and he smiled, kissing her lightly in reassurance. He needed time to control the flaming passion in his body and feared that her touch alone would bring quickly to a conclusion what had just begun.

He urged her toward the bed and lay beside her, placing gentle kisses on her face as he stroked the thick, soft mass of her chestnut hair. He could sense the urgency within her, but stayed her hands when she would have touched him, until he felt once again in control of his body.

He kissed her deeply before rising from the bed to shed the last barrier that kept him from her.

When he returned to her, he allowed her hands to roam across the wide, muscled chest and down the corded, flat stomach. She hesitated only for a moment before her hand closed about his aching manhood.

"No man should be so beautiful," she whispered with awe as his mouth took possession of her own and passion could no longer be delayed.

His hands found her breasts and kneaded them gently, teasing the rigid points with his thumbs. He felt her shudder and knew her pleasure as his lips replaced his fingers, his tongue torturing until she grasped his head and told him in gesture of her need. His lips closed over one firm peak, and she arched against him as he gently suckled at her breast.

He urged her thighs apart and moved between them as he turned his attention to the other breast. Instinct now guided him, and as she lifted her hips, he thrust into her eager body. For a moment they remained still as Lottie's body adjusted to the fullness of his manhood. Then she began to move beneath him, urging him, begging him to still the ache that rose from deep within.

He was male in its most splendid form as he moved inside her; it was as though he had been born with the knowledge of how to please. She felt the tremors begin and held her breath as fulfillment brought her upward against him. She cried out. So lost in her own rapture, she was unaware of his own release until he fell heavily upon her and the sweat from their bodies mingled.

She began to sob, and he held her gently, remembering her strangled outcry. "Dear God, Lottie, did I hurt you?"

The alarm in his voice stopped her tears and she reached up and lovingly traced the handsome planes of his face with her fingertips. "Oh, no, it was wonderful. More wonderful than I ever dreamed it could be. But I fear that in gaining a lover I have lost a dear friend."

Devlin gently brushed the tears from her face. "Nothing could change what I feel for you, Lottie. You've only made yourself more dear to me."

His words caused alarm, and she sat up, suddenly realizing how vulnerable this young man was. "I don't want to hurt you, Dev, but I must be honest. I'm not in love with you, and I don't want you imagining yourself in love with me."

He reached for her and hauled her playfully back into his arms. "Hush, woman. What happened just now was wonderful for both of us. Don't spoil it by worrying it to death."

Devlin began to rise much earlier on the days he went to Lottie's. The stolen moments in the early dawn were precious to him as Lottie taught him every way possible to please a woman and increase his own enjoyment. But the greatest lesson she taught was that caring, tenderness, and respect brought a greater satisfaction in the act of love than a thousand hurried couplings paid for and delivered in the rooms above a tavern.

It was for both of them many things. For Devlin, it erased the memory of his first time—he awkward, the Billings whore mechanical, and the whole thing reeking of falseness like the cheap perfume she wore. For Lottie, it was a chance to experience the woman in herself again. But for neither was it a forever kind of love. In time Devlin felt her begin to draw away from him, and she seemed to nurse a worry too deep for him to touch.

One morning when he arrived early, as had been his custom for nearly a month, Lottie met him at the door, dressed for the fields. If Devlin felt any hurt, it was softened by Lottie's face, freed somehow of the anxiety that had etched it in recent days.

"Dev," she said gently, drawing him outside where they could speak without waking the boys. "I made myself a vow, and I think you should know about it. You and I both know that what we have between us some people would call a sin . . ." Devlin opened his mouth in protest, but she silenced him with a glance. "What the good Lord sees it as is His alone to tell. I've been waiting for a sign from Him, and I guess you've noticed that it's been worrying me." She paused now, looking for and finding understanding in those kind blue eyes.

"If we made a child . . . you knew we were risking that, didn't you?" A fearful comprehension suddenly dawned on Devlin; his jaw tightened though he kept his gaze steady. "Well, I just decided that that would be God's judgment on us. But we haven't, and I believe that's the Lord's way of saying we had our pleasure, but now it's time to stop. I vowed I would, Dev, if my time of month came—and it has."

Devlin felt a mixture of regret and relief, but he knew to his depths that Lottie was right to end it. Whether it had to do with God and sin or something less mystical, he knew that in time their friendship would have burned out along with their passion. That friendship was more precious to him—and to her, he sensed—than fleshly gratification.

Chapter Eight

Jennifer followed her father out onto the porch. She watched him closely as he pulled a cigar from his breast pocket, struck a match on the heel of his boot, and then settled himself on the railing while the fragrant smoke curled about his head. Anyone who knew him less well might think him a man totally at ease with his world, but Jenny sensed a tension within him. The worry wrinkle between his thick brows seemed to be permanently fixed. He smiled frequently, but the smile never quite reached his eyes. His booming voice had a forced joviality.

Jennifer joined her father on the railing. Linking an arm with his, she lay her head on his shoulder. She desperately wanted to believe that the cattlemen's meeting in Billings today was only the routine bull session James insisted it was, but this morning's private conference with Devlin and Sam, behind closed library doors, was too reminiscent of many such meetings in the past year.

She had tried hard these past months to be the daughter James wanted her to be. By degrees she had even come to feel a certain pleasure in her femininity. But for all the dresses and her new role as the belle of Yellowstone County, the Jenny of the tumbled hair, boyish clothing, and wild ways lurked beneath the surface. A secret smile touched her lips. It was her sixteenth birthday, and if she felt the woman she was becoming inside her, she also knew the tomboy was somewhere there as well.

The smile faded. She had acceded to all of James's

demands in exchange for his approval, a sign of love she desperately needed. But his refusal to share what worried him threatened to damage the growing bond between them.

Lifting her head from James's shoulder, Jennifer studied his profile. James Douglas was a worried man. "Are you telling me the truth about the cattlemen's meeting?" It was a straightforward question boldly asked.

James tossed away the half-smoked cigar. He tried to avoid her direct gaze by absently dusting imaginary particles from spotless trousers. The question put him on the defensive. Was he wrong not to tell her? Perhaps if he threw her a crumb of the truth, she'd stop studying his every gesture.

"The Triple S is missing a few cows, so naturally Herb Walters wants to throw the entire county into a panic about cattle rustlers and desperadoes. Personally I think Herb is a bag of wind who keeps sloppy records."

If James had placed every treasure in the world at her feet, Jennifer could not have been more pleased than she was at this moment. "Is that why you've looked so worried lately? Do you think there's a possibility of cattle rustling?"

James's eyes rolled upward as if asking for divine guidance. "Lord, girl. Don't *you* go making mountains out of molehills."

He grabbed Jennifer and hugged her with the gruff tenderness of a tame grizzly. "The only thing I'm worried about today is getting old. Every time you have a birthday, my old bones creak a little louder."

Sam approached, leading two saddled horses. "Mornin', James—Princess." The plug of chewing tobacco between gum and cheek made speech difficult. "You ready to ride into town, James?"

James gave Jennifer another quick hug. "Honey, I wish you wouldn't ride out too far today." Seeing the alarm in her eyes, he covered his warning tone with a hearty chuckle and a gentle tap to her chin. "You've got a big party tonight, or did you forget the shindig we've been planning. I don't want you looking tired and ragged. I've been looking forward to showing off my girl."

Jennifer remained on the porch until her father and Sam

were out of sight. Looking down at the brown spittle Sam had left near the porch, her brows drew together in disgust, the smooth skin on her forehead creasing exactly as James's had done. But the Douglas worry wrinkle was not one whit less alarming than the brown tobacco juice staining the ground. Sam indulged himself in the revolting habit only when he was troubled.

When James knew he and Sam were out of sight of the house, he pulled the roan to a halt. "How many?"

The plug of chewing tobacco was being worked vigorously. The pale blue eyes looked like winter in a blizzard. "I estimate about forty to fifty head."

James whistled between his teeth. "Are you absolutely certain?"

The white-haired man bent over his horse, expelling the entire wad of chew. "Damn that Maggie! Nags at me till I give it up and now there ain't no pleasure in it anymore."

"Damn it, Sam. I asked if you were certain."

"You want to count 'em yourself?"

Ignoring the biting tone, James removed his hat and raked his fingers through hair he was certain had this moment sprouted fresh gray. "Let's keep our losses to ourselves for the time being. If we give Walters fuel to throw on the fire, there's bound to be trouble."

The older man hooked his knee over the saddlehorn. "Dev's checking the fences to see if there's a break to account for our loss. Ain't got much faith in fences anyhow. Cows are just God's creatures like the rest of us. You pen any animal up and he's bound to try and bust free."

If there were hidden meanings in Sam's sage observations, James ignored them. "We better get into town before Herb starts looking for farmers and drifters to hang."

The wind whipped her hair free of its confining ribbon. The sun on her face, the speed of the little pinto, and the rush of joy at riding free and proud across her land made Jennifer's spirits soar as high as the hawk in the azure sky above.

As she crested the hill, she pulled the pony up. Leaning over his neck, she whispered to her co-conspirator. "We've come too far, but you've gotten fat and lazy." Dismounting, she rubbed the ache in her buttocks. "And I've gotten soft."

The sun was high. The rumblings of her stomach told Jenny it was time to head back home. But too many hours trying to be a proper lady made this minor rebellion enticing. She took the reins and began to lead the pony down the other side of the hill.

She hadn't walked far when she spotted a man beneath a grove of trees bordering the fence of the south pasture. Shading her eyes from the noonday glare, she easily identified the tall man as he struggled to repair a downed fence.

Thirst and an empty stomach overruled any personal objections to approaching Devlin as he labored. She knew she would find food and water. The men seldom returned to the ranch for the midday meal. An audacious grin matched the twinkle in her eye. She'd practice the art of flirtation and cajole Devlin into sharing his ration of food.

The thick grass muffled her approach. When she was a few yards away, Jennifer halted abruptly. Devlin had discarded his shirt. Bronzed skin was stretched taut across shoulders that looked even more impressive unconcealed by cloth. Muscles bunched, knotted, and glistened with sweat as Devlin worked at resetting the fallen post.

Jennifer had never before seen a man's body that had the same lithesome grace as a blooded horse. Long powerful legs, lean flanks, and a majestic form sent foreign feelings through her body.

When he shifted his position, the right side of his back was no longer shaded by a tall oak. Jennifer's throat constricted painfully. The network of puckered scar tissue marring what had seemed perfection made her cry out softly in protest.

The sound spun Devlin around. The handgun he had strapped to his thigh was in his hand and aimed at the point between silver eyes before his mind registered the identity of the dark-haired vixen.

Blue eyes darkened with the knowledge of his sudden

vulnerability. A part of him wanted to grab up the shirt and cover the naked evidence of his degradation. With only a word or look she could reopen those old wounds. Pride made him stand firm, braced for the inevitable questions, the jeering remarks.

"What do you want?" His tone was hostile. It took him a few moments to realize he still held the gun in his hand although he'd lowered it to point at the ground. He slid the firearm back into its holster and casually reached for his shirt.

"I . . . I was thirsty. I thought you might—"

"Canteen's over there." He pointed to where his horse, Shannon, was tethered.

"Thank you." Her voice was a mere whisper as she approached the tall chestnut. She could feel Devlin's hatred wrap itself around her heart. When she reached the grazing animal, her hand stroked the proud neck lovingly. The taste of salt as a teardrop touched the corner of her lips was the first awareness that she was crying. Unobtrusively she wiped her moist face on the sleeve of her blouse. Devlin would not thank her for these unaccountable tears of pity. But who could have treated him with such barbarity? Flesh must have been cut nearly to the bone to leave such horrible scars. The pain must have been unendurable.

The wind rustled the leaves on the trees, and a girl's silent sympathy reached to touch and ease the man who watched her so guardedly. He pulled on his shirt, his footsteps silent as he approached. "Are you hungry too?"

Jennifer shook her head. Her appetite was gone, but she accepted the canteen he handed her. Keeping her eyes lowered, she sipped the cool water, keenly aware of the masculine form towering over her.

A single, crystal teardrop remained on the velvet cheek. Absently, Devlin's knuckles brushed it away. When she lifted her head in surprise at the gentle touch, he smiled hesitantly. It never ceased to amaze him that her pale gray eyes could be so expressive; not cold and frigid as one would expect. As if they were windows to her mind, those eyes reflected all the questions she didn't voice. He felt compelled to say something, if only to acknowledge his gratitude at her continued silence.

"My father used to tell me, 'Son, keep your eyes on the road ahead 'cause where ye been is just a place to pass through to where you're going.'"

Jennifer returned his smile. "And just where are you going, Devlin McShane?"

"Going? Well, right now I'm going over there to fix that fence." He didn't question her presence as she walked beside him.

"Don't you think it's strange that this entire section of fence gave way?" Touching the barbed points of the wire, Jennifer turned to Devlin, her unease growing to alarm. "This fence has been cut."

"Looks that way, doesn't it?" There was little point in denying the obvious.

"Have we lost cattle?"

Devlin considered his answer carefully. "Possibly."

Jennifer made a face. "You wouldn't give me a straight answer if the range had been stripped bare. The conspiracy to keep little Jenny ignorant continues."

Whatever brief truce had existed between them was broken. Jennifer regretted the sympathy she had felt for a lost boy as she recalled her loathing for the man who had replaced her in her father's heart. Pushing the canteen into Devlin's hand, she whirled around and made for her horse. As she mounted she called over her shoulder, "Thank you for your kindness, Mr. McShane—for the water and"—her teeth were gritted—"the valuable information."

Devlin watched her ride away and then, a look of wry amusement masking his pain, returned to his work.

Seated before her dressing table, Jennifer fastened a pearl earring while her foot tapped in time with the fiddler's lively tune. The sounds of music and laughter drifted upstairs as she put the finishing touches on her preparations for the first grown-up party of her life.

There was no need to pinch her cheeks, as her color was high with anticipation. Her eyes sparkled with the brilliance of diamonds. Maggie had swept, twisted, and piled the seemingly impossible length of her hair high atop her head. Soft waves of ebony satin, held firmly in place by pearl-tipped hairpins and ivory combs, accented the finely drawn features she had once considered a curse rather than an asset.

Standing, Jennifer twirled before the mirror to get the full effect. The ivory silk dress hugged her youthful figure where it should hug, and flowed gracefully over layers of petticoats. The demurely scooped neckline with its six-inch fall of lace allowed a modest display of her graceful neck and upper chest.

She tugged at the neckline of the dress until she managed to reveal a half inch of bosom, and then wrinkled her nose as the décolleté disappeared when she released her hold on the garment.

Suddenly bored by her own reflection, and slightly perplexed by this sudden vanity, Jennifer stuck out a childish tongue. It didn't give her courage, but she felt infinitely more comfortable with herself as she left the safety of her room.

At his station by the door, James glanced up as his daughter descended the stairs. His heart swelled to bursting as he stepped forward to take her hand. Bowing in homage to her fresh beauty, a proud father led his daughter into a room filled with neighbors and lifelong friends.

A hush fell over the room, followed by admiring gasps as James Douglas presented his only child, introducing her to a world that acknowledged her a young woman. Jennifer turned to her father with eyes shining, her face glowing with joy and gratitude.

Close to the fireplace, away from the main group of well-wishers, Devlin stood, his face shuttered as he watched the varying reactions to the full bloom of Jennifer's beauty. Stuart Walters and Tom Davis looked like they had both been struck by Cupid's sharp arrow. To claim that his own senses were unaffected would be to deny life in his obviously healthy body. He was thankful that he, unlike those two raw lads, was a mature man of twenty-one with enough experience to think with his head instead of his loins. Jennifer was a child. An unbelievably lovely child who possessed the face and form of an enchantress, but a child nonetheless.

Jennifer took a glass of champagne and giggled as the bubbles tickled her nose. A tentative sip caused her lips to pucker prettily. The somewhat bitter wine reminded her of persimmons. She couldn't know how this artless pursing of lips would draw masculine eyes and turn masculine thoughts.

Over the rim of the glass, her eyes swept the room until they rested on a tall figure leaning casually against the mantel. The muscles in her stomach knotted involuntarily when Devlin lifted his own glass in a silent toast. Her heart fluttered as he began the journey across the room. When he stood before her there was no mockery in his smile. But when she looked into his eyes there was also no matching warmth. Had she imagined that moment of affinity this afternoon when his hand gently touched her cheek? Lowering her eyes, she studied his polished boots.

"Excuse me, sir." Devlin drew James's attention. "I'm sorry, but I can't stay. One of the mares is in foal. Davie needs my help."

"Surely one of the other men can give Davie a hand if he needs it." James sounded disgruntled.

"It's Shannon's foal . . . my responsibility."

Jennifer listened to the quiet argument going on over her head. Let him go, she silently screamed. If he prefers horses to my party then I don't want him here.

Before Devlin left he did remember to acknowledge Jennifer, if somewhat absently. "Happy birthday, Princess."

Jennifer barely responded to his courtesy. She turned toward Stuart Walters with a blinding smile, which brought the young man running to her side. When she turned again, Devlin was gone.

Accepting Stuart's stammered invitation to dance, Jennifer tried not to cringe visibly when he stomped on her feet.

She determined that nothing was going to spoil this evening for her. She even attempted to ignore the huddle of cattlemen in a distant corner of the parlor, but time and time again her eyes strayed to those ranchers. Eventually her father claimed his dance.

"Is anything wrong?" she asked him. The downed fence, the cut wire, and Devlin's evasive answers continued to nag at her.

"Tempest in a teapot," James reassured. "Now don't you start worrying your pretty little head about men's business."

The curtain fell. Somehow the pain was less than she had expected. Miss Hastings had prepared her well for a woman's place in a man's world. Lifting her chin, she determined that she would find her own place. There would be no further self-deception.

When James turned her over to Tom Davis, she looked into the young man's adoring hazel eyes and accepted in that moment the only power she would ever wield. She tested this weapon on Tom and then, later, Stuart. It was not the way she would have chosen, but clearly it was effective.

Both young men nearly came to blows trying to bring her a glass of punch. Three fathers looked on this scene with tolerant smiles.

"A woman's weapons," Maggie had said. Dear, wise Maggie. Sorrowfully, Jennifer had been slow to learn.

The house was dark and silent. Jennifer sat fully dressed in the chair by her window. The air was still; the tree outside her window motionless.

Suddenly she felt stifled. She picked up an old shawl and crept silently through the house.

It was only moderately cooler on the porch. She draped the shawl across the railing to protect her silk dress and perched herself as she had that morning with her father. Wrapping her hands around the carved post supporting the roof, she leaned back and began to sway in an effort to produce her own cooling breeze.

There was still a light on in the barn. Was there trouble

with the new foal? Concern mixed with curiosity sent her across the yard, holding her skirts high. She was halfway to her destination when the light was extinguished. Jennifer froze, not certain she wanted to be discovered.

The pale ivory of her dress was like a beacon to the man who emerged from the barn rubbing the tense, knotted muscles of his neck with his hand. With the stealth of a panther he approached. His tone was less than friendly as he demanded, "What the devil are you doing out here at this time of night?"

Jennifer lifted her head with an almost regal grace. Her face was bathed by the lambent glow of moonlight. "There's no need to assume that tone with me, Mr. McShane."

Sounds like the princess born, Devlin thought. Looks it too. "Sorry. Guess I'm tired and a little cranky."

Glory be! Had she actually heard him apologize? "Is . . . is everything all right with the foal?"

Taking her arm, Devlin led her back to the porch. "It's a fine colt. Every bit as noble as his sire."

"You sound like a proud papa," Jenny commented conversationally.

Devlin grunted some response as he delivered her safely to the porch. "Good night, Princess."

"Wait . . ." The plea had been impulsive. Now she wanted to snatch back the hand that clutched his arm.

"Is something wrong?"

At the genuine concern in his voice, she lowered her guard. "No. I couldn't sleep. Could you stay and talk with me for just a minute?"

Devlin leaned back against the pillar. "What should we talk about?" Even in the dim light he could see her blush slightly. "Did Cinderella meet her prince at the ball? Are the pangs of first love the root of your sleepless state?"

Jennifer made a disparaging sound. "All men are toads!"

Devlin grinned, chuckling at her vehemence. "I can see that you didn't believe the fairy tales of your childhood. Don't you think a princess can kiss a toad and turn him into the man of her dreams?"

The smile and the laughter in his voice signaled that he was having himself a great good time at her expense. The truce was indeed ended. "You're the biggest toad I know. Would a kiss transform *you?*"

"Maybe . . . maybe not. Want to give it a try?" That ought to send her flying for safety. He was dog tired. All he wanted was to flop down on his bunk and sleep.

With a boldness that shocked him, Jennifer grabbed his shirt and lifted her face, pursing her lips in anticipation of a kiss. He fought the laughter that bubbled up inside. Grabbing her shoulders, he pulled her roughly against his chest, fully expecting her to bolt and run. When she didn't, he became more determined to call her bluff. "You're a bold lass, and in need of a lesson. Brazen little girls usually come to a bad end."

Eyes that had been tightly shut flew open. "And typical of the Irish, you're full of blarney. You don't have the guts to kiss me, McShane."

"I believe I've warned you before. Never dare an Irishman." He was getting nervous. When she didn't struggle or attempt to pull away, he slid his arms about her waist and lifted her off her feet.

Jennifer nearly cried out when her feet left the solid security of the porch. He wanted her to quail, and she wouldn't give him the satisfaction. She forced her body to relax and wound her arms about his neck.

She'd backed him into a corner. He'd be damned if he would cry uncle. He brought his mouth to hers with anger, but the anger didn't last. This was a girl's first kiss, and it should be remembered fondly even if its bestower was not. Gently he taught her the way of it.

Somewhere between fright and stubbornness, Jennifer began to enjoy this new experience. Devlin smelled of hay, horse, and the lingering scent of soap. When the brute force gentled and his mouth began to move persuasively against her own, she determined this kiss to be one of the sweetest, entirely pleasant sensations of her life.

Thinking himself an experienced man of the world instructing a child, Devlin soon found himself being taught a lesson he'd remember for a lifetime.

She smelled of wild flowers, spring, and new beginnings. The firm thrust of her breasts against his chest seared him like a hot brand. Her mouth was petal soft, flowering beneath his own as her lips parted gently. He knew he would forever remember the special taste that was Jennifer.

Tentatively he sought the tender inner rim of her mouth with his tongue. Wildfire desire tore through his body until he thought his knees might buckle. With a desperate groan, he pulled away, holding her firmly at arm's length. Never again would he deceive himself that Jennifer was a mere child.

He was trembling; his voice unsteady. "My God, girl. You're supposed to slap my face. You are *not* supposed to kiss me back."

A little dazed, Jennifer smiled at him rather vacantly. "Slap you? Why should I slap you? It was nice."

The foul word Devlin muttered made her recoil as he turned on his heel, leaving her to stand alone on the porch with her mouth agape. Eventually the night grew chill, driving Jennifer back into the house.

Stretched out beneath the sheets, Jennifer decided that if all men kissed like Devlin McShane, it might be an enterprise worth cultivating.

Devlin was waiting when Jennifer emerged from the house for her daily ride. He'd saddled Dusty and stood holding the pinto's reins.

A wide-brimmed hat, set low on her forehead, hid any expression in her eyes. Without speaking she accepted his assistance as he gave her a foot up into the saddle. Beneath the rim of her hat she could see the slight flush of embarrassment beneath the bronze of his skin. She wanted to crow with delight as he cleared his throat not once, but twice before he managed to speak.

"About last night . . . I . . . I'm not in the habit of molesting little girls. It won't happen again."

Jennifer pushed the hat back on her head. She stared until she could almost feel him squirm inside. "That's too bad, Dev. I was looking forward to another McShane lesson."

Jerking the pinto around, she urged the horse to a gallop, kicking dust into Devlin's face.

She didn't hear his low nervous whistle. Nor did she see the slow grin of admiration before he tipped his hat in tribute.

Chapter Nine

In the back of the wagon, Jenny sat on a blanket holding tightly to her straw hat with one hand while the other gripped the railing. Her legs dangled over the back edge, swinging to and fro in rhythm with the sway of the awkward transport as it lumbered along the road toward Billings.

When a wheel dropped into a deep rut, the sudden lurch nearly tossed her off the edge. Forced to use both hands to save herself, she was helpless when a sudden gust of hot wind stripped the little hat from her head, bringing the carefully pinned mass of hair tumbling into her face.

"Lose something, Princess?"

She didn't need to look up to identify the deep, slightly patronizing voice. "My hat." She said it flatly, without emotion. The small victory she had won over this man a few weeks ago now seemed a mere pinprick on his granite hide. If anything he seemed more indifferent than before.

"Hold up, Sam," Devlin requested, turning Shannon to begin the search for the girl's hat, wishing he had ridden ahead with James to attend the cattlemen's meeting.

When he returned, hat in hand, Devlin tied his horse to the wagon. Easily hoisting himself to sit beside Jennifer, he requested, "Move on, Sam."

When a strong arm slipped about her waist, Jennifer opened her mouth to protest. A glance over her shoulder confirmed the audience of two. Giving Maggie and Sam a rather lame grin, she remained silent, distrustful of this sudden show of chivalry while Devlin announced, "I'll hang on to you while you fix your hair and secure that pretty little hat."

As the wagon lurched again, the arm about her waist tightened, the fingers spreading beneath her breasts. Helpless, she swayed into his embrace, gritting her teeth at his low, throaty chuckle.

When the hat was again securely pinned, she gave this false gallant a withering look, fully intending to dismiss him. Suddenly both of his hands were about her waist as he half lifted, half shoved her farther back into the bed of the wagon.

"You're less likely to fall out on your face," he drawled, stretching out his long legs, bracing his back against the opposite side of the wagon. "Are you looking forward to the big Fourth of July celebration?"

Mumbling the appropriate response, Jennifer found herself unable to meet and hold the direct gaze. Without doubt, Devlin was making a declaration that the kiss they had shared meant nothing. Her mind raced, seeking a method to assure the Irish bastard that he had no cause to worry about her feelings on the matter. Lunacy seemed to be the only explanation for her bold behavior, and a person couldn't be held responsible for actions born of moonshine madness.

"You planning on laying a wager on the horse race, Sam?" Devlin heard his own voice like an echo as he and Sam discussed this year's horses and riders, but all the while his eyes never left her face.

A simple kiss, but it had turned his world upside down and made him question everything he thought himself to be.

During the day it was easy to chase the feelings away. Then suddenly the day would be gone, and in darkness he would be haunted once again by the smell, feel, and taste of her. At the party he had facetiously branded her enchantress, smugly thinking himself immune to any spell cast by the girl. How could he have been so wrong?

"Hey . . ." Sam's voice seemed to echo across the plains. "You sleepin' back there?"

Both Jennifer and Devlin started visibly, their eyes shifting to the man perched high on the bench of the wagon.

Sam's eyes narrowed. He wasn't so old he didn't remember looking at a girl and feeling his insides turn to mush. Had the expression on his own face been as obvious as the one Devlin was wearing? He trusted this boy, but experience had taught Sam Smith that a hard pecker had no conscience. The look he gave Devlin was more than just a warning.

The threat blazing from Sam's eyes nearly made Devlin cringe. The older man was fond of him, but his first loyalty would always be to the princess. With a simple nod of his head, Devlin yielded to Sam's silent command.

The men were gathered around kegs of beer. The women congregated at long tables filled to overflowing with cakes, pies, and enough food to feed half the population of Montana. Clucking their tongues, the ladies glared with blatant disapproval at their husbands, sons, and brothers. High spirits and a beverage that robbed a man of his good sense once again scandalized the good women of high virtue.

Seated at the end of one of the tables, Jennifer tuned out the vociferous gabble. Her eyes swept the crowd until they rested on James and Sam standing in a gathering of other men. But while the others gulped, refilling their mugs time and again, James Douglas and his foreman seemed content with their half-empty mugs.

Not one man who had attended the second cattlemen's meeting this morning had breathed even a hint of its subject or outcome. Whatever had troubled those men in June seemed to have found its own resolution.

Tired of women's chatter, Jennifer politely excused herself and stepped up on the wood-planked walk. With her hands clasped behind her back, she traversed the town of Billings, peering into merchants' windows, greeting neighbors, and searching for something to allay the growing boredom.

She was admiring a small replica of a carousel displayed in the window of Rodgers' General Store when the stale smell of beer assaulted her nostrils. Swinging around, she faced a young man swaying precariously as he fought to maintain his balance. Stuart Walters's eyes were glazed and red-rimmed, his lopsided grin nearly contrite when he reached out to grab hold of the only stationary object in his spinning world.

The mere force of his hands on her shoulders nearly sent her to her knees. But when he continued to totter forward, she was powerless against his superior weight as they went tumbling down together.

Jennifer pushed and shoved at the dead weight keeping her pinned to the walk. "Get off me, you lout . . ."

Stuart's weight disappeared as he was lifted with ease by the mighty strength of Devlin McShane's anger. Devlin's face appeared to be carved of stone, the deep blue eyes as hard and cold as sapphires.

A trip to the top floor of Slater's saloon, and the overpainted, overperfumed whore who had been the recipient of the fire kindled by this brazen little chit, had proven ineffective in righting Devlin's topsy-turvy emotions. The anger he directed at himself he now shared in full measure with the girl who lay flat on her back for all the world to view. "You don't learn very fast do you, Princess?"

Jennifer recoiled inside at the scathing tone. He judged her guilty, but what was her crime? Her own eyes smoked with fury as she watched him hoist Stuart over his shoulder. The consoling words he spoke to the limp form as he walked away cut Jennifer like a knife.

"Let's go get you sobered up, Stu. A man needs all his faculties when he tangles with a shameless hellcat. Boy, she'd gobble you up and spit you out. . . ."

The words grew indistinct. Rising slowly to her feet, Jennifer slipped into the open doorway of the store to cover her humiliation. She nearly jumped out of her skin at the sound of a voice.

"Come on in, honey. Sit a spell and pour yourself a glass of lemonade."

With a hand over her heart, Jennifer expelled a sigh of relief.

The rocking chair groaned beneath the strain of Ada Rodgers's girth. Sixty years of life was etched into the full-fleshed face. Twinkling eyes were wise and all-seeing.

"Looked like you had a little tussle with Stu Walters." At Jennifer's shrug, she continued. "Don't pay no mind to Devlin's harsh words. Sounded to me like he was more than just a bit jealous."

Trying to turn the conversation, Jennifer poured herself a glass of the offered lemonade, casually commenting, "Things are getting rough and rowdy out there."

Ada chuckled. "Honey, I've seen Fourth of July celebrations that fairly blew this town apart. Folks must be gettin' old like me. This is a church picnic compared to the old days."

Settling herself in the empty rocker next to Ada, Jenny sipped the tart beverage. She relaxed a bit in the cool dimness of the general store. She'd always loved coming here as a child, drawn as much by Ada's easy welcome as by the brightly colored treasures to be found on the shelves and in the display cases that lined the walls of the shop. Memories of sitting on Ada's knee, stuffing her mouth full of oatmeal cookies and being petted to the point of being spoiled rotten, brought a smile.

Jennifer had a special place in Ada's heart as well. Her own children, two girls, were grown and one had even married a wealthy shipbuilder and lived back east in a place called Bridgeport. She rarely saw her grandchildren, and Jennifer seemed at times to stand in their stead.

They talked some more about Fourth of Julys past, about Jennifer's birthday party, and about the way Billings was changing. Ada was convinced it was surely for the worse, though she and her husband, Zeb, would benefit from the influx of business as the population boomed.

Ada muffled a yawn. "Think I'll take me a short snooze so I can push my drunken husband around when the music starts up. Zeb ain't much for dancin' when he's sober."

"Can I leave my hat in the back room?" Jennifer was already out of the rocker.

"Sure 'nuff, hon."

Brightly lit Chinese lanterns were strung across the street. Any man with a fiddle was encouraged to play. Jennifer stood next to her father, her laughter joining with his, watching wives drag husbands who could barely stand out onto the street. They would have their dancing if they had to carry their partners.

James smiled down on Jenny. Her shoulders swayed in time with the music. Taking her hand, he drew her into the street. Round and round they twirled until, laughing, she begged him to stop.

Dizzy, her head on her father's strong shoulder, Jennifer knew a contentment she hadn't felt since the morning of her birthday. This was her place, and all the world looked bright and wonderful.

When Davie waltzed by with a very handsome, chestnut-haired woman in his arms, Jenny peered over her father's shoulder. "Who's the lady with Davie?"

Turning, James smiled and nodded in the couple's direction. "That's Lottie Thomas. I'm surprised your curious nature hasn't spurred Dusty to the Thomas farm. If I remember correctly, you were ready to take her side against me back in the spring."

"You were wrong to try and take her land away from her. Just because she's a woman. . . ."

"Hush," James commanded softly, placing a gentle finger on her lips. "That's all behind us now." Slipping an arm about her shoulders, he began to move toward Davie and his attractive companion. "Come, I'll introduce you. You can meet her boys, too. They're over there horsing around with Dev."

At mention of Devlin's name, Jennifer halted in mid-stride, her body rigid.

"What's the matter?" James asked, puzzled by this sudden change in temperament.

Jennifer shrugged free of her father's arm and glared at

Devlin. All she needed was for him to mention the incident with Stu Walters in front of her father or, worse, say nothing but look knowingly at her. "I'll meet her another time," she mumbled, then pushed her way through the crowd.

Unaware of the silver-eyed scrutiny, Devlin was preoccupied with tickling the six-year-old boy on his lap until the child squirmed, giggled, and begged for more. When his mother approached, little Saul Thomas scrambled off Devlin's lap, and giving his mother a disparaging glance for having interrupted his fun, he joined his brother, Joshua, on the walk. The adoring look Josh gave Davie Garrett made Saul sneer. Each brother had picked the man he'd most prefer as a second father. Saul really had nothing against Davie except that he was a stickler for seeing the chores done. His almost daily admonishment to "mind your mother" hit a sore spot with a boy who began and ended most sentences with "Do I have to?" Devlin was more fun; he didn't give orders. Although Saul admitted he'd never put Devlin's temper to the test. Most times a mere look from the man who seemed as tall as a tree ended any argument before it began.

Rising from the walk, Devlin towered over the couple standing before him. His deep blue eyes glinted with humor. "You do some mighty fine high steppin', Sprout," he drawled, mimicking Davie's Texas accent.

Davie grinned, cocking one eyebrow. "I've heard the Irish dance a fair jig." It was a quiet challenge.

"Some do" was the evasive answer.

The smile on Lottie's face widened. Boldly, she reached for Devlin's hand. "Dance with me, Mr. McShane."

Jennifer had lost herself in the crowd but she heard Lottie Thomas brazenly ask Devlin to dance. She felt a sudden white-hot stab of savage dislike for the woman she'd never met. Vehemently she denied the sting of envy as Dev's arm slipped around the buxom woman, and she turned her back on the dancing couple.

Two men from the Douglas ranch stood nearby. "Is that what they mean by two left feet?" one said. "Looks like Dev's got more than just two the way he's going about it," his companion replied with a hearty laugh. Neither was surprised a few minutes later when Lottie Thomas threw up her hands in defeat.

Jennifer was trying to regain her poise and escape the sweaty press of dancing people when she was startled to hear her name.

"Miss Jennifer"—an uncertain voice near her shoulder carefully pronounced each syllable—"I think I owe you an apology?"

Jennifer turned and eyed Stuart Walters critically. He'd cleaned up. His hair was slicked down, the rumpled and soiled jacket he'd been wearing earlier discarded. His hangdog expression brought a smile in spite of her irritation. "Yes, you do, Mr. Walters."

"Well . . . I . . . well. . . ."

He looked so abject that pity overruled common sense. "I forgive you, Stu." The look of relief on his face was her reward.

"Will you dance with me?"

It never occurred to Jennifer to question his sobriety. He seemed quite lucid when he led the way. But the minute he put his hand on her waist, she recognized the sour scent of beer coming from a mouth far too close to her face.

He was no longer blind drunk, but he was unsteady on his feet. She'd learned the night of her birthday that Stuart danced with a heavy foot at his best, and he surely wasn't at his best tonight. If she survived this one dance, she would not risk another.

When Stuart began waltzing closer and closer to Devlin and the people Jennifer now called his little family, she tried to turn him in another direction. So intent was she on this purpose, she did not see her young partner's face change as her lithe, full-breasted body brushed against him time and again in her efforts to redirect him.

Stuart's head was reeling, his body inflamed by each brush of her soft woman's body. His groin ached painfully, his befuddled brain recalling those times she had ridden the boundaries shared by Douglas and Walters land. He saw again a young girl in tight trousers, her hair cascading down her back in a riot of windblown curls, and the ripe, pointed breasts bobbing beneath a thin cotton shirt. As if to quell the ache in his loins he pulled her roughly against him.

Jennifer's head snapped up as she was suddenly aware of a foreign hardness pressing against her thigh. For the first time in her life she saw lust mirrored in a man's eyes. She pushed at his chest, her eyes searching the crowd for aid.

With relief she saw Devlin rise, set aside the children on his lap, and move slowly in her direction. This time she would welcome his interference, would warmly acknowledge his rescue. But Devlin passed them by, nodding an indifferent greeting. Jennifer's hope turned to panic. Both of Stuart's arms were about her waist now. Searching hands were sliding upward. Jennifer froze when Stuart's hips ground into hers and his avid mouth placed a slobbering kiss on her face. Arching away, she nearly retched with disgust.

Suddenly James's voice knifed through the din, echoing in the street as if it were a canyon. But this was not an isolated gorge; it was Main Street, and it was filled with people she knew. Her stomach flipped over as she looked from face to face. She found censure, shock, and outrage. No one seemed concerned about the young man dangling helplessly, being shaken as if he were a rag doll, and then tossed aside. All eyes were on Jennifer Douglas.

"Get your things!" James roared again.

The muttered comments of those who had witnessed this shameful scene brought tears to her eyes. Lifting her skirt, she began to run.

"Well, I'd never have believed it."

"Wanton, absolutely wanton."

"Douglas better marry her off quick."

"I'd like a piece of that for myself."

When the wagon pulled up in front of the Rodgerses' store, Jennifer stood in the shadow of the doorway, mauling the straw hat she grasped in her hands. As Devlin jumped down from the bench, she pressed even closer against the wall. "You didn't help me." Her voice was whisper soft.

"Help you?" He snorted, reaching to drag her out of the

safety of the shadow. "Did you need assistance? It didn't look like you needed my help in making a fool of yourself, your father, and that poor boy."

His words struck her like a blow. "It wasn't my fault."

"Of course not." Devlin sneered. "The little princess can't *ever* be wrong. It's perfectly acceptable for you to prance about in tight pants and shirts that make a man's eyes bulge until he loses all reason, and his job, for daring to say what every man within a hundred miles is thinking. There's no danger in daring a man to kiss you in the moonlight either, because not one male soul on this entire earth would think of taking up an offer made by a saucy, hip-twitching little slu—"

"That's quite enough out of you, Dev," James warned as he stepped onto the walk. "I'll chastise my daughter if I think there's a need."

"Fine with me," Devlin grumbled. "I'll let *you* play nursemaid to her virtue from now on. I'll save the knuckles on my hand."

"Get your horse and get back to the ranch." James's voice was acid, his eyes dark as thunderclouds. "You're out of line, McShane."

Jennifer was surprised she felt no joy as she witnessed the first breach between her father and Devlin. Fleetingly Devlin's mask of self-possession slipped, and she saw raw pain in his eyes at James's stern dismissal. His footsteps echoed a hollow victory on the wooden walk.

The trip home from Billings was the longest Jennifer had ever experienced. When the wagon finally rolled into the yard, she was beginning to feel justified in her outrage at the unanimous front of condemnation she faced. Sam refused to speak at all, and Maggie's tongue clucked between endless sentences detailing her disappointment at Jennifer's behavior.

Having traveled by horseback, James was already closeted in his library when she entered the house. "Daddy . . ." She was frightened by his black look, but stood firm in her own defense. "It was *not* my fault."

108

James was feeling every one of his years and then some. "I'm not totally blind, Princess." Running his fingers through his hair, he conceded, "I can't fault you for not having the benefit of a mother's guiding hand. But it's little comfort when the entire population of Yellowstone County has witnessed my daughter behaving like a shameless hussy."

Jennifer hung her head. If her father could believe her capable of such behavior, the citizens he mentioned would have a heyday for months, maybe years, to come.

"Go to your room, daughter." James's voice was lifeless.

The letter in his hand was dog-eared. The lawyer's handwriting stared up at him—straight strokes without curlicues or flourishes.

He'd written Grayburn the morning after the July Fourth fiasco. In his angry state, Maggie's hesitant suggestion of an eastern finishing school seemed the only way to quiet the gossip.

With Arthur's influence, Jennifer had been accepted at the Stapleton Academy for Young Ladies in Boston. But a week ago James had determined to put Arthur's letter to the torch, discarding the idea as a moment's madness. Then the cattle began disappearing from the ranges again. What he and the other ranchers had hoped was an isolated incident now looked like a craftily contrived plan to strip the range of beef, one cow at a time.

His own men, armed for the first time in years, now patrolled the boundaries of his land. Civilization had barely begun to tame this territory, and the tranquil surface could be torn away in the blink of an eye. For this reason alone he wanted Jennifer out of harm's way.

Moving to the window, he spotted his daughter perched on the corral fence, watching Davie put Devlin's new colt through its paces. Oblivious to the change about to occur in her life, she hadn't questioned the ban on her riding. She probably thought it was punishment and was relieved to get off so easily.

He dreaded telling her, had put it off until less than two

weeks were left before they would have to board an eastbound train. He should call her inside right now. Get it over with. But later was soon enough, he reasoned. Just as soon as she came in would be plenty soon enough.

The door slammed behind Jennifer when she entered the house. Devlin's early return forced her inside. He had disliked her before. Now that she'd driven a wedge between him and her father, Devlin didn't attempt to mask his contempt, becoming more short-tempered and impatient than ever in her company. She avoided him whenever possible. But then she seemed to be avoiding everyone lately.

The strain of walking on eggshells was beginning to wear on her nerves. In spite of her effort to show she was mending her ways, the forgiveness she'd anticipated was withheld. Her father ignored her, and Maggie and Sam acted as if someone had died.

"Jennifer, come in here. I have something to discuss with you."

Hope dawned. She entered the library expectantly, but as she watched her father squirm in his chair, clear his throat several times, and fasten his eyes on a point just above her head, a mounting anxiety welled up within her. After his first sentence the blood drained from her face as a cold blanket of dread settled about her.

"I won't go! I won't!" Her scream shook the walls, piercing James's heart.

"Honey, you're not thinking clearly. I promise I don't mean this as a punishment. I'm only thinking of your future."

Her eyes were wild, tears falling in a torrent down her cheeks. Flying through the door, she crashed into a man who had covered the distance between the corral and the house at a dead run when he heard her scream.

A doubled fist hit Devlin squarely on the chest. "It's *your* fault!" she yelled. "I wish whoever put those marks on your back had beaten you to death!"

The words, more than the ineffectual blow, caused him to

stagger, allowing Jennifer the space needed to escape. He called out a warning, but he was too late to prevent her from vaulting onto Shannon's back.

No man other than Devlin McShane could have tamed the spirited chestnut, and no man with any sense would attempt to ride him now. But Jennifer Douglas had a spirit to match the firebrand stallion's. At breakneck speed they disappeared over the horizon as the sunset turned the sky crimson.

A lesser animal would have dropped at the pace she set. Even with his great strength, Shannon was lathered and wheezing when Jennifer reached her sanctuary and slid from his back.

Throwing herself down beside the small stream Robert Douglas had christened Silver Creek in honor of his grand-daughter's eyes, Jennifer released the howls of despair. She cried until she retched, until only dry sobs tortured her throat. Then she bathed her face in the crystal-cool water and dropped onto the warm, sweet-smelling grass to seek the oblivion of exhausted sleep.

The song of a cricket awakened her. Rolling to her back, she stared up at the night sky with its silver crescent moon. Her body felt heavy. As she watched, storm clouds obscured the starlit sky and the sounds of night became ominous. Fear crept into her leaden limbs.

Slowly rising to her feet, Jennifer looked about her. The untethered horse was probably already back in his stall munching oats. To set out on foot was madness, for this secluded grove was at the farthest corner of her father's property. Impulsive, foolish, and stubborn to a fault, Jennifer still had enough good sense to await the men who surely searched. It brought little comfort to remember that few knew of this place or her fondness for it.

The wind began to gust, building strength as the storm approached. In the distance lightning streaked across the sky. Rumbling thunder made the earth, and a frightened young woman, tremble.

Jennifer heard the horse approach long before she could

111

identify its rider. She drew farther back into the shadow of the tree she had taken shelter beneath, daring not to breathe until he called out her name.

She rose, her voice unsteady. "Over here."

She heard the groan of leather, saw the tall shadowy form, and then she was caught up in an embrace that threatened to crush bones.

"Are you all right?" Devlin released her, trying to peer through the darkness. "Did Shannon throw you?"

"Perhaps it would have been better if he had." There was no life in her voice.

The fingers on her arms tightened. Jennifer feared her head would rock off her shoulders as Devlin shook her, yelling at the top of his lungs. "What a damn stupid thing to say! Your father's half out of his mind with worry. Maggie is in bed with a migraine. Sam's roaring like a wounded cougar, and every man in the territory has been out looking for you since dusk."

Frightened, cold, hungry, and filled with despair, Jennifer was unable to tolerate more abuse. Drawing back her foot, she kicked Devlin squarely on his shin. The cry of pain, coupled with her sudden release, brought a smile of momentary victory to her face.

The smile faded when she was jerked to the ground and hauled, face down, over Devlin's knees. She made no sound as the first blow landed on her backside, but by the time he had given her five hard whacks, she was howling like a banshee.

His control near the breaking point, Devlin used a heavy hand to count out ten blows. His own hand was numb when he finally pulled her to her feet. "I'm doubtin' that ye've ever felt the flat of a good hand applied properly to your backside." With his anger, the carefully drilled diction disappeared. The heavy brogue of his childhood was liberated along with the fabled Irish temper. "I'll be settin' myself up as the first volunteer should you have need of such a paddlin' again."

Jennifer jerked away. Her movements were stiff as she

staggered toward the big tree. Sinking to the ground, she covered her face with her hands.

Never in his lifetime had Devlin heard such sounds. Her sobs gave birth to a kindred pain that made his own eyes grow moist.

Easily subduing her halfhearted struggle, he drew her into an embrace so filled with tenderness that its comfort was transmitted and welcomed. Jennifer burrowed into the safe haven of Devlin's arms, oblivious to the storm lashing out in full fury around them.

He held her for what could have been hours or mere minutes. Soaked to the skin by driving rain, and a girl's tears, Devlin's first awareness was the chill making strong arms tremble while he rocked Jennifer. He crooned a rhyme remembered from childhood. The memory of Maureen McShane, little Sean at her breast, rocking, singing, and smiling gently at the older son who watched in awe, seemed not so painful with this slip of a girl in his arms.

Eventually Jennifer too became aware of the wet cold. Reluctantly she left the steady comfort of Devlin's heartbeat. The storm had passed, and once again the glade was bathed in soft moonlight. When Devlin set her aside she felt bereft, watching silently as he moved toward the tethered horse. When he returned with two dry blankets she didn't protest the hands on her blouse as he quickly stripped the soaked garment from her. But she stayed his hand when he touched the ribbon of her chemise.

Devlin turned away, stripping off his shirt, wrapping himself in the dry warmth of a scratchy blanket. When he turned back, a chuckle erupted from his throat at the sight of Jennifer's tiny form cocooned from chin to toe in wool. "You look like a papoose," he commented, lifting her onto his lap, pressing her head into the warm hollow of his throat.

"Talk," he murmured into the dampness of her hair, using a corner of his own blanket to dry the soaked strands.

When she stubbornly remained silent, he continued to prod until the story poured from her with the purgative

113

cleansing of a summer rain. She held back nothing, sparing the man who shared the greatest burden of her pain little. From the grandfather who had named her Princess, to the orphaned boy who embezzled a father's affection and stood as substitute for the son James would never have, Jennifer journeyed through the years with her tale.

There were painful truths, half-truths, and groundless fears aplenty. But as he had never once in all the years stopped to consider or question the reason for this girl's hatred, he admitted his own culpability. James had restored his dead soul, healed his tortured body, and provided a way of life that made getting up every morning a glory. Only this girl in his arms put a blight on his contentment, and he had always resented the thorn of her contempt.

He sighed heavily, shaking his head in self-reproach. "Oh, Jenny, we've a tangled mess to straighten out between us."

Jennifer laughed without humor. "It all seems pretty simple to me. I'm off to Boston, banished by the king for misdeeds. You will remain, the favorite, high in the king's favor."

Devlin's embrace tightened. "You carry a lot of childish, silly notions in that pretty little head, my Princess. First of which is the assumption that I've claimed James to replace my own lost father. Patrick McShane was my sire. I'll not deny him as long as I draw breath."

"You don't understand yet, do you? It doesn't matter what we think or want. *You* are the son of my father's heart whether you will it or not."

Devlin pondered her words. "If that be the truth then it's time I moved on." He smoothed the damp hair away from her brow. "What I owe your father I've done my best to repay. I don't owe him my identity."

She clutched at the blanket around his shoulders. "Why should I trust you? How do I know you're telling the truth?"

Devlin leaned back against the trunk of the tree. The sky was no longer filled with stars. It was that time shortly before dawn when all things were cast in hues of gray. "Truth is much like that sky up there—gray, obscured, and clouded by opinions." He captured her chin and, when his hand met resistance, used both hands to force her to face him. He didn't care that the blanket about his shoulders slipped, baring his chest. He didn't care about anything but taking the pain from the girl's face. His smile was rueful, he was handing her the final victory. "How much time will you give me to pack up and move on?"

Humbled, knowing he would stand behind his words, Jennifer blinked back the tears. "What purpose would your leaving now serve? I'm not as empty-headed nor as deaf as everyone seems to think. We've lost cattle again and that means trouble. Daddy needs you." Her voice softened. "And I need you to watch over him."

Devlin looked down at the small, feminine hand resting on his chest. He picked it up and placed a gentle kiss on the palm. "Go to Boston, Princess. Come back a fine lady, and you'll step into your daddy's shoes without even a whimper from men who would rather starve than take orders from a little hellion in skirts. You can have your kingdom, Princess. But first you'll have to learn how to behave like a queen."

Disturbed by his words and the touch of his lips upon her palm, Jennifer struggled to rise. Fighting the blanket, she made it only to her knees.

Devlin easily swooped her up into his arms. "It's time to go."

"My clothes," she protested. "They're still wet."

"Then you'll ride like a papoose."

"What will Daddy think? I . . . I'm naked beneath this blanket." She giggled.

He sat her on the saddle and mounted behind her. "As you trust me with your father's well-being, so he would trust me with your own."

"And the others who might see us ride in together? What do you think they'll say about your bare chest?"

There was no mirth in Devlin's laughter. "They'll say we got caught in a rainstorm. Any man who would venture another opinion . . ." He didn't need to finish the sentence. They both knew the penalty for underestimating an Irish temper.

They were halfway back to the ranch when her head lolled and then rolled back over Devlin's arm. He memorized every feature of that sleeping, well-loved face. All his actions toward her had been brotherly, but deep in his gut he knew there was nothing resembling that sibling affection within him.

He shifted the girl in his arms until her head lay upon his chest, her breath softly caressing his skin. He turned the horse toward home.

Chapter Ten

The vision before James's eyes began to blur; the figure of the girl on the platform grew smaller and smaller as the train pulled away from the Boston station. He was somewhat reassured when the woman at Jennifer's side put a comforting arm about the girl's shoulders. Had the headmistress also sensed that the overbright smile, the cheerful, almost aimless chatter, was a ruse to protect a grown man's feelings?

Jennifer's intent at making this parting easier on him sat like a great weight upon his heart. The pride he felt at her show of courage dimmed in the realization that when he saw her next, she would be a woman.

Furiously he wiped the tears away. Taking a handkerchief from his pocket, he blew his nose. It was going to be one hell of a long journey home.

Amy Stapleton watched Jennifer carefully as they returned to the carriage. Observing partings was not a new experience for her. Why then had this particular separation of parent and child touched her so deeply? Was the bond between this father and daughter different from the others? Were the silent, tearing grief within the man and the courage shown by the girl something unequaled by past experiences?

Jennifer Douglas had not been sent to the Stapleton Academy because it was fashionable or because it would provide an opportunity for new wealth to mingle with old.

No, Jennifer Douglas was something else: a rough-cut diamond, ready to be polished into brilliance. The challenge both excited and saddened Amy Stapleton. For the first time since opening the doors of the Stapleton Academy twenty years ago, she said a silent prayer that she would not be entirely successful.

Throwing back the covers of her narrow bed, Jennifer glared at the sleeping form of her roommate with murder in her eyes. The girl's restless tossing and mumbling continued as they had each of the countless sleepless nights that had passed since Jennifer had been assigned to this room. An entire herd of bellowing cattle could not possibly make more noise than this one highborn girl who, by day, was the unchallenged queen of the society misses.

Stifling an urge to smother the girl with a pillow, Jennifer pulled on her robe and stood at the window as dawn's early light bathed the room. Would those prim young ladies, who followed the auburn-haired Allison Armbruster like a gaggle of geese, think her so wonderful if they could hear the monstrous noises that came from her throat between the hours of midnight and morning?

Returning to her bed, Jennifer awaited the knock that would signal breakfast. The numbness of the early weeks had progressed to bitterness and then resignation.

During those early, miserable days it had been easy to slip back into the comfortable habit of blaming Devlin. But Jennifer was no longer an immature girl with a convenient scapegoat to blame for her father's shortcomings. Here, in this foreign world, she began to see and accept things as they truly were.

From the moment of her birth, James Douglas had conceived an image of his only child. Although she bore little physical resemblance to the mother who died giving Jennifer life, James was determined that Louise's child would, in deportment, echo her mother's gentle, ladylike manner. With equal stubbornness, Jennifer had made it her goal to smash his dreams to dust.

But how could any father, no matter how well intentioned, banish someone he professed to love to this lonely, wasted existence? Clasping her arms about her knees, Jennifer sighed heavily and glanced toward the other bed. When Allison snorted, a small smile appeared on Jennifer's face. Perhaps she should awaken the other girls along this hall. Should she charge a fee or grant free admission to this concerto of pandemonium? The thought brought the first genuine amusement in weeks. Nearly light-headed from this reawakening of high spirits, she picked up her pillow and flung it with all her strength as yet another rumbling snore emerged from Allison's open mouth.

Allison's alarmed cries were muffled beneath the pillow. Sitting upright, she stared at Jennifer, bewildered by the sudden glint of amusement within those strange pale gray eyes.

Sitting primly in her straight-backed chair, her hands clutched in her lap, Jennifer ground her teeth together while Miss Templeton recited Dickens in the same nasal monotone she reserved for all works of literature that did not meet her approval. It was a sacrilege to murder those beautifully written words until Oliver's story became an exercise in endurance, instead of the deeply inspiring tale the author intended.

When the gentle but morally misled Nancy met her death at the hands of a brutal lover, only approval was voiced within this classroom. What should have torn at the heart brought snickers.

Without moving her head, Jenny's eyes surveyed her classmates. She was struck once again at the shocking sameness of expression. A girl was taught to titter, never laugh. Open merriment, the expression of which fully employed the facial muscles, was almost a sin. These little imitations of humanity were even taught the accepted way to cry. Red, puffy eyes, watering noses, and trembling lips gave way to delicate hankies catching tears as gentle as a soft rain. Any strong emotion that might cause premature wrinkles—and make these wooden puppets seem alive—was viewed as improper.

As she studied their faces, they began to blur, like wax figures melting in the sun. Jennifer shut her eyes tightly as if to escape the living nightmare that she would in time become like them.

"Miss Douglas." The nasal voice danced on Jennifer's spine. "Are we boring you? Is Mr. Dickens not to your liking?"

Silver eyes opened slowly, reflecting the girl's distaste for the affected mannerisms that surrounded her.

"I asked a question, Miss Douglas." Alice Templeton detested this ill-bred child, the only thorn among her roses.

Jennifer rose gracefully, as she had been taught. "Mr. Dickens's novels could never *bore* me, Miss Templeton." The vehemence in her tone was not lost on the imperious instructor.

An eyebrow lifted in cool disdain. "Perhaps I'm not interpreting the passages to your satisfaction. Perhaps we might all be enriched by hearing *Oliver Twist* read with a western twang."

The laughter seemed deafening, although mere titters escaped from prissy little mouths. Jennifer approached the teacher's stool and accepted the proffered volume. Her eyes swept the room as she took Miss Templeton's place. A pair of emerald eyes near the desk glittered in open amusement. Jennifer met Allison's silent laughter with determination. She began to read.

Soon she was caught up by the story, forgetting that the exercise had begun as punishment. When the clock chimed to end the hour, she looked up from the book to find odd expressions on those usually impassive faces.

One by one they left the room in their orderly fashion. Only one girl took a moment to comment. "That is the first time I've enjoyed a literature class." Both girls smiled at the outraged gasp from their teacher.

"Thank you, Allison," Jennifer whispered gratefully.

The book was suddenly yanked from her hands. "A full report of your impudence will be made to Miss Stapleton."

The words were calculated to strike terror in a young girl's heart, but to Jennifer they were a challenge. Only her promise to her father to try and stick it out kept her from behaving so abominably that they begged her to leave. She rushed from the room, forgetting that a lady never rushed; reaching the stairs, she lifted her skirt and took the steep staircase at a dead run.

In the sanctuary of the small room she shared with Allison, Jennifer viewed her own reflection. From the hem of her blue serge skirt to the high prim collar of her pleated blouse, she was a duplicate of those girls she belittled. Her raven hair was braided to form a coronet so tightly pinned that her brows were pulled upward in a perpetual startle. The sun-kissed complexion had faded to a proper pale porcelain.

Suddenly she wanted to strip the hated uniform from her body and tear the pins from her hair. "I don't belong here," she cried softly. Grabbing her cloak, she rushed out of the cell-like room to seek the freedom of sun and sky.

Standing on the front stairs of the huge stone mansion, she touched the marble lion guarding the entrance, her fingers caressing the cold beast as though it were something warm and alive. There was no sun to warm her. A heavy mist, tasting of salt and sea, enveloped her with a dampness that seemed to seep into every pore. Jennifer began to long for the icy cold blast of a Montana blizzard. It was honest in its attack. It didn't sneak into one's bones like a thief, robbing a body of warmth.

Amy Stapleton quietly approached the lonely girl. Again she felt a tug at her heart for this lovely child. Isolation from friends, family, and what was familiar caused homesickness in all the girls for a time, but Jennifer seemed unable to adapt, and the problem was not mere homesickness. "Jennifer, come inside and share a cup of tea. It will warm you."

Never had Jennifer sensed anything but kindness from the headmistress. Her blue-gray eyes were intelligent, sensitive, and sometimes very sad. Her golden brown hair showed not even a hint of gray although Jennifer knew she must be close to forty, and her complexion remained supple, smooth, and unlined. The drab clothing could not hide a nicely rounded figure. Amy Stapleton was still a beautiful woman.

Jennifer followed her inside. In the warmth of Miss Stapleton's private parlor, she was able to relax for the first time in weeks. She did not fear this woman or the authority that radiated from her stately pose.

Privately, Amy Stapleton was seething. Alice Templeton was a pompous ass. It had been unnecessarily cruel to humiliate this girl in front of the class. As soon as a replacement could be found, Miss Templeton would find herself on the front stair, bag and baggage.

"I heard some very nice things about your reading, Jennifer." Amy Stapleton smiled over the rim of her teacup. "You have inspired Allison Armbruster to vow to read every one of Mr. Dickens's novels. Getting Allison to read anything more challenging than the *Lady's Gazette* is no small accomplishment, I assure you."

Silver eyes danced with mirth. "I'm so pleased I could be of service to Miss Templeton."

A knock at the door interrupted their conversation. A young girl peered in. "Miss Templeton wanted me to remind you that she's still waiting to see you."

The headmistress maintained a blithe expression. "Thank you, Renee. Please ask Miss Templeton to continue to wait. Miss Douglas and I haven't finished our tea."

In the evenings, after dinner, there were long, empty hours to fill. Jennifer did not join the other girls in their gossip, or their singing about the piano in the music room. Instead, she composed long letters home. The letters to her father were vastly different from those she wrote to Devlin.

When the mail came, Jennifer would smile ruefully as she read James's cheerful missives. Father and daughter played at the same game, neither wanting to worry the other. Only with Devlin was she completely honest and only Devlin replied with the same candor.

With the approach of winter the cattle rustling had once again stopped. But the range was a powder keg, ready to explode should the criminals make an incautious move. Devlin predicted things would remain quiet throughout the winter months. He was less optimistic about the approach of spring. He wrote:

"All the ranchers are hiring additional men to patrol. Some of these men tread the line between the law and lawlessness very carefully. So far your father hasn't resorted to the use of these hired gunslingers. Hopefully, the need won't arise for us."

He always ended his correspondence, "Affectionately yours." Jennifer smiled at the valediction. Never would she have dreamed that affection could exist between them. His honesty earned her respect, and with respect also came the rebirth of an emotion a small girl had felt for a tall, gangly boy.

One evening, as she finished her letter to Devlin, she impulsively wrote, "Love, Jennifer."

The days passed slowly, one into the other as winter approached. Very soon it would be too cold, the snow would come, and the only pleasure Jennifer had found in this school would be denied.

She sat stiffly upright, her knee hooked over the pommel of the saddle, while the gray mare plodded down the trail. The skirt of her blue velvet riding habit was draped gracefully across the broad rump of this old nag. The high plumed hat, cocked jauntily on her head, completed the aristocratic facade.

Inside a girl born to the saddle railed against the absurd convention. Adapting to the sidesaddle had been child's play, since the creatures they misrepresented as horses moved at a snail's pace along the well-marked paths surrounding the school, often stopping and refusing to budge unless tempted by a carrot in the riding master's hand. Only Jennifer's innate love for this species of animal kept her from improvising a spur to attach to the dainty boots on her feet.

She watched the girl ahead of her with undisguised amusement. Allison was not, nor would she ever be, an equestrienne. The girl who could walk across the room with the bearing of a queen, bounced and rolled on her mount's back, sliding across her saddle as if someone had greased it with lard.

Jennifer saw the mare's ears twitch and felt its nervous shudder before she heard the high-pitched yelps of dogs in pursuit of quarry. Instinctively she tightened her grip, settling herself more securely on the saddle. As the dogs broke into the clearing the horses began to prance skittishly. The riding master gave a warning yell just as a frenzied cat streaked beneath hoofs, the dogs closely pursuing, yipping and yapping until even the gentlest mount was wild-eyed and dancing with panic.

Suddenly the desperate cat left its feet, trying to escape the jaws of death. Jennifer watched in horror as it dug its claws deep into the flank of Allison's mount. The pain-maddened horse bolted, nearly unseating its rider as it crashed into the forest.

Jennifer barely glanced at the riding master, who was fighting to maintain control over several animals. Swinging her right leg over the saddle, she dug her knees into the side of the mare, slapping her viciously on the rump. Her urgency must have communicated itself to the beast because soon they were racing through the wooded copse. She leaned over the mare's neck to avoid the overhanging branches, urging a swifter pace until the proud blood of forgotten ancestors sang in the horse's veins.

They were nearly abreast of the runaway horse when Allison's mount stumbled, going down on its knees and tossing the girl over its head to land hard on the rain-soaked earth.

In its panic the crazed animal would have trampled Allison, crushing that lovely face beneath its hoofs if Jennifer hadn't leapt from the back of the mare and begun shooing the horse away. She finally got close enough to grasp the reins, putting her own self in danger as she distracted the horse.

Eventually the animal responded to her. He was as gentle as a lamb when Jennifer tied both horses to a nearby tree and rushed to the still and lifeless form. Allison's eyes opened slowly, then widened with panic. Remembering another time, a faraway place, Jennifer held the girl's shoulders to the ground as she reassured, "Lie still. You've had the wind knocked out of your lungs."

When Allison's breathing returned to normal, she struggled to rise. Hampered by the sodden riding habit, she would have fallen face first in the mud had Jennifer not been there to catch her. "Cowgirl . . . you saved my life."

Instinct had spurred Jennifer to attempt what had turned into a futile rescue. Honesty spurred her tongue now. "Nonsense. I might have saved you from drowning just now, but any horseman worth his salt would have caught that stupid beast *before* he tossed you."

"True," Allison agreed with equal candor. She did not miss the instant flash of distressed anger. Throwing her arm about Jennifer's shoulders, she leaned on her heavily. "But I do appreciate the effort."

Walking the auburn-haired aristocrat to a tree stump, Jennifer fought the hostile feelings that were suffering a rebirth. Was Allison's left-handed compliment sincere, or was it laced with ridicule? "I'm surprised you managed to hang on to that nag. You can barely maintain your seat at a crawl."

A slow grin spread across Allison's face. She held out clenched fists and then slowly opened them as if in offering to reveal long, thick strands of black horsehair. She'd held on for dear life, taking handfuls of mane with her in the tumble.

Jennifer began to chuckle, then broke into a full-throated laugh. Soon the tears rolled down her cheeks as she clutched her stomach howling with unsuppressed mirth. Caring nothing about future wrinkles, or proper behavior, she dropped to the ground.

Bell-like laughter, music to the ears, soon joined her own as Allison slumped on the ground beside her. They were both snorting in a most unladylike manner when a dark shadow loomed above them.

A whiplash voice reverberated. "I can only assume this vulgar display is caused by hysteria."

Instead of finding the riding master's words sobering, the girls clasped each other, gales of laughter erupting anew as they rocked to and fro.

The incident produced the vehicle for the brand of high drama on which Allison Armbruster thrived. The surprise was that Jennifer now stood center stage while the auburn-haired girl stood in the wings, applauding louder than the others.

Jennifer became a heroine, and the girls who had once shunned her now clamored for her favor. But it was Allison's true friendship that became the treasure. The older girl took Jennifer under her wing, and life became one madcap adventure after another. Beneath the patrician crust was a mischievous imp crying to be free. A close brush with death and a dark-haired soulmate released Allison's true nature from its prison of conformity. Jennifer feared these stately walls might crumble each time those emerald eyes lit with the plotting of yet another prank.

With surprise Jennifer found herself greeting each new day with enthusiasm. Miss Templeton had offered her resignation, and her replacement was a joy, the literature class a celebration of enlightenment.

Soon the other trappings of society seemed not so distasteful. And Jennifer learned that Allison's nightly bellowing could be endured by sleeping with her head thrust beneath her pillow.

The elegant carriage continued down the winding maple-lined drive that led to the Armbruster estate. Palms perspiring, mouth dry as cotton, Jennifer was beginning to regret accepting Allison's invitation to spend the Christmas holiday with the Armbruster family. She felt like Cinderella on her way to the ball without a fairy godmother to protect her. She envisioned a forbidding family who would probably send her packing the minute she opened her mouth.

Her spirits sank even further when the mansion came into view. She wanted to go home—all the way home—to the ranchhouse that would fit in one tiny corner of this imposing structure.

When the carriage stopped, Jennifer hung back in spite of Allison's impatient urgings. But eventually she placed her hand in the footman's white-gloved palm and allowed him to assist her from the carriage. If she hadn't been so terrified, she might have chuckled. A girl who had often crawled on and off a wagon twice the height of this carriage was being helped down one step by a man dressed in an aquamarine coat with brass buttons.

She followed Allison through the stately portico, her mouth dropping in wonderment as the mirrored walls, the marble floors, and the chandeliers of gold and crystal transported her into a storybook world.

She was vaguely aware of the maid removing her cloak. When Allison gently led her into the parlor, she felt the peasant being ushered into the palace for an audience with a king and queen. The imagery was so strong that she felt an overwhelming urge to curtsy when Allison presented her to the waiting Armbruster family.

Feeling gauche and completely out of her element, Jennifer responded to polite questions with a wavering voice. She was too awestruck to see the warmth in Eleanor Armbruster's eyes, nor did she notice the amused glance Mrs. Armbruster gave her husband when Aaron Armbruster bowed low, bestowing a cavalier kiss on trembling fingers.

Eleanor Armbruster looked queenly in a gown of blue velvet, her silver hair piled high atop a regal head. Allison had inherited her mother's beauty. Aaron Armbruster was tall, perhaps even taller than Devlin. The flame-colored hair was thinning, sprinkled with gray, but his emerald eyes were wise, piercing, and very much aware of Jennifer's discomfort. It was his suggestion that the two girls retire to their rooms to rest before dinner.

Ushered into a room fit only for a princess, Jennifer turned to Allison. "Allie, I can't stay here. I want to go back to school."

There was honest dismay on Allison's face. "Why?"

Jennifer was miserable. "I don't belong here."

Understanding dawned. "Shame on you, Cowgirl. You disappoint me."

Jennifer pleaded. "I'll do something to embarrass you. Your parents will hate me. They might even demand that you be assigned a different roommate."

Allison's green eyes glittered dangerously. "You're making some pretty harsh judgments about the character of my family. How dare you assume we are unmitigated snobs unable to overlook a backwater mistake or two?"

The words were sharp and edged with hurt. Allison's tirade continued for a full five minutes before she dealt a parting thrust. "If you still want to leave in the morning, I assure you there won't be a single person blocking the front door." She slammed the door behind her.

Jennifer sat down in a blue velvet chair and stared at the gilt molding of acanthus leaves adorning the bedroom wall. Her shame was greater even than she had felt at the hands of Stuart Walters. There had been ignorant innocence in *that* horrendous blunder; she could not excuse herself anything now.

Woodenly she changed her dress, fixed her hair, and rehearsed an apology inside her head. Promptly at seven o'clock she made her way to the drawing room. Fighting panic and her own stubborn reluctance to admit a mistake, she stood frozen for long minutes near the bottom of the curving staircase.

Jennifer was unprepared for the earsplitting yell originating above her. Spinning around, her heart pounding with alarm, she watched as a young boy slid down the banister on his stomach to land in a heap at her feet.

Thinking him hurt, she immediately dropped to her knees beside him. The freckle-spattered face sported a grin so wide it was hard to resist the temptation to loosen a few of those very healthy white teeth. But before she could give in to the impulse, Eleanor Armbruster swooped down on the boy like an avenging angel. She picked him up, shook him, and paddled him with enthusiasm.

"John, I've told you time and again that you are going to

kill yourself with that stunt. I'll not tolerate another scare. If I see you attempt the banister again, I'll lock you in your room until you grow into some good sense."

Jennifer watched the woman spank her child, lecture, and then hug him. When he went off in a sulk, Eleanor turned to Jennifer.

"I won't apologize for my temper. There are days when my children drive me to the brink of insanity with their pranks. If I *ever* get them raised all in a piece, I'm going to retire to a quiet cottage deep in the woods, where they'll never find me."

Jennifer was grinning by the time Eleanor Armbruster took a breath. The ice was broken.

Seeing the broad smile on the girl's face, Eleanor opened her arms, clasping the tiny girl tightly when she rushed into the embrace. "Welcome, my dear. Welcome to what I hope will become your second home."

Tears were in Jennifer's eyes, but she managed a giggle. "Will you spank me if I'm bad?"

A gentle swat on her backside was part of the response. "Regularly, if needed."

Across the miles a young man reclined on his bunk, his bare feet crossed at the ankles. After finishing the letter he'd been reading, he leaned over and pulled a box from beneath the bed. He folded the letter and placed it among the others.

Devlin was hardly aware of Sam's entry into the cabin. He did not notice the dusting of snow on the man's hat and coat, although his toes curled at the cold blast of air.

"Somethin' bothering you?" the older man asked.

Devlin shook his head, closing his eyes. The letter from Jennifer had been filled with the exploits of the Armbruster family. He felt relief that she was no longer bitter or unhappy, that she was beginning to get used to her new circumstances. He *wanted* her to be happy, he told himself over and over again.

He pounded his pillow with a closed fist and flipped over

on his side to stare at the rough-hewn log wall. The Armbrusters and Bozworths of the world were always standing by to remind a McShane of his place. For a time, a damn short time, he'd forgotten the split between the haves and the have nots.

His gut twisted as he let go of a dream.

Chapter Eleven

The winter months passed quickly, catching Jennifer unprepared for spring. Silently, painfully, she watched new friends depart. Some would return again in the fall; others, like Allison, were released to the bosom of home and family.

A solitary set of footsteps echoed in the dormitory as a tomblike hush fell over the Stapleton Academy. Restless nights were spent in a room grown too quiet without the comforting, familiar sound of Allison's sonorous mumblings.

Letters delayed by winter blizzards arrived daily for a time. The cheerful missives had been written by the light of a blazing hearth while the howling wind and drifting snow provided a natural fortress against the menace of man's greed. But now that spring had stripped winter's blanket of safety from the earth, those she loved would become vulnerable.

Suddenly the letters stopped. Two full months—longer if she allowed herself to count backward to the date of her father's last correspondence—passed without any word. June drifted slowly into July with an agonizing disregard for a girl's increasing anxiety. She began to have nightmares: vivid imaginings of violence that turned her blood to ice, leaving her shivering on the balmiest of nights.

Amy Stapleton watched those lonely gray eyes carefully. Day trips to local museums and places of interest proved unsuccessful in distracting the child from worry. When Jennifer continued to refuse invitations to spend weekends with the Armbruster family, the headmistress used her authority to bully the girl into accepting. Strong wills clashed, but Jennifer relented when Miss Stapleton promised to personally make the trip to the Armbruster estate should a letter or wire from Montana arrive during her absence.

But no letter came. Mothering instincts Amy Stapleton didn't know she possessed rose to the surface when Jennifer returned from her holiday looking like a mere shadow of the young woman she had grown to love. When Jennifer's appetite disappeared, Miss Stapleton called her personal physician. Turning a deaf ear to the girl's protests, she administered the prescribed sedative and sent off a blistering letter chastising James Douglas for his cruel silence.

Making the upward climb from a drug-induced sleep, Jennifer's body felt leaden. It seemed an eternity before she could force her eyelids open.

"Awake now, are we?" said a voice nearby. "I'll notify Miss Stapleton."

The housemaid took her leave. The minute the door closed behind her, Jennifer rolled to the side of the narrow bed. Ignoring the throbbing ache in her head, she draped herself over the side and lifted the coverlet to peer beneath.

Hidden beneath the bed was a carpetbag, packed and ready for travel. A calendar slipped between the folds of stationery within her desk marked the date, the limit to her endurance.

"I didn't bother to unpack for you," quipped a cheery voice from the doorway.

Jennifer watched Miss Stapleton glide across the room. She was the perfect lady; the absolute role model for her students. When the woman reached the side of the bed, Jennifer saw the smile in her eyes, watched the tiny lines fan outward, marring the seemingly ageless complexion. When Amy Stapleton held out her hand, the joy on her face made her the most beautiful woman Jennifer had ever seen.

Snatching the folded slip of paper from her hand, Jennifer read the succinct message. "It's over. All are well. Due process of law in force." No name identified the sender of the wire, but Jennifer didn't need a name. Closing her eyes, she brought forth the image of a face. Mentally she caressed it as she whispered, "Thank God, Dev. Thank God."

"Jen," Allison wailed. "Can't we go in now? I can feel the freckles popping out on my face." The shade from the delicate little parasol was inadequate. A blazing sun on a cloudless August day turned a sandy beach, and the reflecting crystalline water of Cape Cod Bay, into a ruinous menace for a lady's complexion.

Her long skirt draped over her arm, baring shapely calves, Jennifer danced along the water's edge. Selfishly she ignored Allison's beseeching cry. The wet sand beneath her bare toes and the cooling water lapping her heels were the only things that made the heat bearable. Growing braver, she held tightly to the hem of her skirt, walking directly into the surf until it swirled about her knees. She could feel the tide pulling her, wooing her onward. The seagulls overhead seemed to cheer this fearless mermaid who suddenly cast aside all inhibitions, laughing joyously while the ocean played with its new toy.

Allison rose from the blanket, calling a warning. "You're too far out—Jenny!" Her voice rose stridently, heart pounding as Jennifer was lifted on a wave. She lost sight of her friend as she rushed to the edge of the water, mindless of the damp sand staining her slippers, the water soaking the hem of her dress.

The ocean had tired of the play but was in a benevolent mood. Picking the girl up, it nudged her toward shore, hardly wetting the loosened braids before safely returning her to an anxious companion.

"Jennifer Douglas . . . you scared me nearly out of my wits! I never dreamed you'd go plunging into the water like that. The tide's treacherous here. You could have been swept away!"

Walking out of the water proved a greater chore than

133

entering it. Sodden skirts and petticoats clung to her legs and hampered her movements. But she was so delightfully cool and refreshed that she smiled throughout Allison's tirade, nodding and promising with great reluctance to sacrifice this exquisite pleasure for the remainder of her stay.

Tossing the thick braids over her shoulder, Jennifer glanced toward the house. Compared to the graceful lines of the Armbruster mansion, the wooden summer cottage was a hodgepodge of complex shapes and ornamental design. Windows sporting stained and leaded glass were outlined with gingerbread moldings above a wide veranda that overlooked the ocean.

She started to turn back to Allison when her gaze caught and registered the form of a man leaning casually against the balustrade. Shielding her eyes from the sun's glare with one hand, she boldly pointed with the other. "Who's that?"

Squinting, Allison turned toward the house. With a moan of exasperation she slapped at the pointing finger. "Don't do that! If he thinks we've spotted him, he might feel duty bound to join us."

Mumbling something about Allison's crabby mood, Jennifer attempted to lift her heavy skirts away from her legs. What had felt so delicious only moments ago was now acutely uncomfortable. "We can go in now if you want."

Allison marched away, leaving Jennifer to stare mutely at her friend, who plopped down on the blanket and picked up her parasol. Laboriously she made her way across the hot sand.

"Don't drip all over me, for heaven's sake," Allison snapped. "Sit down on that corner."

Following orders had never been one of Jennifer's strong points. She moved closer to the purse-faced Allison, purposefully shaking the water from her skirt. "I thought you wanted to get out of the sun," she said blithely, ignoring dangerously glittering emerald eyes.

"I'll stay out here until I melt."

Jennifer sighed wearily and lowered herself to the blanket. "If we stay out here much longer, I'll turn into a pillar of salt. Does your reluctance to return to the house have anything to do with our visitor?"

"He won't stay long. We're too tame for the flamboyant Mr. Armbruster. He's here on business, and Adrian's business always comes second to Adrian's pleasure."

"Armbruster? A distant relative, I presume." Jennifer was intrigued by Allison's obvious dislike for this man.

"Not distant enough. I liked him better when he put the distance of this ocean between us. But since Uncle Charles's death, the prodigal son has returned from exile. And to answer the next question burning in those curious eyes: No, I don't like him—never have."

Jennifer had more questions, but Allison's mood was such that she let them go for the time being. Another quarter hour in the boiling sun brought the feared freckles to Allison's milk-white skin. There wasn't an inch of Jennifer's body that didn't itch unmercifully, and the slightly fishy smell rising from her damp dress caused her to announce, "You can melt if you want to. I'm going to find a tub of clean water." The look of horror Allison gave her didn't need interpretation. "Don't worry. I'll go in through the kitchen and sneak up the servants' stairway."

The kitchen door was bolted. Now, who would have dreamed of finding a *kitchen* door locked? Jennifer knocked softly, tentatively, and then waited a few moments before knocking again. Surely one of the maids or the cook would be somewhere in the proximity of the kitchen.

Eventually the door opened. With an audible sigh of relief, she slipped through the door, a quick glance over her shoulder confirming that Allison remained on the beach.

"How convenient," drawled a deeply masculine voice. "A fish presenting itself at the kitchen door."

The cultured richness of the voice, coupled with distinctly British overtones, kept Jennifer's eyes downcast, as though looking for a hole big enough to crawl into. There was a deep, throaty chuckle before a slender, long-fingered hand cupped her chin, forcing her face upward.

For weeks to come she would squirm with the mortifying

135

memory of her mouth dropping open to stare with puerile adoration at the most entirely beautiful man she had ever seen.

Amber eyes held her transfixed, sparkling with undisguised mirth while they appraised their bedraggled captive. The dark mustache above a mouth that must have been chiseled by a gifted sculptor quirked slightly before straight white teeth blinded her with a dazzling smile.

She searched for a flaw in this face. Although noses were seldom things of beauty, she could find no fault with this one. The dark brown hair, curling softly above arched brows, completed a picture of male beauty. The blood rushing through her veins, the sharpening of all her senses, and the lazy sensuality manifested within those strangely colored eyes made her aware of every nerve in her now trembling body.

When he removed his hand from beneath her chin, her knees nearly buckled. It was as if that featherlike touch had been the only thing keeping her upright. To save herself from falling at his feet in what could easily be misconstrued as worship, she dashed around him, leaving a trail of sand in her wake.

Perched on the window seat, Jennifer watched Aaron Armbruster bid his nephew farewell. Through the leaded glass the world outside looked distorted and unreal. Leaning her cheek against the cool glass, she shut her eyes and sighed heavily. Never would she accustom herself to the climate or the customs of this fairytale world. A rueful smile touched her mouth. Mr. Adrian Armbruster with his worldly manner had brought Jennifer Douglas out of the clouds and back down to solid earth. Why did she *always* make a fool of herself in the presence of any man under the age of forty? Since most of those humiliating incidents had occurred around Devlin, she'd always had a convenient excuse —it was *his* fault. Today had certainly proved that to be untrue.

Jennifer rose from the window seat and stood before the mirror. Lustrous ebony hair, released from the binding braids, curled damply about a face as red as one of Maggie's pickled beets. Laughter erupted as silver eyes glistened within that sunburned face. The alabaster skin was ruined beyond redemption for weeks to come. Not once during her frolic in the sea had she given thought to the care of her complexion. Impulsive, rash, headstrong—Jennifer Douglas was alive and awaiting the end of her separation from endless rolling plains and their constant challenge to her spirit.

On her fingers she counted the months until she could go home. Not so long now. Closing her eyes tightly, she traveled the miles. Never again to be encased within stone walls. To ride free like the wind, one with the earth and the sky, was what her spirit hungered for.

PART III

Chapter Twelve

With the exception of a long, lean form stretched out on a solitary bench, and three giggling young girls, the Billings depot was deserted. The others who awaited the overdue train had long ago taken shelter from the hot wind and dust in the hotel or saloon down the street.

At the faint sound of a whistle the figure on the bench tensed perceptibly. The slight movement caught the eye of one girl, and she turned away from her friends. Bored with their chatter, she watched the reclining cowboy, amused by his fruitless attempts to fit his tall form comfortably on the unyielding, splintered wood.

He was dressed as a common cowhand, but the boots peeping from beneath the edge of his trousers were polished to a bright luster. A dark brown Stetson, pulled forward to shade his eyes, covered the upper portion of his face. With the second, more audible blast of the train's whistle a muscle in the man's cheek began to work vigorously.

The sound of the approaching train filled the air, reverberating within his head. At the third blast Devlin removed his hat, wiped the beads of moisture from his brow with the back of his sleeve, and swung his legs off the bench. Rising, he dusted the particles of grit from his clothing before settling the Stetson firmly in its place. He took a deep breath and let it out slowly as he made his way across the platform to lean against the post supporting the overhang. In spite of the heat his hands were cold. Rubbing them together, he frowned to discover that his palms were damp. Another deep breath did not relieve the tight knot of apprehension twisting at his gut. When the dark speck with its rising column of black smoke rounded the last bend on its approach to Billings, Devlin wiped his sweaty palms against his trousers before folding his arms across his chest, burying icy fingers beneath his leather vest in an attempt to warm them.

For a thirteen-year-old girl in Billings, summers were long and without excitement. Meeting the weekly train and watching passengers come and go was, at times, the highlight of an otherwise dull existence. Making up stories about the people she watched had become a passion. Her fertile imagination went to work on the cowboy. Anticipation began to build. Eagerly she moved to stand beside him, watchful as troubled blue eyes flickered downward to give her the briefest appraisal before returning to stare at the length of track and a train that seemed to approach with an agonizing slowness.

James's heart swelled with pride as his daughter, his beautiful grown-up child, made her way down the narrow aisle of their compartment. When she took her seat beside him, he grasped her hand and gave it a gentle squeeze. "You look beautiful."

Jennifer's smile was tremulous, her heart's gladness shining within her eyes. "Did I get my hat on straight? I had to share the mirror with three other women."

James pretended to examine the silly little concoction sitting at a precarious angle atop glossy black hair. Women's fripperies seemed to be growing more preposterous with the passage of time. One good blast of wind and that bird perched on the side of her bonnet just might learn to fly. He couldn't repress a chuckle at the thought.

With an exasperated groan, Jennifer reached up and extracted the hatpin. "I thought you liked this hat," she complained when he smiled approvingly at its removal.

"I like your pretty hair better." He continued to grin, skillfully avoiding the issue of the hat.

Jennifer looked down at the apricot traveling costume she had donned this morning. It was slightly wrinkled, but otherwise spotless.

"I said you look beautiful," James reassured, feeling a little guilty for his earlier criticism. He was so proud of her he felt like bursting. She had developed a poise and an assurance of self that had made her seem a stranger those first weeks in Boston. He'd felt all thumbs handling Mrs. Armbruster's delicate teacups, sometimes with disastrous results. Jennifer had never reproached him for his clumsiness, soothing his embarrassment with kind reassurances.

Looking at her now, he remembered how easily she seemed to fit within that alien world. He began to wonder whether she would be content with the simple, sometimes tedious, often uncompromising life to which she was born and was now returning. Recent statehood would not bring Montana enlightened civilization. He might, in his lifetime, see telephone wires stretching across the plains, but it would take many more years than he had left for this wilderness to catch up with the advances occurring daily in the East. For James the thought was comforting. He became less adaptable with every passing year. But the young had a way of reaching out to grasp change with both hands, not content with the tranquility of the present. He voiced his concern.

"Will you miss that life, Princess?"

Silver eyes met his searching gaze without hesitation. "Everything I am, everything I want, is here."

The rising steam from the locomotive temporarily cloaked the man waiting on the platform, momentarily obstructing his vision. When the cloud of steam lifted he was caught unprepared. His breath was suspended in his throat, and the tight knot inside him seemed to coil painfully when she stepped onto the platform. The promise of a young girl's beauty had been fulfilled, and for the first time in many years he knew fear, real fear. He didn't move, had doubts that he could move, when she began to search through the crowd. When James joined her, distracting her from the search, he was given a few moments reprieve to master his feelings. He pushed himself away from the post, forcing his feet to cover the too short distance. Years of harsh self-discipline, and a strong instinct for survival, stood him in good stead. When he stood at her side and she lifted her face, he knew his expression revealed little of the turbulence he felt.

"Dev." She whispered his name, joy leaping into her eyes.

Keep the conversation light, he cautioned himself. Don't talk at all unless you have to. "You've grown up some, Sprout."

Jennifer felt as if she'd been dashed with cold water. He was clasping her father's hand, pumping it vigorously, barely giving her a cursory glance. He acted as if it was James who had been absent for three long years. When the two men left to gather the luggage, chatting amicably about the weather, the cattle, and easily slipping into that exclusive male comradery, Jennifer felt the old animosity begin to rise.

"No," she whispered to herself, fighting against anything that could dampen her joy.

The hot wind gusted, lifting the arid soil, peppering the three who traveled the open road with smarting clouds of dust. Seated on the wagon next to her father, Jennifer turned her face away from the abrasive particles stinging her skin and eyes.

"Looks like this wind might blow up something more than dust soon!" James shouted at the horseman who rode slightly ahead of the wagon.

Shielding his eyes, Devlin peered through the spiraling dust. Black storm clouds, approximately an hour away, were visible on the horizon. He turned Shannon and rode back to James. "I think we'll make it ahead of the storm."

"Whoa!" James shouted to the team of horses, pulling firmly on the reins. Sensing the approaching storm, the animals wanted to run but were burdened by the trunks in the wagon. "Take Jenny up with you, Dev. No sense in all of us getting soaked to the skin."

It was a reasonable request; Devlin could find no logical reason to refuse. He pulled his rain slicker from the saddlebag and tossed it to James. "Climb aboard, Princess."

The skirts and petticoats made it awkward, but Jennifer somehow managed to scramble from the wagon and onto Shannon's saddle with damned little assistance from Devlin. The only concession he made to the precariousness of her position was to brace her back, holding on to the pommel with his right hand while he held the reins with the other. When the powerful horse lurched forward, she would have slid from the saddle if she hadn't slipped her arm about his waist to clutch his belt tightly.

With each mile the wind seemed to grow stronger, until Jennifer hid her face against its punishing gusts on Devlin McShane's broad chest. It was sensible, even necessary, that both arms go about his waist. She felt the involuntary shudder, heard the acceleration of his heartbeat against her ear. Lifting her head, she ventured a glance at the strong, masculine face.

Knowing his expression would betray the blood-hot desire flowing throughout his body, he shoved her head back down upon his chest, praying that the voluminous skirts she wore would provide an adequate barrier between her and the surging, uncomfortable evidence of her effect on him.

The musky male scent of him, the muscles rippling beneath her fingers with every movement of the horse, made her suddenly aware of Devlin the man, and herself the woman. She hugged him tighter.

Devlin was going mad. Her cheek, that velvet soft cheek, was brushing across his chest much as a cat rubbed when it wanted stroking. She was a sorceress, a devil, his own private demon.

The sudden jerk on the reins almost brought Shannon to his knees in an effort to obey his master's abrupt command. Jennifer squealed, nearly sliding from the saddle before strong hands hauled her back. He held her firmly away, his eyes searching, but finding only innocence and sincere affection in the lovely face.

"I've missed you, Dev. I've missed you so much." Her

arms went about his shoulders. She pressed a kiss to his cheek.

Giving in to the torment of his famished heart, he clasped her tightly to him, lowering his lids over eyes that might say too much. "I've missed you, too, Princess."

Then he was repositioning her to ride astride, her back braced against his chest. "Hold tight," he whispered in her ear before urging Shannon to a full gallop.

The wind whipped at her skirts, baring her legs, flaring the little bolero jacket of her suit. A muscular arm was clasped tightly beneath her breasts, shifting, moving to keep her steady as they rode hard and fast across the rolling plains.

Racing time, racing the storm of nature and the storm of emotions, neither thought beyond the moment as they traveled together across the earth they both loved. Jennifer leaned back against Devlin, lifting her face to the sky, letting loose with an earsplitting whoop of joy that echoed throughout the valley. She was home.

The sky was black with clouds when they rode into the enclosure. Devlin dismounted and easily lifted Jennifer from the saddle, watching her closely as her eyes caressed every detail of every building before they began to fill with tears. She reached out for his hand, squeezing it with a strength that surprised him. She smiled with trembling lips, but the joy in her face was there for all the world to see.

Suddenly the empty yard filled and a wall of noise surrounded them. Devlin winced as Maggie's voice rose to a pitch guaranteed to cut through solid rock. Men filed from the bunkhouse, talking too loudly, their rowdy welcomes covering deeper feelings.

Devlin's departure went unnoticed as he quietly led Shannon toward the dark sanctuary of the barn. Closing his mind to the sounds outside, he quickly tended his animal. When the horse was curried and fed, he walked toward the cabin he shared with Sam. He needed some time for solitude, time to come to grips with this new reality. All the

146

years, the labor, the loyalty, had been only a pittance upon his debt. The toll was due in full now . . .

Sam had waited until the first wave of welcome was over. When the men began to make their way back to the bunkhouse, he stepped forward. Jennifer would have launched herself at him, but he kept her at a distance, walking around her, turning her this way and that. "Told James they couldn't make no silk purse outta an old sow's ear."

"I love you, Sam," Jennifer said huskily, her tears flowing freely down her cheeks.

As if she were still a very small child, Sam lifted her, twirled her about, and then hugged her so fiercely that she made a soft protest.

"You stay put, Jennifer Douglas. Just stay put from now on."

The slightly musty smell of rain-washed earth and a dawn more beautiful than any she'd ever seen only increased Jennifer's restlessness. Sitting on the porch stairs, elbows on knees, chin pillowed in her hands, she proceeded to pout. Being ordered not to ride her first day home hadn't exactly been an auspicious beginning to what she hoped would be a new attitude toward her privileges and rights.

James had left the breakfast table with his mouth set in a firm line. Jennifer's anger and disappointment found no outlet when Maggie began to scold. "Your daddy should just have tossed his money in the pond. Three years of schoolin' hasn't changed you even a little bit. You're just as stubborn and pigheaded as you ever were."

Storming from the house with the intention of riding alone in spite of her father's orders, Jennifer had made it as far as the front porch.

"I've seen longer faces in my time, but not often," said a deep voice behind her.

Jennifer turned slightly, shrugged, and then observed, "You didn't ride out with Sam and my father."

Devlin sat down on the stairs beside her. "Nope. My day to ride the fences."

Jennifer didn't attempt to make conversation. Those confusing feelings of yesterday were still fresh within her memory, making her squirm with dismay at the brazen way she had clutched him.

"Some get-up you have on there," he drawled. "Is that the latest style back in Boston?"

The expensively tailored fawn-colored breeches were not quite loose enough to hide the slender, shapely curve of her thighs. The blouse she wore was of the softest ivory cotton, high collared and pleated down the front. It emphasized the lush ripeness of her bosom while still managing to look demure and virginal.

Three years of whalebone and tight braids encouraged this rebellion. The secret fittings, the bribery to keep the dressmaker silent—unwise, foolish, senseless. Three years of schooling and a father's expectations squandered for a pair of silly trousers.

She smiled ruefully. "Did you know that I'm a thick-headed mule?"

Devlin chuckled. "And who would be sayin' a thing like that about our Jenny?"

"Most everyone who's ever had the pleasure of my acquaintance. Yourself included, Mr. McShane." She stood up suddenly, arms akimbo. "Miss Stapleton said that I tend to run headlong at life, butting my head against obstacles when I could just as easily walk around them."

"And what is Jennifer's opinion?"

"Jennifer thinks if she'd been born a man . . ." Pausing, she looked down on his golden head. "I would never step aside or go around anything."

Devlin looked up, his eyes traveling slowly upward, giving her a thoroughly male appraisal. He was rewarded when a very feminine flush stained her cheeks. "Being a man wouldn't solve *all* your problems, Jen." His smile was rueful. But it sure as hell might solve a few of mine, he conceded silently.

148

She watched him stand, admiring the innate grace in his movements. He *was* the perfect male specimen. His rugged, chiseled features held not a trace of prettiness, the kind of prettiness Allison's cousin had. No, he was handsome, superbly so, in a completely virile way that made her acutely aware of her own femininity.

The sun peeped out from beneath a stray cloud, catching the pale gold streaks in Devlin's hair and gilding the down on his muscular forearms. A queer kind of ache began to throb inside Jennifer.

Devlin was drowning in the misty depths of her eyes. He grappled with his demon, losing ground, then regaining his soul by the sheer force of will. He turned and walked away.

She caught him halfway across the yard. "Take me with you today. Please . . ."

The struggle continued. He fought the urge to fling her away and run. "No." His voice was harsh, strained with the sensations coursing through him from the simple touch of her hand on his arm. "No," he repeated.

"I won't be any trouble . . . I promise you." She hated pleading, but was compelled to grasp on to this moment. There was little understanding within her, only the instinctive knowledge that she was on the brink of some new discovery.

"Please . . ." The whispered, desperate entreaty immobilized Devlin's defenses. He turned to her, stoical resignation stamped on his features. "Go tell Maggie you're coming with me." She had already turned away, but was stopped by a hand on her shoulder. "Jennifer . . ." The warning died in his throat. "Have Maggie make some sandwiches. We'll be out all day."

Nodding, Jennifer ran to the house. She didn't see a man slam his fist into the barn wall or hear the crack of splintering wood.

They rode the perimeters of Jennifer's land, stopping when Devlin would spot a section of fence in need of attention. Jennifer helped him by marking a map with a piece of charcoal. Riding the fence was a year-round job. It took a keen eye and a tough backside to cover the seemingly endless acres.

Devlin watched her as she rode, her hair hanging down her back, the leather tie ineffectual in keeping the heavy mass restrained. Often he allowed her to race ahead, knowing she needed to reacquaint herself with the land. She was like the wild flowers of this prairie—beautiful, untamed.

Eventually the sun rose high in the sky. "Time for a break," he called out.

Jennifer whirled Dusty around. When Devlin urged Shannon to a gallop, she spoke words of encouragement into the pinto's ear. "He's strong and his long legs eat up the ground. But you've got heart enough to match his stride."

Not trusting himself if he touched her, he didn't offer to help her dismount. Pulling on the leather ties holding the blanket to his saddle, he noticed the cautious movements of her dismount. His lips quirked in a smile when she surreptitiously rubbed her backside.

Jennifer's eyes drank in the beauty of this, her special place. She trailed her fingers lovingly over the bark of a tree before leading Dusty to the crystal water of Silver Creek. Cupping her hand, she let the cold water trickle over her palm, then drank thirstily of the fresh spring-fed stream.

Devlin stretched out on the blanket. Lying on his side, his legs crossed at the ankles, he too assuaged a thirst, filling his eyes with the warm, vibrant beauty that was Jennifer. The shapely buttocks that were presented to his view when she bent to drink from the stream caused a tightening in his groin. He accepted what he had been fighting since she stepped off the train yesterday. Jennifer was a woman. Her youth no longer protected either of them. He tried to steel himself against the endless, tortuous days ahead.

Jennifer tied Dusty to a nearby tree and joined Devlin. Plucking at the grass, she inhaled deeply, filling her nostrils with the clean scent of this place. Her eyes were lambent when they rested on Devlin. "Thank you," she whispered. "Thank you for letting me come."

Swallowing hard, Devlin shifted his eyes away from the swell of her breast. He sat up, his voice raspy as he said, "Let's eat."

Jennifer was still nibbling on her sandwich when the wind began to gust. The leather tie holding her hair could not withstand the force of the breeze and soon she was plucking long black strands out of her mouth with every bite.

Having lost his appetite sometime around noon yesterday, Devlin had long since finished. "Come over here," he commanded from his resumed reclining position.

Intending to change places with her, he had barely crooked a knee when her back was braced against his chest. "You make a wonderful chair," she said impishly before proceeding to finish off her lunch with the enthusiasm of a hungry lumberjack.

Fresh air and a full stomach made her languid. She muffled a yawn with her hand and then stretched upward, lifting her arms above her head, arching her back to relieve the little ache at the base of her spine. Throwing back her head, she used a muscular forearm as a pillow while she watched puffy white clouds dance across a cerulean sky.

If she had but glanced his way, Devlin knew she would have seen the wretchedness caused by her arching breasts, the torment of that silken hair against his skin. The innocence, the immunity to throbbing desire, inflamed him further. He resented her casual indifference to propriety, the confidence she placed in ol' reliable Dev's restraint. He picked up a strand of her hair and rubbed it between his fingers, testing the silken texture. Still she did not look at him.

Jennifer found nothing alarming about the way he toyed with her hair. She giggled when a callused finger traced the shape of her ear, tickling the sensitive skin at the nape of her neck. She swatted the hand away, much as she would dispatch a bothersome insect. But when the long fingers of his hand began to massage the stiff muscles of her shoulders, she abandoned herself to the soothing touch. His body shifted and he moved to kneel behind her, pulling her against his chest, using both hands to work their magic, moving down her spine, then upward again. His voice was a deep rumble in her ear. "No woman should be this naive."

"Hmm?" she answered sleepily. Suddenly she was flat on her back with the entire weight of him pressing her to the ground, robbing her of breath. She shifted beneath him, eyes widening as the bold, male shape of him pressed more urgently at the juncture of her thighs.

"For God's sake, Jen. I'm not a damned eunuch!" he groaned as she wiggled provocatively beneath him. The arms braced on either side of her head trembled. "Hold still!" It was a plaintive whisper. When she ceased to wriggle, he eased himself away, covering his eyes with his forearm as he rolled to his back, breath ragged, blood pounding in his ears.

Jennifer sat up, clasping her arms tightly about her knees. He had been right; she was not that naive. Shame brought hot color to her cheeks, which flamed to burning when curious eyes strayed to the mysterious bulge of his masculinity.

When Devlin rolled to his knees and began stuffing the remains of their lunch into a saddlebag, Jennifer reached out, touching his shoulder. "I'm sorry . . . I didn't think. I . . . you must think I'm . . ." Her voice trailed away.

Sitting back on his heels, Devlin dropped his head before turning to her. She seemed so willing to take the blame for his lustfulness. He touched her cheek gently, his thumb sliding over the tender curve of jaw. "Stop looking at me that way." He turned to her, cradling her face, seeing within her eyes what he had always dreamed of seeing. "Stop it, Jen . . . stop. . . ."

The touch of his hands compelled her. "Am I a wanton, Dev? I *wanted* you to kiss me. I still want you to kiss me."

It was so short a space to her lips. Her chin tilted, the lips parted, and he was lost. Hungrily his mouth covered hers, famished for the taste he could not satisfy if he lived three lifetimes.

Jennifer slowly rose to her knees, her hands now resting on the wonderful strength of his biceps. The kiss was at one moment hard, then soft; demanding, then incredibly tender. When he would have pulled away, it was she who stretched upward, threading her fingers through the thickness of his hair.

As if the sound came from a very distant plane, she heard his groan before he gathered her to him. Everywhere they touched throbbed with life of its own.

The taste of her sweet mouth robbed Devlin of his troublesome conscience. Expertly he parted her lips, his tongue hesitantly searching until he found the honeyed well of her response. Dreams and reality scrambled inside his head until the only real thing on this earth was this very essential woman pressing against him.

His hands moved over her hips, pulling her more intimately against him, spreading his knees to fit her more securely to his growing need. Then her breasts were beneath his hands, the nipples budding, thrusting against his palms like daggers. "Sweet, so sweet," he murmured against her mouth.

A strange heat seemed to be radiating upward from the center of her being. When his thumbs began to move in lazy circles across the bodice of her blouse, Jennifer began to tremble. Any protest she might have made was silenced as his kisses became deeper and deeper, consuming her with the fires of a passion she had unleashed. When she felt his hands working at the buttons of her blouse, she began to panic, grabbing his wrists.

"Let me touch you," he pleaded, using his superior strength to ignore her ineffectual hold. The blouse parted easily, the ribbon on her camisole fell away. He touched the velvet softness of her young skin, cupped the breast, and lifted it free of the thin undergarment. His mouth swooped downward.

She was bent backward, crying out when his mouth found

her. Involuntarily she arched upward as the gentle suckling seemed to draw her from herself until she feared he would take the very essence from her soul. Tears trailed down her cheeks when she failed to deny him, failed to deny herself this rapturous pleasure.

He took her lips again in a shattering kiss that swept resistance away. Jennifer's arms went about his waist, and she folded into him in an age-old gesture of surrender.

The taste of salt on her lips eventually penetrated the fog of his desire. Lifting his head, he looked down into her face. She was his. This beautiful creature who had plagued his youth, haunted his dreams while she blossomed into womanhood, and filled his heart since her sixteenth birthday was his. The sky would witness their joining. The rich earth would be their marriage bed. Montana earth. *Douglas earth*.

He loved her with every fiber of his being, but he let her go. He covered the beautiful breasts and pulled her onto his lap, crooning as he had done three years ago, holding her until the trembling stopped.

When he left her, she folded herself into a tight ball. A kiss, a simple gesture of affection asked for and received. She wanted to laugh at herself.

Devlin stripped the kerchief from his neck, dipped it in the cold water, and returned to Jennifer. He knelt down beside her, urging her upright to bathe her face. Rebuttoning the blouse, he avoided her searching gaze. "Stay away from me, Jen."

"Why?" Her breasts still tingled from his touch. The passion in her young body had awakened, and she trembled anew as his fingers hovered over the bodice of her blouse.

Dropping his hands, he turned away, determined to avoid her forthright question. When it was repeated he attempted to cocoon himself in anger, his words carefully chosen for their ability to wound. "Because eventually I'll take that luscious body of yours. I'll forget that you're the boss's daughter and I'll thoroughly enjoy what you so generously offer. . . ."

He heard the rustle of cloth as she scurried off the

blanket. When he looked up again she was mounted and riding toward him. He rose, gathering the blanket.

Jennifer pulled Dusty to a halt. "Am I doing it right, Dev? Isn't this the place where I take fright and flee, grateful to have escaped the beast McShane? Why is it that I don't scare that easily anymore? Could it be that your bark has lost its bite?"

He grabbed the bridle, genuinely angry now for being so transparent. "I'll not offer you marriage." His free hand slid up her thigh, a salacious grin twisting his handsome features. "But if you insist, I'll guarantee satisfaction for services rendered."

The bellowing of a cow penetrated through the haze of tumultous thoughts. Turning Dusty toward the sound, Jenny let the animal's pained bawls direct her.

Entangled within a torturous prison of wire, a young calf struggled vainly to be free of the pointed barbs embedded in its hide. Rivulets of blood seeped from fresh wounds. The soulful brown eyes were so pitiable that she plunged without thought into the tangled web of wire. She cursed the ensnaring spikes that snagged her trousers, pierced her palms, and shredded her blouse.

When the cow scampered away, still bawling loudly, Jennifer gingerly disentangled herself. The post lying flat upon the ground seemed to challenge. Determination stamping her features, she wrangled with the heavy wood until it stood upright once again.

With a smug smile, she remounted. Never again would she countenance the attitude that such a task was beyond her ability. She took the map from her pocket and placed a large "X" to mark this place before turning the horse toward home.

Chapter Thirteen

"Yes, sir, James," Herb Walters drawled. "Your Jenny turned out pretty as a picture. The wife and I just might give some consideration to sending our Molly off to that school."

Leaning back against the corral railing, James drew deeply on his cigar before tossing it into the dust and grinding it beneath his heel. He wore a smug smile. "Your son sure seems taken with her." The little sonofabitch, James thought privately. Stuart Walters had cornered Jennifer as soon as the tables had been cleared of food, fueling the town gossips once again. Speculative glances from Billings' female population while they scurried about clearing plank tables, packing away baskets of food, brought James's blood to the boiling point. The purpose of this welcome-home party had been to put those old rumors in the grave.

"Yes, sir, your little Jenny has grown into quite the young lady," Herb continued, mentally calculating the financial advantages should Walters and Douglas lands merge in a marriage.

The father of the girl on display watched her scan the assemblage, catching his eye with a silent entreaty. "Excuse me, Herb," he said, dismissing himself from the men who loitered near the corral to smoke and swap stories.

A fixed smile, a somewhat dazed look, and vague responses did not dampen Stuart Walters's enthusiasm for his tale. "You should have seen him, Jennifer," he gushed, eyes rolling wildly. "Whip Morgan, he called himself. Pa said he was the meanest bastard—excuse me—gunman this side of the Yellowstone. Faster than greased lightning with a gun. Used that whip he wore wrapped around his waist like a demon outta—"

"He was a cold-blooded murderer." James's voice flayed Stuart to silence. "Personally I hope this county has seen the last of his kind."

Jennifer popped out of her chair. "It's growing cool. I think I'll get myself a wrap."

Once safely inside the house, Jennifer leaned against the wall, giggling at the lame excuse she'd used to make her escape. It had to be at least one hundred degrees in the shade.

The buzz of women's voices drew her toward the kitchen. "Can I be of any help?" she asked of the four women—five if you counted Ada twice—who washed, dried, and stacked mountains of plates.

Within seconds she was being hustled from the room by Ada Rodgers's bulk. "Just how many women do you think it takes to do a piddlin' batch of dishes? Already threw Lottie out. Ain't gonna get it done with a parade marchin' through the kitchen every five minutes."

Behind the house a riotous game of blind man's buff was in progress. "Looks like fun," Jennifer commented with a shy smile to the woman who stood watching the merriment.

Lottie Thomas returned the smile. "I don't know who's having more fun—the children or those two grown men supervising their game."

Devlin and Davie were in charge of the blindfolds. Both seemed to be in their element as they mischievously shouted encouragement or misleading information, depending upon the circumstances and the age of the victim.

Jennifer watched Devlin bend his tall form to whisper into a little girl's ear. When the blindfold was in place, he gave her a tiny shove and then grinned from ear to ear when the child walked directly up to Davie, grabbed him tightly about the knees, and yelled, "You're it!"

Cheers erupted. Davie's protests fell on deaf ears while Devlin tied the black cloth over his eyes. He was turned round and round, and then given such an enthusiastic shove he nearly fell to the ground.

Arms outthrust, hands sweeping the empty space before him, he seemed to take an unwavering path. The children howled with anticipatory laughter as he moved closer and closer to the house and the two women watching their game.

Lottie and Jennifer stepped apart, ducking those seeking hands, darting away when he came too near. The determined set of Davie's mouth warned that he knew exactly what he was about.

When he came too close, Jennifer squealed. At the sound, Davie whirled in the opposite direction, trapping Lottie against the house.

"Davie Garrett," the woman chided. "You just watch your manners . . . and your hands."

A lopsided grin appeared before the bandanna was pulled down to reveal the twinkle lurking in those mischievous green eyes. "Now *you're* it."

Lottie gave him a shove. "Get on with you. Go and play with the children."

"I'd rather play—" A surreptitious pinch on his forearm cut off the rest of his teasing. "Beg pardon, ladies." He attempted a contrite smile before loping off to rejoin the game.

"I think we'd best put ourselves out of harm's way, don't you?" The smile on Lottie's face faded. The young woman next to her seemed to be cast in stone, the expression in her eyes making Lottie seek the cause.

A silent, almost tangible cord of communication flowed between Devlin and Jennifer. "The eyes are windows to the soul," Lottie muttered to herself, recognizing the dark yearning in the deep blue eyes.

Davie also witnessed what would be evident to anyone over the age of twelve. He stepped behind Devlin and covered those revealing eyes with the black cloth. "Goddamn, Dev, why don't you just get yourself a chair made of dynamite and start smokin' cigars."

Devlin didn't pretend to misunderstand. "Is it that obvious?"

Davie began to turn his tall friend round and round. "I'll make you a sign to wear around your neck. When the hell did this come about?" He remembered the fights, the snarls, the open warfare of the past.

"Forever ago." Devlin planted his feet wide, refusing to go another turn. "But it's not going any further, Davie. It stops here and now."

Released from the bondage of Devlin's eyes, Jennifer turned away. Slowly she became aware of the swish of skirts and the woman who walked at her side. There was compassion in Lottie Thomas's soft brown eyes. Chestnut hair glistened with rich copper highlights in the blaze of the afternoon sun. The very attractive face revealed a generous heart and a deep-seated integrity. Jennifer wanted to pour out her heart to this kind woman.

Seeing Jennifer's intent, Lottie hushed her quickly. "This isn't the place to talk. Too many ears."

Jennifer nodded. "May I ride over some afternoon?"

Lottie linked her arm with the girl's, feeling a comradeship, yet knowing their common link could never be revealed. "Just pick a day when Dev and Davie aren't working."

Jennifer stood at James's side, waving good-bye as the last wagon disappeared over the hill. With a sigh of contentment father turned to child. "Tired?" he questioned, dropping an arm about her shoulders. "Did those women wear you out with their chatter?"

"Mmmm." Jenny dropped her head onto his shoulder. "Did you know," she said quietly, "that sugar, not salt, is the secret of Ada's pie crusts?"

"What?" James looked down into laughing silver eyes. "That bad, huh?" He chuckled with her. "Well, it might not seem like much now, but that little bit of information just might catch you a husband." The smile left her eyes. He grabbed her hand before she could turn away. At her yelp of pain, he examined the hand, horrified to find large white blisters oozing with fluid. "Good Lord, child. How did you come by these?"

"A cow was caught in the fence. I couldn't let the poor animal suffer."

James's eyes narrowed. "That explains the scratches and the punctures. But it doesn't explain the blisters."

Jennifer shrugged. "The post was down. I replaced it." Her very posture declared her right to perform such chores.

"Do you think I sent you back east to learn how to put in fence posts? You could have stayed right here, chopped off your hair, and learned how to spit tobacco good as any man if that's what I'd wanted for you." How could any woman look so dainty and have the strength—or the stubbornness —to attempt a man's chores? "I don't want to see you in a pair of trousers again. It's time you started thinking about settling down, getting married, and . . ." He was losing ground beneath the steely glint in her eyes.

"And what, Father? Have a passel of babies to keep me in line? Then surely you won't object if I give Tom Davis permission to call upon me. One stallion is just as good as another . . . don't you agree?"

His mouth dropped open at her crudity. But before he could find the words to remonstrate, she had flown past him, disappearing into the house.

A man standing in the shadows of the porch let go with a loud guffaw. James whirled on him. "What's so damn funny, Sam? Didn't you hear what that girl said?"

Sam continued to chortle. "Sure 'nuff put you in your place, didn't she? Always said that girl had spirit." He stepped up to James. "Leave her be, Jamie. Ever since she turned sixteen you've been tryin' to ride herd on her, make her fit some kind of image you're carryin' round in your head." He started to walk away.

James pulled him up short. "Image? What the hell are you talking about?"

"I'm talkin' about a pigheaded fool who can't seem to recognize the kind of strength and determination it must have taken for a little slip of a girl like our Jenny to take on barbed wire and reset a downed post." Ice-blue eyes were piercing. "Louise is dead, James. Ain't it time you buried her? That girl ain't her mother all over again. Fact is . . . she's one hell of a lot like her pa when he was a young man. Think about it."

Jennifer gagged at the stench of charred hair. The bawling calf was released, and trotted back to its hollering mother. She shuddered slightly, closing her eyes as yet another animal was tossed down and held for the iron.

Bob Tucker handed her the glowing brand. "You sure you wanna do this?" She was pale as death.

"I can do it!" Jennifer insisted through clenched teeth, grabbing the iron from his hand and deftly applying it with light pressure, searing the calf with the Douglas brand.

The bile rose in her throat when the animal was released. Pulling her kerchief over her nose, she blinked back tears while fighting to maintain the contents of her stomach.

In his role as flanker, Davie Garrett tossed another calf. Gray-green eyes narrowed at the tight-jawed expression on his partner's face while the two men immobilized a white-faced calf.

Devlin banked his rage. But when the iron sizzled this time, the girl's touch wavered, causing the animal more pain than was necessary. He was on his feet, wrenching the brand from her grasp. "Enough, Jen! You're about ready to pitch over into the coals!"

She shook free of his grasp, taking deep swallows of air to control the nausea. "I can do it, Dev!" She marched back toward Bob and Davie.

Witnessing the breakdown in labor, James spurred his horse. "What's the trouble here?" he demanded, sweeping the idle group with smoking eyes. His daughter's colorless face made him pause, but he hardened in his resolve. He was only giving her what she wanted. When no one responded, he gruffly ordered, "Get back to work then." He didn't miss the murderous rage blazing from deep blue eyes before he turned his horse, riding away from the smell of smoke, sweat, and singed hair.

Davie attempted to lighten the tension, easily tossing a

calf on its side, admiration for the plucky young woman growing with every application of the brand. "First time I joined in a roundup, I spent half my time heaving up my insides. You get used to it after a time." He received a wan smile for his efforts. Looking at Devlin, the mischief was back in his eyes. "I'd say that the Princess is a woman to ride the line with . . . don't you agree, Dev?"

Devlin looked up into gray eyes above a blue bandanna. They were asking for some word of tribute. Averting his gaze, he ignored the silent plea. Instead he nursed his rage at a father who would subject his own daughter to the hardships of the roundup, working her harder and demanding more than he'd ask of a seasoned hand.

He felt the heat from the branding iron, felt his own blood begin to simmer in the sweltering heat of early September. There was irony in this new development. He'd thought himself safe for a time, thought he could bury himself in work, avoid the face that turned him inside out.

When the calf was released, Devlin's eyes strayed to shapely hips beneath a split deerskin skirt. Upward they traveled to firm breasts beneath a sweat-stained shirt. A loud cough diverted his gaze just as Sam relieved Jennifer of the branding iron.

"You get back to the chuckwagon and help cook with the chow." Sam's tone brooked no argument. Few men would have dared debate the order, but Jennifer was not the typical cowhand.

"I'll finish what I started," she stated defiantly, reaching again for the iron, repeating, "I can do it."

"So you've proved." The tone softened slightly. "But I'm the ramrod here, and you'll follow orders just like everybody else. Now either you get yourself over to the chuckwagon or hightail it back to the ranch."

When she had gone, Sam's cold gaze swept over Davie and Devlin. "I don't think I need to remind you boys to keep a civil tongue in your heads around that girl." The ice-blue gaze lingered on Devlin. "Or to keep your eyes on your business." Handing the brand to Davie, he put two fingers in his mouth and gave out with a shrill whistle while motioning a man away from the herd. "Time's a wastin'! Ain't got the whole damn year."

Jennifer choked on the doughy biscuit, washing it down with a swig of coffee that tasted acrid and looked like mud. She pushed beans flavored with salt pork about the tin plate. The smell of charred flesh and singed hair still lingered in her nostrils; it clung to her clothing and mixed with the odor of unwashed flesh. Her stomach rolled over, and she tossed the plate aside. Rising stiffly from the hard ground, she moved away from the campfire, away from the scents of unpalatable food, male bodies, and a good downwind dose of cow manure.

Every inch of her skin crawled, begging for a hot bath. Three days of working and sleeping in the same clothing, having to walk or ride additional agonizing miles just to find the privacy needed when nature called, and the seemingly endless hours of labor beneath a broiling sun combined to test her fortitude. It was a clash of wills between father and child. James had set out to prove she was unfit to do a man's labor; Jennifer was equally determined to prove him wrong. The score was tied.

A lonely scrub oak beckoned. Seating herself beneath its branches, Jennifer closed her eyes and gave in to over-whelming fatigue. She was sound asleep when strong arms lifted her from the ground. She did not feel the butterfly kiss on her brow or see the gentle longing in a man's eyes. She did not even awaken when she was placed on her bedroll nor hear angry words exchanged over her head.

"What in the hell is this all about, James?" Devlin's voice cut through the darkness of a dimming campfire. "Have you lost your mind making her work like a common cowhand?"

James's tone bristled in reply. "I'm not making her work; I'm *letting* her work. Look to Jennifer for your answers. Talk some sense into that stubborn head if you can." He turned away.

Devlin made the transition from slumber to full aware-ness in the blink of an eye. Davie crouched at the edge of the bedroll, a worried expression making him look every one of his thirty-two years.

"Jennifer." Davie's voice was barely above a whisper, jerking his head toward an empty bedroll. "Took off bareback, heading northeast . . . away from the ranch."

Devlin rubbed his eyes with the heels of his hands, shaking his head to clear his brain. Throwing back the blanket, he reached for his boots. Within seconds the two men were striding away from the camp toward the tethered horses.

"Shouldn't I wake Mr. Douglas?" Davie was uncertain in his new role of nursemaid and not the least bit reluctant to dump the responsibility on Devlin.

Devlin tossed the saddle onto Shannon's back. "I think I know where she's headed. I'll have her back before James can miss her."

The tone more than the actual words brought alarm. "Dev, take it easy on her. She's had a rough time."

Devlin laughed humorlessly from his mount. "And a rough time is usually what she asks for." He turned Shannon toward the northeast.

The full moon illuminated the glade with a silvery radiance, reflecting its face in the crystal water. Stripped down to her undergarments, Jennifer sat beside the icy stream, splashing handfuls of water over hot, sticky flesh. When her skin became accustomed to the chill, she gradually maneuvered herself into the water. Only two or three feet deep during the rainy seasons, the frigid water now barely covered her hips when she sat on the rocky creek bed.

Catching sight of her near-nude body as he rode into the glade, Devlin felt his breath stop in his chest. The wet fabric of her camisole was transparent in the moonlight, revealing the generous curves of her breasts, the hardened nipples tempting a man's resolve. When she rose proudly from the stream like a goddess, he could see the dark shadow of her womanhood.

The tightness in his chest radiated downward to rest in his groin when she lifted her arms and began removing the pins from her hair. Her tresses drifted like a dark cloud down her back, and he ground his teeth in an effort to control the wildfire desire racing through his body once again.

The groan of leather brought Jennifer's head around with a snap. Covering her chest with her arms, she felt her heart race with fear and a strange anticipation as she watched Devlin stride purposefully toward the stream. Paralyzed by the impenetrable expression within his eyes, she made no protest when his hands went to the buttons on his shirt. His movements were unhurried, deliberate, as he stripped the shirt from his body, baring his muscular torso. Next came the boots. When his hand rested on the buckle of the leather belt, her eyes flickered away. There was the soft splash of water and a startled gasp when bare feet submerged in the frigid stream.

Jennifer kept her eyes downcast, not daring to speak or look at the man making discordant sounds deep in his throat.

Just what the doctor ordered, Devlin thought with silent amusement. Sitting down in the water, he let the icy stream cool his passions, wondering if he sizzled like a hot poker dipped into water.

"Get dressed, Jennifer," he ordered. "I can't stay in here forever."

The harsh tone mobilized her. She leaped from the water and pulled on her skirt. The plaid work shirt was in her hands when he rose from the stream. He was not completely nude as she had feared, but wore faded red longjohns that he had chopped off at the knees.

Water ran in rivulets down his muscular calves. The wet woolen fabric clung to his male shape, outlining the mystery from which all young girls should be protected. The ridged muscles of his stomach rippled with the force of indrawn breath when Jennifer's eyes moved up his body in a survey so complete that fire returned to cooled passion. Pride would not allow him to turn away to hide the response that surged against the wet fabric of his underwear.

Her entire body flushed with embarrassment. She trembled with a strange mixture of awe and alarm and whirled away, covering her flaming cheeks with hands gone frigid with trepidation.

Devlin knew her unease. "Sorry you witnessed that, Jen. But I'm afraid there are some parts of me that just seem to have a will of their own." He reached for his discarded clothing. "Don't worry. The beast McShane—isn't that what you called me—isn't going to toss you down and slake his lust on that inviting little body of yours."

The distance he maintained between them and the apparently unperturbed tone of voice reassured her. Curiosity overruled common sense, and she turned back to watch him dress.

"For God's sake, put your shirt on!" he snarled. The swell of bosom above the camisole and the pouting nipples straining against the thin fabric sent another fresh surge of heat to his loins. Grabbing up his boots, he presented his back.

Jennifer watched him pull on his clothes while she stuffed her shirttails into her skirt. Lust? Did the term apply only to men? She said the word beneath her breath, testing the sound of it while she watched the play of muscle in his back as he pulled on his boots. Her breasts tingled just watching the hard muscles of his arms knot and bunch. She wanted those arms around her, wanted to press her cheek against the solid wall of his chest, wanted to run her fingers across the taut, bare skin. Was this lust?

He could feel her watching him. Grabbing up his shirt, he asked, "What's going on between you and your daddy?"

"I don't know what you mean." She feigned ignorance. It was a private battle.

"He said I was to talk some sense into you. Maybe you need turning over my knee again."

Jennifer walked to Dusty, grabbed his mane, and vaulted onto his back. "I'd attempt to explain if I thought I could penetrate your thick Irish skull, but I'll not waste my breath. You, my father, sometimes even Sam . . . none of you are capable of understanding." Her voice wavered. Unbidden tears stung her eyes. She was so tired of fighting for just a particle of understanding. She kicked Dusty in the flanks.

Devlin went after her, fearful that the horse would stumble in the dark. He caught her easily. "Slow up, damn you. A gopher hole will break the pinto's leg at that speed."

The unimpeachable logic caused her to slow the pinto to a walk. There was no conversation between them. Devlin seemed thoughtful as he rode at her side. When they reached the camp, Jennifer slid from Dusty's back. She did not see Davie slip back into his bedroll and cover his head.

"Looks like you weren't missed," Devlin commented.

She started to walk away, but then stopped. "Sometimes it's very lonely in an ivory tower." There was power in the husky, whispered voice; brilliance in the silver eyes, liquid with tears. "If my father should ask, tell him the Princess has fled the tower."

Chapter Fourteen

Summer slipped into fall without the usual gradation of seasons. Heavy October frosts turned the grasses a premature brown. Howling winds, pushing downward from northern plains, stripped the trees bare of foliage. While the temperature dropped daily, men worked against time to prepare for a winter that threatened to be long and severe.

It had been spitting snow since noon. Jennifer pulled the bulky greatcoat together where it gaped at the neck. The hands on the reins of the pinto were stiff from the biting cold. Her nose seemed to drip perpetually, and she wiped it against the rough fabric of her sleeve until it felt raw.

She chased a calf that had broken from the herd, running it into a gully before cutting in front of the animal, turning the pinto sharply, and driving the calf back toward the herd.

James watched the expert horsemanship with an admiration he would have denied. "Where'd she learn to ride like that?" he commented to Sam.

"In the blood, I guess," the man replied, searching the gray overcast sky. "We'll have us a blizzard before dark."

His prediction brought no argument. Already snow dusted the brim of hats, clung to coats, and rose in spirals from the ground. The stacks of hay being tossed from the back of a wagon would keep a cow from starving to death—if it didn't freeze in its tracks. "Look's like things are in pretty good shape here. What about the south pasture?"

"Dev's up there with Hank and Curly lookin' for strays," Sam replied. "They're cuttin' a pretty wide path. Hope they have enough sense to get back before this storm breaks loose."

James watched Jennifer rub her gloved hands together, blowing on them to bring life to cold fingers. "I'll send the princess home. Think she'll go without a battle if I tell her to help Maggie get a pot of stew going?" The smile on his face was genuine.

"You best *take* her home." Sam grinned. "But if I was a bettin' man, I'd lay a wager that the only way you're going to get her off this range is to promise to peel 'taters yourself."

The snow was falling heavily by the time they reached the house. James pulled Jennifer from the pinto and nudged her toward the front door. "You and Maggie get started. I'll take care of the horses." He was shouting to be heard over the howling wind.

By the time James crossed the yard from the barn to the house, visibility was difficult. Stamping the snow from his boots, he hung his coat on the peg near the door. The lure of a blazing hearth drew him into the parlor. Suddenly Jennifer was at his side, her eyes searching, asking for some kind of reassurance. Death was outside the door. There were no assurances he could give her.

"Well, daughter, don't just stand there. Let's get to cutting vegetables."

"I've seen worse storms," Maggie commented to the first group of men seated around the kitchen table. "But not often."

Dog tired, their faces red and stinging from exposure, the men ate hurriedly, grateful for steaming mugs of coffee and the generous portions of stew. But for the scrape of eating utensils on china, there was no sound to answer the ferocious roar of white death outside.

Muted words of gratitude were voiced and plates were

cleared from the table. Finally every man made the journey to the bunkhouse to lie awake and await in silence those three who had not returned.

Jennifer curled in the chair before the fire. Shudders having little to do with the cold shook her body until she trembled visibly. When the front door flew open, banging against the wall, she leapt from the chair, grasping the mantel to hold herself upright.

James and Maggie were suddenly in the room, and three awaited the news.

Davie unwrapped the muffler. Ice crystallized on the new mustache he sported. Red-rimmed eyes were bleak, weary, and blinking furiously against the light.

"We found Hank and Curly, Mr. Douglas. Their butts were near froze to their saddles, but they'll be fine once they thaw out."

"What about Dev?" It was James who spoke the question in everyone's heart, his voice reverberating tonelessly within the room.

"No sign of him. Hank said they split up before the worst of the snow started, thought to cover more ground that way. Sam rode out to look for him—"

At Maggie's keening cry, Jennifer's hand clutched her tight throat. The thought of Devlin lost was an agony, but Sam—Sam gone too was more than anyone could bear.

"We tried to stop him," Davie protested. "Said it was crazy. . . . It's death out there, Mr. Douglas." His eyes were pleading.

"You did the right thing, Garrett. Now get yourself some chow, you look about to drop."

Maggie walked heavily toward the kitchen. James followed, bringing Jennifer along with him. When Davie was seated at the table, the bowl of stew ignored before him, James spoke. "We'll start searching the minute this blizzard lets up. Have the men take turns keeping watch. Be ready to ride."

Davie nodded. He managed a few bites of Maggie's stew, drained a mug of brandy, and took his leave. Stopping in the doorway, he looked back at the pale threesome staring silently at each other.

"We'll be ready, sir. First sign of it slowing or first light . . . we'll be ready."

Her mind wanted to hold on to this oblivion, to continue to cocoon itself with the comfort of dreamless slumber. But the cramping muscles in her neck were pulling her into wakefulness, and Jennifer met the new day with the dread of one facing his own execution. Slowly her eyes opened; cautiously she moved muscles that protested the lumpy sofa.

Seated at the window, staring at the mountainous drifts of snow, Maggie didn't hear the girl's question, "When did they leave?" until it was repeated. Optimism, however slight, had dwindled with each passing hour of the night. She prepared herself for the reality of what the men might find. The real terror was that they might not be found for weeks—perhaps months—to come.

"They've been gone about two hours." Maggie's voice was hoarse from hours of crying while the girl slept.

The child still living inside a woman's body needed comfort. Jennifer walked to Maggie's chair, dropped to her knees, and put her head on the woman's lap. Maggie had always been able to heal the wounds, kiss the hurts away. She didn't cry when Maggie absently stroked her hair, saving the tears, hoarding them, refusing to relinquish that tiny, stubborn shred of hope.

In the end it was Jennifer who gave Maggie comfort when sobs tore through an exhausted body, eventually fading into slumber. Sometime in those hours of vigil, Jennifer released the last hold on childhood, becoming a woman, waiting, keeping the hearth fires burning brightly for the return of her man. She prayed for them all—those lost and those seeking. But her heart held to the image of mocking blue eyes, and she waited.

The sound of a rifle shot had Jennifer covering the distance between the kitchen and thigh-high drifts of snow at a dead run. She covered her mouth to muffle the sobs tearing at her throat at the sight of two horses, limp burdens tossed face down over the saddles, being led into the yard. Tears crystallized on her face. The biting wind stung her exposed skin. She was barely aware of the woman standing behind her, or the pain when Maggie's fingers dug into the tender flesh of her shoulders.

Light faded and she felt her body sway when those lifeless forms were carefully lifted from the saddles. The roaring in her ears prevented her from hearing her father's booming shout. "Damn it, Jennifer!" A bearlike hand reached out to slap her from blackness. "Open the door for Christ's sake. They're still alive!"

The world was an endless void of white. He drifted through the colorless haze. Afraid . . . he was so afraid. An unseen specter clutched at his boots, pulling, clinging, forming a suction from which he could not escape. Falling, he was falling backward. He cried out when thousands of needles seemed to hurl out of that void, striking him, pelting him with innumerable, excruciatingly painful stinging wounds.

"Dev!" The voice led him away from the peril. A hazy shape began to take form and he rushed toward it, arms outstretched, reaching, finding, grasping that dark cloud, hiding from the blinding glare of white.

"Dev?" The voice again. The dark cloud wrapped around him, and he drifted to a peaceful slumber. The pain was gone. He'd fought with death, and he'd won.

Finger by finger, Jennifer pulled his hands free of her hair. Her scalp hurt, and she fully expected to find long black strands still entwined in his hands when she lifted her head. The sound of soft snoring in her ear assured her that he slept peacefully.

She reached for the towel on the bedside table and dabbed at the moisture beading upon his brow. She rested her cheek against his to check for fever and was relieved to find none. After readjusting the quilts, she left the bedside.

She didn't need a mirror to tell her she looked like a hag. With her hands, she did what she could to restore some semblance of order to her hair.

The sounds of doors opening and closing, footsteps rushing in the hallway, drew her away from the window. She opened the door and peered out just as James reached the top of the landing with a bucket filled with snow. Silver and gray eyes met.

"How is Dev?" James asked tiredly.

"Sleeping now. What does Maggie say about Sam?" For the time being at least, Dev was safe. Her worry was for the man who labored for breath in her father's bed.

"His fever is high, Princess," James said, a worried shrug telling all. She knew he could not offer her anything more.

Jennifer closed the door softly and turned back toward the bed. Sitting up, anguish reflected on his face and deep within his eyes, Devlin croaked in a raspy voice, "How is he?"

Jennifer crossed to the bed and pushed him down. "Alive, but very, very ill."

Devlin's eyes closed, he swallowed with difficulty, and then those deep blue orbs searched the lovely face, unwittingly caressing, tender, while he memorized features he had thought never again to see. "My fault." He struggled to free the words from a painfully raw throat. "We were headed back. Still had plenty of time. Shannon went down . . . don't know why. Sam wouldn't leave me. Old horse couldn't carry both of us; snow was too deep. We found the hay wagon and used it for shelter." He grinned slightly. "Damned Sam talked my ear off trying to keep awake. When his throat gave out, he kept poking me in the ribs so I'd talk. Never talked so damned much in my life." His laugh was harsh. "I don't even remember what the hell I said."

"Shannon?" Jennifer was afraid of the answer.

Devlin turned his face away. "His leg snapped." No need to tell her how the horse screamed in pain, or of the merciful bullet that silenced the stallion.

Jennifer laid her head on his chest. The bare skin was soft beneath her cheek. She could hear his heartbeat slow, feel the rhythmic respirations of slumber. She started to rise, but his arms clutched her. He awakened with a start. "Don't leave."

Never had he asked anything of her, never had he needed her. Strong arms trembled with effort as she was pulled onto the bed beside him.

She curved into the circle of his arms as if she'd been made to fit that achingly empty space. Devlin rested his chin on her head, reveled in the feel of her breath upon his chest. He would hold her for just a little while. Surely that was not too much to ask of heaven. Just a little while . . .

Maggie found them hours later still sleeping in each other's arms. She prodded Devlin awake with her finger, answering the question that flashed into his eyes. "The fever has broken." Tears trickled onto her cheeks, the mouth attempting to smile quivered with emotion. "Started complaining already, so I know he's going to make it."

"What?" Jennifer's head came off Devlin's shoulder just as the door closed behind Maggie.

"Sam's better," he whispered, drawing her more closely into his embrace. "Hush now. Go back to sleep." Like a trusting child she complied without argument. He lay awake for a very long time, glorying in the feel of her. Maggie's calm acceptance at finding Jennifer in his bed puzzled him. He'd expected outrage or at the very least a cluck or two of her tongue. After a time he slipped farther down in the bed so he could look his heart's content at the sleeping, well-loved face. Eventually fatigue overcame him. He slowly drifted into deep slumber, reaching out in dreams to embrace the will-o'-the-wisp.

Jennifer awakened to the feel of his warm breath on her face and the dead weight of a bare arm resting across her breasts. Fearful of awakening him, yet knowing she could not remain, she moved cautiously, gingerly lifting the heavy arm to slide beneath it. Slipping from the bed, she watched his hand grasp the pillow to pull it snug against his body. She felt bereft, her stomach twisting with regret, when he enfolded and fully embraced the inanimate object, the dream of her own soft warmth reflected on his face. At the door Jennifer turned back and wondered again how she could have ever thought she hated this man.

Chapter Fifteen

There was little light to make her journey across the room hazardless. She muttered a soft curse when her booted foot hit the brass footboard of the huge bed. Holding her position, she waited until her eyes adjusted to the dimness before moving to the bedside table to gather the breakfast tray she'd been sent to fetch. When she lifted the tray, a fork resting on the edge of a dish clattered noisily to the floor.

"Damn if you ain't about as quiet as a maddened bull in a china factory."

The voice was too strong, too filled with humor to belong to one suddenly awakened. "Now, you wouldn't be playing possum, would you, Sam Smith?" Jennifer teased, placing the tray back onto the table.

Sam rolled over and gave her a confirming grin. "Thought if that woman saw I was asleep she'd give over that nasty brew she keeps poking at me all hours of the day and night." He pulled himself into a sitting position and didn't seem to mind Jennifer's cosseting while she fluffed the pillows behind him. When she gave him a wicked smile and pulled a bottle of Maggie's home remedy out of her pocket, the face he made was nearly obscene.

Jennifer uncapped the bottle and poured out a measure of the medicine. "You haven't lived long enough to outsmart Maggie, old friend." Sam grumbled, but he took his medicine like a man.

"Since you're here and filled with the milk of human

176

kindness, I'd be grateful if you'd take those damn shrouds off the windows. A little sunlight ain't gonna blind me."

"My, my . . . aren't you just the model of sweetness and light," Jennifer chided as she began to pull away the heavy dark cloth that had been draped over the curtain rod. The room was flooded with sunlight. When she turned back to the bed her heart constricted. Dark circles surrounded eyes now tightly shut against the glare. Naturally lean of build, Sam's body looked gaunt in one of James's nightshirts.

Catching the look on her face, Sam snorted. "Don't need to read the expression on your face to tell me I came real close to shakin' hands with the devil." He noted for the first time that she was dressed for riding. "You goin' some-place?"

Jennifer shrugged. "Not likely. It seems I've been con-fined to quarters for the duration of the winter . . . longer if my father's attitude of the morning is any indication of his feelings."

Sam shook his head. He'd been alert enough the past two days to know that a warm chinook sweeping in from the northwest had melted most of the snow. He also knew what James expected to find out there. "Finding and buryin' frozen carcasses ain't exactly a rancher's idea of a high time. Can't blame your daddy for wantin' to spare you that."

That comment brought another expressive shrug before her chin jutted with an almost predictable stubbornness. "Oh, yes, please spare dainty Jennifer the harsh realities of life." Her eyes glittered with righteous indignation. "Not to mention the fact that she'd probably just be a hindrance . . ." Her voice trailed away. She stared at the man on the bed for long moments before hissing between clenched teeth, "It's my right!"

Sam's eyebrows rose. "Maybe . . . but—"

"But what? Haven't I proved myself worthy yet? Not once—by word or gesture—has my father conceded that I can . . . that I proved . . ."

"That you can pull a man's share of a hard day's work," Sam finished the halting sentence. "Well, Princess, if you're waitin' for applause and praise, then you'd best consider a career on the stage." He patted the edge of the bed. "Sit yourself down and let old Sam give you some hard facts."

Jennifer started toward the door. "I'm not in the mood for a lecture, and you're not up to giving one."

"Get your butt back here . . . pronto!" Sam smiled smugly when she obeyed instantly. "The men who work here get a decent place to sleep, three squares a day, and a pay envelope once a month. Ain't nothin' said as long as they do their job. When they don't they get asked to just ride on out. Your Daddy paid you the only compliment you're likely to get when he didn't send you home first week of roundup. Fact is, I thought he was being damned hard on you . . . harder than he'd be on a green boy. But you got grit, girl. You proved yourself or else he would have sent you packing."

Jennifer closed her eyes and sighed. "Sam, I don't want compliments. I just want simple acceptance."

"And I say you don't know what the hell you want from one minute to the next. You been fighting one thing or another since you left old Prune Face's schoolroom. Now why don't you tell me what's *really* chewin' on you. Get it off your chest."

"It's mine!" Like an active volcano she erupted. "Grandpa promised. But I can't have it, can I? I keep swimming upstream against the current. A woman can't own property. A woman can't do anything. . . ." She pounded the bed with a closed fist. "Why won't I learn and give up the fight?"

With effort Sam struggled upright, grasping her shoulders and giving her as good a shake as he could muster. "Don't be a fool, child. Ain't no man owns the land. We just borrow it for a time. Only way you can be a part of God's earth is to be six feet under."

Hearing his rasping breath, Jennifer urged him back down onto the pillows, cringing with guilt when he began to cough. When the violent barkings calmed, her voice was contrite. "I'm sorry, Sam. Now don't you fret on this." She held a glass of water and helped him drink. "Rest now."

Sam grasped her arm, refusing to let her leave. "Listen to me, Jenny. There isn't a single blade of grass on this place

178

that's worth drivin' a wedge between you and those you love. You can't own the land, but it sure as hell can own you. Don't get caught up in the same trap as old Robert. This land cost him a wife . . . you remember that. He forgot about what was really important when he went off to seek his fortune. You can't love a damn rock or a tree. You can appreciate it, but it ain't gonna keep you warm on cold nights. Ask your daddy. Ask him if he wouldn't give every square mile of it away for just the chance of holding your mama one more time."

Her face was turned away from him. Sam made one last effort to blast through years of wrong thinking. "But maybe you're not woman enough yet to understand." When she still refused to respond, he released his hold. "God help you, girl, if you don't have enough sense to be willing to chuck it all for a man who really loves you."

Jennifer had plenty of time to reflect on what Sam had said on that morning that now seemed long ago. Winter was a great provider of idle time. It was also a great enforcer of the hard facts Sam spoke of. Fact number one was that Devlin skirted around her when they met with the agility of a boxer in the ring. Always courteous, painfully polite, he gave out daily messages that what had passed between them, though not forgotten, would not be repeated. It seemed another door had been firmly slammed in her face. She found the shutting of that second door more painful than the first.

Sam was wrong. She *was* woman enough to understand. And it was tearing her apart inside. But she knew Devlin was a man with a tenacity that surpassed her own. She could not force love where love did not exist.

When the spring thaw began, she made not even a token attempt to join the men in their chores. This quiet admission of defeat was heartily approved. The princess was back in her tower where she belonged.

Chapter Sixteen

It was a long time after Lottie Thomas held out the olive branch that Jennifer finally took it up, but when she did she felt she had found the only person who understood the painful realities of being a woman in a man's world. Often she sought the companionship of this patient woman, who listened more than she spoke and thereby earned Jennifer's confidence. For indeed, though the younger woman was certain she had found a soulmate, to Lottie there seemed not a single issue on which they shared a viewpoint. She had fought for her land because she had nowhere else to go. It had been a simple matter of survival, for herself and her children; women's rights hadn't a thing to do with it.

On the subject of Devlin especially, Lottie kept her opinion to herself. She tried to be fair, taking into account her young friend's lack of experience, but how any woman could miss recognizing a love so painfully evident was beyond Lottie's comprehension.

On that particular day, Lottie looked up from her mending, shaking her head in consternation, wishing she had the courage to blast some sense into the two heads sitting across from each other, trying for all the world to pretend that the other did not exist.

Jennifer was stirring her tea impatiently, much as a cook stirs gravy waiting for it to thicken. Devlin had come in from the field and was eating his lunch with the singleminded devotion some folks kept for religion. Neither looked at the other, but the tension in the room was as heavy as the air before a Kansas twister.

"When do you think you'll be ready for planting?" Lottie asked Devlin, desperate to break the silence.

"Davie says another week," Devlin replied, rising from the table to carry his plate and cup to the sink. "Thanks for the meal, Lottie." He paused at the door. "I'll see you back at the ranch, Jennifer."

When he was gone, Jennifer turned to Lottie. "Do you see what I mean? That godawful politeness is driving me insane! It's almost as if he sees me as an afterthought."

Moving to the open doorway, Jennifer stared at the man returning to the fields. Every step of Devlin's powerful stride was measured, the muscles in his haunches tensing, the powerful thighs flexing.

Lottie put her mending down on the table and rose. She joined the girl, dropping an arm about her shoulders. "Sometimes you have to hit a mule to get his attention."

Jennifer laughed humorlessly. "Are you referring to Devlin or myself?" With a heavy sigh, she moved away from the door. "I'd better go home."

Lottie walked Jennifer to her horse. When the young woman repeated the invitation to bring the boys to the Douglas ranch some afternoon, Lottie replied, "We'll do that. Just as soon as the crop is in the ground."

When Jennifer had gone, Lottie began to make her way across the plowed furrows of her land. Had her sons been nearby, they might have scattered at the expression on their mother's face, recognizing the tight-lipped determination.

Devlin was watching the retreating figure on horseback, and so was unaware of Lottie's approach. Suddenly a firm grasp on his arm spun him around. "You're coming back to the house with me. It's time we had ourselves a little talk."

Devlin followed. He recognized that tone, having heard

her use it often enough with the boys. And like the children, he was not looking forward to what was to follow.

Jennifer nearly missed the young man who had come to call. Tom Davis was climbing aboard his ma's shiny new surrey when she rode into the yard.

"Thought I'd have to leave without seeing you," Tom said, hopping down and hurrying across the yard to help her dismount. "Came over to show off our new rig. Thought you might like to take a spin."

The gamin grin, and the admiration blazing from hazel eyes, were like a tonic. Jennifer accepted the invitation, taking pleasure in the gentlemanly manner with which Tom assisted her aboard the vehicle. She took note of the high polish on his boots, the firm crease in his trousers, and the heavy scent of bay rum all about him. His ginger-colored hair had been slicked down, but a wayward lock curled attractively on his wide brow. By comparison she knew she looked unappealing in her dusty riding clothes.

With a flick of the reins, Tom turned the buggy. When they cleared the gate he spoke. "Ma wanted me to ask . . . I mean, *I* wanted to ask if you and your father would come to supper this next Sunday."

His earnest tone touched something deep within Jennifer, and she felt a warm glow begin to dissipate the depression of the past months. There was little doubt about his intent. Tom Davis was asking if he could court Jennifer Douglas. She studied his profile and suddenly realized that he was no longer a gangling boy, but a man. A very attractive man. "That would be lovely, Tom. Thank you."

He rewarded her with a smile as wide as the Yellowstone. That smile never faded during their ride, and when he returned her to the ranch, she could hear his cheerful whistle long after the surrey disappeared over the hill.

In her rocker on the porch, knitting needles flying, Maggie watched the two riders descend the hill. Her lips quirked downward. The frown in no way reflected her opinion of the man with Jennifer. Tom Davis was a fine boy from a good family. And he was sick with love for a girl who didn't deserve such sweet devotion. Her needles slipped, dropping stitches when Jennifer clung to Tom's shoulders after the young man had helped her dismount.

Maggie rose from the rocker and walked to the end of the porch. Her lips pursed as her suspicions were confirmed. Devlin stood in the doorway of Sam's cabin.

From the window of the library James had witnessed the young couple's return. He stepped out onto the porch, watching his daughter and her beau walk arm in arm toward the house.

"Do you hear wedding bells, Maggie?" he asked softly. Her disparaging snort brought his brows together. For reasons she kept to herself, Maggie seemed to oppose this match.

"Afternoon, Miss Maggie," Tom drawled, removing his hat in deference to the older woman before turning toward James. "Mr. Douglas."

"Hello, Tom." James grasped the young man's hand, pumping it with enthusiasm. "How's the family?"

"Fine, sir. Ma and Pa send their regards." The slight flush of color beneath his tan was caused by the press of Jennifer's breasts against his arm. The public displays of almost possessive affection unsettled him, especially since she was considerably more reserved when they were alone.

"I've asked Tom to stay for supper," Jennifer said with an almost syrupy sweetness. She didn't miss Maggie's quelling glance or the gleam of approval in her father's eye. She gave Tom's arm a parting squeeze. "If you'll excuse me, I think I'll change out of these dusty clothes." Her voice dropped seductively.

Maggie followed her to the door. "James, why don't you yell over to Dev and ask him and Sam to join us. We'll have us a little party."

Devlin waved, nodded, and then yelled, "We'll clean up and be right over." Stepping back into the cabin, he slammed the door shut with such force that the old timbers trembled. He stripped off his shirt and wadded it into a tight ball before throwing it forcefully across the room. Drawers were opened and closed so vigorously that the old wardrobe rocked with the vibrations of Devlin's fury.

"Breaking up the place ain't gonna cure what ails you, boy," Sam drawled.

Devlin whirled around. His mind had been so filled with the vision of Jennifer pressing herself against Tom Davis that he'd forgotten Sam was in the room. "I don't know what the hell you're talking about." Taking a deep, controlling breath, he pulled on a clean shirt. "We've been invited for Sunday supper."

Sam rolled off the bunk where he'd been napping before Devlin had set the rafters to ringing. "All you have to do is declare yourself and throw that young'un off the place. Or do you intend to suffer in silence until she marches down the aisle on some other fellow's arm?"

"We've been invited to supper . . . not a wedding," Devlin snarled, tucking his shirttail into his pants, silently cursing his stupidity in losing control over his temper.

Sam anticipated Devlin's retreat. With the agility of a man years younger, he moved to stand in front of the closed door. "It's a wedding we'll be attending next unless you choke down some of that pride of yours and tell her you love her." Sam grinned at the expression on Devlin's face. "You don't remember what you said when we were freezin' our asses off in that haystack last October, do you?"

Devlin tried to push Sam aside. "Neither do you, old man. We were both half crazy. You were dreaming if you thought I said something like that."

A finger was placed dead center of Devlin's broad chest. "Don't you flimflam me, Devlin McShane. I remember every damn word you said." Sam punctuated his words by poking his finger into Devlin's chest again and again. "And if you hadn't told me over and over again just how much you loved that girl, I'd have had you horsewhipped and castrated by now. Ain't much you left out of the tellin' of that story. You put hands on the princess. Now it's time you did the honorable thing."

The fight went out of Devlin. His shoulders slumped and

he turned away. "Leave it be, Sam. She's not been harmed. I'm not that much of an animal." He looked back at his old friend. *"Please,* just leave it be."

"Why?" Sam questioned softly. "The girl loves you. Any fool can see that. Seems to me you're makin' something simple awful damn complicated. Do you want her to marry Tom Davis or some other yahoo like Stu Walters?" When Devlin merely shrugged, Sam jerked him around. "Where the hell is your head, boy? She wants *you!"*

Years of bottled emotions, years of wanting, loving, and keeping a tight rein, exploded as Devlin roared, "Me? And just who the hell do you think *I* am?" He began to pace, then stopped suddenly. "I guess you think it would be just fine and proper for me to go down on my knees and say, 'Jennifer, give me your love, your land, and your birthright —thank you very much.'"

Understanding dawned, but Sam just grinned. "Sounds about right to me. James looks on you as a son. Might as well make it legal."

Devlin closed the distance between them, towering over Sam. There was little doubt about the threat blazing from those darkened blue eyes. "Stay out of this, Sam. Don't stick your nose into my business."

"You threatening me, tyke?" Sam drew himself up; his eyes were chips of ice. "Unless you intend to marry that girl, you keep your hands off her. I catch you messin' with her and I'll find that old bullwhip of mine and add a few more stripes to that stubborn Irish hide."

The color drained from Devlin's face. Sam reached out, his anger gone, an apology on his lips. But Devlin shoved him aside. Again the door rattled on its hinges.

Devlin's closed fist slammed into the corral fence. The pain radiating up his arm was overshadowed by the hurt inside. He bent down to pick up a clod of Montana earth, squeezing it within his powerful hand until it turned to dust. Dust like the dreams that plagued his sleep. A fine powder with so little substance that a gentle breeze scattered the particles when his clenched fist opened. He stared at his empty palm.

Loving Jennifer was an empty dream, and a man needed a dream he could grasp, something that wouldn't turn to dust.

It was time, past time, to move on. One more summer, he promised himself, one more roundup. He'd given James twelve years, and there was no debt left to pay. But before he left there was one last score to settle. If Sam was right, if Jennifer loved him, he had to turn that love back into hate. He might carry her memory to the far corners of the earth, but he'd not leave her to the same fate.

Jennifer accepted the dram of sherry her father offered. She despised the lady's drink, barely sipping it while she basked in the heat of Tom's admiring gaze. She'd changed her attire and looked prim and proper in a high-necked rose-colored blouse. The wide band of the skirt, flaring moderately at the hips, emphasized her slender waist. She'd drawn back the sides of her hair, tying them near the crown of her head with a velvet ribbon, allowing the remainder of her curls to cascade down her back. The perfect caricature of a Stapleton lady, she proceeded to charm Tom Davis right out of his wits.

James Douglas watched his daughter as intently as a fox watching a henhouse. The complete turnabout in Jennifer's behavior was welcome, but the cause was suspect. His eyes narrowed when Jennifer flicked a speck of lint from the leg of Tom's trousers. He began to squirm inside as he remembered her comment of last summer about "any stallion." Tom was obviously uncomfortable, his eyes darting about the room.

Suddenly Tom Davis stood up, moving across the room, hand outstretched. "McShane. Good to see you." The relief in his voice was undisguised. James looked at Jennifer, who plucked at her skirts.

"Why don't you give Maggie a hand in the kitchen, Princess," father suggested to daughter. "I'm sure Dev and I can entertain Tom while you ladies get supper ready."

"Of course, Father." Jennifer didn't miss the steely tone. Placing the glass of sherry on the table, she rose gracefully, giving Tom the sweetest of smiles. But her eyes lingered on Devlin's face, unguarded for just a fraction in time.

Maggie was carving the roast when Jennifer entered the kitchen. "Daddy sent me to help."

Maggie put down the carving knife and wiped her hands on her apron. "Aren't you the least bit ashamed? Playing with that nice young man's affections. You don't fool me, girl. You better stop leading that boy on or else I'm not even going to claim you."

Jennifer turned toward the cupboards, pulling china from the shelves. "How do you know I'm not seriously interested in Tom? As you say . . . he's really quite nice."

Maggie wagged her finger at the young woman she knew too well. "Just you remember, missy. We often get paid back in kind when we start stompin' all over other folks with no regard for the hurt we cause." The older woman had the satisfaction of seeing Jennifer's eyes drop. "You stew on that thought for a while. I sure wouldn't want to live with your conscience."

During supper Jennifer did little more than push the food around on her plate. The conversation between the men was lively. Devlin was positively garrulous, talking easily with Tom as if they'd always been the best of friends. She kept her head down and her mouth shut.

James, too, was puzzled by Devlin's glib tongue. It didn't surprise him, for Devlin could charm the birds from the trees when he took the notion, but James had the uncanny feeling that he was observing an actor playing a role. To what purpose? He looked at Sam. No help there. Sam looked as though someone had loaded his chair with cockleburs.

Jennifer helped Maggie serve dessert. She had just placed Tom's dish of cobbler in front of him when her gaze locked with the man directly across the table. An exquisite ache tore through her body. With a mere glance he could reduce her to quivering jelly. Looking down on Tom, she saw confusion within those kind hazel eyes. The smile she gave

187

him was filled with the genuine affection she felt. How simple life would be if Tom's gentle kisses could inspire the kind of passion she had found within Devlin's arms.

It was no surprise when James summoned the men into his private sanctum for brandy and cigars. Maggie refused Jenny's help with the dishes. "Sugar, I don't want to say more than I have already. Guess I'll just have to trust you to do the right thing. Besides, I know you well enough to know if I tell you one thing, you're sure to do just the opposite."

Jennifer braced her arms against the porch railing, looking upward at brilliant stars in a cloudless night sky. The soft creaking of the door caused her to turn. Devlin stepped onto the porch.

"James won't keep your young man much longer." He sat down on the railing next to her. Inhaling her sweet fragrance, he tested his own resolve.

"And who says he's my young man?" Jennifer challenged, moving closer to Devlin.

"He's a good man, Jen. You could do a lot worse."

"For instance," she purred. Her hand touched his shoulder; a single finger ran down the length of his arm. "Does he have your personal stamp of approval? Is he the man you would choose to share my bed?"

Devlin flinched. He wanted to slap her. He wanted to kiss her. "Who you choose to stud your bed isn't my concern."

Jennifer turned to escape from those hateful words. She didn't get far, crashing into Tom just as he stepped onto the porch.

"I've got to be going. Thank you for your hospitality, Jennifer. Good night, McShane."

Wondering just how much Tom might have overheard, Jennifer grabbed his arm. "I'll walk you to your horse." No opposition was offered, but there was an unusual tension in Tom's stride as they crossed the yard.

She waited by the barn door while Tom saddled his horse. "Is anything wrong?" she asked, disturbed by his continued silence.

Leading his horse, Tom walked toward her. The perfect features of her face were illuminated by the coal-oil lamp hanging near the door. "You are so very beautiful," he whispered.

Tears burned her eyes. "And you are very, very nice." She leaned forward to press a kiss to his cheek.

Suddenly Tom's arms were dragging her into a bone-crushing embrace. "If we're going to give a performance, let's do it right." There was no softness in his tone nor in his kiss.

Jennifer accepted the brutal force without a whimper, giving a man back his pride at the cost of her own. It was far less than she deserved.

Tom lifted his head, feeling slightly sick at his own violence. "I knew you didn't love me." He paused, his voice breaking with emotion. "But to use me to get at McShane . . ." Anger made him lose all reason. His mouth swooped downward again, plundering her lips. He pushed her against the doorframe. At her cry of pain he released her quickly.

Jennifer's head hung with shame. "I'm sorry, Tom. I really never meant to hurt you."

"Didn't you?" He mounted his horse. "Well, I'm sorry for you, Jennifer. Sorry as hell that you can't have what you want. McShane will never come to heel when you crook your finger. Lucky man. I think he knows you far too well."

She watched Tom ride out of her life, knowing she had lost a friend of great value. Hands clenched at her side, she returned to the porch feeling like a snake. A dirty lowdown slimy snake in the grass was what she called herself over and over.

Devlin had remained. "I sense a momentous announcement in the air." The tone was light. Inside he was dying.

His words were intolerable. *He* was intolerable. A light burst inside her head, blinding her to any foreknowledge of her actions.

Before Devlin could duck, a closed fist struck him squarely, painfully, on the jaw, nearly knocking him backward off the rail. The second blow landed on his shoulder while he struggled to right himself. He didn't give her a third chance at him.

Grabbing both of her wrists, he thrust his shoulder into her midsection and stood up in one fluid motion. He ignored the screams of rage as he carried her toward the horse trough. He was impervious to James's bellowing command, and insensitive to the men who filed from the bunkhouse in various stages of undress.

Her legs imprisoned by a muscular forearm, her wrists shackled by a grip of steel, Jennifer shrieked impotently when she was shifted off his shoulder. Glancing downward, she began to buck violently while he dangled her above the slimy water.

"Are you going to cool that spitfire temper?" Devlin snarled. "Or do I cool it for you?"

"What in the hell is with the two of you?" James grabbed his daughter, pulling her forcibly from Devlin's threat. "Dev?" His tone demanded an answer.

The minute she gained her freedom, Jennifer resumed the attack. Devlin easily sidestepped her blows. "Was it something I said, Princess?" he cooed.

"Jennifer Louise!" James physically restrained the spitting wildcat he no longer recognized. "Stop this nonsense or I'll finish what Dev started!"

She froze. Looking at Devlin's tall, implacable form, she felt trapped like a fly crashing time and again against a closed window, beating itself to a slow death in an attempt to reach the unreachable. "Let me go, Father," she said firmly.

James slowly released her, ready to spring again if she should lose control. He watched as she smoothed her tousled hair, straightened her shoulders, and walked away totally composed, looking for all the world as if she'd just left a church social instead of a free-for-all. He briskly ordered the men back to the bunkhouse before turning to Devlin. "Now you can start explaining just what the hell is going on here?" He was talking to a stone wall. "Don't you think I deserve an explanation?"

A pugnacious Irish chin thrust outward. "I owe you many things, sir. But an explanation isn't one of them." It would have taken more than one man to stop Devlin. He left James standing with his mouth agape.

James would have gone after Devlin had Sam not stepped in front of him. "Let it go, James."

Angry gray eyes swept the men still loitering in the yard, and lingered on Davie and Sam. "Can anybody tell me what the hell is going on around here?" The question was purely rhetorical. Three sets of jaws clamped firmly shut.

Bob Tucker elected himself spokesman. "Ain't none of our business." One by one the men followed Bob back to the bunkhouse. Davie hesitated, then joined his comrades.

James's eyes narrowed on Sam, who was wearing a smug expression. "I'd be willing to bet you could tell me what that was all about."

"Maybe," Sam returned vaguely. "But maybe I'll just let you figger this one out for yourself. You got brains, and you got eyes. Try using them for a change."

Argument was pointless. A hot brand wouldn't make Sam Smith talk. James turned on his heel, grumbling as he retraced his steps to the house.

He was tempted to call Jennifer from her room and demand an explanation. Instead he poured himself a healthy shot of brandy, lit a cigar, and then stared at the wall. He was puffing his cigar, the smoke rising, the tip glowing red-hot, when one of his pa's favorite sayings flashed into his mind.

"When you see smoke, you can usually find a fire." James leaned forward in his chair, surprised at the sudden direction of his thoughts. For the next several hours he alternately dismissed, then confirmed the suspicions dawning inside his head.

Fatigue and brandy eventually dulled his brain. But when he stretched out on his bed, just before dropping into a deep slumber he whispered, "Jennifer and Devlin." He continued to smile even in sleep.

Chapter Seventeen

Jennifer's eyes burned from lack of sleep. Throughout the long, restless night she'd seen Tom's face over and over again in her mind until he became the symbol of everything that was wrong in her life. Wracked by a guilty conscience, she realized that she always coveted anything denied, fighting to possess the forbidden, rebelling against restrictions.

The need for a friendly, unbiased opinion had spurred her to Lottie Thomas's farm. When she closed the gate that separated the farm from her own land, she said a silent prayer that Lottie would be able to help her put these tumultuous thoughts into some kind of perspective.

Lost in her own thoughts, Jenny didn't see the horse tied behind the barn. Waving to Joshua, who was playing with his dog, she knocked on the door and then entered without waiting for an answer. Suddenly time was frozen as the two occupants of the room turned slowly to stare at the girl silhouetted in the doorway.

Devlin rose from the chair, naked from the waist up, his magnificent bronzed torso illuminated by a beam of sunlight infiltrating the room from the open door.

Seeing the stricken expression on Jennifer's face, Lottie stepped into that beacon of light, her hand outstretched. "Jenny," she pleaded softly. "Please don't jump to conclusions . . ."

Tears blinded her eyes, but not before they registered a woman dressed only in a nightgown and a threadbare robe.

Jennifer backed away, nearly falling when her foot slipped off the single step. Alternately tripping and stumbling, she ran across the yard and vaulted onto the pinto.

Lottie stood in the doorway, gripping the man's shirt in her hands, totally oblivious to the needle stabbing into her palm.

Devlin pried the shirt from white-knuckled fingers. He snapped the single strand of thread, and the button she had been replacing dropped to the floor, rolling away.

He was pulling on his shirt when Lottie turned to him. "Go after her, Dev. Make her understand."

His mind was in turmoil. How easy it would be to let Jennifer's assumptions go uncorrected. It was the very thing he'd been searching for. But looking at Lottie, he knew an attempt must be made to save a good woman's reputation. Jennifer was quite capable of destroying Lottie with a few vicious words. "Not now, but later—if she lets me get close enough—I'll try."

Lottie put a restraining hand on his arm when he started to leave. "She loves you, Dev. And you love her."

"I know," he said wearily, admitting what he had vehemently denied a few weeks ago. "That's what makes it so damned hard."

She stood in the doorway long after Devlin had gone, staring without seeing until the barking of the hound and the laughter of her oldest son brought her back to the reality of her comfortable, uncomplicated life.

"Josh!" she yelled. "Go find Saul. You two boys still have chores to do."

Jennifer returned to the house in a daze. Needing activity, she hauled buckets of water upstairs and began scrubbing down walls and floors until her hands were raw and her back ached without mercy.

Maggie watched this frantic burst of energy in silence. Instinct told her Jennifer was working off some kind of demon. When the girl requested a tray in her room rather than joining the rest for supper, there was no argument. It was Maggie who shushed James's questions, making lame excuses. And it was Maggie who covered the sleeping girl whose face still bore the tracks of tears.

"Poor little love," she whispered, extinguishing the lamp. "My poor little love."

Awakening abruptly, Jennifer rolled to her back, staring into blackness while a cruel mind flashed images of Devlin and Lottie. She said the two names aloud, the whispered words grating in her ears, tearing through her heart.

Throwing off the single blanket, she found the matches and lit the lamp on the bedside table. Trembling fingers worked the buttons of her work-stained dress, tore at the ribbons and fastenings of her underclothing until she was naked. She poured water into the wash basin and bathed heated flesh in an attempt to cool the seething rage ignited by humiliation and betrayal.

The chambray nightgown she pulled over her head felt cool and soft against her skin. Not bothering to fasten the buttons at the high neck, she sat down at the dressing table to pull a hairbrush through the tangles of hair, punishing her scalp with sweeping, hurtful strokes. Unable to look at her own reflection, she saw instead a man and woman laughing, pointing at the comical figure who stumbled awkwardly, tripping over her own feet to flee her own blind foolishness. How transparent her expression must have been.

She'd poured out her heart to Lottie Thomas. Had there been laughter or pity behind those unwavering brown eyes? Maggie's prediction that her carelessness with Tom would be paid back in kind was coming true. The devil had received her due in spades.

Accepting that further sleep would be impossible, Jennifer looked for something to read. A book of sonnets—a gift from Tom—was the only volume in the room.

Her bare feet made no sound in the carpeted hallway or on the staircase. The house was silent, the other occupants in their beds.

She paused when she saw the light beneath the library door. Cautiously she peered inside. The room seemed deserted in the glow of the desk lamp. The ledger book was open, as if her father had grown suddenly weary and gone to bed without thought to the lamp.

Making her way toward the bookshelf, Jennifer scanned the titles, stretching upward on tiptoes to find her selection just out of reach. A dull thud to her left made her start with alarm.

Dropping his book to the floor, Devlin swung his legs off the leather couch. Without speaking he moved toward her, hating the way she flattened herself against the shelf, hating the expression blazing from frigid gray eyes.

"What are you doing in my house?" she demanded. He towered over her, blocking her escape with his overpowering size.

"I often read in here late at night. Sam claims the light bothers his sleep." The tone was soft. He kept his eyes on her face, ignoring the full breasts pressing against the thin gown, trying to forget the vision of shapely ankles, fighting an insane desire to touch the silken fall of her hair. "Can we talk?"

Jennifer made a move away from the bookshelf. Devlin moved faster. Arms outthrust, palms flat against the shelf, he neatly prevented her escape. She pushed against one of the hard-muscled arms braced on each side of her shoulders. "Get out of my way," she spat through clenched teeth.

"Not until we talk," he insisted with quiet determination. "You need to be straightened out about what you think you saw this morning. I doubt I'll get another opportunity like this one."

Jennifer laughed derisively. "I'd say you're a man who makes his own opportunity, McShane. Now let me pass." She wasn't looking at his face but at the broad expanse of chest revealed by the gaping unbuttoned shirt.

"You're going to listen whether you want to or not. Lottie and I are friends . . . nothing more. She was only sewing a button on my shirt."

"Of course." The sarcasm was heavy in her voice. "And I suppose that button just couldn't wait for Maggie. Please

195

don't insult my intelligence." She pushed at his chest. It might have been a stone wall. "There was guilt written all over Lottie's face."

Hands gripped her shoulders, hauling her away from the shelf. "All you saw was a woman mending a shirt!"

In spite of the evidence, she wanted to believe him. "Why were you there? It wasn't your day to work." She shook her head to and fro. "Lottie wasn't even dressed. A decent woman would not entertain a bare-chested man in her nightdress. A decent woman wouldn't have an intimate relationship with a man not her husband."

Devlin's voice dropped to a husky whisper. "And what of sharing his bed, him naked as the day he was born?" He knew she would remember the night they'd spent after the blizzard. "And what of a girl in a thin nightgown, and a man with his shirt unbuttoned? What would you make of that, Jenny?" When she gave him no answer, he released her to perch on the corner of the desk.

"Tell me you've never shared her bed." She needed to hear him say the words.

Devlin looked down, studying the hands resting on his knees. "Would you believe me? Would that be the end of it?"

"Yes," she admitted. "You're capable of many rotten things, but I've never known you to lie."

"I've never shared her bed." Although softly spoken, the lie exploded within the room. He watched her flinch in reaction. Reaching out, he grasped her shoulders. "Listen, Jen. It was a long time ago. Lottie was very, very lonely, and I was . . ." He needed desperately to make her understand. "It just happened." Silver eyes were hard as diamonds, the flesh beneath his hands unyielding. "Surely after what almost happened between us last summer, you can't convict Lottie for simply being human, for needing—"

"Nothing happened between us last summer! How dare you toss me into the same basket with your whore!" She was like a wounded animal—vicious, deadly.

Devlin pulled her closer, a sneer marring the handsome

face. "Nothing happened because I called a halt. You were begging for it!"

"Don't delude yourself, McShane. I was merely curious as to what the mystery was all about. You never touched my heart. And you certainly didn't stir my passions. It just amused me to let you think yourself the great lover."

"And that makes you better, rising above the base needs of mere humans?" Devlin pulled her hard against his chest. "How simple life must be for the virgin princess, protected from the filth of animal passions."

Jennifer began to struggle, her heart thumping wildly. "Let me go, Dev. You're hurting me. Please . . ."

He shoved her away. "I could prove you wrong. I've felt the passion in you, felt you arch against me." His voice was harsh. He was weary of fighting Jennifer, fighting feelings. Although he loved her, he often didn't like her very much.

Not once during his speech did he look directly in her face. He didn't dare. He stood and moved toward the door, pausing with his hand on the doorknob. "One word . . . if I hear one solitary word against Lottie from your mouth, I'll make you wish you'd never been born." The door opened.

"Dev." She spoke his name softly, but the command in her voice made him turn toward her. "Touch me again and I'll put a bullet in the place where your heart should be."

The look in her eyes was lethal. He nodded, stepping through the door, closing it softly behind him.

"I think he's plumb lost his mind," Davie spat through clenched teeth. "That devil horse is going to kill him."

James agreed. The Appaloosa Devlin had brought back from Helena to replace Shannon was a high roller, refusing to be broken to saddle, displaying a streak of crazy meanness. The old scars visible on the mottled hide were either the cause or the result of this wildness. James could understand Devlin's empathy with the animal, but this was suicide. He climbed the corral fence, throwing his leg over the top rail. He intended to put a stop to this contest between man and horse.

Devlin hit the ground again, harder than before, his teeth, bones, and brains rattling until he saw stars. The Appaloosa stood over him. Shaking his head to clear his vision, he looked eyeball to eyeball at a horse who looked back with bold challenge.

"Give it up," James commanded, hauling the stubborn young man to his feet before the horse could stomp his stupid brains into the dust. "Put him out to stud. It's all he's good for."

Dusting his backside, Devlin was half inclined to agree. If James knew the animal's history, he'd not have him anywhere near the corral. The former owner had suffered a twinge of conscience after taking Devlin's money. Never had this animal been ridden. The man who had put those scars on his haunches would never ride or walk again. But when Devlin looked at this animal all he could see was Jake slowly taking the belt from his trousers, hell blazing from his eyes.

"He can be tamed." Shrugging off James's restraining grasp, he flashed the man a cocky grin. "It's my butt to bust. Stay out of it."

Returning to the rail fence, James looked at Davie and shrugged his shoulders wearily. "Boy has a stubborn streak a mile wide."

A crowd began to gather. All watched while Devlin talked softly to the skittish animal, his voice a singsong. Running his hands over quivering flanks, he attempted to accustom the animal to his touch, his scent, and the reassuring cadence of his voice.

Having been drawn from the house by the uproar, Jennifer rested her arms across the top railing. "Has Dev finally found a horse he can't manage?" she asked lightly.

Davie took exception to her tone, giving her a scathing look. "That's no ordinary horse. That animal is the son of old Lucifer himself." He blamed Jennifer for Devlin's obsession. His friend had changed since she returned from Boston, becoming short-tempered, indulging himself in black moods, and being a general pain in the ass. Devlin had started no less than three fights while they were in Helena.

It was as if he wanted somebody to knock his head off his shoulders. But it was a hard head, and most sane men didn't tackle a mountain. Drinking, fighting, and whoring when given the opportunity was part of the cowboy creed. But it wasn't Devlin McShane's creed any more than it was Davie Garrett's.

"Get out of here before he sees you." Davie was afraid for his friend. "He'll never quit with you standing here." His hand was on her arm, intending to draw her away by force if necessary. He didn't care about the boss or the possible loss of his job.

Suddenly the mood of the crowd around the corral altered. Davie muttered "Shit" beneath his breath.

The horse had quieted. Devlin quickly grabbed its ear, distracting it long enough to get his left foot into the stirrup. His right leg never made it across the saddle. The horse left the ground, coming back down hard on all fours. Devlin felt his mouth fill with blood and knew he'd bitten his tongue. He was still attempting to straddle the Appaloosa when it reared over backward.

Jumping free, he saved himself from being crushed beneath the thrashing animal. He landed hard on his shoulder and felt the separation of bone and muscle as his arm was wrenched from its socket. He heard a scream and vaguely wondered if it was his own before losing consciousness.

He awakened to agony. His head was pillowed on something soft. Pain-glazed eyes registered Jennifer's face above him. Someone was forcing a piece of rawhide tied around a stick between his teeth.

"You must hold very still," Jennifer warned softly, leaning over his upper body.

James took hold of his arm. "Hang on, son," he said, already feeling Devlin's pain inside himself. "Jenny, maybe it would be better if Davie held him down."

"No." She insisted, knowing the fiber of the man. "He's too stubborn to move." Not one man gave argument to her statement. "Isn't that right, Mr. McShane?"

Devlin blinked, nodded, and then closed his eyes. He

199

turned his head into the curve of Jennifer's shoulder and prepared himself for the pain. At the first tug, he nearly bit through the rawhide. A cold sweat beaded upon his brow. When the separated joints were once again merged, the rawhide was removed. Fresh blood from the pressure of his injured tongue against the stick ran down his chin.

Gently Jennifer dabbed at the trickle of blood with the hem of her skirt. "Davie, go find something to make a stretcher. Tear off a door if you have to."

A wooden gate was found, and Devlin was carried to the cabin. Maggie was waiting with bindings to strap his injured arm to his chest. "This will do until we can fetch the doctor from town," she pronounced. "No sense in taking a chance with a man's arm when a good doctor is around." She forced a dose of laudanum down his throat.

Davie went for the doctor. Jennifer waited in the doorway until Maggie shooed her away. "He's sleeping now. You best see to your daddy. He went out of here with murder in his eye."

Puzzled, Jennifer obeyed as ordered. She was just about to enter the house when the door swung open, nearly knocking her off her feet. James held a rifle in his hands. Guessing his intent, she ran after him. "No!" she shouted, grabbing at him. "You can't. You don't have the right!"

James whirled on her. "That damned animal nearly killed him. Do you want to see him dead, his neck snapped or his back broken!"

Putting both hands on the rifle, she confronted James's black rage. "He'd not thank you for your interference, no matter how well-intentioned."

James released his grip on the weapon. He studied his daughter's face. Over the past few weeks he'd watched Jennifer and Devlin with hawk eyes, growing more disheartened with each passing day. They behaved like cat and dog around each other. He'd just about decided that the brandy, Sam's ambiguous words, and his own wishful fancies had invented a romance between his daughter and the man he loved like a son where none existed. What he'd witnessed today confused him.

Dropping an arm about Jennifer's shoulders, he sighed heavily. "Thank you, child. I guess you're smarter than your old man—at least when it comes to knowing that boy." If Jennifer's face reflected an emotion other than relief, James did not recognize it.

The small portion of brandy James poured his daughter was intended to loosen her tongue. They sat in the library, an uneasy silence signaling their anxiety as they waited for the doctor. James leaned back in his chair, propping his feet on the desk, trying to appear casual as he broke the silence. "Why did Tom suddenly stop calling?"

Closed silver eyes snapped open. "I . . . I'm not sure. Perhaps I didn't appeal to him after all."

"Bull," James scoffed. "That boy followed you around like a long-eared pup. What happened?"

Jennifer stood, walking to the window to avoid his eyes. "I'm often not a very nice person." She smiled ruefully to herself, taking another fortifying sip of the brandy. "But I don't think I have to tell you that. Tom just finally saw what everyone else already knows about me."

"And the argument between you and Dev . . . did that have anything to do with Tom?" James had the bit between his teeth, and he intended to run with it.

She emptied the glass and placed it on the table. "Dev and I have always fought," she parried, moving toward the door. "We try not to . . . but if we spend more than a few minutes in each other's company . . ." She shrugged.

"Sit down, Jennifer," James ordered. When she hesitated, he repeated the command. "Why don't you get along? There has to be a reason."

Flopping onto the chair, she curled her legs beneath her, searching for explanations that would be reasonable, acceptable, and would have the ring of truth. Her father was not stupid, although he was often blind.

"You mostly," she answered truthfully, looking him directly in the eye. "I used to hate him for being the son I could never be to you."

James's feet hit the floor with a thud. "You were jealous of Devlin? Good Lord, girl . . . that's nonsense."

"Is it?" Her brow lifted. "Why then does Devlin know everything about the running of this ranch, while I know almost nothing? Why do you always turn to him in times of trouble and slam doors in my face?" She leaned forward in her chair, hands clutched tightly in her lap. "Ever since he came here, I've been passed over."

The dismay on her father's face was real. "Passed over? In what way? Do you think I hold Dev in higher esteem than my own flesh and blood? Is that what's been sticking in your craw all these years?"

Jennifer shook her head wearily. Could he possibly understand? She opened her mouth to explain, but James was already on his feet, walking around the desk. "Honey, I love you more than anyone or anything on God's earth. It's only your happiness I want. You shouldn't have to worry about a man's business or problems. Matter of fact, you should be grateful to Devlin for taking the responsibility he does around here. Surely you don't want to worry your pretty head about . . ."

His voice droned on and on. She deliberately shut out the meaning behind the sound. No, her father would never understand her need to have or express an original opinion. And more than anything, she wanted her thoughts, her feelings and opinions, to be of some consequence . . . to someone.

"Someday you'll have a family to worry over," James finished. "You'll be too busy to fret about ranching business. That's a man's province, Princess."

"Of course," she whispered, rising from the chair to smile at him sadly. "Maggie will be with Dev until the doctor arrives. I'll go start lunch." Women's work, she thought bitterly.

His hand on her arm stalled a quick retreat. "What I wanted to say—before we got sidetracked—is that if there's something going on between you and Dev, I wouldn't have any objections to seeing the two of you get together."

"You wouldn't?" she said dryly. "No. I imagine not. Well, please don't get your hopes up, Daddy. Rat poison has more appeal to Devlin McShane than I do. And please, for all our sakes, don't repeat your blessings to Dev. He'd walk straight into hell for you, even if it meant taking me as part of a bad bargain." She kissed his cheek lightly and left him to gaze after her, more confused than ever.

When Allison's letter arrived a week later to announce her forthcoming marriage and beg her best friend to be part of the wedding party, it seemed heaven sent. It took Jennifer only five minutes to make a decision—a little longer to work out the necessary details. But she was determined to get away, from Devlin and her father, from the chaos of the present and the uncertainty of the future.

Finally, with her careful plan in motion, Jennifer appeared at the library door and announced, "I've decided to travel to Boston for Allison's wedding."

"That's nice," James muttered absently, scratching his head, wondering why the column of figures in his ledger wouldn't add up to the same sum twice. it was a few moments before Jennifer's announcement penetrated his befuddled brain. He looked up to find the doorway empty. Rising from the desk and slamming the ledger shut, he went in search of her. He found her in the kitchen.

"You're just chock-full of surprises lately, aren't you?" James was quickly losing patience with the lightning changes his daughter made on a daily basis. He'd picked up the paragon of the perfect lady last spring in Boston, and found himself only a few months later saddled with a headstrong female cowhand. During the winter months she'd seemed to settle down into some kind of reasonable pattern. But lately he'd felt as if he were living with a total stranger. "I suppose you expect me to drop everything and escort you across the country, just because your friend is getting herself married?"

Jennifer smiled blithely. "You underestimate me, Father. I know very well how impossible that would be. With Dev laid up for heaven only knows how long, I'm fully aware that you've lost your good right hand."

"You're not making the trip alone."

Again that smile. "Everything is arranged." She patted his arm. "Ada Rodgers has been nagging Zeb to take her to Bridgeport to see the grandchildren. So you see . . . I'll be properly chaperoned during the journey."

James's mouth opened and closed several times. What objection could he make? "Since when did you start making decisions without discussing them with me first?"

His protest was met with an exasperated sigh. "We did talk about it. Don't you remember? I mentioned it to you one evening right after Allison's letter arrived. You didn't voice any objections." It was an outrageous lie; she couldn't meet his eyes.

James didn't completely buy her neat story, but neither could he deny it. He did remember her saying something about Allison getting married. "How long do you intend to be gone?"

"Only until September. I'll be back long before the hard weather sets in." Desperation drove her to deceit. She needed time away from here to come to terms with her feelings for Devlin. Time to put her life into some kind of bearable order.

James placed a finger beneath her chin, tipping her face upward. "I thought you swore never to go farther east than the Mississippi ever again."

Somehow she managed a bright smile. "A girl can change her mind for a friend, can't she?"

He was struggling to get the lid off the tin of coffee, cursing his incapacity, when she entered the room. Devlin turned, surprised to find her standing there. Not once since she'd held him so gently while James snapped his shoulder back into place had she even stopped by.

She was dressed in the same pretty outfit she'd worn when

he had picked them up at the Billings station a year ago. The only addition was a ridiculous hat perched atop her neatly coiled hair.

Jennifer crossed the room and took the cannister from his hand. Easily she lifted the lid and began spooning coffee into the pot. "I came to say good-bye," she said softly, glancing up, hoping to catch some glimmer of reaction, finding nothing. "I'm leaving for Boston. Allison is getting married."

He adjusted the shirt that was slipping off his injured shoulder and walked across the room to sit down on the bed. It was for the best, he told himself. At least they'd be out of each other's way. If one of them didn't leave—and it couldn't be him until his shoulder mended—eventually she'd touch him or he'd touch her and all hell would break loose between them.

Jennifer set the pot on the stove. Inside her heart was screaming, Tell me not to go. Please ask me to stay.

Devlin cleared a suddenly tight throat. "James told me about the horse. Thank you for interceding." He looked up to see her standing before him. Her eyes were asking eloquently for something he could not give.

She touched his shoulder. The almost caress was light, but he closed his eyes as if in pain. "Does it still hurt?" What had possessed her to come here?

"Not much," he replied, opening his eyes. When she turned to leave, he grabbed for her hand, clenching it tightly. "Jen . . . that night in the library"—the hurt in her eyes was killing him—"I was angry and said hateful things. Everything that happened was my fault."

"You spoke the truth," she admitted, pulling her hand away. "But you misjudged me in thinking I'd spread tales about Lottie." Jennifer turned and walked to the door. "Good-bye, Dev."

From the doorway, Devlin watched Sam help her onto the buckboard. She didn't look back when the wagon moved out of the yard.

Maggie saw him standing in the doorway. She walked

over, seeing within his eyes what he was now incapable of hiding. What foolishness kept these two young ones apart? "She'll be back in September."

Devlin smiled sadly. "September," he repeated. Touching his sore arm, he turned to escape the woman's comfort. By September he would be gone.

PART IV

Chapter Eighteen

Jennifer looked pityingly at Zeb and Ada Rodgers. The couple were exhausted. The strain of the journey and the discomfort of the last hour showed on the pinched, pale features of the robust woman and her angry husband. The hard wooden bench in the crowded Boston station provided little comfort for an old woman whose muscles already protested too many hours of sitting. Zeb's expression warned of a short temper on the verge of an explosion while he stood guard over their luggage.

Another glance at the large clock confirmed their long wait. Jennifer practically bounced off the bench, her own patience at an end. "You two sit tight. I'll find a porter and make arrangements for transportation to the hotel."

Zeb grunted with relief. Ada tried to soothe Jennifer's temper. "Honey, maybe your friend didn't get our wire."

"Maybe," Jennifer grudgingly conceded. But it was possible, in fact more than likely, that Allison was just being her usual tardy self. Whatever the cause, Jennifer had no intention of making Zeb and Ada suffer further.

The porter had difficulty keeping pace with the young woman's brisk stride. The wooden heels of her hightop shoes tapped a furious tattoo on the glossy surface of the floor. He listened politely to her brusque orders, and his black face radiated with a bright smile when she pressed a generous tip into his hand. He hurried away with a promise for a quick return.

The stale air trapped inside the cavernous waiting room

209

was oppressive. When another half hour passed, Ada leaned over and whispered, "I don't think that man is coming back. Maybe you should have waited to part with your money *after* he'd done his job."

Feeling incredibly naive, Jennifer pressed her fingers to pounding temples. "I'll find someone else."

"The hell you will." Zeb's voice rumbled throughout the station. No less than forty shocked eyes turned to stare at the rough-looking man who shouted obscenities in this very public place. "I'll find that lazy bastard! He'll get our luggage and find us a cab if I have to—"

"Hush your mouth, you old fool." Ada reddened. Jennifer was too tired to care. She swept the crowd with a haughty stare.

Suddenly an auburn-haired whirlwind was pushing her way through the crowd. Behind her came a tall young man.

Allison threw herself at Jennifer, hugging her tightly, breathlessly apologizing. "I'm sorry we're late. We were looking at townhouses and simply lost track of the time. Have you been waiting long?" She took a breath. "Stephen, help these poor people with their luggage. Find a porter." Turning back to Jennifer. "Oh, I'm so glad you're here!"

Jennifer didn't know whether to scream or laugh or choke this exuberant, predictably outrageous girl who wasn't even attempting to stop the flow of joyous tears coursing down her face. She hugged her instead.

A deep cough distracted the embracing women. Allison released Jennifer to pull her young man forward. "Jenny, this is Stephen Shepherd." Her eyes were filled with pride and love. "Stephen, meet my dearest friend . . . the cowgirl."

Wanting to be fair, Jennifer tried not to be critical of the perfectly ordinary looking man who was taking her hand and kissing it in cavalier fashion. But it was impossible to completely hide her dismay that Allison, gorgeous, flamboyant Allison, could fall in love with such a nondescript young man. In spite of excellent tailoring, the suit he wore seemed to hang on his tall, lanky frame. She could see the cowlicks swirling in his brown hair as he bent over her hand. But when he raised his head, the dark brown eyes were gleaming with mischief.

Stephen's face split in a wide grin, easily reading her thoughts. "I'm not sure I understand it either, but the woman thinks I'm fairly beautiful."

The smile transformed him, producing two dimples and an endearing lopsided grin. It was the kind of smile that reached out with the promise of friendship and a wealth of humor. She instantly revised her initial opinion. He *was* beautiful all the way to his soul.

Jennifer placed her free hand over the one he continued to hold. "I must agree with Allison. You are attractive beyond measure."

Stephen's smile merely widened. "As modesty is not one of my virtues, I'll bow to your judgment." The arm draped easily over Allison's shoulder; the loving look bestowed on her upturned face said so very much more.

Very quickly a porter was found and they were bustled outside. Stephen was solicitous of the older couple, graciously putting them at ease in these unfamiliar surroundings.

Jennifer watched Ada pluck at the folds of her wrinkled skirt, knowing she must be comparing herself to the parade of fabric and fashion passing by. Looking down at her own peach traveling costume, she too felt frumpy and unfashionable. A glance at Allison's cool beauty made her cringe at the comparison.

"Allison!" A rich musical voice caused heads to turn. "Are you coming or going, cousin?"

Reflexively, Jennifer began to inch her way behind the taller Allison. Reluctantly her eyes shifted toward the man moving toward them with an easy, almost swaggering stride.

"I could easily ask you the same question, *cousin.*" The well-modulated tones of Allison's voice held no warmth. "But I doubt if either of us really cares."

Adrian Armbruster seemed totally oblivious to his relative's frank rudeness. "Oh, yes, I remember your father mentioning that you were picking up a friend today." The pale amber eyes swept the group gathered around Allison.

Forced to make introductions, Allison was icily polite. Her animosity toward her cousin seemed to escape Ada and Zeb's notice, but Jennifer was acutely aware of the tightly coiled tension within her friend.

Adrian, however, was gracious, tarrying to chat until Stephen returned with a cab. He made his farewells, those magnetic eyes lingering on Jennifer's face. Her toes curled inside her shoes.

Inside the carriage Jennifer watched as the well-tended lawns and the stately bricks and brownstones of Boston's old wealth passed by the window. She smothered a smile when Ada commented to Allison, "Your cousin is some fine-lookin' hunk of a man." Ada sighed heavily. "If I was just twenty years younger and forty pounds lighter. . . ."

Zeb bristled. "You'd make a fool of yourself."

Allison laughed lightly. "Well, she would have a lot of company. More than half the female population on the eastern seaboard would throw themselves at his feet—if their husbands didn't keep them on a short leash, that is."

No one noticed that Jennifer remained strangely quiet. She was remembering penetrating amber eyes and a flashing, teasing smile. Did he also remember a silly, open-mouthed, waterlogged girl?

The scent of roses was heavy in the soft breeze. The only sound to disturb her solitude was the trickle of the fountain and the faint hum of honeybees gathering nectar.

As she threw back her head, the unbound hair cascaded down her back. The sun bathed her face and neck with radiant warmth. A soft sigh escaped her lips while she gloried in the first moments of tranquil peace since stepping off the train.

Alone in the Armbruster garden, the servants the only possible witnesses to her immodest behavior, Jennifer kicked off the kid slippers, stripped off her stockings, and plunged her feet into the tepid water of the small reflecting pool, shedding the ladylike veneer as easily as she'd shed her shoes and stockings.

The marble bench beneath her buttocks offered no soft

comfort to aching muscles. But the sun was too bright, the air too sweet, to hide within the dimness of her room.

The dark circles of fatigue beneath her eyes were genuine. There had been no argument when she'd begged off yet another garden party in honor of Stephen and Allison. The matrons of Boston society were in full swing, competing to outdo, outshine, and outspend their peers. Allison Armbruster's approaching wedding was the social event of the season.

Jennifer had arrived at the Armbruster estate nearly dead on her feet after a week in Boston with Ada Rodgers. With the same pioneer spirit that had spurred Ada west, she'd taken on the Boston shops. Jennifer had wanted to collapse in Stephen's kind arms when they finally put Ada and Zeb on the train for Bridgeport. She'd been allowed a day's rest before being thrust into the social whirl surrounding Allison's engagement.

Exhausting though it was, the hustle and bustle had been a tonic. She had very little time alone to brood about unrequited love. And the eager attentions from attractive young men were a balm to her bruised ego.

Pulling her feet from the soothing water, she stretched out on the bench. The hot stone burned her skin beneath the thin cotton dress, causing her to arch and shift until the shade of her own body cooled the marble.

Yawning, she threw her arms above her head, wriggled her toes, and allowed the trickling water from the fountain to sing a soothing lullaby.

Standing at the entrance to the garden, a man was enchanted by the uninhibited beauty before him. The muscles of his stomach tightened involuntarily when she arched upward, thrusting her full ripe breasts against the thin fabric of her dress. A midnight cloud of hair floated free over the end of the bench. Creamy skin was bathed in the sun's golden hue. Adrian Armbruster lived life by the moment, and this was one of the most pleasant he'd experienced for some time.

Jennifer drifted in her dreamy haze. She was no longer in a rose garden, but lying in the thick, fragrant grass beside her beloved Silver Creek. A soft, warm breeze whispered across her cheek like the caress of a soft-spoken endearment. Her lips parted expectantly, awaiting that phantom kiss of a sweet dream.

Kneeling beside the sleeping girl, Adrian filled his nostrils with the fragrance of her sun-warmed skin, finding her natural scent more potent, more enticing, than any perfume manufactured by man. Desire, stronger than any he'd ever experienced, surged through him as he released pent-up breath. When those exquisitely formed lips parted in invitation, he touched his mouth to hers, intending only to give a simple kiss of awakening.

She wanted to lift her arms and draw him closer, but found they were too heavy. Sleepy eyes refused to open at the soft touch of his mouth. The butterfly kiss was disappointing and she groaned softly in protest, then was rewarded when his lips took full possession.

It was the sense of smell that finally penetrated Jennifer's sleepy trance. Her nostrils flared at the unfamiliar spicy scent of a man's cologne. Long black lashes fluttered against her cheek; her brows drew together. Suddenly she was completely alert, every nerve in her body registering the ticklish, but not unpleasant, sensation of a man's mustache against her upper lip. Eyes flew wide to stare into golden-brown eyes filled with mirth.

"Are you the real sleeping beauty, or has my imagination conjured the perfect fantasy?"

The deep voice, silken, resonant, galvanized her into action. In a single fluid motion she was sitting upright. But again fate conspired to defeat dignity as the hem of her skirt caught on the pointed edge of the bench, baring her shapely legs to the knees before a violent jerk rent the cloth. A heavy veil of unbound hair hid a deep flush of mortification while she struggled to regain control over her skirt.

"No, not a sleeping beauty. You are a nymph, a goddess of nature, or maybe Aphrodite herself."

The taunting amusement in his voice brought Jennifer's head up with a snap, tossing the black mane back over her shoulders. The silver eyes glinted. "And I suppose you fancy yourself to be Adonis." Her tone was waspish. Allison's cousin seemed to have a particular talent for catching her when she looked worse than a common street urchin.

"It seems we are fated to meet under unusual circumstances, Miss Douglas. I apologize for not being able to resist the temptation of teasing you." The smile faded, the amber eyes darkened. "But I won't apologize for the kiss." When she remained silent, he asked, "Would you like me to leave?"

"I have no authority over visitors in this household, Mr. Armbruster." She rose from the bench, acutely aware of the shoes and stockings lying on the path between them.

Adrian made a half turn and then looked back over his shoulder. "Shall we begin again, Miss Douglas. Join me for tea in the parlor." He moved away with the grace and arrogance born of generations of breeding. "The parlor . . . fifteen minutes." It was a command.

When he disappeared through the open doorway, Jennifer grabbed her shoes and stockings. The inlaid stone walk bruised the tender soles of her bare feet. Taking the side path, she slipped into the dining room and scurried through the kitchen, ignoring the curious stares of the staff as she sprinted up the servants' back staircase.

Inside the blue and gold room, she stripped off the drab, colorless dress. Within minutes she had bathed and doused herself with cologne and was standing before the mirror smugly. The lavender-sprigged muslin flattered her figure, complemented her complexion, and brought a hint of color to her pale gray eyes. A lavender velvet ribbon, tied at the nape of her neck, restrained her flowing hair.

She didn't pause to consider her unquestioned obedience to Adrian Armbruster's command. Within the allotted time she presented herself in the parlor.

His eyes were clearly approving as he handed her a delicate china cup. "Cream and sugar?" Did he know that his velvet voice sent tremors up her spine?

"Sugar, please," she replied, quite pleased with herself for managing to accept the offered tea without rattling the cup within its saucer.

Adrian studied her with candid appreciation. There was not a trace of coyness in her level gaze. "You fascinate me, Miss Douglas."

The cup rattled. Allison's cousin was a far cry from the uncomplicated young men she'd met in the past weeks. He was a mature man in his early thirties, a rogue who knew how to use his charm to its full potential. It was a mere game to him. He enjoyed watching her squirm beneath those long, long lashes while he dazzled her with a mesmerizing smile. She returned the cup and saucer to the table. "Now, why would a simple girl from Montana interest a man who has the entire female population of Boston—or was it the eastern seaboard—swooning at his feet?"

Untroubled by her blunt question, Adrian took a sip of his tea and then settled back more comfortably against the sofa, crossing one leg over the other. "I see that Allison has been championing my virtues." There was a lazy sensuality in his movements. "Obviously my powers are highly over-rated. You do not seem inclined to swoon." He smiled wryly. "In fact, it's my impression you would prefer to toss the tea service at my head."

He was flirting with her, and Jennifer liked his manner. The superbly tailored buff-colored trousers hugged lean legs, but she strongly suspected that the padding at the shoulders of his honey-brown jacket gave the illusion of a muscular build. He was just a little above average in height, and slenderly built. But what he might lack in physical attributes was overshadowed by that overwhelmingly hand-some face. She gave him an honest smile. "Then your attraction for women . . . and their attraction for you is mere vicious gossip?"

He laughed outright. "Not at all. Not at all. I absolutely adore women. Women, I find, love to be adored. But I assure you, Miss Douglas, I'm hardly the blackguard Allison paints me."

Jennifer added another lump of sugar to her cooling tea.

"To be fair, Mr. Armbruster, Allison rarely mentions your name. I was merely repeating something overheard, and hearsay is not a reliable source of information."

Another wry laugh. "My lovely young cousin can barely stand the sight of me." He became very serious. "But then I'm often quite unlikable."

A nerve had been struck. Jennifer attempted to turn the conversation. "I'm being very rude to cross-examine you in your uncle's home. Please accept my apology."

Adrian was gracious. Jennifer began to relax, telling him a little about herself, prompting him to reveal a little of the man beneath the polished veneer. Soon they were talking easily with each other.

Adrian leaned forward, resting his hands on his knees. "With my father's death a few years ago, it occurred to me that there was very little substance to my life. I returned from England and stepped into his position at the family bank. Much against my nature, I have become a man of business. The transformation has not been an easy one. Old habits die hard." The amber eyes were serious. "It was not my intention to kiss you in the garden, but I've lived by impulse too long to resist such a delectable temptation." He ignored her blush.

When he rose to take his leave, she accompanied him to the door. The air seemed charged with a strange electricity. Standing beside this man, she sensed a common bond. All her life she'd been dwarfed by the men who moved within her world—by their size and by the force of their personalities. But her head was level with this man's shoulder, and he was an admitted maverick who flaunted convention with enthusiasm, freely confided his faults, and seemed tolerant of those who judged and found him lacking.

"Should I give your aunt and uncle any message?" she asked when they reached the front door.

His smile was enigmatic. "You might tell them I've never enjoyed a visit to their home quite as I did this one."

"That would hardly be kind, Mr. Armbruster." Her flip reply brought him around. He tipped her face up with a single slender finger beneath her chin.

"My name is Adrian, Jennifer. Mr. Armbruster was my *father*. He's quite dead."

She did not miss the scathing tone with which he spoke the word *father*. The lack of remorse coupled with the fervent expression flaring deep within his eyes caused her to back away a few steps.

"I'm leaving for New York in the morning," he informed her quite calmly. "I'll be back before the end of the week."

Was he telling her he was planning to see her again? She couldn't find the courage to ask, and he left without a single word of confirmation.

When the last course was cleared from the table, Jennifer muffled a yawn, hoping it would not be noticed. Having been granted a day of rest, she could hardly plead fatigue and excuse herself from the table. And as cousin Adrian seemed to be the topic of conversation, she had, she admitted to herself, an intense interest in remaining.

"Adrian is shaping up quite well," Aaron Armbruster asserted, defending the slurs against his nephew's character, heatedly delivered by his only daughter. "I think Charles underestimated the man's fiber."

Eleanor ignored Allison's snort of disbelief. "Charles treated his only son abominably. It's no wonder he rebelled against such harsh discipline. Your brother was abusive, and Isobel has been totally inadequate. I've never known such an unnatural mother."

Eleanor's words explained the bitterness Jennifer heard when Adrian had referred to his father.

"What does *abomdimal* mean?" asked twelve-year-old John Armbruster. He looked daggers at his sister when she went into a fit of giggles.

"Abominable is the subject of our discussion, John," Allison said between chortles. "The word very accurately describes Adrian."

Aaron and Eleanor quickly changed the subject, pointedly ignoring their young son's continued questions and eventually dismissing the determined youngster from the table.

John gave Allison a nasty pinch on her arm before stomping out of the room. Both parents turned on their daughter, but with the agility of a cat, she sprang from her chair and grabbed her silent fiancé's hand to escape into the moonlit garden.

Retiring to the parlor, Eleanor took up her sampler, but her eyes often strayed to the garden doorway. Aaron snoozed in his big stuffed chair. Jennifer attempted to read, but her heavy eyes kept closing.

Soon an angry male voice blending with female laughter drifted in from the garden. Then there was another long silence. Jennifer looked at Eleanor, who was staring at the open doorway.

Suddenly the quiet of the night exploded with a thundering roar and simultaneously a loud splash; nervous tinkling laughter followed. Within minutes Stephen burst into the parlor dragging Allison behind him.

"What in the world?" Eleanor rose halfway out of her chair, her voice strangled by the sight of Stephen's drenched body, wet clothing clinging to his lanky frame. Little puddles formed about his feet as he thrust Allison in front of him.

"Wake your father," he ordered. "We have things to discuss."

"Don't be silly, Stephen." Allison tried to placate him. "You're overreacting."

"Wake him!" The forcefulness and volume of his voice accomplished Stephen's goal. Allison's father practically leapt from the chair. Green eyes glinted, taking in the situation with a single keen glance.

Stephen faced his future father-in-law with damp dignity. "Sir, Allison and I are going to be married by the end of the month. I know this will cause a hardship on you. I know this will ruin many of your plans, and I apologize. But your daughter will be my wife by the end of July."

"Impossible." Eleanor was on her feet now. "The arrangements have been made. The invitations are at the printer. It's simply impossible."

Stephen ignored Allison's mother, facing her father

squarely. "You know me to be an honest man, sir. And I hope you'll forgive my bluntness. If you force us to hold to the September date, I cannot promise you will be giving away a virtuous bride."

Allison groaned, hiding her face. Eleanor gasped and sat down hard. Somehow Jennifer managed not to collapse onto the floor with laughter. She'd watched Allison tempt and torment this easygoing young man for three weeks.

Eleanor was the first to recover. "What have you done, Allison?"

"Me?" Allison squeaked, looking for support from Jennifer, but finding only open enjoyment of her predicament. "I . . . I haven't done anything."

Stephen pulled his wet clothing away from his body. He too began to smile. "You, my love, are a consummate tease. You turn a man inside out with sly tricks until he's dying of wanting. Then you dunk him into a pond to cool what you've expertly started. My patience is at an end. If you expected me to play this foolish game, you picked the wrong man."

The mischievous glint returned to Allison's eyes. She reached up to sweep a damp lock of hair from Stephen's forehead. "I didn't make the wrong choice." Love was shining in her face.

"No, daughter, you certainly didn't." Aaron Armbruster crossed the room, extending his hand. "The arrangements will be made, Stephen." He hushed his wife's strident protest. "Eleanor, unless you want to see your daughter married in something other than white, I suggest you stifle yourself."

Jennifer clamped her hand firmly over her mouth to hide the laughter that could no longer be contained. Aaron and Stephen solemnly shook hands.

"I'll keep my part of the bargain, sir." The lopsided grin appeared. "Unless she pushes me beyond human endurance."

Aaron shrugged. "If you're married quickly, I don't see that it would make much difference one way or the other."

Allison looked positively radiant. Not for one minute did Jennifer doubt that this dramatic scene had been carefully planned and executed by one of the world's finest actresses.

Jennifer fidgeted while the dressmaker made the final adjustments to the bridesmaid's dress, but the defeated expression on the woman's face brought a smile. It had been a battle, hard fought and bloody—Jennifer's skin still bore tiny puncture wounds—a war of pins and needles. But now she stood victorious in a dress that had been stripped of the voluminous sleeves, preposterously draped skirt, and lavishly frilled bodice that had made her look like a midget wearing a tent. Allison could wear the current fashion with flare, but Allison was tall and stately.

A slave to fashion, the dressmaker had refused to change the original design in any detail. Equally stubborn, Jennifer had made her own sketches, but the dressmaker had ignored the crude drawings. The gown had been near completion when Jennifer appealed to Eleanor Armbruster, putting her faith in the older woman's level judgment and astute taste.

Eleanor had surveyed the dress, lips pursed. Finally she had turned to the dressmaker. "Change it, for heaven's sake. That dress makes Jennifer look like a stuffed clown."

The lovely dress she now wore was admittedly daring. The bodice of the apple-green silk underdress scooped low, revealing the upper swell of Jennifer's bosom. The overdress of matching tulle veiled her creamy skin but did not completely hide what the dressmaker considered an immodest display on one so young. The long sleeves retained a fashionable fullness, but the diaphanous fabric clung to slender arms. A wide band of emerald satin cinched the tiny waist, the streamers flowing gracefully to a ruffled hem. On the day of the wedding, fresh daisies would be attached to the waistband and entwined within dark curls.

With the dressmaker's help, Jennifer stepped carefully out of the dress. She made an attempt to mollify the woman. "You've done a wonderful job, Mrs. Lanier. All of Boston will think you quite original."

"Or quite mad," the sour woman replied. "I only pray that Mrs. Armbruster has the consideration to forget my name."

With a swish of skirt and a slight shudder of the door, the woman swept from the room. Left standing in her chemise and petticoats, Jennifer didn't bother to dress. She pulled on a wrapper and returned to the desk and the chore of addressing invitations to the wedding.

The original list of guests had been drastically cut and revised. The wedding would be held in the rose garden of the Armbruster home, and only very close friends would be invited to the ceremony. There was little doubt that a great number of Bostonians would have their noses out of joint for some time to come.

Writer's cramp eventually drove Jennifer from her task. Flexing her fingers, she strolled the room, wondering how to fill the remainder of what could turn into a very long day. There had been too many long, empty days lately. Weddings were famous for setting the mood of romance. Watching Allison and Stephen together was a painful reminder of her own shattered hopes and dreams.

During the day she was able to look at her feelings for Devlin objectively, deciding that she'd given her infatuation for him more importance than was its due. But at night her dreams were filled with him. The warm summer air brought back vivid images of his ruggedly handsome face, the natural grace of his muscular body, and the remembered passion on a summer day. She would awaken from those disturbing dreams to find her body pulsing with a need she didn't understand. Even now, fully awake, she could feel her breasts swell at the briefest thought of his hot mouth against her skin. She shuddered, crying out against the curse of Devlin McShane. She seemed unable to relinquish the hold he had on her heart.

A knock on the door interrupted her reverie. One of the housemaids peered around the door. "Miss Jenny," the young woman said breathlessly, her fair skin unusually flushed. "Mr. Adrian has come to take you riding. Mrs.

Armbruster sent me up to ask if you wish to see him or if she should make excuses for you."

Jennifer opened her mouth to tell the maid that Mr. Adrian had come three weeks too late to take her anywhere, but something, perhaps boredom and a need to escape her own tortured thoughts, stopped the heated words. "I'll change and be down shortly."

When the door closed, Jennifer's lips curved in a devilish smile. The velvet riding habit was out of the question in this heat. Quickly she crossed the hall to John's room. The smile never wavered throughout her search through the boy's closet.

She pulled out fawn-colored breeches and held them up to her body. The boy was tall for his age. Perhaps, just perhaps . . .

Eleanor Armbruster's eyes flew wide with shock, and a bejeweled hand clutched her throat. Adrian merely rose from his chair and crossed the room to greet a young woman whose shapely hips were attractively revealed in very tight boy's trousers. The frilly white blouse merely emphasized the pure femininity before him. A single long thick braid hung down her back. But it was the challenge in those crystalline eyes that stirred him to a depth of feeling that was almost frightening. He was beginning to regret this impulsive call, but quickly masked his feelings.

"Jennifer!" Eleanor found her voice. "Surely you don't intend to step outside in those . . . dressed like . . ."

Out of respect and affection, Jennifer reassured the woman. "The manner of dress might be a bit unconventional for Boston, but I assure you that it is quite common back home. I would have brought something more appropriate if I'd given it some thought."

Adrian chimed his reassurance. "We'll stay to the grounds of the estate."

Eleanor could only nod in mute agreement. "*You* will behave as a gentleman, I trust, Adrian?"

"Of course, Aunt Eleanor," he promised easily while lazy

amber eyes traveled appreciatively over a very shapely body. Escorting Jennifer from the room, he leaned close to murmur in her ear, "You enjoy shocking people, don't you?"

When they stepped through the doorway, she pulled away from the hand too boldly caressing her arm. She opened her mouth to remind him of his promise to Eleanor when her eyes spied the most majestic animal she'd ever seen. Except for a blaze of white on the horse's nose, the coat gleamed blue-black in the afternoon sun. The beauty of Adrian's mount was the equal of his master's.

"My God," she whispered with awe. "He's magnificent."

Adrian watched with astonishment when Jennifer hurried down the staircase toward the black Arabian. Before he could shout a warning she was running her hands over the animal's lean flanks, stroking his nose.

"Careful, missy," the groom warned. "That beast likes the taste of human flesh."

Adrian joined them. "It seems beauty has tamed the beast, Jones." The animal was resting his head on the girl's shoulder.

Jennifer sensed the change in the horse, stepping back to slap him firmly across the nose just as he would have taken a chunk of flesh from her shoulder. "You need to teach him some manners, Adrian." She extended her hand, demanding the sugar cubes Jones always kept in his pocket. "What do you call him?" She continued to stroke the horse's neck while he gently removed the cubes from her open palm.

"Diablo." Adrian's tone was curt. He envied the loving attention being bestowed upon a dumb beast. "Do you think you could manage him?" It was an offer made from pure selfishness; he wanted to divert her attention from horse to master. Sparkling eyes, filled with gratitude, rewarded the gesture.

"I'll not give you a chance to change your mind." Her foot was already reaching for the stirrup. She hoisted herself onto the horse easily without aid. The Arabian reared slightly when her weight settled upon his back, but Diablo ceased his prancing as he realized that the knees pressed against his flanks held the firmness of command.

Mounting the timid mare the groom had saddled for Jennifer, Adrian followed the girl and the stallion down the lane toward the open field beyond. Very soon he was cursing the nag beneath him. Jennifer raced ahead, urging the spirited stallion to a full gallop while the mare wheezed in protest at a mere trot.

Jennifer circled Adrian, her laughter ringing in the soft breeze like a symphony of bells. Her face radiated joy. Golden sun-washed skin was flushed pink from the exercise.

Adrian laughed at her efforts to contain herself and the Arabian. Pointing to a copse of trees visible in the distance, he shouted, "Have yourself a good run. Meet me beneath those trees."

She swung the animal around, leaned her body into the rhythm of his strong strides, and displayed an excellence in horsemanship superior to anything Adrian had ever witnessed.

Seated beneath a large maple tree, Jennifer was attempting to rebraid the hair that had loosened during her wild ride when he approached.

Adrian tied the mare next to Diablo, then sank down on the grass beside her, uncaring of the stains that would ruin his light trousers. Gently he swatted her hands from her task and began to entwine the silken strands himself, reluctantly releasing the heavy braid when she retied it with a ribbon.

"Diablo is a wonder, Adrian. Thank you for allowing me to ride him."

She kept her eyes averted. His hand curved around the nape of her neck, forcing her to look at him. "Then you won't mind if I demand a small boon of appreciation," he said huskily, slowly lowering his head.

She twisted away from him, scrambling to her feet. "A simple thank-you is all I am offering. I merely rode the animal; I didn't steal him."

The way she tossed her head reminded Adrian of the way

Diablo pranced while in a temper. It had not been the beauty of the blooded animal that had tempted Adrian to risk all with that last throw of the dice, but the spirit of the beast that made the prize, and the winning, worth the gamble.

Slowly he rose to his feet, advancing toward her, ignoring the warning she uttered. "I told you old habits die hard, Jennifer." His hands captured her shoulders. "My reputation as an unprincipled rakehell was well earned."

She tried to break free of his grasp but was surprised by the strength in that slender body. "But you're trying to reform," she reminded him bravely. It was a false bravado, but pride would not allow her to show fear. His mouth was tracing the curve of her jaw. The hands were now holding her head in a viselike grip.

He found her mouth, but could not coax a response from lips pressed firmly together. "Relax and let me kiss you." There was a not so subtle threat in his tone. "You only dare me to take more by refusing so little." He gently bit the deliciously full lower lip, taking advantage of her gasp of surprise.

She conceded his unequaled skill in the art of seduction. The mustache was unexpectedly soft against her mouth. He used his mouth and tongue persuasively. She allowed the bold kiss, all the while comparing it to Devlin's artless mastery of all her senses. When Adrian pulled her firmly against him, every inch of her body rebelled against the press of his slender frame, craving hard muscle instead.

For a time Jennifer's complicity deluded him. But soon it became apparent that her response lacked genuine feeling. There was total surprise in his expression when he lifted his head. Not since the age of fifteen had he found a woman to be completely insensible to his sensual skill. Male pride told him that she was frigid, instinct told him that there were fires within this girl yet unleashed. He stepped away. There would be other days, other opportunities to resolve pride and instinct. Taking her hand, he led her toward the tethered horses.

Neither spoke until they reached the stable. As Adrian

lifted Jennifer from Diablo's back, he declared, "The next time we ride together, I'll see to it that you have a mount worthy of you. We'll race to see who is the better equestrian."

The challenge in his eyes went deeper than a simple horse race. "I hope you are a good loser, Adrian," she taunted.

"As a matter of fact," he drawled silkily, "I'm a very poor loser when it comes to something I want badly. But then I usually win, so I won't worry it overmuch." He mounted the black stallion. "Until the next time, Miss Douglas."

Chapter Nineteen

Someone handed Jennifer another glass of champagne. She stared at the golden bubbles in consternation. Did a graduate of the Stapleton Academy and Allison Armbruster Shepherd's maid of honor dare get stinking drunk? Would all of Boston point their patrician fingers and cluck their superior tongues? Already her lips felt peculiarly numb, her reflexes sluggish. She began to look for a place to discard the crystal wineglass and then groaned inwardly when another idiot cheerfully yelled, "I propose one more toast to the bride and groom!"

Tears filled her eyes when she looked at Allison and Stephen. So much love flowed between them; dreams were being fulfilled; a bright future was promised. She downed the glass of wine in a single swallow.

Her legs felt funny when she finally found an abandoned chair in a quiet corner of the parlor. Did she dare escape to her room, throw herself onto the bed, and give vent to the tears of self-pity that had threatened since Allison and Stephen had solemnly pledged their lives to each other?

Why today, of all days, had she been unable to banish the dark shadow of Devlin McShane? Closing her eyes, she damned him for the thousandth time, loving and hating him with a passion that was both capricious and obstinate.

Obstinate? Her brows drew together, wrinkling a smooth forehead while she pondered the notion. Was her love rooted in simple stubbornness, just as the years of hatred had their basis in an old habit of childhood? Looking back, she acknowledged that very little justification existed for a young girl's animosity. Was there even less reason to claim a woman's love? A few kisses, a moment of ill-considered abandonment, instantly regretted by the man, perhaps treasured beyond reason in a fanciful heart—was this the foundation of her love? Or did Devlin merely represent a challenge, an impossible peak that demanded conquering because it stood tall, proud, and unattainable?

"Jennifer." The velvet voice demanded attention. "Where have you gone?"

Throughout the day Adrian watched her walk as if in a fog, passing him by several times without a flicker of recognition in those misty eyes. "Do weddings always affect you this way?" he teased, carefully masking the anger seething inside. "Have you any idea how painful it is for a man—even one with my tremendous ego—to have a woman walk by a dozen times or more without seeming to be aware of his existence?"

"Did I do that?" She feigned horror. "Shame on me."

Taking her hands, he pulled her to her feet. "A walk in the garden will soothe my wounded feelings." The admiration in his amber eyes banished Devlin's image for the moment.

"Do you think my reputation will survive?" It was a coquettish remark. She was surprised by the pained fury that flashed in his eyes.

"A smart girl wouldn't take the risk," he said acidly, dropping her hands and turning away to enter the garden alone.

Quickly scanning the room, Jennifer discovered an audience glowing with silent approval of what they assumed to have been a proper setdown for the black-sheep Armbruster. Even Adrian's mother inclined her regal head, smiling in support of the wisdom of spurning her son.

Lifting the hem of her skirt, Jennifer practically ran toward the garden door.

"Adrian," she called breathlessly, catching him. "I didn't mean it."

The setting sun bathed her in coral radiance. He pulled

229

her into the shadows gathering along the west wall. Pushing her against it, he released the hurt and anger that had lived inside him throughout this day. There was no gentleness in his kiss as he ravished her mouth, forcing her lips apart to accept the demanding thrust of his tongue.

Instead of being repulsed by the angry force, Jennifer was shaken to find her arms creeping around his shoulders, her mouth giving succor to his pain. She took his hurt inside to merge with her own until it was cleansed from him and he became the gentle lover once again.

Adrian's heart was pounding, his body trembling with the need to possess every inch of this loving, giving creature. He had not known himself before to be so empty, bereft of real emotion. Trembling fingers caressed her face, neck, and shoulders. He pressed soft kisses on the mouth he'd bruised, wanting to heal the hurt he had caused. Foreign, these feelings were so foreign.

Laughter, loud and nearby, broke them apart. Adrian allowed one more touch, running his fingertips over lips that looked well and thoroughly kissed. "Slap me," he commanded softly. The voices were nearer now. When she continued to look at him in bewilderment, he laughed softly. "You were right about your reputation, my love. Now be a good girl and make my ears ring."

Jennifer smiled. She kissed his cheek, then followed the kiss with a blow that echoed throughout the garden. She watched him blink back the tears that sprang unbidden to his eyes from the force of her slap. "Are your ears ringing?"

"Is my head still attached to my shoulders?" he asked, looking at her with a strange mixture of dismay and admiration. Then he turned on his heel, fixed his face in an expression of fury, and stormed from the garden.

"I won't stand for it, Adrian." Isobel Armbruster was livid. "Not that girl. If we lose your uncle's favor, every door in Boston will slam shut in our faces." Her voice was rising to a hysterical pitch. "Without their support we would be ostracized, outcasts because of your alley cat nature."

Adrian stroked the cheek that still bore the imprint of

Jennifer's hand. He smiled a secret smile, looking at his mother with open contempt. But the dark interior of the carriage hid his expression. "My father's family has damned little to do with the opinion of society. We're Armbrusters. The name alone will open any door we care to enter." He leaned forward. "When did you begin to care about social acceptability?" The contempt she couldn't see was in his voice. "Was it when you grew too old to collect young lovers?"

The carriage stopped in front of the townhouse. Adrian graciously opened the door, assisting his only living parent. In the moonlight he could see her agitation.

"Please leave that girl alone. She may have no breeding or wealth, but while she remains under your uncle's protection—"

The smile Adrian bestowed on his mother was malignant, hushing her immediately. "You underestimate Jennifer, mother dear." The grip on her arm was bruising. With very little effort he'd discovered that Jennifer was not only the most delightful, desirable woman he'd ever known, but also one of the wealthiest. "Have you never heard the term *cattle baron?*"

"I will not allow you to seduce that child!" Brave words, but her face was quite pale with fear.

"I have no intention of seducing her. Jennifer is going to be my wife."

Isobel tried to break free of her son's merciless grip. "Please don't try to convince me that you love the girl. You aren't capable of such tender feelings."

Adrian pulled her along the walk that led to their front door. Did he love her? The very idea of love made him vulnerable. He remembered the tenderness between them, the strong urge to protect and cherish. "Is the pot calling the kettle black, Mother?" he snapped. "What would you know of love or tender feelings?"

She grasped his arms, turning him to face her. "Leopards don't change their spots. Listen to me, son . . . I've lived with you too long. For some people change is impossible."

He unlocked the door and thrust her inside. "I think it's

time for that European tour you've been considering. Yes, I think an *extended,* perhaps indefinite, tour of the Continent is quite timely."

"Adrian!" she shrieked, halting him midstride as he started up the stairs.

He turned, smiling at her. "Go to Europe, Mother. Find yourself a lusty young man to warm your bed and feed your ego. Go to hell for all I care. . . ."

Adrian's courtship was like a stampede upon Jennifer's uncertain feelings. Not a day passed without her spending some part of it in his company. Four weeks of whispered words of love, burning glances, and stolen kisses passed too quickly. But each day brought her another day closer to September, and a decision she was still reluctant to make.

In the wake of Allison's precipitous nuptials, the elder Armbrusters had asked Jennifer to stay on as originally planned. She sensed that they welcomed the presence of a spirited young woman in their household now that their own daughter was gone. And for Jennifer it was the opportunity to maintain that needed distance from Devlin. Even with the diversion Adrian offered, her feelings for Devlin were still too confused, too heated to risk a reunion.

Jennifer's fingers toyed with the piano keys, grateful to be alone. Adrian had suddenly been called to New York on business, and the Armbrusters had left for an impromptu two days at the Cape. She was determined to spend the time trying to sort out her feelings—about Devlin, about Adrian, about herself.

Sensing that she was being observed, Jennifer looked up, eyes widening when she saw Adrian himself leaning against the doorframe, the heat of his passionate gaze blistering her.

"You . . ." she sputtered. "You are supposed to be in New York."

He attempted to look sheepish, failed at that, and then crossed the room with his characteristic swagger. Joining her on the piano bench, he brushed a stray wisp of hair from her cheek. "I lied," he whispered, lowering his head to nuzzle the sensitive area beneath her ear.

Jennifer arched away but was ineffectual in preventing the sensual exploration of her neck. "But Aaron took you to the station," she protested, her voice unsteady.

He chuckled, giving her a gentle nip. "He didn't see me board the train." Adrian reluctantly raised his head. "My aunt and uncle have been hovering like two guardian angels; we've not had a moment alone. When Uncle Aaron said they had planned a visit to Cape Cod to coincide with my scheduled New York trip, I seized the opportunity to invent an earlier, false trip."

"You, sir," Jennifer scolded, sliding to the edge of the piano bench, "you are an unprincipled rogue."

A strong arm snaked around her waist, hauling her hard against his firm body. "Have I ever denied it?" The amber eyes were smoldering. "We need time alone."

Jennifer swallowed hard and nodded in agreement. She was paralyzed by the look in his eyes. Suddenly the intensity faded. The mature face turned boyish. "I've something to show you."

He pulled her from the bench and practically dragged her to the front door. "Shut your eyes," he ordered. When she hesitated he laughed at the look of mistrust, then pretended to be wounded. "If my intentions were dishonorable, I can assure you they wouldn't be altered by whether your eyes were open or not. Now, please, be a good girl and shut your eyes."

She obeyed. She heard the door open, felt the sun on her face. When he lifted her off her feet to carry her down the stairs, she burrowed her head into his shoulder, secretly pleased by this show of masculine strength.

Adrian was glad she couldn't see the strain her slight weight brought to his face. An occasional outing on Diablo was his only exercise. He spurned the boxing and fencing clubs of his peers, living by his wits rather than his physique.

He put her down, moving to stand behind her with his hands on her shoulders. "Now you can open your eyes." Would she notice the slight breathlessness in his voice?

Temporarily blinded by the sudden light, Jennifer blinked several times before her eyes registered the snow-white Arabian next to Diablo. Adrian's hands were moving off her shoulders, down her arms, and then he pulled her tightly against him. "The man who sold her to me promised that she lacks neither speed nor spirit." His fingers spread beneath her breasts, the thumbs precariously flirting with what was deliciously forbidden. "I told him she was a gift for a lady who could ride like the wind." He reluctantly turned her in his arms to study her stunned expression. "She's yours. No one else on earth can match her for spirit and beauty. You were made for each other."

"I cannot accept." Her heart was in her eyes. "It isn't proper."

He gave her a little shake. "You can and you will. A betrothal gift is quite proper." Adrian silenced her protest with his mouth. "And if I remember correctly, you challenged me to a race." Again she attempted to protest. He hushed her quite effectively. "I can stand here kissing you all day, and you can keep right on protesting. Take her. She's yours . . . no strings attached. Now go change into that darling little riding outfit or run the risk of being kissed to death."

Jennifer moved away. "Only for today, Adrian. Just today."

They were both breathless and laughing, the horses lathered when they reached the copse of trees that ended the race. Adrian and Diablo had beaten Jennifer and Fatima by mere inches. Swinging her leg over the beautiful silver-studded saddle, Jennifer slid off the horse unassisted. "I'm rusty from lack of practice. You won't beat us next time."

"You accept my gift then?" Adrian questioned softly.

"She's captured my heart," Jennifer claimed at the same moment he took her into his arms.

"Lucky beast," he whispered into her hair.

Move slowly, he cautioned himself. His blood was high from the race. The scent of her and the sweat-dampened shirt clinging to the soft curves of her breasts brought a wild desire. Very slowly he claimed her mouth. When he felt the stirring of her response, he began a teasing motion with his tongue, slipping it in and out of her mouth in a parody of the love act. When her fingers threaded through his hair, his hands slipped down to cup her slender, rounded bottom, pulling her into his desire, thrusting his hips against her, duplicating the rhythm of his tongue.

Jennifer felt no fear, only delicious pleasure. She abandoned herself to the artful persuasion of his lovemaking. That ache, that demanding searching throb of half-forgotten passion, was being reborn, building in intensity until her hips voluntarily ground into his.

It was the invitation he'd been waiting for. He lowered her to the ground, fitting himself between her legs, carefully controlling the motion of his hips while his fingers worked the buttons on her shirt.

He was so adept that she was unaware of his movements until slender fingers were curving over her rounded breast beneath the thin covering of her camisole.

The sudden rigidity of her body caused him to moan. "Let me touch you." He lowered his mouth to the velvet skin above her underclothing. "I love you, Jennifer. Let me show you how good it will be for us."

It was madness not to stop him, but she had to know, had to make that final comparison. Adrian's lips were warm against her skin, moistly avid with the urgency to taste and touch. The hardness pressing at the juncture of her thighs was the same . . . yet not the same. The mouth nibbling the skin of her breasts stirred her, but did not rob her of her very soul. She wanted that soul-rending passion, needed to lose herself in the mastery of his mouth. As if reading her thoughts through the eloquence of her flesh, he took what she offered, feasting upon her breasts until the pale nipples were firm, pouting, and shaded deep pink from his expert suckling.

Her young body reacted. Healthy passion throbbed. But still it was not the same. "Stop . . . please, Adrian." She drew a ragged breath. "No more."

He rolled away, angered at her rejection. He wanted to

lash out. Instead, he rose to his feet, walking to cool passion, to quell the urge to commit rape. "I need to ride," he growled over his shoulder, clumsily climbing onto Diablo's back, wincing with pain when the hard staff of his arousal came in contact with the unyielding saddle. His eyes strayed to where she lay on the grass, the blouse open to expose those perfect pointed breasts. In that moment he came close to hating her for the torture of his body. He spurred Diablo, cruelly laying a sharp slap across his haunches.

When he returned, Jennifer had composed herself; she looked cool and completely untouched. She didn't reject the arm he draped about her shoulders when he lowered himself to sit beside her on the grass. "I'm sorry if I frightened you, but I haven't had to pull back like that for a very long time." He touched her face. "Marry me, Jennifer."

She shook her head. "I need more time." Her eyes pleaded for understanding while her heart twisted at the hurt registering on his handsome face.

"Who or what stands between us?" he demanded angrily.

Her hand automatically went to the velvet carpet of grass. She plucked a handful, raising it to her nostrils to inhale its fragrance. "It's sweet," she said absently, more to herself than him. "But it couldn't sustain cattle." She tried to make Adrian understand. "The land, the tall grass, the endless sky, are part of me. They nurture me, feed my soul. Can you promise me that I won't go hungry, that I won't wither up inside and die by degrees inside dark buildings, shut up in a city where the sun only casts shadows?"

Adrian pulled her to her feet. The fury in his face caused her to shrink in terror. "This obsession with land and smelly animals is beyond my comprehension. I cannot fight it because I cannot understand what to me amounts to pure nonsense. You either love me or you don't." He turned away. "Obviously you don't."

She raced after him, catching him before he could mount Diablo again. "Please, Adrian . . . more time. I *do* love you." It was the first time she'd admitted it even to herself.

He crushed her to him, taking her mouth with a fierceness that left it bruised. "We've run out of time, Jennifer. Make your choice. But be very sure what you want. I won't take just bits and pieces of your heart. I want it all. I've never loved anything in my life before you. I'm possessive." He shoved her away. She stumbled, landing hard on her backside. There was no remorse in his face as he vaulted onto the stallion's back. "My train leaves for New York on Friday morning. That gives you four days. Be on that train with me or go to Hades. I'll not ask again."

Jennifer was in the stable grooming the Arabian when Allison and Stephen returned from their honeymoon. Her face bore the strain of two sleepless nights spent tossing and turning within her bed, unable to make the decision Adrian demanded. The only release she had found was in the wild rides on the magnificent animal she now soothed.

Allison entered the darkened stable with trepidation. Her mother had eagerly filled her in on the details of a blossoming romance. Eleanor was an incurable romantic. Allison was a realist, and the weight of her own guilt set heavily upon her shoulders. In her haste to wed and bed Stephen, she'd abandoned Jennifer to Adrian's unsavory charms. Mentally she kicked herself while caution insisted she tread carefully. To vilify Adrian now might accomplish the very thing she dreaded with her whole heart.

"If you're not careful, you are going to brush the hair from that poor animal's hide." Allison's voice was soft in an attempt not to startle.

Jennifer squealed with delight, launching herself at Allison. Allison reared away with distaste, pinching her nostrils in protest against the odor of horse sweat and manure.

"I smell like a cowhand." Jennifer laughed, pulling Allison out of the stable. "Come upstairs with me. We can talk while I rid myself of the stench you find so offensive."

Allison stretched across Jennifer's bed, searching for a way to casually introduce the topic of Adrian. She was saved when Jennifer announced, "Adrian has asked me to marry him."

Shock and stunned disbelief rendered Allison speechless. Seduction she had expected, but a proposal of marriage. . . .

"For heaven's sake, Allie," Jennifer defended. "He's not Bluebeard."

When her heart began to beat again, Allison swung her body off the bed. "Well, he sure isn't Prince Charming either. Marriage? My God, Jen, how can you be so . . . so . . ." She searched for an appropriate way to voice her thoughts. "Surely you're not that stupid." The blunt words tumbled from her mouth as she began to pace. "What I can't understand are his motives. *Marriage?*"

"Am I so unlovable?" Shoulders squared, Jennifer refused to let Allison see how much her careless words had hurt.

"Don't be ridiculous!" The auburn-haired woman stopped pacing. "With a crook of your finger you could have any man in Boston crawling on his knees. It's what Adrian wants that worries me. He's simply not capable of falling in love." She turned to Jennifer, green eyes glittering with an almost maniacal fervor. "The man is an aberration! He's foul inside!"

"He loves me," Jennifer replied with quiet assurance. Then anger, held in check, overflowed. "Foul? Aberration? He's a man, Allie. He can love, hurt, and feel. What has he done to you that makes you strip him of simple humanity?"

Allison bit her tongue, squelching the urge to answer Jennifer's question and unburden herself in the process. Would she be believed? No. If loving parents could charge her with a jealous nature and an overactive imagination, Jennifer would never accept memories she often doubted herself. Had she truly found in Adrian a convenient scapegoat for treasures broken or misplaced by a clumsy, absentminded child? And the puppy—had its unfortunate escape from her arms to be trampled beneath the hoofs of Adrian's horse been the sad accident he claimed? Or had it truly been the vicious murder a brokenhearted little girl claimed it to be? The adult she was now could not yet reconcile the veracity of those young memories.

"Perhaps he does love you, Cowgirl," she finally ventured. "But do you return his devotion?" She rose from the bed and grasped Jennifer by the shoulders. "Stephen is my mate. We complete one another. Does such a bond exist between yourself and Adrian?"

"I'm not certain I want to love or be loved so totally," Jennifer admitted in a small voice. "My father loved my mother so deeply he never resigned himself to her death." She looked up into Allison's eyes. "Sometimes I feel an indefinable comradeship with Adrian that touches something deep inside. I've never felt that way before. I can't explain it . . . I only feel it. I'm significant to Adrian. And . . . and that's important to me."

Allison embraced the smaller woman. "Jenny, don't settle for even a fraction less than you can give or receive. You talk of feelings, but you've said nothing of romance or passion, even though my cousin's reputation in the art of seduction is nonpareil. No . . . don't pull away. Please, hear me out. For a woman, passion flows from love just as a stream merges into a river to become a single powerful whole. Do you feel this for Adrian? If not, then you're about to make a mistake you'll long regret."

Without another word, Allison walked from the room, leaving Jennifer with a wild tangle of thoughts and feelings. Still, the ring of truth chimed inside her head.

She knew Adrian's feelings ran deeper than her own. The passion Allison spoke of existed but was one-sided. Had she never known such depth of emotion, she might be innocent of its import. But with Devlin she had experienced such mind-emptying desire that her body still ached with the remembrance.

Whom could she believe? Devlin, who denied the beauty, casually defining what happened between them as nature's urges—more crudely called lust? Or Allison, who believed passion and love were inseparable?

Dropping across the bed, Jennifer cried softly until she fell asleep.

Two letters arrived for Jennifer the next day. For reasons she would ponder later, she opened the one from Ada first.

Ada's brief letter was filled with chatty information about her daughter and grandchildren. But the last line brought a smile: "Honey, I've just loved being with my kids. But I can't wait to get home, put my feet up, and take off this damned corset my girl insists I wear. I haven't taken one good, deep breath since leaving Montana."

Ada and Zeb would be in Boston next week. They expected that Jennifer would return with them.

She avoided reading her father's letter for an hour. Fear that this missive from home might sway the decision she must make kept her turning the unopened envelope in her hands. Eventually she took a deep breath and opened the letter with trembling fingers. It began innocently enough. James asked about her welfare, sent his regards to the Armbrusters, and wished the bride and groom good fortune. But the innocuous tone changed suddenly:

My heart is heavy, daughter. Devlin is leaving as soon as the roundup is finished. No amount of arguing has been able to sway his decision so far. He won't even give me a good reason except to say he's lived off my charity for too long.

Sam says he's been to the bank to see about a loan for a place of his own. Why wouldn't he come to me? I'd help any man that had been with me as long as Devlin. But the boy's more like family than hired help. Old fool that I am, it never occurred to me that he might leave this place. Should have known he had more fiber and grit in him. Always was a proud one, even when he was a skinny, barefoot orphan fending for himself.

Forgive your father's romantic dreams—but I always hoped that something might spring up between you and Dev. You two always struck sparks off each other, and I had a foolish notion that might mean there was deeper feeling there. Sounds silly now.

We start roundup in a few weeks. Dev's arm has mended, but he's still working with that devil horse. Has even named him Lucifer. Says he wants to start breeding him.

Jenny, I've been skirting around the real reason for this letter. It's come to my mind that you'll get married someday, and that your husband's home and a new family will take priority over this ranch. That's as it should be. Louise gave up everything to start a new life with me. Princess, I'm thinking about offering Devlin a partnership. I'll sell him that land up by Silver Creek— never use it anyway—for his horses. He's too smart not to turn a profit at whatever he sets his mind to. I'll accept a down payment, and then he can start paying off the loan after his money starts coming in. He can split his time between this place and his own.

Devlin would never cheat you or yours. He would always see to Sam and Maggie. I wouldn't want to hurt you for the world, but you were right about this being a man's world. Without a son, a strong man to fight nature and the government, this place could be gone in the blink of an eye. Dev would always be right there behind you, guiding you through the rough times. Even a good husband might make the wrong decisions with all the best intentions in the world. But nobody will ever pull the wool over Devlin McShane's hawk eyes or get around his stubborn nature.

Now I'm not foolish enough to think he's just going to jump at this idea. His first thought is going to be how you might react. Believe it or not, the boy does have a real regard for you. May not be exactly what I'd always hoped, but he certainly looks on you like a little sister.

If you've read this far I expect you're in quite a temper by now. Just think on it, and I know that you'll realize that we need him. You should be home before it's time for him to leave. I'll try to wait until you get here, but *may need to play my ace just to hold him. I'm praying that you'll lend your voice to mine and support me. Dev's proud. He'll need some convincing to get him to agree. I'm counting on you to use your head, and not fly off in all directions and let emotions overrule good judgment. I'm doing this for you.*

I love you, daughter. We sure have missed your pretty face.

Jennifer let the pages fall to the floor. Her pretty face had been missed. That last line certainly said a great deal about her place in the world.

There were no tears. She couldn't even summon anger or resentment. She was loved. Her father was only trying to see that her future was secure, the land protected from the ineptitude of a female child.

She went to the desk, pulled the stationery from the drawer, and began her letter. It wasn't a difficult task, and she put her heart into words a very steady hand spread across the page. She pleaded with Devlin to accept her father's offer. She released him from the promise made to a sixteen-year-old girl who had dreamed of standing upon a hill, looking out over the wild beauty of the Montana landscape, knowing that she belonged. Jennifer gave him her sincere blessings and wished him good fortune and a happy life whatever his decision. Then she sealed the letter and gave it to a housemaid for immediate posting.

Tomorrow Adrian was leaving for New York. She intended to be on the train with him.

Chapter Twenty

"Here, darling," Adrian said as he thrust a glass of brandy into his bride's hand. "Drink this. It will soothe those bridal jitters."

Jennifer accepted the amber liquid and the kiss her new husband placed upon her brow. She did not bother to contradict Adrian's natural assumption that she was a tight knot of virginal apprehension. A dutiful wife, she lifted the potent liquor to her lips, drinking deeply, shuddering when the brandy settled warmly in her stomach.

"That's a good darling," Adrian crooned. "Drink it all down while I'm in the bath."

When the door to the bathroom shut behind him, Jennifer tossed the remaining liquor down her throat and moved to the richly draped window. The electric lamps, twinkling up at her from the street below, mocked her, increasing the growing sense that she had been transported into an alien world.

Lifting her left hand, Jennifer studied the circlet of gold on her marriage finger. There had been no minister to give his blessing to the union of Jennifer Louise Douglas and Adrian Arthur Armbruster. Only a slightly disgruntled justice of the peace and his portly wife had toasted the future of the happy bride and groom. This luxury hotel, the romantic dinner by candlelight, the negligee, were all attempts by a loving husband to make up for the joyless reality of their actual wedding.

Unable to banish the feeling that she was slightly outside

of herself, Jennifer moved to the mirror, squinting when her eyes refused to focus. Pulling the ribbon at the throat of the silken robe, she shrugged out of the garment and began a critical survey of the body clearly revealed by a diaphanous gown. The filmy fabric emphasized rather than hid her nakedness. Tiny pink satin ribbons held the silly confection to her body. A mere tug at the bows on the shoulders and—*whoosh*—the gown would be gone.

The soft click of a door and the smell of a man's spicy cologne alerted the bride to her husband's entry. She turned at the sound of his indrawn breath.

She is more beautiful than I dreamed, Adrian thought, his eyes sweeping the diminutive perfection of Jennifer's body. How many nights had the thought of those slender hips, the curve of thigh, the high breasts with their thrusting nipples, kept him awake while his blood pounded furiously through his body. His fingers tingled in anticipation of her velvet skin.

She felt no fear when he approached. She was lighter than air, floating. Her numbed lips perceived the soft brush of his mustache, her mouth accepting the searching, teasing exploration of his tongue. When her eyes closed, the room began to spin, and she sighed with relief when his mouth moved to her neck. The glazed silver eyes fastened on the formidable bed that dominated the room. The dark oak four-poster seemed to beckon, and she swayed toward it, slightly irritated by the masculine form blocking her path.

"Whoosh," she muttered softly, almost giggling when the opalescent pink gown slithered to the floor. Randomly her fingers played in the dark curls on the head now nuzzling at her breasts. The muscles in her legs quivered from the effort of holding her upright.

Adrian smiled when he felt her tremble. His expert tonguing had brought those pert little nipples to life, bringing the seed of Jennifer's passion to bud. His hands moved over the swell of her hips, the soft roundness of her stomach, to explore the downy delta of her womanhood, finding the velvet warmth that would soon assuage the burgeoning ache of his eager maleness.

Jennifer's knees buckled. There was a roaring in her ears when she was lifted and carried to the bed. Her eyelids were heavy, her brain benumbed as she fuzzily comprehended a male form rising above her. A thick pelt of dark curling chest hair was pressed against her breasts at the same moment she felt a burning sensation between her thighs that spread upward into the core of her being. The alcohol-induced fog seemed to evaporate, and she pushed against Adrian's chest, crying out when he invaded her body, tearing through her virginal veil, punishing her again and again with each hard thrust of his body.

When he collapsed upon her, breathing heavily, quaking with the tremors of his own ecstasy, it took every ounce of her willpower not to shove him aside.

"My little virgin," he whispered, kissing her with tenderness. "Next time will be better, I promise."

The bed that had once seemed so inviting now seemed part of an ominous threat. "Next time," Adrian had whispered before rolling away to drop into deep slumber. Jennifer held back the tears, refusing to give herself release, holding the hurt inside until her throat and nose stung as sharply as the tenderness between her thighs.

Turning to her side, she studied the sleeping form of her husband. *"Husband,"* she whispered, testing the word on her tongue, knowing herself for the cheat she was. Should he awaken now he would see only remorse, not the love that was his by right of law and God.

Sometime during the hours before dawn, Jennifer made a vow, a vow more sacred than those made in self-deception before a justice of the peace. The sun would herald the beginning of a new day. Tomorrow all her yesterdays would cease to exist.

She awakened to the sound of a man's singing. It pounded through her aching head with the force of a hammer. Her eyes reacted violently to the bright sunlight, and she rolled to her stomach to burrow beneath her pillow.

Suddenly the bed sagged and the pillow was tossed

halfway across the room. "You're beautiful." The coverlet was swept from her body. "All over beautiful."

The deep voice was husky with renewed desire. Warm lips traversed her spine before moving to the rounded flesh of her soft bottom. At his urging she turned, reaching for him, offering freely what his body now demanded he possess.

Healthy, young, and eager to put yesterday behind her, Jennifer welcomed this joining. When the promise of less pain was fulfilled, she took it as a sign that Adrian's vows were no less consecrated than her own. Soon she was matching his rhythm, awakening to the artful mastery of his body. But too soon the race was lost. Adrian rushed on ahead, leaving her poised on the threshold of discovery.

Rolling to his back, Adrian gave in to the lethargy brought by the warm afterglow of lovemaking. The sheets beneath his heated body were cool, the mattress delightfully soft, and his heavy eyelids closed, never realizing that a door that had been opened to him shut softly while he snored.

Two wires left the New York telegraph office later that same afternoon. One traveled to Boston to assure the Armbrusters of Jennifer's newly married state and well-being. The other traveled a much greater distance.

Chapter Twenty-One

The late afternoon sun was blistering. Perspiration dripped off Devlin's brow and trickled into his eyes, temporarily blinding him while he worked to repair the corral's railings. Muttering curses, he dropped the hammer and wiped his face with a sweat-drenched kerchief, blinking furiously until his vision cleared.

The Appaloosa snorted and pranced within the enclosure. Devlin glared at the animal while rubbing the stiff muscles of his left shoulder. He had none but himself to blame for the reinjury on muscles newly mended, nor the railings kicked loose during that last fierce battle.

A rueful smile touched his lips. Putting two fingers into his mouth, Devlin whistled shrilly. Lucifer whirled, stopped, and then obeyed the command of the man he now accepted as master. Tossing his proud head, he walked slowly toward the railing, receiving the spoken words of praise and the hand that stroked his nose while still snorting fire. A precarious truce had been declared. Neither horse nor man could claim victory, but both retained pride and spirit.

Giving the horse one final pat, Devlin retrieved the hammer, pulled the nails from his pocket, and again began the chore of repairing the corral.

The telegraph operator in Billings drummed his fingers on the table, watching the clock that was slowly crawling to the end of his shift. The sudden, unexpected staccato tapping of the key startled him. Within seconds he was scrawling the message on the paper next to the machine.

"I'll be damned," he said to the empty room, the bored expression fading from his face. He grew impatient and increasingly irritated when the clock chimed the hour. Ten minutes later, when his replacement sauntered in the door, the man grabbed his jacket and snarled, "If you're late again, I'll report you."

"What's the godawful hurry, Ben?" retorted the other man.

Ben Phillips was already on his way out the door. "I just got in a wire that can't wait. I'm headed for the Douglas place if anybody asks."

Reading the hastily scrawled message that would serve as a file copy, the man who sat down behind the desk mumbled, "Holy cow."

Dust billowed upward when Ben Phillips pulled his horse to an abrupt halt in front of the tall cowhand. "Is your boss around, McShane?" He slid from the animal's back and led him toward the watering trough.

"Should be back in an hour or two," Devlin responded, his brow already puckering with worry. "What brings you out here, Ben?"

"Got a wire from the girl." Ben pulled an envelope from his pocket. "Didn't think it ought to wait until somebody wandered into town."

Within the blink of an eye the message was snatched from the telegraph operator's hand. "Hey," he muttered in feeble protest when Devlin tore open the envelope. The opportunity for these small moments of glory was rare. Ben had the sinking feeling Devlin was about to steal his thunder. "Hard to tell if it's good news or bad," he ventured in an attempt to make conversation with a man suddenly gone ashen beneath the dark bronze of his skin.

Wordlessly Devlin folded the message, stuffed it into the pocket of his denims, and left the telegraph operator standing near the corral. In a daze he entered the welcome darkness of the barn, saddled one of the stock animals, and led the horse out into a world suddenly shrouded by the heavy darkness inside his heart.

"Whose damn fool idea was this anyway?" Sam grumbled. It was like an oven in the windowless shack. Not even the hint of a cooling breeze could be felt through the open doorway.

James merely grinned while he continued his task of stacking the tins of food that could sustain a man through weeks of bad weather. Never again would any man on Douglas land be caught without shelter nearby. During the summer months three crude but serviceable shelters had been erected in key locations. James would never again risk one of his men to the whim of nature.

"Bakin' my damn brains so I don't freeze my ass. Make any sense to you?" Sam put the last nail in the frame that would support a straw mattress. "Don't know why I couldn't put this thing together outside."

"Because you couldn't get it back through that door you cut," James replied, heading for the wagon and another load of foodstuffs. When he stepped into the doorway, he saw the horse and rider approaching. "Wonder what Dev wants," he said over his shoulder.

Sam rose to his feet at the question, joining James in the doorway. "Maybe he got lonesome." They both moved outside to approach the advancing rider.

By the time Devlin had ridden to the south pasture, some of the color had returned to his face. But the haunted expression within his eyes couldn't be masked.

"What is it, son?" James asked worriedly, accepting the envelope being thrust at him.

With trembling fingers James slipped the message from its envelope. Quickly he scanned the words written on the paper and passed it to Sam. Without comment he turned and walked back toward the shack.

"Shit," Sam snarled, fixing an ice-blue stare of accusation on Devlin's face. "You happy now?"

The angry words stripped Devlin of his cocoon of numbness. A gnawing ache settled in his midsection. It was a familiar pain; an old friend returning for an indefinite visit; a grim future filled with emptiness.

Davie climbed the stairs. The saloon keeper was right on his heels, braying like the jackass he was. "Who's gonna pay for all that damage?" The man's voice was grating. Davie's teeth clenched when the man grabbed hold of his arm. "Did you see what he did to my place?"

"Shut up, Harry," Davie spat, violently shaking off the man's restraining hand. "I'll make good the damages. Now where the hell is he?"

Harry pointed to one of three rooms that housed the more profitable business of the saloon. "He's in there with Tillie."

Davie opened the door, grimacing at the sight of Devlin's inert form lying crosswise on the bed, arms outflung, legs dangling over the side. Three days' growth of beard couldn't hide the purpling bruise that discolored his chin. Hard, accusing green eyes turned on the saloon keeper.

"Took three men to bring him down," Harry defended. "Nearly busted my hand on that iron jaw of his." Garrett had a murderous glint in his eyes. Harry slowly backed out of the door. "Don't want no trouble. You just get him out of here."

When the door shut behind Harry, Davie's eyes slid to the woman curled up in a chair near the window. "Did he do you any hurt, Tillie?" The cutting tone he'd used on Harry was gone. On the surface it appeared that the whore had escaped the unnatural violence that had been unleashed with devastating results on the room below.

Tillie easily read the direction of Davie's thoughts. Rising from her chair, she stepped into the light, a sly smile tipping the corners of her painted mouth. "Only thing I got to complain about is your taking him out of here."

Leaning over Devlin, Davie wrinkled his nose in protest at the foul stench of unwashed flesh and the reeking odor of cheap whiskey. "Is he unconscious or just dead drunk?"

"Does it really make a difference?" Tillie's eyes made a quick survey of Davie's slim, wiry strength. "You might manage an ordinary man, but you ain't gonna carry this one out without some help."

There was no argument from Davie. He stroked his mustache. "Fetch me some black coffee."

"Already tried that." Tillie indicated a copper pot on a table. "He's dead to the world. More's the pity—thought we'd have another go afore you got here."

Davie dug deep into the pocket of his trousers and withdrew a wad of bills. "See if you can hire two strong backs to help carry him to a horse." The number of bills he handed the woman was generous. "Keep whatever you don't use for your trouble and your kindness."

The woman touched Devlin's limp hair in a gesture of tenderness. "I'll bring you back the change. He did me more service than I did him." Her voice was sad.

"Don't think he knew who I was half the time." Pausing at the door, she looked at the unconscious man with genuine pity. "Kept calling for a Jenny."

"Poor dumb bastard," Davie mumbled when Tillie had gone. "Maybe going home tied across your horse will shake some sense into that thick, stubborn head. While you're puking up your guts, you might just spit out that poisonous little bitch."

Devlin was awake for some time before he braved opening his eyes, knowing with dread certainty that the dull, throbbing pain inside his head would explode with the lifting of his eyelids. He wasn't sure where he was, and had very little memory beyond the moment he'd walked into Slater's. Very slowly he opened his eyes. The pain he anticipated nearly split his skull, and with a groan, he attempted to roll to his side. A face wavered above him, but it was impossible to focus.

"Where you been, boy?" Sam thundered in Devlin's ear.

Flinching away from Sam's roar, Devlin swallowed the bile rising in his throat. "To hell, Sam," he croaked. "Straight to hell."

"Well, I'd guess you ain't seen the last of that place. But I don't hold with kickin' a man already down. Pull yourself together. James is just chock-full of questions. Wants to see you."

Sam smirked when Devlin wobbled as he attempted to sit upright, his head falling into his hands the minute his feet touched the floor. "Hope you can think up a real good story. Or better yet, just admit you're an asshole. That explains it all."

Lifting his head from his hands, Devlin offered Sam the license to crow. "Why don't you say 'I told you so' and get it over with."

With a shrug Sam moved to the door. "Don't need to. You said it yourself." He stepped outside and closed the door, slamming it shut with sadistic force.

Devlin rose to his feet by careful degrees before moving across the room at a snail's pace to reach the washstand. Leaning over the bowl, he poured the entire contents of the porcelain pitcher over his head. The shock of the icy water cleared his brain while his stomach protested so violently it nearly sent him to his knees. Taking deep breaths, he lifted his head to the mirror, feeling nothing but disgust for the bearded, battered reflection staring back at him.

It took almost an hour to accomplish what normally would have taken only minutes. By the time Devlin left the cabin, washed, shaved, and dressed in clean clothing, he had little doubt he was going to die.

The few yards between the cabin and the house seemed like miles. Explanations rattled inside his head until he feared his brain would burst. He rejected them all.

While pulling himself up the porch stairs, he saw Maggie rise from her rocker, her eyes filled with compassion. But when she would have reached for him, he waved her away, feeling undeserving of her pity, preferring instead Sam's honest contempt. With a resigned nod, Maggie stepped back to allow Devlin into the house.

Seated in a stuffed chair near the cold and empty hearth, James watched the young man enter. Gone was the assured stride, the innate grace of movement. "You look like very hell," he stated flatly. "Sit down, for God's sake, before you fall on your face."

It was a near thing, but Devlin did manage to lower himself onto a chair before his legs crumbled beneath him. The pungent odor from James's perpetual cigar aggravated his violent nausea. When a full glass of brandy was thrust beneath his nose, Devlin gagged.

"Hair of the dog," James explained. "Go on . . . drink it."

Devlin shook his head, turning his face away until the liquor was withdrawn. James watched the already pale face turn a sickly hue. "If God serves judgment for the sins of the flesh, it would appear you're getting double the customary sentence. What got into you, son? Was it Jennifer's marriage?"

Red-rimmed eyes focused on James's face. No excuses were attempted for uncharacteristic behavior. Neither did Devlin respond to that astute final question. No point in denying what would now be obvious to anyone . . . everyone.

"The cost of repairing Slater's place will be considerable," James said coldly. "It will be deducted from your pay."

"I'll make up the lost work as well," Devlin managed with effort.

"Damned right you will. Now get your butt out of here before you make a mess on Maggie's carpet."

The brandy Devlin had refused slid easily down his own throat in a single gulp. Oblivious to the younger man's lurching retreat, James reached again for the decanter. He drank away the pain of what might have been, should have been, not understanding any of it, not really wanting to know the answers.

"What the hell difference does it make now anyway?" he growled into his brandy glass.

Sam's anger faded and was replaced by alarm when Devlin continued to retch violently into the chamber pot. When the sickness didn't subside, he fetched Maggie.

Several hours later Devlin's exhausted body gave in to a deep sleep while Maggie soothed his brow with cool cloths.

"He'll be fine," Sam pronounced. "In time."

Without protest, Maggie allowed Sam to lead her from the cabin. "Will she come home again? Or is she gone from us forever?" A comforting arm slid around her waist and she returned the gesture, seeking Sam's strength, sharing the loss of the young woman they both loved and might never again see.

At the kitchen door Sam wiped the tears from her cheeks with callused fingers, pulling her into his arms to kiss her brow. "You're a pretty thing in the moonlight, Miss McGee."

She pushed him away. "You might have turned my head with those words once, Sam Smith, but I'm too old to be swayed by them now."

The teasing banter was not unfamiliar. It was the expression in her eyes that made him reach out and grasp her by the shoulders. "Maggie?" A thousand questions were posed with just the utterance of her name.

Maggie's emotions were too raw to hide what had been so skillfully concealed all these many years. "Dev ain't the only blind, pigheaded idiot on this ranch, Mr. Smith. Matter of fact, you've been a champion ass for quite a number of years now."

Stunned, Sam's hands dropped away from her shoulders. She used the advantage to slip into the kitchen. For nearly an hour he walked in the moonlight, seeing Maggie's face as it had been tonight and all those other nights and days. How had he missed the signals? More the point, why had he purposely ignored what now seemed so clear?

Booted feet did not falter as Sam entered the house. He opened the door to Maggie's room and stepped inside.

Fully awake, Maggie determined that the thud of a man's boots, the rustle of clothing being dropped to the floor, was the song of the angels. When the quilt was lifted and a hard male shape curved spoon-fashion against her womanly form, she turned eagerly to face the man she had loved forever. "Now, go easy. I ain't waited half a lifetime to have you overtax your old heart and die on me now."

Sam swatted and then caressed the soft, rounded bottom.

"I've got a few good years left in me yet, Maggie my girl. Don't plan on cheating you or myself out of the time that's left to us." His hand was moving upward over her hip to find the fullness of her breast. "Now, why don't you skinny out of that nightgown so we can get on with the business of living."

It was a full hour past dawn when James entered the kitchen. The pot on the stove was stone cold. "What the . . ." he mumbled. Stepping to Maggie's door, he knocked softly. When there was no response, he became alarmed. "Maggie? Are you ill?" Shoving the door open, James nearly tripped over the pile of discarded clothing near the door. His mouth dropped open when Sam's head reared off the pillow.

There wasn't even a flicker of embarrassment in Sam's pale blue eyes. "Shut the door and your mouth, Jamie. You're causin' a draft."

The wedding, held a week later in the parlor, was treated with all the dignity befitting the occasion.

The bride was radiant, eyes sparkling with youth restored by the love of her man. Her voice, as she spoke the vows, held a reverent softness alien to men who had often flinched when Maggie was in a temper. The groom's voice shook the very timbers of the house when he pledged Maggie his love.

Afterward, when the wedding feast was scraps and bones, the keg of beer nearly empty, plank tables were cleared from the yard and young Hank was encouraged to bring out his fiddle. Drunken enthusiasm compensated for Hank's lack of talent while the bride was passed from cowhand to cowhand. When her feet could no longer take such punishment, the men, too far gone in drink to care, began to dance with each other.

Standing apart from the merriment, Devlin was studying the first star to appear in the dusky sky when the swish of silk and a woman's gentle touch brought his gaze to warm brown eyes filled with concern.

"I was going to find a place of my own, Lottie," he said

softly, sharing with her the dreams he'd kept only for himself. "It wouldn't have been much—not for a while. I wanted to come to her as a man, with something to offer . . ."

Her fingers tightened on the arm he had braced atop the corral rail. Devlin took that hand and began to lead her back toward the others. When they stood in the circle of men falling and stumbling against each other, he swung her into his arms, moving gracefully, as she had taught him, in the steps of the waltz.

"Why couldn't I have loved you?" He pulled her closer, ignoring her soft protest to his question and the intimacy of his embrace. Over her head Devlin's eyes searched, and then locked with Davie Garrett's murderous glare. "Trust me," he whispered against Lottie's cheek before closing those scant inches between them to bring her flush against his chest.

"Dev?" Lottie started in confusion just when the sharp rap of determined knuckles glanced off Devlin's shoulder blade.

"I'm cuttin' in," Davie snarled, his fists knotted, feet spread and planted for battle.

Devlin stood back but did not release his hold on Lottie's waist. "Sprout, you'd better do better than cut in on a dance. Matter of fact, if you're smart, you'll cut this one out of the herd and put your brand on her quick before somebody else gets the same notion."

Lottie's eyes flew to his face, her cheeks crimson with embarrassment even while she understood his intent. Devlin's lips pressing against her palm, and the wink only she could see, stifled any denials she might have voiced.

"Don't wait too long, Sprout," Devlin emphasized. Turning on his heel, he didn't wait to hear Davie's response, his own mistakes mocking that, for some, wisdom came too late.

"You need some help?" Sam's voice cut through the still darkness of the porch.

"I can manage," Devlin grunted, hauling James out of a

chair to sling the inebriated man's arm across his shoulders. "You might get the door though."

Sam noted the thin, grim line of Devlin's mouth while he half carried, half dragged James into the house. "Putting him to bed this way is gettin' to be a nightly thing, ain't it?"

Devlin didn't have the breath to answer. James was dead weight, and dead drunk . . . again. Once inside, he propped the nearly unconscious man against the wall at the foot of the staircase. Then, with a silent, inward groan, he lowered his shoulder and hoisted James up over his back. "He'll be all right, Sam." His voice was tight with the strain of two hundred pounds. "Go to your bride. I'll look after James." A mumbled curse heralded Sam's departure.

By the time Devlin tossed James across the middle of his bed, back and leg muscles were quivering from the effort of navigating the stairs.

"You give me hell," he grumbled, pulling off his employer's boots, "then start getting yourself sotted blind every night."

With a sputtered groan, James suddenly reared upright. "What the hell . . ." he slurred, his bleary eyes squinting in the dim light of the single lamp. "Is the party over?" He rubbed his face and shook his head to clear an alcohol-fogged brain, pushing Devlin's hands away from his shirt-front. "Don't need you treating me like a helpless babe, goddamnit!"

The frown lines around Devlin's mouth deepened. What the hell was eating at James? he wondered, not for the first time. Better than most he could understand this man's misery, but James's behavior was extreme, and sometimes Devlin saw more than remorse in the smoke-gray eyes; something very akin to a guilty conscience. He was stymied for the cause.

In the end James was forced to concede the need for assistance with his trousers. When he was tucked in and Devlin had bent over to extinguish the lamp, the question a father had been afraid to voice burst from his lips. "Did she know you love her?"

There was a moment's hesitation, a gust of breath plunging the room into darkness, before James received an answer.

"No. But it wouldn't have made a difference if she had." That had been the hardest—admitting that he'd misread the depth of Jennifer's feelings.

Devlin didn't see some of the haunted anguish leave James's features. This much, at least, he didn't have to suffer. "Guess it's only right chicks leave the nest to make their own way," he stated dully. "Suppose you're still determined to leave right after roundup?"

Was he? Devlin wasn't sure of anything anymore. The reason for leaving had been removed. Whatever had given any meaning to his life since leaving Ireland was right here, except for the one he'd stupidly sent away.

No, that wasn't quite true, he reminded himself again. Of her own volition Jennifer had left; of her own free will she had chosen another man to share her life. If once she had felt tender feelings, if once she'd felt passion, his own foolish pride had seen that those emotions were ruthlessly destroyed.

"Maybe not," Devlin finally answered. "On the condition you'll keep yourself away from the brandy. My back won't survive many more trips up those stairs with you slung over it."

"Thank you," James whispered, both of them knowing that what was done was done.

Chapter Twenty-Two

Adrian tossed a coin to the driver of the cab, ignoring the man's insolent mumblings over the sparsity of the tip. Picking up his bag, he opened the gate and moved up the walk toward home. With each step the weariness in his body seemed to drop away. Not since he was a boy of eight or nine, returning after long, lonely months in cheerless schools with unfriendly companions, had he felt any joy in a homecoming.

By the time he reached the front door, there was a smile on his face. He muttered an impatient curse when the key in trembling fingers clattered noisily onto the step. His aching back protested when he bent to retrieve what would unlock the obstacle keeping him from Jennifer. With the eagerness of a very young man, he thrust open the door, dropping his bag on the floor.

The gloom of the entry hall was dispelled by the sound of footsteps. He turned eagerly in anticipation of Jennifer's glad cry at his early homecoming but saw instead his housekeeper appear in the doorway of the parlor.

"You're home earlier than we anticipated, Mr. Armbruster," she said, taking his coat and hat.

He flashed a warm smile. "I took the last train out of Buffalo last night instead of waiting for the morning." Adrian had already turned toward the stairs. "Is Mrs. Armbruster still abed?"

"She's out, sir. Mrs. Shepherd called an hour or so ago.

They went shopping together." Mrs. Johnson witnessed the immediate change in her employer's mood. A muscle twitched in his cheek while he ground his teeth. "We didn't expect you until late this afternoon." She felt an urge to defend the young mistress.

"Have Johnson bring up my bag." All warmth had left his tone. "Tell the cook to prepare a light breakfast and a pot of tea. I missed the morning meal in my rush to get home to my eager, adoring wife." He was snarling with resentment.

"Right away, sir," the housekeeper replied as he disappeared up the long staircase. With a heavy sigh she went in search of her husband. Had it only been last evening that he had remarked about the change in Adrian since his marriage?

"That girl is going to make a difference for us. She is a ray of sweet sunshine in this house. If the elder Mrs. Armbruster will keep herself in Europe, maybe Mr. Adrian has a chance at happiness."

Dear, sweet Harold Johnson was a born optimist. Twenty years in this household hadn't jaundiced his outlook on life. Lifting her skirts, Agatha Johnson descended the narrow, twisting staircase that led to the kitchen and the servants' quarters. Her realistic view of Adrian's marriage was that in time his jealous love would eventually smother the life from his innocent bride.

Entering the kitchen, she found her husband sharing a cup of coffee with the cook. "The *master* is home, Harold. He wants his bag carried upstairs and will most probably want you to draw a hot bath." She turned toward the rotund woman who was always batting her silly eyelashes at the unsuspecting Johnson. "He wants breakfast and a pot of tea, Celia. When it's ready I'll take it up."

"Yes, Mrs. Johnson," Celia hissed. "Right away, Mrs. Johnson." Nondescript blue eyes shot daggers at the skinny woman who looked down her beaked nose at Celia Dawbar as if she were a speck of dust on the spotless floor. "Old crow," she muttered when the Johnsons left the room.

Black hair, black eyes, and the black dress she considered

appropriate to her position had earned Agatha Johnson the nickname Celia had bestowed upon her within a week of employment. It was irksome that a man with Harold Johnson's qualities could look so tenderly upon that shriveled-up old bird when a plump pigeon like herself remained unplucked.

A soft knock on the kitchen door interrupted her private harangue against the housekeeper. Celia waddled to the door and flung it open to glare at a young woman with freckles and carrot-red hair. "What do you want?"

"I've come . . . I've come to speak with Miss Jennifer," the young woman sputtered, her rich brogue and her obvious distress garbling the words.

"And what would the likes of you have to say to the mistress?" Celia hatefully mimicked the accent, enjoying the rare opportunity to vent her spleen on someone even lower than herself. "We don't hire Irish."

Not the least bit cowed by the cook's enmity, the girl pushed her way into the kitchen. "My business is with Miss Jennifer. I'll not be wastin' my breath on the likes of you."

Having witnessed Celia's setdown from the doorway, Agatha Johnson smothered a smile. "The mistress is out, girl. And she's Mrs. Armbruster to you and all else. State your business or be on your way."

Recognizing the authority in the new woman's tone, Daisy O'Manion felt her nerve begin to waver. "I'm a housemaid for Mr. Aaron Armbruster," she explained hastily. "I've come to return something to your mistress . . . Miss Jennifer that is." Her head tilted downward. "And since I be owin' her an apology to go along with it, I'll not turn it over to you."

The distress on the girl's face belied the cocky tone. Mrs. Johnson shrugged and pulled a chair away from the table. "Suit yourself, child. Celia, pour our guest some coffee. She might as well be comfortable while she waits."

"Will it be long?" Daisy asked hesitantly.

"Several hours, I would imagine. Mrs. Armbruster has gone shopping with Mrs. Shepherd."

"Oh, dear . . ." The housemaid plopped down on the chair, ignoring the fat woman's hateful glare as a steaming mug was slammed down on the table. "I can't be stayin' here the whole day. It's me day off, and Mum's expecting me to look after the little ones while she delivers her ironing." She fingered the mug. "The customers won't be happy if they have to wait on their laundry."

Neither woman offered a solution, ignoring her completely while they silently went about their duties. She reached into the pocket of her coat, pulled out the envelope, and studied it before making a decision based on necessity. "Will you see this put in your mistress's hands? And tell her that Daisy O'Manion won't be blamin' her if she should feel the need to report me to Mrs. Eleanor. It was negligence pure and simple, and I'll not excuse myself by sayin' the excitement of her elopement with Mr. Adrian was the blame." Daisy placed the letter on the table. "If I hadn't torn the hem on me summer uniform . . ." Tears sparkled in the hazel eyes, followed by a loud and expressive sniff. "It was only the other day that I found a few spare minutes for the mending. This letter was in the pocket still. It's sorry that I am, but that's the long and the short of it."

"Well, you'll get the sack for certain, missy," Celia cackled. "Typical to your race, you have no sense of responsibility."

"Hush, Celia," Mrs. Johnson snapped, irritated that anyone could crow so loudly over another's misfortune. "Why didn't you simply mail the letter once you found it? Who would have been the wiser?"

Daisy rose slowly from the chair, and a smile quirked at the trembling lips. "I'll not deny it crossed my mind . . . but it's cursed honest I am." With another loud sniff, she touched the letter. "Devlin McShane," she read aloud. "At least I can tell Mum that it was one of our own that was party to me downfall. Though I doubt she'll see much comfort in that when we're both workin' until we drop at the factory."

"I think I'm about to cry," Celia dripped sarcastically.

It was at that moment Adrian stormed into the kitchen, his mouth set in a grim line of annoyance. "Does it take half a day to scramble an egg?"

Without thought, Agatha Johnson snatched the letter from the table. "If you want secure employment, girl, then you'd best make certain this letter reaches the proper party." Taking Daisy's elbow, she began to propel her toward the door.

"Always follow your first instincts, child," Mrs. Johnson advised while she wrapped the girl's fingers around the envelope. "Good luck."

Daisy was practically thrust into the cold. Stunned, she stood on the back step for long moments before shoving the envelope back into her pocket. The O'Manions had just been given a bit of luck this day. With a clear conscience, she started walking toward the trolley stop that would take her past the post office.

Agatha Johnson turned back to her employer. "Irish," she said simply. "Celia told her we didn't hire Irish."

"They're God's curse on this country," Adrian sneered. Amber eyes flickered over the silent women. "Have my breakfast upstairs in five minutes or join that girl on the street."

"Yes, sir," Mrs. Johnson replied, frosting Celia Dawbar with a glare. When he left the kitchen, Agatha let go with a sigh of relief. "Thank you for keeping your silence, Celia."

"Didn't do it for you," the fat woman snorted. "I was only thinking of poor Harold."

Jennifer had the door of the carriage open and was standing on the sidewalk before the driver could climb down from his perch. "Come on, Allie. It's starting to drizzle." She shivered, pulling the hood of her blue velvet cape over her hair, stuffing her hands deeper into the fur muff she carried.

"Maybe next time, Cowgirl." Allison peered up at the darkening sky.

"It's *always* next time." Jennifer grasped Allison's arm

263

and tugged. "I promise I won't let Adrian bite you even if he should arrive home early. Having tea after our shopping was part of the bargain."

Reluctantly Allison stepped from the closed carriage. "Our friendship is in a sorry state when I have to bribe you to spend a few hours in town." She looked at the townhouse where Jennifer lived and frowned with distaste. "How do you stand living in that mausoleum?"

Jennifer avoided the question by turning to the driver. "If you take that side path, it will lead you to the kitchen. Tell Miss Dawbar that she's to give you a hot drink to warm your bones."

"Yes'm," he replied with a jaunty tip of his hat, watching the two young women move up the walk. A man had to be quick to stay a step ahead of Mrs. Jennifer. He'd managed to beat her to the door of the carriage only once during their many stops.

Jennifer smiled warmly at the butler, who had anticipated their arrival and was standing in the open doorway. "Good afternoon, Johnson," she said as he took both capes. He was an odd little man who somehow seemed just a bit out of touch with the world. His expression was perpetually complacent, but the stooped shoulders and the cautious movements of his body spoke of a man who lived with pain. The damp cold had to be torture for the aging butler.

"Is there a fire in the parlor?" Jennifer asked. At his nod, she pulled Allison down the short hallway. "Will you ask Mrs. Johnson to bring us tea?"

"Of course, madame," he said with a bow so characteristic that it always brought a smile to his young mistress's face. Almost as an afterthought, he turned back toward the girl with the sparkling eyes and rosy cheeks. "Mr. Adrian returned before noon. He is sleeping now. Should I awaken him?"

"Oh, Lord." Allison spun on her heel to make a hasty retreat.

Jennifer reached out and grabbed a handful of skirt. "Whoa there, hoss." She was still smiling, but worried eyes

264

were traveling up the darkened staircase toward the second floor. "No . . . don't awaken him. I'm sure he's very tired. Just bring our tea."

"He won't like my being here." Allison tried to recapture her skirt but allowed herself to be coaxed into the parlor.

"Don't be ridiculous," Jennifer insisted. "He might be a little upset I was out when he returned, but that would be a natural reaction, don't you think?"

The fire in the hearth dispelled some of the gloom within the parlor. The gas jets on each side of the marble hearth sputtered and flickered, highlighting the fading colors in the once garish wallcoverings. Jennifer hated every square inch of this house.

"How do you stand it," Allison questioned, her expression revealing abhorrence for the tasteless furnishings. She was looking pointedly at an arrangement of waxed roses beneath a glass dome.

"I can't very well begin redecorating the entire house within two months of marriage. Adrian's mother still has a few rights." She giggled. "Poor taste, but it is her house still."

The entire room had been decorated at the height of the Victorian era. Reds and pinks clashed nauseatingly. The only item in the room worth salvaging was a handsome chromolithograph displayed on an artist's easel. The heavy brocade draperies of a vivid cerise caught the golden sunshine and then turned it into a sickly shade of magenta that cast a pall over the entire room.

Allison joined Jennifer on the burgundy velvet sofa, pushing aside the fringed satin pillows as if they were crawly creatures instead of items for decoration. "Although I've never seen nor heard a brothel described, I envision it would look much like this room."

"How astute, little cousin," drawled a masculine voice. Adrian entered the room, bussed his wife less than enthusiastically, and then took the chair across from the sofa. "They do say that one's taste in furnishings and dress tell a great deal about one's character."

The tightness in Jennifer's chest was released with a nervous laugh. "I think you enjoy shocking people far too much, darling. Allison and I are wise to your brand of humor. Did you have a good trip?"

The amber eyes were veiled by long, spiky lashes. "It was tiresome" was the noncommittal reply. Adrian never said more about his business than was absolutely necessary.

The long silence was making Allison squirm. She kept looking over her shoulder at the clock on the mantel. "I really must leave soon, Jennifer. Stephen usually leaves his office about now. I would like to be home before he gets there."

The lashes of Adrian's eyes flickered upward. "Ah, the devotion of young love. Inspiring, wouldn't you say, Jennifer, my love?"

The sardonic smile and the angry lights of displeasure snapping from his golden eyes left little doubt that Adrian was determined to be insufferable.

"Very inspiring, darling," she responded with saccharine sweetness. "But then Allison has the unique pleasure of knowing ahead of time when to expect her husband."

Allison bounced to her feet. "I really must leave now, Jennifer. Thank you for letting me drag you around town. I really did need your opinion on that Chippendale."

Jennifer walked Allison to the front door. "I'm sorry he is in such a foul temper. Obviously his trip was less than successful."

"When is he *not* obnoxious?" Allison questioned, planting a kiss on Jennifer's cheek. "You do have a right to escape from beneath his possessive wing, or does he expect you to languish about the house while he travels for weeks at a time?" Her voice was beginning to rise heatedly.

"Hush," Jennifer cautioned. "Let's not throw fuel on the fire. Let me handle my husband in my own way. Now be a good girl and give Stephen a kiss for me."

"I think I'll give him several . . ." Allison was skipping down the front stairs, pulling on her cloak. "Yell at Hobson and tell him I'm waiting in the carriage."

Jennifer turned and practically crashed into Johnson. "Would you call—" She didn't get a chance to complete her sentence.

"He's already been notified, madame. Mr. Adrian gave the word when my wife brought the tea."

Returning to the parlor, Jennifer stood in the doorway, eyes flashing as she watched Adrian spoon sugar into his teacup. "You certainly outdid yourself for rudeness. Why even pretend to be gracious?"

Adrian calmly placed the teacup on the table. "Was I pretending to be gracious?" He rose from the chair. "Somehow I don't remember making a conscious effort."

The handsome features were twisted, the man who was advancing toward her a stranger. "Adrian?" she whispered, alarmed and confused. She backed into the hallway to avoid being pushed aside.

Picking up the hat, coat, and umbrella he'd brought down earlier, Adrian turned back to the woman who watched him with a puzzled expression. "If I feel the need to be lectured on deportment, I'll let you know. Otherwise, keep your sophomoric opinions to yourself."

Jennifer practically had to run to catch him at the door. "Where are you going?"

"Out," he snapped. "But I'll be back. Only next time I won't run up the walk like a stupid, hopeful child." He almost softened when the silver eyes flooded with tears. "We're expected at the Delaneys' at seven o'clock for dinner." With that parting bit of information, he opened the umbrella and stepped out into the cold November rain.

Jennifer stood in the door, ignoring Jenkins's friendly wave of greeting before the wizened little man who was both driver and groom climbed atop his perch on the carriage and drove away. The wind shifted, pelting her face with icy, wet droplets until Mrs. Johnson urged her away from the door, shutting it firmly.

"You'll catch your death in that damp, madame. Shall I bring your tea upstairs now?"

"Please," Jennifer managed to croak, unwilling to let this

haughty woman see her trembling. "Mr. Armbruster and I are dining out this evening. Please notify the cook."

"Of course, madame," Mrs. Johnson replied. When the young woman disappeared up the long, curving staircase, she turned and looked at her husband. With a resigned shrug of her shoulders, the housekeeper made her way toward the kitchen.

Adrian returned while his wife was still in her bath. Perched on the edge of the tub, he watched the water lap at her nipples, the heat of the bath suffusing her milk-white skin with a rosy glow.

Already regretting his harsh words earlier in the day, Adrian plucked a towel from the shelf. "Hurry, my love, or we'll be late."

Stepping from the porcelain tub, Jennifer lifted her arms for the ritualistic toweling of her body. She made no protest, allowing herself to be twisted and turned while her husband alternately used the soft cloth and his tongue to remove the moisture from her skin. Her chin was trembling with repressed tears when he turned her into his embrace and kissed her softly.

"I guess we've had our first real disagreement," Adrian said, pulling the pins from her upswept hair, fanning the heavy mass over her shoulders. "Do you know what is nice about marital spats?" he whispered against her mouth, drawing her slowly into the bedroom. "They provide the loveliest excuses for making up in bed."

Inside she was ice, but she didn't deny him when he pushed her down onto the bed and began to strip off his own clothing. When he finally joined her on the bed, she was shuddering with cold, and neither the warmth of his hands nor the heat of his breath upon her body could banish the chill. Too often his fierce lovemaking brought this response. She embraced him, fighting against the instinctive shrinking of her flesh, blanking her mind when the heavy pelt of his chest hair settled against her breasts and his knee pushed itself between her thighs. Her movements when she arched upward to meet his thrusts were practiced, regulated to increase his pleasure as he'd taught her. But there was no reciprocal quickening within her own body.

Adrian slowed his headlong rush toward release. "Don't deny yourself," he whispered huskily, contorting his body to reach her breasts with his mouth. "Let me give you pleasure."

The words, more than his touch, ignited that tiny spark. She wanted the fulfillment he promised, wanted to give unreservedly what he asked of her. But a spark is not a flame, and again Jennifer failed to match her husband's passion.

Rolling away from her, Adrian was gasping from the ecstasy only Jennifer's softness could bring. All the women before, and since, their marriage could not satisfy the savage hunger he felt at the mere thought of her. When his breathing returned to normal, he pulled himself upright.

The sight of her hands clenched tightly at her sides and tears slipping from the corners of her eyes brought contempt, not pity. "You only deprive yourself of much joy, my lovely wife."

Jennifer sat up, pressing her face against the smooth, white skin of his back. "Not by choice, Adrian. Not ever by choice."

"Perhaps not," he agreed. Never had she turned him away. "Maybe little virgins take longer to accustom themselves to their animal lusts." He turned and kissed her cheek rather absently, his mind already darting to the business matters that pressed upon him with increasing weight.

"Get dressed," he ordered brusquely. "Delaney has an obsession with punctuality."

The word *lust* reverberated in her head. Jennifer closed her eyes and soundly castigated herself for the unbidden memory the word brought. She reached for the underclothing she had earlier placed upon the bed and drew her camisole over her head. She wished she could find some excuse not to go to this dinner party. Sharing a meal with Sean Delaney was little better than facing a firing squad at dawn.

Adrian watched her dress, frowning slightly when she

pulled a modest, almost girlish aquamarine silk dress from the wardrobe. Again his wife would look plain and unsophisticated next to Delaney's daughter, Erica. But until he had the funds to dress her properly, there was little he could say or do about the sorry state of her wardrobe.

"You look very lovely, darling," Adrian said with a bright smile. "Shall we go?"

Somehow Jennifer managed to smile and restrain her desire to cover aching ears. Sean Delaney's grating voice was an offense to the senses, the off-color stories an offense to moral sensibilities.

She looked pityingly at the pale woman who was his wife. Helen Delaney smiled tremulously, often visibly flinching at her husband's coarse language. Untutored ranch hands had better bearing and judgment than this florid-faced boor who spat particles of food and pounded the table in enjoyment at his own wit.

Jennifer was sorely tempted to tell this lout, in language he might comprehend, what a revolting picture he made. At first meeting—before he'd opened his mouth—she'd found him attractive. He was a big man, muscular, even handsome in a primitive way. The Irish heritage and lingering brogue had appealed to her instantly . . . for about five minutes.

Seated directly across the table was Delaney's bright, shining jewel, the apple of his eye. Erica Delaney's silver-blond hair, piled high atop an aristocratic brow, glistened with the radiance of moonlight as it caught the light from the overhead chandelier. Delicately arched eyebrows curved above violet eyes that were currently locked onto Adrian's face. Every so often Erica's tongue would dart out from between sharp, straight little teeth to circle full, pouting lips; it was as though she were a ravenous beast licking its chops before pouncing on its prey.

Although her husband seemed oblivious to the less than subtle messages being telegraphed across the table, Jennifer knew few men could remain insensible to the ample display of Erica's overripe breasts threatening to spring free of the low-cut purple velvet dress.

When their host dismissed the women from the table so that he and Adrian could indulge themselves in brandy and cigars and men's talk, Jennifer followed Erica to the drawing room, admittedly fascinated by the undulating movement of the young woman's hips as she crossed the room.

Ignoring Erica's venomous stare, Jennifer smiled warmly at Helen Delaney. Looking about the tastefully furnished room and back again at Helen, Jennifer regretted that she had stifled Allison's passion for gossip. The story of how this sweet, obviously cultured woman got herself tied to a low creature like Sean Delaney must be one big whopping tale.

"Have you heard from your father recently?" Helen asked graciously while handing her guest a cup of coffee. "He must miss you dreadfully. Sean would be bereft without our Erica."

A wave of homesickness washed over Jennifer without warning, leaving her unprepared to respond to Helen's innocent question without a revealing tremor in her voice. "He's been so busy, I doubt he's had time to miss me . . . yet," she responded huskily.

Would the ache ever ease? Was she well and truly missed with the same tearing heartsickness that was becoming her constant companion through long and lonely days? He had written, wishing her well, supporting her right to choose a husband and a way of life, expressing his hope and prayers for her continued happiness and good health. Hardly the sackcloth and ashes he'd voiced when faced with the loss of Devlin.

She did not realize she had spoken aloud until Helen leaned forward with a puzzled frown. "What did you say, my dear?"

"I . . . I was just thinking about the roundup. It should be over by now. In my father's last letter he said that Davie and Lottie were going to be married right after roundup— Davie is one of my father's ranch hands. Lottie owns a farm adjoining our property. So many weddings . . ." Her voice trailed off.

"Let's hope they are catching." A note of uncharacteristic

bitterness crept into Helen's tone. "I'm beginning to despair of grandchildren."

Sean Delaney continued to grill Adrian about the paper mill he'd been paid to look into. "So the old man has developed a lung disease necessitating a warmer, drier climate? Frankly I don't buy that. The Lowell Mill has been in operation for generations. Why would the family rid themselves of a profitable enterprise simply because one of their members is incapacitated?"

Sipping Delaney's inferior brandy, Adrian was careful to mask his aversion for the liquor and the man who served it.

"Sean, as you no doubt already know, there were only two sons. The oldest died this past year, and with the father's subsequent illness, Bertram Lowell has been thrust into the management of his family's affairs. He hasn't the head for business his father or brother possessed, being something of a scapegrace, and untrained for the position. It's my opinion the young man is also a bit slow-witted. The elder Lowell has probably realized this and wants to salvage what he can before they lose all from Bertram's incompetence."

Throughout Adrian's recital, Delaney's head had bobbed up and down, his mouth curling upward in a satisfied smirk. "Well done, my boy. My assumption exactly. Tell me—were you well received?"

"Everything but the red carpet was rolled out to make me welcome."

"Good. Good," Delaney cackled. "There was no mention of my involvement?" Adrian's denial brought a full smile. "By God, I think I've got that old bastard by the balls." He leaned forward over the table, seemingly unaware that Adrian recoiled from the fetid breath coming from a mouth too fond of garlic.

"I can see my money was well spent when I approached you to make this little inquiry, Armbruster. How would you like to continue our association—up the ante, so to speak? Does an easy twenty thousand dollars sound reasonable?"

Adrian was unaware of how closely he was being observed while Delaney allowed the amount he'd named to tickle and tease the imagination. "Well? Have you nothing to say? Have I stunned you speechless?"

"Honestly or dishonestly, Sean?"

The hesitantly worded question brought an outright guffaw. "I can assure you, Adrian, any dealings you have with me will be no more or less unscrupulous than that little game you're currently operating through the bank."

The finely arched brows drew down before Adrian managed to control his troubled reaction. Delaney looked smug.

"Come, come, Armbruster. No need to panic. Your secret is quite safe. None of your satisfied customers have betrayed you. It was accidental that I happened upon the information during a small . . . ahem . . . transaction of my own."

"I don't know what you're talking about. My title of vice-president is mere window-dressing at the bank. I'm actually little more than Uncle Aaron's errand boy, and compensated accordingly."

"Don't be so modest. You've managed to get your thumb deep into the pie and have become a most valuable asset to certain members of our business community." The older man reached for a silver box and offered Adrian one of his imported cigars. Adrian's perfectly manicured fingers trembled before they steadied around the tobacco. When the smoke curled from two cigars, Delaney leaned back in his chair.

"Adrian," he crooned in a softly chiding tone, "you have no reason to fear me. Frankly, I admire your good sense. Certain information is made available through the bank. You'd be foolish not to see the benefit of selling that knowledge you are privileged to have. Who does it hurt? Certainly not the businessmen who pick up commercial properties on the verge of ruin without the bother of a public sale or auction. Not the bank—they get their money right enough. And think of the reputations you've saved; the families who've avoided the stigma of having their financial reverses be fodder for this week's gossip."

"I'm a veritable saint," Adrian said gracelessly. "Make

your point, Sean." The man was obviously well informed, and dangerous.

"The point I'm attempting to make, Armbruster, is that you and I share a common viewpoint in many areas, especially when it concerns overcoming life's unfair obstacles. While you carry a name that stands with Carnegie and Rockefeller, your finances are severely limited. I, on the other hand, am as rich as Croesus, but my humble beginnings deny me entry into the world you take for granted. Both of us are saddled with the liabilities of our birth, but have managed, by our wits and brains, to compensate. Perhaps we can combine our individual assets toward a profitable venture. Are you interested?"

"Go on." In fact, Adrian was very intrigued. It was true that Adrian supplemented his meager income by putting selected associates in touch with others who were deeply in debt and desperate to avoid scandal. But it didn't pay enough to live in high style, nor to dress his wife as she, and he, deserved. Twenty thousand dollars was tempting beyond belief.

Delaney went on to explain. "I want that paper mill. As we've discussed, old man Lowell and I go back a long way. Suffice it to say we had a misunderstanding, which I see no reason to detail. Let's just say Lowell has an aversion to my name. However, the proud, untarnished name of Armbruster will get you right into that old bastard's parlor."

It was an uncomplicated plan, so simple that Adrian could already feel the weight of Delaney's money in his pocket. Delaney wanted Adrian to represent himself as the buyer while he remained a very silent partner. When the legalities had been observed, and it was too late for Lowell to discover the truth, Adrian would begin the process of changing the title on the contracts. Easy money indeed.

"I'll give you ten thousand dollars right now, the remainder to be paid when our business is completed."

"What happens if Lowell should discover our conspiracy, or take another offer?"

Delaney's face darkened. "The only way he'll discover my involvement is through you. That won't happen." There was a strong hint of menace in his tone before he smiled again. "If he deals with someone else, you keep the advance regardless. Now . . . do we have a deal?"

It was a workman's hand Delaney extended. Adrian stared at it, his mind confused. Ten thousand dollars in exchange for a name that had never been worth more than a line in the social register. "Can I think about this?"

"Take my hand, Adrian. You won't ever again get a better offer than this one . . ."

Adrian saw his arm extend itself, felt the tight grip of Delaney's hand. A puzzling chill shook him when his new partner said, "Good. How soon can you return to Buffalo?"

Chapter Twenty-Three

Adrian felt right at home in this smoky Buffalo casino. The cut-glass tumbler he held in his hand was filled with the mellowest blend of fine whiskeys. From a dimly lit stage, a buxom redhead dipped and swayed, her throaty rendition of a naughty ballad barely audible above the hubbub. On occasion the frustrated contralto would raise her voice, straining vocal cords only to be outshouted by the inevitable "Place your bets, gentlemen!"

"Our lovely songbird seems to interest you, Adrian. If you'd like, I'm sure an introduction could be arranged."

Amber eyes moved lazily to the cherubic young man seated across the green baize table. "I'm a married man, Bertram."

"Your glass is almost empty," Bertram Lowell lisped, his speech impediment more apparent with his overindulgence. The plump fingers were unsteady, causing the neck of the bottle to clink loudly against the leaded glass, spilling the pale golden liquid. "Come on now, drink up. This is a celebration."

"Indeed it is." Adrian lifted his glass. "To your father's recovery, and the warm sunshine of New Mexico."

"I'll certainly drink to the sun after the foul weather we've been enduring."

"Well, it is December." Christ, Adrian cringed silently, surely we're not going to make inane conversation about the damned weather. Verbally, however, he continued to act the jolly good fellow, discussing snow and ice as if it were the subject dearest to his heart.

Six weeks he'd endured this buffoon's company, playing the role of boon companion by evening while spending his days with a seemingly never-ending string of bankers and attorneys. Never had he dreamed the negotiations would consume so much time. But the old man drove a hard bargain.

Fortunately the Lowells never questioned the weekend trips to Boston. After all, it was to be expected that a bridegroom of a scant three months was eager to see his wife. That was a laugh. Sean Delaney monopolized nearly every moment with his scheming, and Jennifer was anything but pleased with the current state of their marriage.

Finally, this past weekend, Delaney had written a figure on a scrap of paper. "Tell them this is your final offer. It's a good deal more than Lowell could have dreamed, and far less than I was prepared to pay."

Now with the signed contracts in his pocket, and another ten thousand dollars waiting in Boston, Adrian was hard-pressed to suffer Bertram Lowell's tedious company another minute. Tossing down the last of his whiskey, he flashed a congenial smile. "I've a very early train, my friend. Although it pains me to cut this last evening short, I'm afraid I really must bid you farewell."

Adrian removed the contracts from his breast pocket and passed them across the table. "Per our agreement, the funds will be transferred before the end of this week."

Lowell doubled-checked the signatures in an uncharacteristic display of caution before his baby features reverted to his customary pout. "I'd hoped we could spend this evening together at the tables. Can't I sway you into staying just a little while longer?"

"Shame on you, Bertie." Adrian clucked his tongue, sickened by his own affected mannerisms. "You're determined to lead me to corruption. First it's women and now the vice of gambling."

Both men stood. Amused by Adrian's teasing, Lowell

giggled. "I'd suggest you come visit when your honeymoon is over"—he spread his hands, palms up—"but I'll be in Mexico—New Mexico, I mean—before then."

Adrian quickly took his leave, weaving his way through the crowded room, his path taking him past the flashy redhead who had just finished her performance. Their meeting between the narrow spread of tables appeared quite innocent, even though the woman's face immediately flushed with a glowing warmth. Adrian was, after all, an uncommonly handsome gentleman.

Only Bertram Lowell witnessed the surreptitious press of hands and read more into the brief exchange of words than mere banter. Because Armbruster's departure was being carefully monitored, he saw the songbird toss a hotel room key from one hand to the other the minute Adrian was out the door.

But not once did Adrian look back toward Lowell's table. If he had, he might have seen an innocently bowed mouth curl in contempt before the youthful face went lax with a most profound expression of relief.

Across the miles a man turned his horse into the gusting wind, making that last turn from Douglas land toward the farm. Heavy gray clouds hung low in the sky, seeming to wrap the earth in a perpetual shadow that matched the darkness of Davie Garrett's mood.

A black day, one he wished had never begun. Davie shuddered as his oilskin snapped and billowed, spurring his mount to reach home and the solid sanity of Lottie and the boys. He needed a woman's strange logic to make sense of the events he had witnessed.

The morning had dawned bright, actually mild for mid-December. The journey into town had been slow and unhurried, the gathering of mail for the Thomas farm and the Douglas ranch routine.

Davie accepted the two bundles from the postmaster, stuffing them into his saddlebags with little interest before stopping off to pick up Josh's cough tonic from Doc Harrison.

Even he would swear well into old age that not a cloud was visible on the never-ending blue of the horizon when he made his journey across Douglas land.

The letter, that cursed overlooked packet of paper and ink, deceptively innocent as it waited in ambush to destroy a bond between two men and unleash the violence three strong men could barely contain.

It was then the sky had darkened, the sun eclipsed by the fury set loose upon the land and the dead sound of one man's curse against the other. "Damn your soul to hell, James." Devlin had pulled himself free from those who held him. "I could kill you for this."

To a man, they felt a chill; the very wind cried soulfully at the threat smoldering deep within midnight-blue eyes.

Chapter Twenty-Four

*Above were cerulean skies. Sun-warmed grasses undulated in
the softest breath of a fragrant breeze. The prairie was alive
with the calico colors of spring.*

*In the distance, dotting the horizon, a human figure was
waving a joyous welcome. In her heart was recognition, and
she knew his eyes would rival the indigo flowers growing wild
and free all around her.*

*The overhead screech of a lonely hawk captured the
essence of this moment, and her spirit joined its flight to soar
over the earth. Higher and higher they flew, carried upon the
wind toward the blinding sphere of the sun.*

*The glory was too great, and she turned away to shield her
face from the light. It was then she felt the chill and knew her
loss. Again she was shackled to the earth, but it had altered:
Towering rocks jutted in grotesque formations, projecting
skyward to surround her with dark, monstrous shadows that
shifted, wavering upon the ground, growing closer and
closer . . .*

Jennifer bolted upright in bed, the harsh rasp of her
indrawn breath splintering the silence. Tears streamed down
her cheeks, and her body shook with the violence of her
nightmare, the image of which she could never remember.

Then Adrian was at her side, and she buried her face in
the curve of his neck, grateful for the reality of his presence
and the tangible evidence of shaving lather smearing her
cheek and caking in her hair.

"The dream again?" he asked when her trembling abated. "Can you remember this time?"

"No," she groaned, still breathless from a panic she could not explain. "I think that's the most frightening . . . not being able to remember."

Adrian lowered her to the pillows. He removed the towel draped around his neck and wiped her face and hair free of the lather. "Perhaps you should see a physician."

"For a dream?" Now that her terror had faded, the idea seemed ridiculous in the extreme. "What earthly purpose would that serve?"

"He could give you something to help you rest, something for your nerves."

"Nerves?" She reared off the pillow. "I'm not a hysteric, Adrian. And I have no intention of being treated as one."

"Make an appointment, Jennifer. I grow weary of your nightly tossings and turnings."

At the blunt order, he strode away to separate himself from her by more than the distance to the bath. The subject was closed: women and other inferior life forms need not comment.

Jennifer slipped from the bed and moved to the window, wishing again for an open, panoramic view instead of the distorted shadow of this townhouse silhouetted against the brownstone of their neighbor, a man who remained nameless and preferring his own company to that of the world. If she were a child, his aloofness would be felt an open challenge. And that carefully trimmed hedge would be a perfect hiding place. These silly musings brought a smile. Her hand slid over the still-flat plane of a tummy already harboring the mischiefmaker who would someday make Mr. What's-his-name's life a misery of chaos.

With a sigh she moved to the dressing table and picked up her hairbrush. When Adrian's reflection passed in the mirror, she made a concession. "I'll make an appointment to see a physician right after the holidays."

Like a child afraid to tell a parent of a scratchy throat before a longed-for outing, Jennifer guarded the knowledge of her pregnancy for fear of being forced to miss out on the fun.

"I hope this delightful weather holds until after tomorrow," she said with cheerful eagerness. "After we arrive at your aunt and uncle's I don't care if it snows buckets."

He grumbled a response, and she twisted around to watch him dress. Her husband was not altogether thrilled about spending the holiday week with his family. "You look extremely handsome this morning."

The unexpected compliment softened the harsh set of his jaw, and he gave her a brilliant smile before his attention reverted to the tie he knotted at his throat. Always his male beauty fascinated and charmed. She found herself wishing for more moments such as this where communication flowed beyond the mere physical, and thoughts and mutual goals joined as did their bodies in the marital bed. Would they then find the key to unlock the door that separated their diverse worlds, keeping them divided even while united in the most intimate union?

"Will you be home for dinner?"

"I'll send word." Adrian was shrugging into his jacket, brushing at the tiny specks of lint that were drawn to the gray wool.

Jennifer bit down hard on her lip to prevent a belligerent tongue from lashing out at his casual indifference. Her world revolved at his whims, and her need to be more than a vessel to receive his sexual needs began to grow in direct proportion to his adamant refusal to consider her in any other role. During these first months of their marriage, they'd been apart more than together. And in some ways Jennifer felt she knew him less now than on their wedding day. Did all wives find themselves married to men different from the ardent lover who wooed and won their hearts? For that matter, didn't husbands suffer the same disenchantment? Jennifer knew she fell far short of Adrian's expectations.

Her spark of temper gone, she smiled up at him. "I'll need the carriage for a few hours this morning. There are still a few items left on my Christmas list."

With a final adjustment to his waistcoat, Adrian gave her a look of displeasure. "You'll bankrupt us with such generosity. I was under the impression we'd set limits to your spending."

"How stuffy you sound, Adrian." The hands in her lap curled into fists. "Or are you laboring under the misconception you've married an imbecilic spendthrift? You needn't patronize me. For your information, darling, I've kept my purchases well within the tight little budget you dictated."

"Jennifer, I'm only trying to point out how unnecessarily magnanimous you're being. The servants don't expect personal gifts. It simply isn't done." His own ears could hear the lecturing tone. And his wife's rigid back announced, without words, her exception to his condescending attitude. With a sigh of resignation he crossed the room to stand before her. "But in spite of my grumblings, I love you enough to indulge you in the ruination of my household."

Drawing her to her feet, he dropped a kiss upon her brow. "Now will you stop scowling and give me a kiss?"

Stubbornly Jennifer held herself away. "Adrian, you must stop treating me as if I were a child. I'm your wife, and I resent being indulged almost as much as I loathe being instructed." The hands on her shoulders fell away at the waspish tone, and anger flared within his tawny eyes.

"I'll place Jenkins and the carriage at your unlimited disposal," he said curtly, raising that invisible but impenetrable wall between them.

Again she felt the burden of her own mercurial temperament, which had become his excuse for spending hours at the club, to dine with his clients, and thereby avoid that most unlovable of creatures—the hair-splitting, argumentative, ill-tempered wife.

But Jennifer choked on the apology that might have insured his company. "Please *try* to come home early." She despised the pleading tone that crept into her voice, but pride made a lonely companion.

"I'll try" was his noncommittal reply. No promise had been made, so there was none to break. In this way he dealt honestly with his wife.

She accepted his perfunctory kiss, and the apology she could not voice was in her eyes for him to accept or reject. He left her to engage himself in the mainstream of life while she schooled herself in the arts of common sense, reason, liberality, and *tact*—all foreign to her nature and, according to highly regarded experts on marital bliss, excellent qualities for a wife to cultivate.

The morning's bright sun had disappeared behind a heavy layer of thick gray cloud when Jennifer stepped out of the dressmaker's shop and into the waiting carriage. The sway of the vehicle as Jenkins slowly maneuvered through the heavy traffic of last-minute Christmas shoppers soothed tired muscles and alleviated the tight band of pain around her brow that warned her afternoon nap was overdue.

As the carriage rolled onto the quiet thoroughfares of residential Boston, Jennifer felt the release of tension caused by the final battle with the stubborn Mrs. Lanier. She smiled to herself as she remembered the shudder that had coursed visibly through the gifted seamstress when she'd first stepped into that shop several weeks ago. Warily Mrs. Lanier had suggested designs and fabrics, slowly relaxing as Jennifer chose her new wardrobe with only an occasional quibble over excess fullness in a sleeve, or a fabric too dark or heavy for a petite frame. But the armistice had come to an end over scarlet silk, black lace, and the dyed plumes of a naked ostrich. In the end there had been a compromise, and the creative blending of two intractable natures was a breathtaking evening gown that would undoubtedly be the shocking highlight of the Armbrusters' New Year's gala.

For Jennifer the gown had become a symbol of the grand finale for a young woman's rebellious spirit—before 1892 and the era of the matron began at the stroke of midnight.

The carriage halted, and without opening her eyes Jennifer waited, grateful for Jenkins's assistance as he pulled her from cushioned comfort.

"You look exhausted, madame." Too often lately, she

knew, her remarkable eyes were rimmed with dark circles of fatigue.

Jennifer didn't contradict him. "Why do women claim shopping to be a pleasurable pastime? My feet are threatening to swell out of my shoes. I have the most excruciating ache right here"—she pointed to the area between her shoulder blades—"not to mention nerves abraded by ceaseless contention from an opinionated seamstress, who is deaf to instructions and blind to line and style."

"Are there no other dressmakers in Boston?" Jenkins asked, giving her a toothless smile before stretching out his arms. She then filled the area between his elbow and chin with boxes.

"Not for me," Jennifer slung over her shoulder. Opening the gate, she teased him by refusing to leave her post. "For heaven's sake, Jenkins. Don't stand on ceremony when I can barely stand on these feet. Lead the way." With a wave of her hand and a bow, she continued to tax his sense of propriety. Heavily creased eyes rolled before his spindly legs preceded her up the walk.

Jenkins—she'd never been able to coax him into revealing his given name—was her one true friend in this household. He was an odd little man who carried something of a mystery about him, encouraging her nonstop conversation while keeping as closemouthed as a clam about himself. He looked like a wizened troll, but his perfect diction and an easy acquaintance with classical literature spoke of an education far above the humble positions of coachman and groom. An enigma was her Jenkins.

When the front door opened, she greeted the butler before directing Jenkins to dump her purchases in the seldom used, nearly barren library.

"Is there any mail, Johnson?" She rushed toward the hallway table, where a single piece of correspondence rested on a silver tray. Picking it up, her emotions swept from anger to hurt and back again. Mr. Adrian Armbruster received letters regularly from his mother, but not once had the old bat acknowledged her son's wife even indirectly.

"Was there nothing else?" Jennifer couldn't prevent the slight quiver of her chin. There had been no word from home in over a month. If the winter weather was severe, it might be spring before that link between Montana and Massachusetts would open once again.

"There are two gentlemen waiting to see you, madame," Johnson said somewhat shrilly. "In the parlor . . ." he added with downcast eyes.

Noting the way he flexed the twisted joints of his rheumatic fingers, Jennifer stifled a groan of protest. "Representatives of another charity, soliciting a donation, I suppose." She took a deep breath and then released it slowly. They came to the door daily, basing their hopes and expectations on the Armbruster name, but the tight budget Adrian enforced permitted only token offerings.

Removing her coat and gloves, she gave the butler a tired smile. While he hobbled off toward the coat closet, she smoothed the deep purple skirt that had been crushed beneath the ankle-length cloak. She quickly checked her hair in the mirror before moving slowly toward the parlor.

She was still fluffing the mauve brocade sleeves of her dress as she stepped through the open doorway. "How can I help you, gentle—"

The greeting strangled in her throat as the man standing before the fireplace wheeled to face her. Knees turned to water, and only the hand she thrust against the solid frame of the doorway kept her from pitching forward. Her vision blurred, and she closed her eyes to the hallucination striding toward her. Impossible, reasoned a mind that continued to rebel against what her eyes had conjured.

She could feel her body swaying, and her nostrils flared when the pungent fumes of cigar smoke teased her senses. Please, God, she prayed wistfully. Please, don't let this be a dream.

"Princess." The husky, vibrating timber of a male voice pulsed its way into her heart. She no longer needed the support of the doorframe. She was caught up by strong arms, crushed with tender fierceness against the massive bulk of James Douglas's chest.

"Daddy," she sobbed, burying her face in his neck, brushing her cheek against the bristles of a dark beard. Her fingers seized his shoulders, curling and clinging tenaciously to the wool fabric of his coat. Lifting her head, she uttered a joyful cry before spreading enthusiastic kisses over darkly tanned cheeks that were wet with unashamed tears.

"You're here . . . you're real!"

"Lord, how I've missed you!" He swung her up, spinning around until her skirts and feet flew out behind her.

She was the child again for a brief time until the woman's delicate condition demanded an end to this turbulent reunion.

"Stop," she gasped when nausea and dizziness became a violent threat. "Please, stop."

"Honey, are you all right?" James questioned softly, alarmed by her pallor before she turned her face away to rest her cheek against his shoulder.

"Dizzy," she explained weakly. "I'll be fine in a minute."

Would she be fine? she wondered when her eyes focused on the darkly tanned and sinewy forearms resting conspicuously against the crimson velvet of the Queen Anne chair several feet away. She swallowed to clear the sudden tightness in her throat. She'd always thought there would be time to prepare for, even avoid this confrontation. Closing her eyes, she clung to her father as a child would cling when faced with the image of her own nightmare.

Too soon, she railed silently. *It's too soon.* She wasn't ready to face the snarled and complex emotions that bore the name of Devlin McShane. Already she was besieged by rapidly changing frames of visual memory, as if a cruel inner eye were determined to present those vivid and painful moments, forcing her to review the past.

She saw herself as a girl again, wantonly demanding that first kiss. There was the almost woman who teased a man to passion beside a sparkling brook, yielding all and then pouting naively when his good sense proved to be greater than her own. And finally, there was the pity within his deep blue eyes while she struggled to bid him farewell, her heart

287

crying out that he ask her to stay—images so clear that they might have been viewed upon Mr. Edison's kinetoscope.

Slowly she forced her eyelids open and studied the arms casually braced just below the elbows against the back of the chair. The hands were tightly clasped in a tension that belied the relaxed pose.

What strange phenomenon was this? Devlin McShane was invulnerable . . . wasn't he? He didn't suffer from uncertainty . . . or did he? Curiously, she felt her own anxiety subside. Strangely, she felt an urge to put him at ease and find some comfortable common ground where they could deal reasonably with each other.

Disengaging herself from James's embrace, Jennifer gave her father a light kiss. "And who's this you've brought with you?"

She took the first step, her eyes drifting upward, and then the second step. He straightened and moved out from behind the chair. As she'd expected, she could find no hint of turmoil on the strongly handsome, now smiling face. The eyes, somehow bluer than memory's recall, danced with the familiar mockery that had always challenged a less wise girl to bold acts.

Her hands extended. "Dev." Her voice was welcoming. Icy fingers disappeared within callused palms that were only a few degrees less cold than her own. The significance of those cool, sweaty palms caused her heart to skip several beats. He *was* uneasy . . . Why? Stop this, she rebuked herself. Devlin is part of the past. What you felt was a mere childish infatuation. Don't complicate your life by digging up dead bones. Remember, remember how it really was.

"You look wonderful!" she exclaimed, flashing him a genuine smile while she openly appreciated the superb cut of his oatmeal-colored twill coat and acknowledged a purely feminine admiration for the way it stretched easily across his wide, wide shoulders. "Absolutely wonderful." A chocolate-brown waistcoat hugged the leanly muscled chest above trousers sharply creased to emphasize the length of his legs.

"Jen," he said simply, his deep voice rolling musically over the shortened version of her name. He bent to touch his lips to her cheek on an impulse that surprised them both. "It's good to see you."

Stepping back, Devlin held tightly to her hands while his eyes swept over her in a brief but thorough appraisal. "You've changed," he stated prophetically. A chill danced up and down his spine while he measured the extent of those changes.

"Yes . . . yes, I have," she reinforced, needing to confirm the absoluteness of his statement. "For the better, I would hope."

Her teasing tone invited a compliment, or a glib retort, but Dev couldn't match her smooth nonchalance. It was the eyes, he decided. Those crystal-silver eyes that had always double-crossed her, giving warning that trouble or mayhem was brewing, were now the color of pewter. What was she hiding with such poised skill that she seemed a stranger? He cautioned himself to go easy, but it was going to be damned hard to play at this game when he wanted to charge like a raging bull and demand answers for the hundred questions her letter had generated.

Jennifer pulled her hands away from a grip that had suddenly grown painfully tight. Turning toward James, she escaped the sudden probe of Devlin's eyes. He wanted something from her; she could feel it. Ridiculous . . . perhaps. Dangerous . . . definitely. But only if she allowed him to be a threat. Only if she gave his person more importance than was his due.

"Has Johnson attended to your luggage? Have you eaten?" Her voice sounded shrill even in her own ears. The numbness of surprise was beginning to crumble along with her confidence.

"Honey, we've registered at a hotel. We weren't certain . . . Hell, your husband might not like his in-laws dropping in from out of the blue. Can't say I'd much blame him." James dropped an arm about her shoulders and shook her with bearlike affection.

"Well, you can just go unregister at that hotel. I want you here with me," she insisted. "If Adrian objects, I'll give him a blanket and directions to the stable."

"Princess, we don't want to disrupt your life." His eyes sought Devlin's face. "We wouldn't spoil your happiness for anything in the world . . . would we, Dev?"

Silence. Devlin didn't even blink. He'd stopped thinking James Douglas was the closest thing to God the minute Davie had put Jennifer's letter into his hands. For a time, he'd felt only blind, killing rage. Eventually his own sense of justice had bluntly pointed out his own considerable guilt. Right now he and James skirted within the bounds of an uneasy truce.

"Pleasant room you have here," Devlin said inanely to the two who awaited some kind of response. Jennifer's eyes made a quick sweep of the room, and then she gaped at him incredulously before a snort of laughter exploded from her mouth.

"Ain't that the mannerly thing to say, Mrs. Armbruster, ma'am?" The western drawl he affected was overdone, but it matched the slack-jawed expression that said this cowboy had been tossed too often onto his head. The tension within the room was dispelled like a puff of smoke from one of James's cigars.

"How I've missed the two of you." Her eyes lost their metal quality, turning the shade of a soft mist on a summer's day. "There is absolutely no way that I'm going to let either one of you get out of my sight. It's a tight leash you'll be feeling."

She moved briskly to the parlor doorway, opened her mouth to suck in air in preparation for a yell, and then with an embarrassed shrug clamped her jaw shut. "They hate it when I bellow," she explained. "I'm going to ask Mrs. Johnson to prepare coffee and cakes. When we've finished, Jenkins can take you to the hotel to collect your luggage. I'll have him deliver a warning to the bank so that Adrian can prepare himself for the menace of in-laws."

When she had gone, James pulled a cigar from his pocket and lit it with trembling fingers. "She seems happy . . ."

"Don't," Devlin barked. "Don't you goddamn dare!" Every word cracked in the room like a whip.

"Listen to me, you bullheaded young—" James stopped short of defaming Devlin's mother. "Answer me this: Can you let her be happy? What if you're wrong? What if she received my letter after she married Armbruster. What then?"

"You don't really believe that any more than I do." Devlin walked stiffly to the fireplace, bracing his hands against the mantel. "But now it's Jennifer's game, isn't it? She's holding all the cards." He looked over his shoulder. "But I'll have the truth, one way or another."

"Dev . . ." James hesitantly reached for the younger man's shoulder, but something within the dark blue eyes caused his arm to fall limply to his side. "The truth won't change anything."

Devlin didn't respond. If what he suspected—if he knew his Jenny at all, it would make a difference. He'd see that it did.

"More wine, Adrian?"

Erica Delaney's purling voice did little to ease Adrian's increasing tension during what was turning out to be a most unusual luncheon.

"You don't visit us often enough." Erica's voice was sugar-sweet. "Don't you agree, Papa?"

Delaney's reply was an incomprehensible grunt. He continued to shovel and slurp his meal with an abandon that disgusted while it fascinated. A sidelong glance at the woman seated on his left easily confirmed the family resemblance. Although Erica's table manners were faultless, the violet eyes watched him with what Adrian could only describe as a primitive avidity. Beneath the concealing drape of a yellow linen tablecloth, Erica Delaney was exploring his masculine anatomy. And to Adrian's chagrin, he was responding, growing hard beneath her determined, talented fingers.

Under the guise of reaching for his napkin, Adrian made another unsuccessful attempt to force her hand back into her own lap, feeling a tingle of both pleasure and revulsion when she could not be swayed. By God, Erica was a slut of the first order. The thought that this bitch had once agreed to become his wife made him lose all appetite for his lunch. Delaney had done him yet another good turn when he paid him to break their brief engagement. A very good turn indeed.

Oblivious to his guest's discomfiture, Sean Delaney gulped down the last of his meal. Swiping a napkin across his dribbling mouth, he gave his only child a doting smile. "Erica . . . Cupcake, would you leave us now please?"

"Oh, Papa," she sulked. "Do I have to? I was having such a good, *good* time."

Adrian's stomach turned while listening to his host's cajoling. He spoke to his twenty-three-year-old daughter as if she were still a precious moppet. Finally Erica puffed up, threw down her napkin, and flounced from the room.

"Shall we adjourn to my study, Adrian?"

Adrian followed his host eagerly, anxious to make this business with Delaney history. The twenty thousand dollars would be well-earned after the hours spent in the company of this toad and of Bertram Lowell. Delaney didn't bother to offer Adrian a chair or a cigar, although he took his good time with the pleasure of lighting and smoking his own tobacco.

All the same, Adrian had seated himself in a comfortable leather chair. But his patience was wearing thin while Delaney dawdled. It was already a full week past the time agreed upon for the Lowells to receive the entire balance due on the mill. Delaney had authorized only a minimum guarantee to close the deal. That he had stalled this meeting, not once but several times, had caused Adrian some uncomfortable moments.

"Everything is in perfect order, Sean," he said, placing the contract upon the desk. "We pulled it off without a hitch."

"Yes, we most certainly did."

Adrian would later remember the deliberate, almost distorted manner in which Delaney drew out those words.

But at this moment he was still under the spell of his own deluded ignorance. "You should feel very gratified."

"Oh, I do, dear boy. Very gratified indeed." Leaving his cigar smoldering in a pewter dish, the older man casually picked up the contract. When the sheaf of papers lay flat upon his desk, he began to read, his mouth forming words without sound while his eyes slowly scanned every line, every paragraph, often two and three times apiece. The smile that appeared every so often was chilling.

A full three quarters of an hour must have passed before Delaney looked up. "It would seem, Adrian, that you've taken on a very considerable enterprise. Frankly, I'm surprised you would take such a risk with operating costs and labor problems being what they are these days. I've always judged you to be a man interested in the easy money, a quick gain requiring little effort. Has marriage changed you so much? Could I have made a mistake in discouraging the match with my daughter?"

Every word, every expression, should have brought Adrian some dawning comprehension. Instead he grew impatient with his host's sense of humor. "I don't feel like playing jester for your entertainment this afternoon, Delaney. So if you'll look over these change-of-title papers I took the liberty of having drawn up, we'll conclude our business and I'll collect my ten thousand."

Delaney lifted a single eyebrow and scratched the side of his nose. "Change of title? Ten thousand? I don't understand, my boy. Are you making me a business proposition, or requesting a loan?"

Adrian popped out of his chair and planted his palms flat on the desk. "Listen here, you sonofabitch, this little drama grows tiresome. I've already received several demands from Lowell's attorneys, the most recent threatening legal action unless full payment is made soon. I've managed to stall them so far, but by the first of the new year—"

There was a loud knock on the study door. The butler stepped in and announced, "You asked me to remind you of your two o'clock appointment, sir. Also, the carriage is waiting for Mr. Armbruster."

"Thank you, Hanes." Delaney rose from his chair, large and menacing. "It's been a pleasant afternoon, Adrian. Although I admit grave reservations regarding your new business venture, I do wish you luck. You're going to need it."

Adrian felt a chilling dampness wet his armpits as the floodgates of understanding began to open. "You *are* joking? Wait a minute, Sean!" His voice was thick with a growing dread. "You wanted that mill, wanted it badly!"

"Now, why would I consider such a foolish investment? Dear heavens, Armbruster. Didn't you do your homework? Old man Lowell has been skirting the edge of financial ruin since before you were born. He's lost contract after contract this past year. Even after cutting his workers' wages—and they're not happy about that, I can tell you—he can barely meet his obligations. You'd better pay off that old bastard. It's a desperate man you've chosen to deal with."

Adrian lunged at the man, grabbing the lapels of his suit jacket. "You set me up! Why?" The blood roared in his ears, his heart pounded violently. "Erica," he breathed. "It's because of that bitch you whelped."

Delaney's hands were suddenly around Adrian's neck. "Bitch? Whore is more apt. And who introduced her to the pleasures of the flesh? Who taught her what she practices with anyone carrying a sufficient bulge in his trousers to ease the fiery itch you started?" His face went purple with rage. "She was an innocent, a good girl! I could have found her a husband with both money and social position. Now she screws every potential suitor before he can get inside the goddamned front door. I'd like to snap your neck, but killing you would bring only a moment's satisfaction. No. I'm going to savor every minute of the legal battles and watch with relish as you become a laughingstock. A name— that's all you ever had. Soon it won't be worth a pile of shit!"

His brain deprived of oxygen, Adrian was barely aware of being dragged through the house and tossed into a carriage.

"We're finished now, Armbruster. But I'll give you a final warning: Come near my girl again, and I'll cut off that thing

294

between your legs and make you swallow it, one inch at a time."

The carriage lurched forward. Wedged between the seats, his head suspended above the paved street, Adrian spewed the contents of his stomach while the unlatched door butted against his head.

Chapter Twenty-Five

The soft glow of candlelight reflected in Adrian's eyes as he moved from the sideboard to stand behind his father-in-law's chair.

"More brandy, Mr. Douglas?" His voice was smooth silk, the perfect white teeth flashing brilliantly when James expressed a high regard for the quality of Adrian's liquor and lifted his glass for a refill.

"Unless I can possess the finest"—he looked pointedly at Jennifer—"I'll do without. Perhaps that's why I remained a bachelor for so many years."

He positively oozed charm, and Jennifer supposed she should feel pleasure at his efforts to make her father feel welcome. But when he stepped behind Devlin's chair, every muscle in her body tensed.

"Are you certain, McShane?" He offered the decanter for the third time, shaking his head as if in disbelief. "An Irishman who doesn't consider a tankard to be an extension of his arm—how rare."

Jennifer silently bristled, unable to look Devlin in the face, mortified by the barbs of bigotry Adrian's smooth tongue tossed at every opportunity. His dislike for anything remotely Irish was hardly remarkable or even exclusive in this city. Still, she bit the insides of her mouth to hold her temper; Dev was quite capable of taking Adrian apart verbally, not to mention physically.

Adrian resumed his chair. "I admire a man who knows his

weakness, McShane. I applaud your restraint. It's a pity more of your race don't follow your fine example."

Her eyes snapped to Devlin's face. His expression remained coolly impassive. He was proud of his heritage, yet refused to utter a single word in defense, almost as if he were unaware of the animosity behind Adrian's civil veneer.

Reflexively, Jennifer's hand wadded the napkin in her lap into a tight ball. "Perhaps," she grated. "Perhaps if their living conditions were less intolerable and their opportunities for education and decent employment expanded, the Irish in this city wouldn't need alcohol to blunt misery."

"Your compassion is admirable, darling, but sadly it is misplaced. Surely you do not believe the tavern owners give away that ale and whiskey. What do you think, McShane?"

Devlin's gaze was on Jennifer, and only she recognized the twitch of his lips and the barely contained amusement. "Oh, I agree with you emphatically, Armbruster. Jennifer *is* compassionate, *and* her admiration is most definitely misplaced."

Jennifer's eyes flew to her husband, fully expecting the foul mood he'd been masking the entire evening to explode at Devlin's adroit insult. To give him his due, Adrian seemed unaffected. But appearances can be deceiving, as she quickly discovered when he shifted his gaze to stare at her for seemingly endless moments. Devlin then received that same intense scrutiny.

"Tell me, McShane . . . how long have you been in partnership with my father-in-law? Perhaps my memory fails me, but I really can't remember my wife mentioning your name or this partnership."

James hastily spoke for Devlin. "The partnership is a recent one."

"Aha, then you are relatively new to the ranch?"

"Twelve years new," Devlin responded wryly, his eyes on Jennifer. His mouth curved in a disagreeable sardonic smile.

James felt as though he'd been caught in the center of a

violent electrical storm. The room crackled with tension as Adrian recognized his adversary. If this were the wild, they'd be snapping and snarling, circling in preparation for combat. "Adrian, Jennifer tells me your mother is currently touring Europe?" James inserted in an attempt to lighten the atmosphere. "Where will she be spending this Christmas?"

"London," Adrian replied tersely.

"You received a letter from her today, darling. Did she indicate when she might be returning?" Jennifer was already regretting her impulsive defense of the Irish. Why had she leapt to Devlin's defense?

"Mother rarely confides her plans."

And so the conversation continued with James taking the lead, dominating the table with the same temperate authority that had always conquered personalities even more mulish than his own.

By the time Mrs. Johnson appeared with a silver coffee service, the threat of a stormy evening seemed to be what Maggie would have termed "a tempest in a teapot."

"We'll have our coffee in the parlor, Mrs. Johnson." Jennifer started to rise and was surprised that it was Devlin who quickly rounded the table to hold her chair.

"Mrs. Armbruster," he said graciously, taking her hand to place it in the crook of his arm. "May I escort you?"

Unsettled by his strange behavior and fearing the return of animosity, Jennifer hesitated, looking to her father for assistance.

"You two go on. Frankly I'd prefer another glass of Adrian's brandy *and* an opportunity to talk to this new husband of yours without you hanging on every word. Unless you have an objection, Adrian."

"Of course not." Adrian smiled smoothly. For a man who possessed a wife with a father rich in land and hard cash—cash desperately needed—jealousy and the loss of Douglas's good will was an ill-advised indulgence.

"Go ahead, darling." Adrian smiled, secretly pleased that she had waited for his consent. He was further encouraged when Jennifer very pointedly withdrew her hand from Devlin's arm to precede him unescorted into the parlor.

Her posture, as she poured their coffee, was wooden and her lips were so firmly set that her lovely mouth was hardened to a thin line. Devlin accepted the fragile cup and saucer but immediately placed it on the table. "You're angry with me, Jen . . . why?"

Because your nearness confuses me. Because I can still feel the firmness of your flesh beneath my fingers. Because your hair is filled with sunlight and you smell of pine instead of heavy cologne. And because when I dare look into the midnight depths of your eyes, they glow profoundly with an unqualified admiration that tears at my heart and threatens my soul to eternal damnation.

"How are Lottie and Davie?" she asked, ignoring his question. She leaned back against the sofa.

"They expect their first child in early summer," he replied, thwarted by her determination to avoid any intimacy, whether a touch or a word between them.

"Has that been difficult for you?" There was no sarcasm in her voice, nothing to indicate more than a casual concern for what she assumed would be a heartfelt loss.

"I gave the bride away, Jen," he answered solemnly. "I explained before about Lottie and myself."

"Yes . . . yes, you did." She rose from the sofa. "I hope you won't think me rude, but I'm very, very tired. We can chat about old friends another time—"

He caught her hand and would have pulled her back. But the purple circles of fatigue beneath her eyes and the chalk white of her complexion were evidence that her claim to exhaustion was not merely an excuse to avoid his company.

"We have a week, Jennifer . . . *and* a great deal to discuss."

Her frown told him that his tone had been forbidding. He softened. "Good night, Princess. I wish you sweet dreams."

Jennifer slept so soundly that Adrian doubted an earthquake would awaken her. No dreams tonight. Sprawled on her stomach with her pillow held snugly within the curve of her woman's body, she looked a child.

Her husband, however, paced the room in a panic, his mood swinging from abject despair to murderous rage. Why hadn't he seen Delaney's trap? But how, how could he have possibly anticipated such an irrational thirst for revenge? And for what? For being the first in a long line to dip into Erica's hot honeypot? He'd been prepared to marry the slut, for Christ's sake!

"Crawl among pigs and be smeared with their slop," he whispered viciously.

If anything, *he* was the wronged party, forced to settle for just enough to pay off his gambling debts at Todd's. It had been at Delaney's demand that he'd given her the heave-ho, keeping little Erica in Papa's good graces—and his will. It didn't make sense. This entire situation was insane.

What to do? Dear God, where was he going to get the money? The contract was binding. The courts would nail him to the wall. If he sold everything he owned, including what was left of his soul, there still wouldn't be enough.

Uncle Aaron? The obvious solution. But his uncle would never grant him fifty thousand dollars without question. He could already see that righteous visage crumble with disappointment. Oh, he'd save his dear nephew. For the sake of the family, and the esteemed name of Armbruster, Uncle Aaron would save Adrian's worthless ass. But there would be a price to pay for that.

Naturally Adrian would be allowed to maintain his position at the bank—for the sake of appearances. He'd keep his empty title, the insignificant responsibilities, and the salary that would forever remain only slightly above that of a common laborer. His wife, of course, would have to be informed. A wife must always be made aware of her husband's shortcomings in order to keep him in line. And should he stray, the family—dear, loving relatives all— would cut him adrift without a qualm or a penny.

Adrian's first solution quickly became a last resort.

Jennifer's father? Now, there was a possibility. Could he interest Douglas in an investment? Perhaps a little wedding gift in a big lump sum? He could win the man's trust. Douglas was a simple man, an uncouth rancher. There was only a week though. Already Adrian might have prejudiced the man against him with evidence of his immediate dislike of McShane.

"Who the hell is McShane? And what's he to my wife?"

As the night rushed toward dawn, Adrian's thoughts grew more confused, whirling and tumbling until only one theme remained.

"I've got to stall Lowell. Find a way to buy some time. Talk to Bertram. That's it. Bertie's my jolly good friend."

Chapter Twenty-Six

Jennifer moved stiffly about the bedroom, her movements jerky while she dressed, revealing how narrowly she walked the line between control and screaming fury.

"Why don't you answer me, Jennifer?" Adrian stepped up behind her when she sat down to arrange her hair.

The hairbrush was slammed down on the vanity. Tossing her hair back over her shoulder, she whirled to face him. "I find your tone offensive and the attitude behind the questions insulting."

"Then I must humbly beg your pardon . . . Princess." He made a sweeping bow while his lips curled in contempt. "Would you please explain why during all those endless hours of prattling about Sam and Margie and others, who will remain forever faceless, you never mentioned even the *existence* of Devlin McShane."

"Maggie!" she shouted, and then quickly lowered her own strident tone. "Her name is Maggie, not Margie. Which only proves how acutely you listen. You can't even remember the name of the woman who was like a mother to me."

Needing desperately to occupy her hands, Jennifer turned to rummage through the drawers. It was either that or throw the entire collection of jars and bottles on her dressing table at his head.

When the floor was littered with discarded combs and ribbons, furious fingers looped and tied her haphazard

choice around the unbound mass of her hair. "Considering
the total lack of interest you've always shown in my family
and my background, how can you be certain you didn't
yawn or doze off and miss what seems so important to you
now?"

"Do you think me a complete fool? The way he looks at
you . . ."

"Looks at me! Me?" She hooted with incredulous laughter, rising from the vanity to face her husband's jealousy
with something akin to amusement. "Well, that's certain
proof that you've allowed your wits to abandon you. If
Devlin McShane has ever seen me at all, it's been as an
afterthought. After Father, the good of the ranch, and most
certainly behind the backside of his favorite horse.

"But, darling husband, if you're truly concerned about
Dev's lustful interest in my person, then you can tell Sean
Delaney you won't be available next week. Stay home and
observe this fierce passion." She clutched her hands over
her heart in a pleading gesture. "Protect me!"

"Your theatrics don't amuse me, Jennifer. My business in
Buffalo has nothing to do with this." She had made the
assumption that his trip to see Lowell was at Sean Delaney's
request. Adrian did not correct her.

"It doesn't? That's peculiar—I seem to remember this
argument began when you informed me of this unexpected
trip." She strode to the wardrobe and pulled out an old
cloak. When he would have prevented her exit from the
room, what little was left of her control exploded. "Get the
hell out of my way!"

He stepped back as if astounded by her behavior. "Well,
well, such language, my dear. I always wondered when your
breeding—or lack of it—would finally surface."

Stopping dead in her tracks, she turned, but kept her
hand on the doorknob. "How dare you . . ." She drew a
ragged breath. "Shall we rattle ancestral skeletons, Adrian?
Attack me, my father, even Devlin, and I'll shake the bones
out of your own closet until this house crumbles about your
pompous ears!"

Opening the door, she gave a very good imitation of her sweetest smile. "Now please stop behaving like a jealous, braying jackass, darling. Try to be nice."

She stormed the stable, attacking the door with a vicious kick when the rusted hinges refused to yield. But her temper backlashed as the old wood, and nearly the toes of her right foot, fractured.

She was still hopping about when the door opened easily and Jenkins stepped out to eye her with dismay. "What in sweet heaven?" he said, taking her arm as she limped inside.

"Will I never learn?" she moaned, dropping down onto a stool to rub her aching foot. "Every time I let my temper fly I only hurt myself. But how much, just how much can a human being tolerate without fighting back? Adrian is behaving like a bigoted, raving sonof—"

"Now, now." Jenkins boldly pressed his fingers against her mouth to stop the profanity. "There's no need to pollute the English language." He turned crimson at his own audacity, but blamed this young woman for encouraging such untoward behavior in her servant.

"The meek will not inherit the earth, Jenkins. Of that I'm totally convinced. And a woman—a woman has no chance at all."

Chuckling, Jenkins squatted down, tipping his head to one side. "If you count yourself among the meek, then it's for certain that I'm the reincarnation of Julius Caesar."

She gave him a weak smile. "For certain." Needing to talk to someone, Jennifer recounted the events of the last twenty-four hours.

"Be patient with your husband, mistress," the groom advised. "I've been with this family for nearly twenty years. Master Adrian has known little of love in his lifetime. These men—father and friend—hold parts of your life and an affection that he can't understand or be party to. He's terrified you might choose them over himself."

She knew he was right. Jenkins seemed to have an astounding insight into Adrian's character. "Poor Adrian

. . . Patience is not one of my sterling virtues. But I know that what you say has merit."

Jenkins pushed against his knees, using them as leverage to straighten joints that were beginning to cramp. Removing his ever-present cap, he smoothed the few wisps of hair remaining on his head.

"What is it?" Jennifer asked, noting his troubled expression.

"I'm too free with my tongue. It's not my place, and if any harm should come—"

She was about to reassure him that only advice taken could do harm when the screech of the door drew their attention.

Devlin stepped inside. Apparently unaware that he wasn't alone, he took a deep breath, filling his lungs with the familiar scent of horse while his mouth curved into a comfortable smile.

"You *are* beauties," he exclaimed with genuine admiration, moving toward the two Arabians. "Proud and fine."

The black snorted, blowing a warning through flaring nostrils. "Ah, yer a pretty one, but nasty tempered like your master."

He turned his attention to the mare. A strong brown hand cautiously touched and then began to stroke the gentler animal from neck to flank. Crooning softly, he recited an old Irish ballad, turning words into musical sounds until the horse was quivering with pleasure.

Jennifer watched the sure movements of the hand as it slid over her animal's flesh in awed silence. Her skin was at one moment hot, then cold. Remembering, remembering. . . .

Jenkins cleared his throat, but Devlin's stroke did not waver. When he finally spoke, it was obvious that he'd been aware of their presence from the beginning.

"The mare looks to have speed, Jen."

"The black, Diablo, is faster," she managed, her voice breaking before she cleared her own throat loudly.

"Perhaps," he mused. "But it would be a very close contest. The skill of the rider might sway the outcome."

"It's been proven, the black is faster." She used the solid

wooden post beside the stool to pull herself upright, not trusting legs that felt strangely weak.

"If you were riding the mare, then I would imagine it was a fair race."

Jenkins, who had been silently watching, saw his young mistress flush with pleasure over the man's endorsement of her skill. "I'd like to see a rematch," the groom stated. "When Master Adrian acquired the mare, she'd grown lazy—almost as lazy as she is now—from too much sweet grass and not enough exercise. I've had them both out, and I think the mare could take the stallion."

With a warm smile and an outstretched hand, Devlin introduced himself to the groom. Jennifer watched Jenkins respond, losing his subservient attitude beneath the easy charm Devlin was capable of—except with her. They talked companionably with each other, horseman to horseman.

Suddenly Jenkins seemed to remember his position. With a touch to his cap, he said, "I forget myself again. The carriage needs polishing, and I'd best see to those other two poor nags. They have a fondness for the neighbor's hedge and would eat their way into his yard unless watched." His grin turned his countenance to that of a kindly troll. "A pleasure to talk horses with you, Mr. McShane. I'd sure love to see you have the chance to prove the white against Diablo. You're the man to show she has the stamina, and Diablo tends to run himself out. It would be a pretty race to watch . . . if the mistress approves, that is."

They both looked at Jennifer. "We'll see . . . if the weather holds."

With Jenkins gone, Jennifer noted the tension that had taken Devlin's features. His eyes wandered aimlessly, as if avoiding looking directly at her.

"You have to prove me wrong, don't you?" she teased. She had his full attention now. He was regarding her with a scrutiny that caused her heart to skip several beats.

"Sometimes, in a single contest, the outcome can be unexpected. A distraction, an error in judgment, any number of factors can call the race. Have you never felt that in spite of your best efforts and intentions, a contest has gone against you, and that given a second chance, you'd do it differently and perhaps even win?" His surefooted stride brought him to stand before her.

His nearness, the sharpness of the blue-eyed gaze, and the ambiguity of the question were poignantly disturbing. Eyes of a hawk—the analogy her father always used now seemed ominously significant.

"It's too early in my day to delve so deeply into the vagaries of human, or equine, nature," she said evasively. "Perhaps after I've had my breakfast. . . ." The hobbling attempt she made to move around him was quickly blocked.

"What's the matter with your foot?" he asked quietly, standing like a solid wall between her and the door.

She took another faltering step sideways, growing irritated when he followed her every movement. "Please stand aside," she demanded firmly, using the same tone that had brought about effective results with her husband.

"Did some insensitive bastard step on your toes, Jen?"

If she'd possessed the swiftness of a young deer, she could not have predicted the lightning-quick rush. In a blink, Devlin had scooped her up into his arms, and she was being carried toward one of the empty stalls.

"What do you think—" Her heated objection died on a yelp, and she quite voluntarily kept a tight hold around his neck as he perched her precariously atop a narrow gate. Her alternatives were Devlin's support or a very large pile of aromatic manure, should she be foolish enough to push him away.

She made no protest when he gently removed her boot, but comfortable rationalization fled when his hand slid beneath her skirt to grasp the garter holding up her stocking. He chuckled at the sound of her strangled gasp.

"Just pretend I'm your doctor . . . or husband," he said with calm reassurance although every instinct he possessed was reacting violently to the velvet softness of her thigh.

"That *might* be easier, McShane," she grated through clenched teeth, "if you weren't taking your sweet time groping for my garter."

Using both hands, Devlin slowly drew the black stocking

down her leg, enjoying every inch of flesh in the process. When the tiny foot was bare, he made a careful inspection, wiggling each toe, his large hands gentle. "Nothing appears broken. How did you injure yourself?"

"I accidently rammed my foot into a door," she answered in clipped tones, already reaching for the stocking he'd slung over his shoulder.

Devlin's hand closed around the foot he held. A slight tug tipped her precarious balance, and he turned to hold her flush against his chest. "A few minutes ago you asked me to step aside. Is that what you did when your father wrote of his intention to offer me Silver Creek? Did you simply step aside?"

"I . . . I don't know what you're talking about," she said breathlessly, her heart pounding violently against the hard muscle that flattened her breasts.

"Don't you? Then I'll try to be more precise." Holding her easily with one arm about her waist, he grabbed a handful of raven hair, not hurting, but refusing to allow her to duck the probe of his eyes. "Didn't you receive that letter and conclude that all your fears were finally being realized? Your father was going to offer me, the surrogate son, the land you prized above all else. Didn't you feel hurt? Betrayed? Didn't you see that offering of land as merely the beginning to my taking over everything that was rightfully yours?"

He could feel her spine stiffen beneath his arm as she absorbed what he implied. "Wasn't your sudden decision to marry Armbruster a way of saying—in essence—to hell with us all?"

"Are you saying that I married simply out of spite—a childish tantrum?"

"Not spite, Jen. But perhaps in defeat."

"No," she denied emphatically. "The letter had nothing . . . nothing to do with my decision to marry Adrian." Her eyes were earnest. She'd lived a long time with her own self-deceit and would not relinquish it to a truth that now stared her in the face. "I wrote to you . . . explained my feelings—"

"Nothing," he said, cutting her off. "Not one damn thing was explained in that very carefully worded two-page note. You didn't mention a husband, new home, or if you were happy or unhappy."

"Perhaps I considered those things to be none of your business. I see no reason to answer to you, Devlin Mc-Shane. My marriage, and the reasons for it, are of no concern to you. In fact, I would think you'd be grateful. My response to Daddy's letter could have been entirely different." Instinctively she knew that her contentious tone would only confirm what he suspected. With a heavy sigh, she gave him the whisper of a smile. "Why do I argue with you? This entire conversation is ridiculous. You have a fine piece of land now, and as Sam would say, 'Don't look a gift horse in the mouth.'"

"Jen, if your father's land bordered heaven, I'd not sacrifice your happiness to possess a single inch." The opaque quality of her eyes cleared momentarily, and in the lustrous depths he saw that flicker of pain and a yearning before they grew hard and cold once again. "You received that letter only a few days—maybe hours—before eloping, didn't you? I had already shut one door in your face. Didn't your father slam the other on you?"

"Let me go, Dev," she muttered, pushing at his chest.

"I will . . . just as soon as you tell me that it was only love that spurred this hasty decision to matrimony."

"And you've always accused me of being stubborn? Oh . . . all right. I'm very much in love with my husband. He's handsome, charming, witty . . ."

"Say it again," he prodded, his features set in grim lines. When she started to repeat the litany of Adrian's virtues, he snarled. "No, just tell me how much you love him. Only next time, look at me, not at that wall over there."

She looked directly into eyes that glistened like shards of sapphire. *"I love my husband."* Every word was sharply enunciated.

"Bullshit," he ground out before his mouth swooped down, covering her lips with a savage denial. He used his only weapon: the elemental, unimpeachable honesty of passion—genuine and uncontaminated by James, the land, and all those other, suddenly inexplicable, factors that had kept them apart.

For but a moment Jennifer's treacherous senses responded to the old lure. But she was rescued by the rising volcano of fury. He'd waited too long to undertake this mission of mercy and save her from the folly of her own impulsiveness. Months too long to give his sincerity any credibility.

When her unyielding mouth refused to part beneath the sensual but tentative flicks of his tongue, Devlin used his teeth to bite down gently on her lower lip. He groaned his victory when suddenly she was giving all, her arms sliding up around his neck. Exultation quickly became pain.

Grabbing both of his ears, Jennifer twisted them with the ruthless strength born of rage. "Let me go, McShane. Or by all that's holy, I'll rip them from that egotistical head!"

The persuasive request brought immediate results. Grabbing her stocking from where it had fallen onto the straw, Jennifer gave no thought to modesty. She lifted her skirt high and jerked the garment up over her thigh, snapping her garter before snatching the boot he offered. "Jen?" he began, his voice filled with an uncertainty she ignored until reaching the door.

The hinges moaned and a shaft of morning sun illuminated the particles of dust in the air, transforming them into tiny flakes of shimmering glory, making a mockery of the darkness within her heart.

"It is *you* who have always assumed too much, Devlin. Not the least of which is that I would take my marriage vows so lightly."

The thud of the door brought a feeling of suffocation. The darkness that followed had, for Devlin, the finality of a coffin being sealed at that last moment before burial.

When there was no answer to his knock, James opened the door to Devlin's room and peered inside. Because of the perpetual darkness that seemed characteristic of all the rooms he'd seen in this house, the shape of a man silhouetted against the narrow window stood out in stark relief—a headless figure with torso, long legs spread stiffly, and arms braced against the wall.

"Here you are," James said lightly. "We've been waiting breakfast on you."

"I'm not hungry," said the headless figure. "Start without me."

The lifeless quality in the voice, coupled with the gesture of defeat, sent James storming across the room. "You've already confronted her, haven't you? Damn you for being a fool! Now she'll be on guard. We'll see only what Jenny wants us to see." He spun Devlin around, sorely tempted to snap that hangdog chin with a hard left hook. "You've accused me of not knowing my own daughter, but I can tell you for certain that her pride isn't one wit less than your own."

"Pride goeth before destruction," Devlin quoted the Bible in the same dead tone.

"And a haughty spirit before a fall," James finished for him, biting out every word. "You've been like a prairie wildfire since Davie put that letter in your hands—unpredictable, out of control. Well, you might just have burned the bridges and our only opportunity to discover the truth."

"She's lying," Devlin whispered, his head rearing up, the slumped shoulders squaring again. "Twice I asked her point blank if she'd received your letter *before* deciding to marry Armbruster. She danced around that question—why?" He began to pace back and forth in front of the window, pounding a clenched fist against his forehead. "I was so goddamned sure, charging at her like an enraged bull, accusing, not asking. Maybe she does love that aristocratic pretty-face. Maybe—"

"Cut it out!" James grabbed Devlin between his shoulders and neck, giving him a hearty shake. "You're not thinking with your head anymore, Dev. You want desperately to see her unhappy. And I don't mind admitting I'd find it easier to sleep at night if you're wrong. Back off. Maybe this time—between the two of us—we'll get the straight of things."

James was still trying to reacquaint himself with the man he no longer recognized. Cool, impassive Devlin, the man he'd always counted on for clearheaded thinking, seemed to have lost all reason. "Come on down to breakfast," he said more gently.

"Not yet. I'm not ready to face her again."

"You've got an hour. I'll tell them you're packing." The puzzled look on Devlin's face brought a smile. "We're leaving for the Armbruster estate in an hour. No need to look like a thundercloud. I can't say I'm wild about the idea myself, but since we're the unexpected guests dropping ourselves down into the middle of plans already made, we'll just have to go along with it."

When the carriage pulled up the circular cobblestone drive, Adrian led his wife into the house, leaving his father-in-law and a gaping young Irishman to stand beside the carriage.

"James," Devlin finally said, swallowing heavily. "Why do I suddenly feel an uncommon urge to polish the toes of my boots against the back of my trousers?"

Rolling laughter and a hearty clap on the back propelled him forward. He stepped beneath the stately portico. "Well, it's for certain I'll be makin' a great fool of me'self now."

Chapter Twenty-Seven

Jennifer stood before the doors leading to the garden. Beneath a fresh blanket of falling snow lay sleeping roses, memories of a trickling fountain and heated kisses in the shadows of a blazing sunset. Perhaps like the roses, she too was waiting for spring and the birth of a new life. It would be a new beginning, and the early bud of passion and love surely would bloom anew.

The thought warmed her, and she pressed her cheek against the frosted glass. "A penny for them . . ." Allison's voice was filled with concern. "You're so pale, Cowgirl." A gentle hand touched a cool brow. "No fever, but you look as if you're not at all well."

"I'm perfectly fine, Allie," Jennifer insisted. "Merely a little fatigued."

Not entirely convinced, Allison was about to press the issue when her attention was drawn by the sound of loud, boisterous male voices and a great commotion within the foyer.

Young John, bundled in layer upon layer of outer clothing, bolted through the drawing room door. "Allison," he exclaimed breathlessly, eyes sparkling above the muffler wrapped about his chin and mouth. "It's bigger than anything ever before. Stephen says that Mr. McShane is really Paul Bunyan." He giggled. "And Papa said Mr. Bunyan would have had more sense."

The item in question turned out to be a fifteen-foot pine

tree that stubbornly refused to fit through any door. After long minutes of futile wrestling, and an equal amount of time spent consoling a disappointed John, the magnificent tree was cut down to a reasonable ten feet.

While Stephen, James, and Devlin worked to set the pine within a special platform, Jennifer brought a mug of hot, rum-spiked cider to her sullen-faced husband.

"That is a very handsome tree," she commented with a bright smile, eager to ease the strain caused by the morning's argument.

"Almost killed me," he grumbled. "*Your* Devlin tried to drop it on my head, then had the audacity to upbraid me for my stupidity. Can you believe such gall? He notches a tree, shoves it directly where I'm standing . . ." He took a deep swig of the cider. "Then he makes himself out the hero by pulling me out of the way. Doubtless he enjoyed nearly wrenching my arm from its socket."

Wisely, Jennifer kept her own counsel regarding Adrian's exaggerated brush with death. No doubt Devlin had been more surprised than Adrian, never imagining anyone would be so foolish to stand downward of a tree about to be felled. But after their morning encounter in the stable, the last person on earth she would defend was Devlin McShane.

When the tree stood upright, Aaron Armbruster passed around mugs of the potent hot punch. "I wish to toast those within this room—family from near and far—and state that their presence enriches our home and the pleasure of this merry season."

"Here, here!" Stephen shouted, lifting his mug high before dropping a companionable arm about Devlin's shoulders as though they were lifelong friends.

"And secondly," Aaron continued, "I want to acknowledge Devlin's quickness this afternoon in preventing injury to my nephew. You'll drink to that I'm certain, Adrian?"

"Most definitely." Adrian flashed that bedazzling smile. "Mr. McShane can never be repaid for what he has done for me." The arm that slipped around Jennifer's waist, its fingers curling so casually beneath her breasts, was a statement of possession. Somehow the rugged young Irishman had relinquished the prize Adrian now fondly treasured.

Relieved that Adrian was going to be magnanimous, Jennifer felt her heart swell with affection for her husband. She turned toward him and closed their embrace. "I'm so grateful you weren't injured," she whispered.

Adrian kissed his wife, warmly and lingeringly. But through the veil of his eyelashes, he saw over his shoulder blue eyes turn black with hurt and jealousy. Laughter bubbled to the surface, and Adrian drew back from his wife, setting it free.

Too many ciders, a sumptuous meal, and a great deal of tomfoolery passed before the great tree was adorned with ornaments made and collected throughout the years, lovingly dusted and carefully tied to the cone-laden branches of pine. The hour was late. John, exhausted from the day's excitement, fell asleep where he sat on the floor with the last and most important of all decorations grasped firmly in his hand. The youngster's protests when his mother gently ordered him up to bed were feeble; he was too sleepy even to muster the energy to affix the star to the celestial summit of the noble tree.

John's final command as his newest hero, Devlin, prepared to carry him from the room was, "I want Jenny to do it." Taking the gilded ornament from his outstretched hand, honored beyond measure, Jennifer placed a kiss on the boy's freckled cheek and brushed the wayward cinnamon-colored lock off his brow.

Would she one day feel this same tender, overflowing love toward her own son as his father carried him off to bed? Looking up into Devlin's face, she suddenly realized it was impossible to see Adrian in her someday fantasy. Only this face, strong yet tender, smiling down upon them both could fit in her imaginings. Pain knotted the womb that lodged reality's child; it was as if the tiny embryo were protesting his mother's thoughts. Tears welled in her eyes, and she hid them with another kiss to a boy's yawning cheek. "Good night, John. Sweet dreams."

A ladder was brought in. Not trusting anyone else with his daughter's safety, James held it still while Adrian and Stephen combined their efforts to hoist Jennifer those few extra inches that remained beyond her reach even from the top rung of the precarious wooden structure.

"Oh, I'm too short," she groaned, her arms aching from that last straining effort. "Allison, you'll have to do the honors."

"And who's to explain the substitution to Lord Johnny?" his sister protested. "A promise was made, and I'll not be the blame for the ruin of a child's Christmas. Besides, he'd probably rather see my head atop that tree."

"Doubtless," her mother agreed. "You tease him unmercifully at times."

"He'd think his sister didn't love him if she started being pleasant," Stephen interjected, wiping his brow while still maintaining a cautious hold upon Jennifer's waist. "I'm good for one more try. How about you, Adrian?"

Adrian was dubious. "I don't know if my shoulder can hold up. I'm afraid I'll drop her."

Jennifer began her climb down the ladder. "Well, we did try, and I'm sure John will understand."

"In a few years, no doubt," Devlin said, pushing away from the doorframe where he'd casually been watching this comedy of errors. "But his heart is set on tradition, and seeing that star up there"—he pointed—"first thing tomorrow morning."

Striding almost lazily across the room, Devlin made his own calculations before he looked toward Adrian. "With your permission, Armbruster," he drawled with mock politeness even as his hands were circling Jennifer's waist. He lifted her high above his head and sat her upon his shoulder. She made no vocal protest, but his jaw was clamped tightly against releasing a cry of pain when she used his thick mane of hair to hold herself steady.

The star was easily looped atop the tree, and when Devlin swung her off his shoulder, applause and cheers abounded. Without a backward glance, he walked away from the throng gathered beneath the tree. Only when he was out of sight did he lift his hands, his brow furrowing as he studied palms that could still feel the imprint of a woman's corset. Why would Jenny, coltishly slender, with a waist no bigger than the circle of his hands, truss her body into such a contraption?

Awakening with a start, Jennifer rolled to her side and clutched her pillow fiercely. In time her heartbeat slowed, the aftereffects of the nightmare easing until all that remained was the mental anguish of being unable to remember.

Still trembling, she slipped quietly from the bed and felt her way around the room until outstretched fingers touched the edge of the writing desk. She found the drawer and the matches and lit the decorative candle she had known she would find. Eleanor had given her and Adrian the blue and gold room she had always inhabited during her visits.

The soft light from the single taper banished any lingering anxiety from her dream and illuminated her husband's sleeping face. How beautiful he was. In repose, without cynicism marring the perfect features, he became again the man she had married.

Easing herself onto a nearby chair, she watched him turn to his back and stretch an arm across her vacant half of the bed. Their argument of the morning pricked at her conscience. She now regretted the hateful things she had said. Although it was true Adrian had never shown any burning interest in or even curiosity about her life or the people who were her family before their marriage, it was also true that Devlin had never been part of her reminiscences of home. Not once since Allison's wedding had she willingly allowed Devlin's name, or his person, to intrude upon her thoughts. Now he was here, flesh and blood, and there hadn't been a single moment since that she'd been free of his presence.

Her husband, the man she had vowed to love and cherish until the end of her days, slept but a few steps away while her mind, and part of her heart, were in that room directly across the hall with a tall, golden-haired Irishman.

More than once since first seeing Devlin in her parlor

yesterday, she'd sworn he would not upend her life, as he'd done time and again since they'd first met. But that was the child speaking to justify a woman's tortured emotions. Devlin had never controlled her father's behavior, any more than he could sway her feelings now from the man she married. Only she had the power to do that. It wouldn't happen. Adrian loved her, needed her, and deserved her whole heart; she'd have him share no part of it with Devlin McShane.

Adrian was her reality, Devlin the fantasy, and now was the time to step away from girlish dreams and begin to build something real.

Now—right now—she needed only to slip out of her silken nightdress and go to her husband without pretense. Her kiss, a touch, would awaken him and silently communicate that there would be no more barriers between their love. He would welcome her with joy, his golden eyes soft with tenderness and love. And if she could free all of her heart, he would then sweep her into that world where nothing existed beyond the fierce need of a breathless desire. They would truly become one being.

She swayed forward with the yearning to put it to the test, needing to give love and be loved. But she was a prisoner, tethered tightly within her chair, gripped by the shackles of old conflicts and emotions that refused to let her free.

Drawing up her legs, Jennifer tucked her knees beneath her chin and vainly tried to choke back rising sobs even while the tears began to flow. She was tugged between mind and heart, duty and desire. It was only two short steps to Adrian.

Time passed and her sobs turned to hiccups as she rocked herself to and fro, soaking her gown with the tears of a senseless misery. Just two steps and one touch would find the warmth of her husband's arms.

But still she sat and rocked, and rocked and cried.

Only two steps . . .

Muttering a curt greeting to the owner of the Buffalo boardinghouse, Adrian ignored the woman's request to wipe his feet with a snort of disdain. Following the trail of other muddy shoes, he climbed the staircase leading to his rented room.

When the door closed behind him, he shrugged out of his snow-crusted coat and went straight for the bottle of whiskey. Not bothering with a glass, he tipped up the bottle and gulped down the fiery liquid until it chased some of the bone-breaking chill from his stiff and shivering body. When heat from the coal-burning stove began to suffuse the dingy room, he stretched out across the unmade bed.

With a mirthless chuckle, Adrian contemplated his altered circumstances, starting with this drafty room in a cheap waterfront lodging house. The way his luck was running, dying of pneumonia might be a blessing.

For the past three days he'd sent message after unavailing message to Bertram Lowell, at the same time haunting the casinos the man had seemed so fond of. The response, when it had finally come, was but two words: "Money talks." So Bertie, the man he had branded a buffoon, intended to skin him alive like the others.

Adrian was a drowning man, on his way down for the third time. "And for what?" he cried aloud, boiling over with rage and frustration. For a life of respectable tedium, one dreary day following another? To prove to the Armbrusters he wasn't the wastrel they'd always assumed him to be? For the love of a woman?

"Aha! There's the answer. For love of lovely Jennifer."

He hurled the empty whiskey bottle across the room. It shattered against the waterstained wall, the fragments scattering like his dreams.

He pulled a full bottle from beneath the bed and downed several more healthy swigs, then let his thoughts wander back to Christmas Day.

The gifts, the laughter, a feeling of family he'd never experienced, had opened within Adrian a yearning never before acknowledged—the need to be a part of the unity surrounding him. For that brief time he had felt there was no problem he could not surmount if only he were never alone again. Even Allison's barbs were tolerable. Adrian felt wanted and safe, and he basked in the glow of Jennifer's devoted attentions, his previous jealousy of McShane seemingly ludicrous.

When Jennifer had excused herself early in the evening, claiming that the excitement had fatigued her, he'd spent an agonizingly long time trapped in a card game with his uncle and father-in-law.

It was close to midnight when he had finally entered their room. Seeing in the firelight his wife's raven hair spilling across the pillow and a bare shoulder glowing with the hue of warm honey, Adrian had been tempted to taste that rich sweetness. Greedily his lips had explored her exposed flesh, but he had not been content. He had drawn back the coverlet and paid homage to her neck, chest, and the swell of her ripe breasts above a silken gown.

His hands had begun to roam beneath the sheets, finding the velvet smoothness of her thighs. Desire, stronger, more urgent—if that were possible with this woman—had driven him to seek her secrets, his own flesh pulsing to bury deep within her body's haven.

"Jennifer," he'd whispered against her throat. "Wake up, my love, my sweet sleeping beauty."

She'd moaned, arching her neck for his access, instinctively moving against his seeking hand even as she continued to sleep.

Her lips parted, inviting his mouth. "Dev?" she'd whispered, and Adrian's universe exploded.

With that single, dreaming utterance of a name, Jennifer had reduced Adrian to a child cringing in the corner, sobbing and terrified by his mother's hysterical wrath.

He'd been twelve, home from school, and too old to be sent to his room for an afternoon nap. After months of rigid rules and the hateful jealousy of his schoolmates, Adrian had ached for a warm touch, a loving caress.

He'd slipped out of his bedroom and skipped down the stairs, determined to inform his mother that he was no longer a baby. Behind the closed parlor door he could hear her voice.

Sliding back the panel, he had stepped inside the room,

only to freeze where he stood. His mother and some strange man were wrestling on the sofa. At first he'd thought the man was attacking her, biting her breasts while she moaned in pain. He had just opened his mouth to scream when his mother had slid off the sofa and freely, willingly taken the man's huge, engorged member into her mouth. It had been then that Adrian had realized his mother was doing things the boys at school whispered about, things only whores did. He'd vomited then and there all over her prized Turkish carpet.

Isobel Armbruster, her heavy breasts swaying above his head, had shrieked curses at her son, calling him every vile name he had ever heard, until he had escaped the close-fisted blows raining upon his head and shoulders.

Now, twenty-one years later, in a rat- and cockroach-infested boardinghouse in Buffalo, Adrian resurrected a conviction formed those many years ago: All women were whores—each and every one.

Chapter Twenty-Eight

"Can't you see them yet?" Allison's question sounded more like a grumbling complaint, which, of course, is exactly what it was.

"Not yet," Jennifer responded, going up on tiptoe, shading her eyes from the sun's glare to scan the eastern edge of the meadow below the open carriage. "Any minute now, I'm sure," she reassured the young woman shuddering beneath a blanket in the corner of the carriage.

"God, I'm so cold my teeth are going to break from chattering."

"Allie, if you'd move about instead of huddling under that blanket—besides, you can't see the race from there."

"Who cares," Allison grunted, but she began to crawl across the seat anyway. "I'm not certain who's the bigger idiot. Me, for letting you drag me out here, or you, for being here at all." She stepped out, hugging herself against the cold.

"Fatima is my horse."

"Oh, that answers everything," Allison said sarcastically. "I'm not referring to this silly horse race, as you very well know. What I'd like to know is why you're here, warming my cousin's bed, when, by all rights, you should be in Montana married to your handsome Irishman?"

"You're wrong, Allie," Jennifer denied sharply, walking away to stand near the edge of the steep hill.

"Am I?" Allison followed, noting that Jennifer refused to

look at her. "Why then have you pasted yourself to my side for the past four days, Cowgirl? Which am I—shield or chaperone? And why would you have need of either one?"

When Jennifer remained silent, Allison persisted. "You can't answer me, can you?" She touched Jennifer's shoulder. "Is it that by responding to any one of those questions, you'd have no need to give any attention to the others? Jenny, you're even avoiding your father. Now I wouldn't be human, or a very good friend, not to be concerned."

"Leave it alone," Jennifer spat. "Please . . ." she finished more softly.

"Talk to me! Tell me what's troubling you. I can see the purple circles of sleepless nights beneath your eyes. Surely you know I wouldn't bring you harm for any—"

"Here they come!" Jennifer escaped the determined cross-examination. She walked briskly to where the hill began its gradual slope, then crawled and slid down the uneven ground, abrading her hands on rocks and the exposed roots of trees. Finally she reached the flat meadow.

At first all she could see were specks of white and black, and then the soft rumble of hoofs slapping the earth became more distinct, beating in tempo with her rising excitement. She would have recognized Devlin's superior horsemanship anywhere in the world; his skill was unmatchable by any western rider. It was the term *western* that qualified what she now realized was a vastly limited exposure.

She felt her heart leap into her throat when a man whose face would curdle milk became beautiful beyond imagination on the back of a horse. Jenkins rode with the stirrups shortened. His knees were level with Diablo's neck, and his buttocks never touched the saddle as he flowed into the rhythm of his mount.

It was an exhibit of excellence . . . and professionalism. She could almost sense his restraint, and when he made that final move, giving the animal his head to streak past the mare, Jennifer was jumping up and down, cheering his victory.

Both riders made a wide turn, circling until their horses

had lost the lust for the race. Then they parted, Jenkins moving up the incline toward the carriage, ignoring Devlin's attempts to call him back.

Devlin headed straight for Jennifer, a wide grin crinkling the corners of his eyes, his blond hair windblown. "My God, Jen, did you ever see anything quite like that before? I'm a hard man to impress, but by damn I'm impressed."

"I'm stunned," she admitted, relaxing some of her guard beneath his boyish enthusiasm. "I swear I didn't fix the race, Dev. I've never seen Jenkins ride before today. I don't think it would have mattered which horse I'd chosen for you—you would have still eaten his dirt."

"But it did prove my point about the rider swaying the contest."

He looked so smug that, without thinking, she playfully smacked his thigh. "Do you *always* have to be right?"

His expression changed, and the face was once again guarded. Kicking his left foot free of the stirrup, he leaned over and extended his arm. "Come on, I'll give you a ride back to the carriage." When she hesitated, his mouth curled in a rueful smile. "I've grown fond of my ears over the years, Mrs. Armbruster. Attached to them, you could say."

Using both hands, she grasped his arm as her toe found the stirrup. Effortlessly she was positioned crosswise on the saddle, her back braced against his arm, her right hand gripping the edge of the pommel.

"You'd better grab hold of something else, Jenny girl," he chuckled as he turned the mare. "Otherwise, this might be one short ride."

Devlin found it impossible to maintain his irritation over Allison Shepherd's continuing role as watchdog. It was his own fault that Jennifer avoided being alone in his company. Besides, he was beginning to enjoy the flamboyant redhead's risqué stories about the ancestors who stared down at them from gilded frames in the hallway outside the ballroom.

"From the pompous, somewhat righteous expression on Great-great Uncle Ralph's face one would never guess that

324

he not only fathered ten children with his wife, but managed also to maintain two mistresses—in separate residences at opposite ends of this city." Allison attempted a disapproving tone. "It's been said that when his overtaxed heart failed him, the entire family gave a collective sigh of relief that the old lecher had the good taste to die in his own bed. Poor Aunt Martha"—she sighed—"never recovered from the loss of her husband, but I will always believe she was consoled with the birth of baby number ten—exactly nine months to the day after her husband's demise."

"Allie," Jennifer scolded, "what a dreadful imagination you have!" The sound of Devlin's laughter rankled somehow. When her father had left this morning to accompany Aaron and Stephen into Boston, it had been Devlin's suggestion they tour the house. She had insisted upon Allison as tour guide. Instead of the disappointment she'd anticipated, he'd seemed quite pleased. Her feminine vanity was wounded, but would mend no doubt.

"Don't lag behind, Cowgirl," Allison quipped. "We have now come to the hallowed hall of knowledge and enlightenment . . . the great library."

"My God," Devlin whispered, spellbound as he stepped inside. Reverent fingers moved over the leather-bound volumes. He scanned titles and subjects that ran the gamut from law to literature. "I am awed. And, I must admit, envious. Do you think your father would object to my borrowing a few of these books while I'm here, Mrs. Shepherd?"

"*Mr. McShane,* I'm not in my dotage quite yet. I would very much appreciate it if you would use my given name."

He was so entranced by the discovery of the library, he barely acknowledged Allison's sharp tone. "Of course."

"Well, Allie . . . we've probably seen the last of Devlin, so your insistence upon a less formal acquaintance was a total waste of time. Mr. McShane will no doubt be found only with his nose in a book until Father drags him onto the train for home."

Was Jennifer aware of the melting tenderness in her tone? Allison watched Devlin, who had been deaf to her own voice just seconds ago, respond fully to Jennifer's, turning away from the books he'd caressed. Deep in his eyes burned a deeper passion.

Caught in the crossfire of strong emotions, Allison felt her own body temperature rising. "Our friendship began with *Oliver Twist,* didn't it, Jennifer?" It was Allison's attempt to cool the heated atmosphere. "I could use some coffee," she trilled loudly. She walked to the bell cord near the door and gave it a hearty jerk. "Father keeps every kind of liquor imaginable in that cabinet behind the desk, Devlin."

"Coffee will be fine," he muttered, moving around the room, examining titles.

Jennifer leaned against the huge mahogany desk, her hands curled around the sharp edge. Allison had taken the chair directly in front of her and was observing too much and missing damned little. She flashed her friend a warning. "Our friendship did not begin in Miss Persimmon Face's literature class," Jennifer insisted. "You simply don't want to acknowledge my heroism and admit what a clown you are on horseback. She's really pathetic, Dev. Such a pitiful sight it brings tears to your eyes."

"So you've told me." The deep voice directly behind her made her start. He'd taken the chair behind the desk. His elbows were propped atop the wood, and his fingers formed a steeple, the apex resting against his mouth. "I've heard many stories about those dull, bleak hours in the academy. Was it really as horrible as Jenny painted it?"

"Bleak? Dull? How could anyone describe beginning each morning with a midget from the Wild West, who breathed fire and brimstone and knifed you with silver-dagger eyes, as dull? On one occasion I was awakened when this child of sweetness and light slammed a pillow into my face without provocation. Bleak—not at all."

"Tell me, Allison," Jennifer said with a sweetly innocent smile. "Is Stephen cranky in the mornings?"

Allison's eyes narrowed, and she leaned forward in her chair. "As a matter of fact . . . But why do you ask?"

"Just simple curiosity," Jennifer said with a shrug.

"Clearly it has been your misfortune to pair up with people who are naturally grumpy before they've had their coffee."

"Speaking of coffee—" Devlin drawled. "Allison, why don't you see what is keeping your servant?"

Catching Jennifer's threatening look, Allison squirmed nervously. "It shouldn't be much longer. Why don't you tell me about the cattle rustling incident, Devlin," she asked in a rush. "Jenny was closemouthed as a clam about the subject."

"Ignorant," Jennifer amended. "And little wiser to this day. It's one of those, 'don't discuss with the little princess' subjects." Bitterness was apparent in her voice. "You wouldn't believe the never ending list of topics shrouded in that dark taboo."

"I'll go check on that coffee." Allison was out of the room before her friend could protest. Jennifer made a move forward.

"Are you thinking of running? What are you afraid of, Jen? Me . . . or yourself?"

"Again you delude yourself, McShane. Surely you realize that it is improper for a married woman to entertain a single gentleman alone at any time and under any circumstance."

Devlin pushed back his chair and rose to walk around the desk. "And, of course, you've always cared deeply about propriety and convention."

Her mouth twitched. She looked up at him from beneath her lashes. "How could you possibly think otherwise?" Her affected primness brought a guttural laugh from the man who knew her too well.

"Would Mrs. Armbruster swoon if I took off this strangling tie?" He pulled at the tight knot. As he was already in the process of removing the necktie and struggling to release the top two buttons on his shirt, her consent was redundant. "Please . . . do make yourself comfortable."

Within minutes his suitcoat lay on the back of the chair, and he was rolling back his shirtsleeves to the elbows. Her eyebrows lifted when he went to work on the long row of buttons on the snug waistcoat. Catching her silent inquiry, he smirked. "No need to sound the alarm, Mrs. Prim and Proper. I'm just giving myself a little breathing space. How you females tolerate all those . . . those under and over things, I'll never understand. It's no wonder you used to prefer trousers and an old shirt. Although there was a time I'd have said you were rebelling—now it seems you were just showing you had good sense."

"Well, glory be. You mean you're actually giving me credit for having sense?" Her sarcasm was softened by the amusement glinting in her eyes. "I'd bet a twenty-dollar gold piece you wouldn't repeat that in mixed company."

Sitting down on the edge of the desk, Devlin crossed his legs, propping his ankle on the other knee, both hands curved lightly around his lower leg as if to hold the position. The muscle twitching in his cheek warned her that he was either angry or getting ready to say or do something she felt certain would be highly unpleasant.

"We hanged ten men, Jen," he finally ground out, turning his head to gauge her reaction to the bald statement he had just slapped her with.

"What?" she choked.

"The rustlers," he snapped. "You've always said you wanted to know. Well, it's time you knew. They were caught and marched, without trial or preacher, to the nearest strong tree. Guess it took a good part of the day to get the job done. It takes ten men a long time to die . . . one by one."

She covered her mouth with her hands as her stomach began to churn. "No." She shook her head in violent denial. "That's not possible. My father would never allow—"

"Vigilante justice?" he finished in a softer tone. "Do you really think anyone asked his opinion? Herb Walters brought in hired gunmen after one of his hands—a boy not much older than Hank—was found next to a cut fence. They'd used the barbed wire—" Devlin's features twisted with the bitter memory. "He'd been dead two days, they figured . . . strangled."

With a cry, Jennifer covered her entire face with her

hands to blot out the pictures her mind was creating. "Dear Lord," she whispered.

Devlin's arm reached out and he hauled her tight into the curve beneath his shoulder. "It was an epidemic of madness . . . over before it could be stopped."

"Why are you telling me this now?" She lowered her hands from her face and grabbed a fistful of his shirt. "Why?"

"Why not? You can't have it both ways, Jen. If you want an ivory tower, don't complain about the restrictions."

She tried to pull away. "Allison should be back any minute."

"I don't think so. Allison and I understand each other better than you might imagine. Strange, isn't it, that your husband's cousin should give me the trust you can't." He lifted his arm from her shoulder. "Run away, little girl. It's what you do best."

"That's not fair, Dev." Even to her own ears, she sounded like a whining child. "Look, I've been protected—and excluded—from practically every major decision or event concerning the ranch. Daddy would pat me on my head and say, 'Don't worry your pretty little head about it, Princess.' Who else volunteered to keep me informed?"

"We told you what we were allowed," Devlin admitted, conceding her point. "However, you *knew* there was trouble brewing with rustlers. You even questioned me about the wire that had been snipped. I'll grant that your father ordered us not to discuss it with his daughter, but you knew better than to run away . . ." He lowered his legs and stood up to tower over her. "My God, Jen. You always acted strictly on impulse, never thinking, always blazing your emotions like they were some damned banner of courage instead of using the brains I *know* the good Lord gave you. I was so crazy with worry that night I didn't know whether to beat you, or kiss you to death when I found you."

"You made the right decision, McShane," she assured, unconsciously rubbing the backside he had walloped with memorable gusto.

"But on *hindsight.*" He smiled, coaxing a responding grin with his play on words. "I did more than my share of acting on my impulses that night—all the wrong ones."

Jennifer lowered her head. She interlaced her fingers and brought them up beneath her chin. "That was the first time I considered you might be friend instead of foe. I don't think I've ever been so glad to see anyone in my entire life. My hero, the golden knight coming to the rescue." She lifted her chin. Her hands dropped back to her lap.

"You hated my guts, Jenny girl. Thought I might go deaf with you screamin' your curses at me day and night."

"You were everything I wanted to be, and couldn't. I kept trying to scratch off some of that luster. But a sapling casts a very insignificant shadow when it's planted beneath a giant oak."

Her smile was the saddest thing he'd ever had to live with, and it tore through him with the force of a sledgehammer. "We talked about truth that night—do you remember?"

"Gray, obscured by hidden things . . . something like that."

"Well, my trusting Jenny, I spun more lies that night than a bagged leprechaun. If it hadn't been for the rain, you'd have seen a cold sweat when I rashly volunteered to pack my things if you but said the word." He raked his fingers through his hair. "The truth is—I'd have stopped breathing if you'd called my bluff. You've not forgotten our talk about truth, but it's certain you have no understanding of it yet."

With cautious movements, he took those few steps that separated them. Recognizing the familiar hesitant watchfulness, she laughed. "I'm not a horse about to shy, Dev."

His hands settled upon her shoulders. "And I'm about as far from perfect as any human creature walking this earth. When I look in the mirror every morning, all I see is the stray your daddy brought home. And most mornings I thank God, the fates, or just the damned luck that gave me a warm hearth and a full belly. Then there are times when I ache to break free of my leash . . ." When he saw her wince from the pressure of his grip, Devlin released her. Turning on his heel, he walked back to the desk and sat down on it again.

Shoulders slumped, he bent forward until his forearms rested against his thighs. "But a good mutt doesn't bite the hand that feeds it."

"Poor little Irish orphan. I think I might cry." Although her words were harsh, her voice was soft, filled with tenderness. Approaching the desk, she continued, "When are you going to put that abused boy and his memories behind you? You said I wore my emotions like a banner; you wear those scars on your back like a hair shirt."

Color drained from Devlin's face. Her words, no matter how gently spoken, cut him all the way to the bone. "You don't know what the hell you're talking about. Nothing," he growled while his insides were being turned inside out, "nothing in your past could give you the understanding of what it's like to be all-the-way-to-the-bone cold, or so hungry that your stomach won't hold even the scraps of food you can forage or steal. Do you know what kind of animal takes the bread from a child smaller and weaker than himself just to spew it up in less than five minutes?" His carefully tutored diction began to disappear beneath the surging wave of loathing and self-contempt. "Did you ever strike an old man down just for the few pennies in his pocket? Ah, that made yer eyes fly wide, Jenny girl." His big hands reached out to curve beneath her chin and hold her firm when she might have turned away. "He was half blind and could barely stand without his cane—the same cane I brought down hard upon his head before I jammed it into his belly to knock him to the street. The scars I wear on my back are that old man's curse upon my soul. I can hear him now, crying and damning me while the blood—" He swallowed several times, looking up at the frescoed ceiling, blinking rapidly to clear the moisture that threatened to unman him completely. "With every lash of Jake's belt, I saw that old man smiling. The beatings were my penance."

Her eyes were flooding with tears, and when he tried to release his hold upon her, she captured one of the hands beneath her cheek and pressed a kiss into the palm.

"Don't," he breathed raggedly. "I'm not deservin' of pity."

Jennifer moved to stand between his thighs. Her hands gripped the tense muscles between his neck and shoulder. "And *you* won't get sympathy, McShane. But will you allow a little compassion for that boy. Can't you see that *he* was a victim himself?"

"It's not that easy, Jen. At thirteen I was already as tall as most men."

"Thirteen? The boy you carried to bed Christmas Eve is only a year younger than you were, a child still." Her arms went around his neck, and she pressed his cheek against her own. "A child, Dev. *He* is deserving of your compassion."

Through her eyes he was able to see himself—only a boy. A very lost, heavily grieved child in a strange land where he hadn't been welcome. His arms encircled her waist and his forehead touched her own while unashamed tears of healing wet his cheeks. But the teardrops slipping from Jennifer's eyes and collecting at the corners of her mouth were not to be borne.

"Oh, Jen," he breathed, touching his lips to that uptilted nose before he pulled back to put a safe distance between them.

Jennifer knew she should move away, but was frozen by the revelation within his eyes. Eyes a pure blue, transparent with love, made her aware that it had been she who had always been blind. When his fingers touched her face, the rough pads of his thumbs chasing tears, moving over the curve of her lips, she flowed toward him.

Their mouths met in the briefest of kisses, breath mingling only for timeless seconds. Then her lips kissed the salty moisture from his cheeks, absorbing the evidence of his lonely pain, as she had absolved the guilt he'd always carried.

He cupped her face. "And this, my lovely Jennifer, is the final truth. Whether we will it or not."

Jennifer moved away. "By your own definition truth is not unclouded by other matters. You are my youth, at once the worst and the best of the woman I'm starting to become. Adrian is my husband, present and future."

With that she turned to leave, knowing all the while that

he had no intention of making it so easy. She flinched inwardly when he caught her just short of the door, spinning her around.

"I can't accept that, Jen. You don't belong here, would never have willingly given up everything you love even for a palace such as this. The letter . . . I have to know. Please, for God's sake, give me the truth. When did you receive your father's letter?"

He'd asked for God's sake; she answered for his sake and her own. "No matter what I tell you, you will believe only what you want to believe. Sam asked me once if I was woman enough to chuck it all for a man who really loved me. Adrian loves me—enough not to hide his feelings because of pride or even uncertainty. But if you must have me say it, the letter didn't arrive until after we left for New York." Gently she removed the hand on her arm. "Dev, if you really care for me, you won't leave me with memories my conscience can't live with."

Knowing with every fiber of his being that she lied, Devlin let her go, perhaps for the final time, although he was not yet ready to accept that her will might be as strong as his own. Hope reborn dies harder the second time.

Chapter Twenty-Nine

"I really don't like the idea of going off when you're not feeling well," James complained to his daughter.

"It's only a teeny little headache, Daddy," she reassured, taking his arm and walking with him to where the others were waiting in the entryway. "You and Devlin have to pick up your clothing for tomorrow night. Allison will stop at the dressmaker's for me. Believe me, it's better I don't wrangle with Mrs. Lanier."

"Borrowed feathers," James grumbled. "I don't know how Dev feels, but I'd just as soon stay in my room and forget that fancy party and your fancy friends." They stepped into the foyer. "Isn't that right, Devlin?"

The man who was helping Allison with her coat twisted his head. "What am I agreeing to now, James?"

Jennifer heard her father repeat his opinion of the New Year's party, but although she saw Devlin's mouth moving, the only audible sound was the rapid beating of her heart when those deep blue eyes fixed upon her face.

"Ready?" James asked, turning to give his daughter a hug. "You set aside some time for me tonight, Princess. You've been harder to get hold of lately than a sinner on Sunday."

The fixed smile disappeared from Jennifer's face as the three departed, Allison's laughter ringing in her ears as she made her way back to her room. Her claim to a headache wasn't entirely false. Every day it became increasingly difficult to hide the fatigue she felt certain was caused by her pregnancy. But it was the dream that seemed to increase in frequency and its ability to terrify, coupled with the tortured thoughts that gave her no peace day or night, that made it imperative that she rest today. It was either that or collapse.

Allison would lead them a merry chase from shop to shop. And Jennifer intended to spend every moment of that time in bed.

As she opened the door to her room, she was rendered speechless by the sight of one of the housemaids digging through her bureau. She quite purposefully let the door close with a thud.

The carrot-haired maid started so violently that the two gold coins in her hand dropped onto the bureau with an incriminating clink.

"What are you looking for, Daisy?"

"Oh, dear Lord," the maid wailed behind the fingers she'd pressed to her lips. "By the saints it's not what it appears, Mrs. Jennifer."

Jennifer picked up the two twenty-dollar gold pieces and turned them over in her hands, feeling their weight. "Where did you get these, Daisy? Certainly not in my room."

The maid lurched forward, both hands spread outward in supplication. "He gave them to me. Told him I didn't want the dirty pay, or the job that went with it. But he was like a crazy man, and I was afraid of what he'd do. I'm no thief. I swear on me father's grave, I'd never—"

"All right, all right." Jennifer gave the distraught young woman a sobering shake. "Now you come over here and sit down. I want you to *calmly* tell me what in the . . ." She pushed the girl into the chair in front of the desk, then sat down in the lyre-back chair and rested her arms atop the polished surface. "Talk, Daisy."

The girl was wringing her hands, shaking her head to and fro. "Oh, don't make me tell you," she pleaded. But at the relentless expression on Jennifer's face, Daisy sniffed loudly, blew her nose on the hanky she retrieved from her pocket, and took a deep breath.

"It was the morning after Christmas. I was cleanin' up the sitting room when Mr. Adrian . . ." Her eyes flickered to

335

Jennifer and then moved away again before she rushed on. "Mr. Adrian put these two coins in my hand and told me I was to watch you and Mr. McShane and report any . . . any strange goings on when he returned from his trip."

It took a few minutes for Daisy's galloping words to penetrate Jennifer's consciousness. Still she could not believe it. "Repeat that, please. Slowly this time."

Daisy was halfway through the second recital when Jennifer's palms slammed down on the desktop and she sprang up out of the chair. "How dare he?" she blazed, cold fire igniting in her eyes. Turning on Daisy with a vengeance, she rounded the desk, hands on her hips. "And just what were you looking for . . . evidence? Did you think to find Mr. McShane in my bureau? Or had you thought to check beneath the bed? Perhaps the wardrobe?"

Daisy was on her feet now, her own temper flaring. "I'm not a spy, missus! I was returning the money, I was. I've still got another month's penance to do for not mailin' yer letter." The girl suddenly paled, causing her freckles to stand out sharply.

"What letter?"

"The letter you gave me to mail just before you ran off to marry Mr. Adrian."

Daisy looked up, her chin trembling. Jennifer was white as a sheet.

"It's not that I didn't mail it altogether," the maid hedged. "Just a wee bit late."

"How late?" Jennifer demanded, waiting while Daisy seemed to squirm for a lifetime.

"Late November," she finally replied.

Jennifer would have been less than human had she not felt the soaring of her heart replace a red fury. It did not require a great mathematician to calculate that it had taken only days, perhaps hours, not the months she had assumed, for Devlin and her father to board that eastbound train after the arrival of her letter. It didn't change a damn thing, but dear sweet Lord, it made everything a little easier to bear. New questions formed in her mind. She pushed them aside. Did it matter now whether Devlin had accepted Silver

336

Creek, and her father's partnership, before or after he learned of her marriage?

Grabbing Daisy's hand, Jennifer pressed the two coins into the girl's palm. "Keep the money. And when my husband requests his report, you can tell him Mr. McShane and I wore the carpet thin sneaking back and forth across the hall each night."

"Oh . . . no . . . I couldn't say that. Ye don't mean it?"

"Keep the money anyway, Daisy. Adrian will believe what he wants in any case," Jennifer stated coldly, pushing the maid from the room and slamming the door before the tide of warring emotions crested in a tempest of outrage and despair.

She alternately raged, then cried, paced the room, and sat very still, staring vacantly. Finally, drained of all emotion, she stripped off her clothing and fell exhausted onto the bed.

Jennifer awakened slowly, laboriously making the upward climb from a dreamless sleep. Her eyelids fluttered open, but the body remained in its weighted state while she watched the changing patterns of reflected firelight dance on the ceiling above her bed. Her stomach growled noisily with hunger, and with a final yawn she stretched her arms above her head, straightening her legs and curling her toes.

Immediately she arched upright as the calves in both legs knotted with a violent cramp. "Damn, damn . . ." she muttered, grinding her teeth as she flung aside the covers.

The man sitting unseen in the chair before the fire approached the bed, his smoky gray eyes filled with concern. "What is it, Princess?" he asked, alarmed by the twisted features and the eyes filled with pain.

"Cramp . . . my legs. Jesus, they hurt like hell."

Within seconds her legs were across her father's lap and his large, strong hands were kneading the aching muscles, massaging the spasms until she sighed with relief. "Don't point your toes," he warned, swinging her legs off his lap to let them dangle over the side of the bed. "Better now?"

"Much," Jennifer breathed as the last of the ache disappeared. "I've never had cramps like that before. At least not without cause." She smiled at her father. "Thank you, Daddy."

Testing the legs that had rebelled so violently only moments before, she cautiously moved to the open wardrobe. She took her robe from the hook inside the door and pulled it on over scanty pantaloons and a camisole. Even a father's disinterested eye might notice the bloom of the figure she'd kept restrained within a tight corset.

When her stomach growled again, she laughed. "What time is it? I'm ravenous."

"Past midnight. But I had the cook leave a plate of cold chicken and muffins just in case you decided to wake up." He nodded toward the towel-covered mound resting atop the desk.

"Why didn't someone get my lazy bones out of bed?" she questioned, already brandishing a chicken leg in one hand while the other was stuffing an entire muffin into her mouth.

"Tried." He shrugged, moving to stand near the fire. "I was beginning to think you'd found a new way to keep me at a distance. Told you to save some time for me . . . so you slept that time away. No excuses necessary that way."

She gulped down the chicken, turning away to wipe her fingers on the towel. "I wasn't avoiding you. I'm . . . I'm terribly sorry if that's the impression—"

James made a disparaging sound deep in his throat. "You can cut the hoity-toity manners with me, little girl. Every time Devlin or I start getting too close to a subject you think you might not like, you get up on your high Mrs. Armbruster horse. Well, this time you'll not put me off stride, Princess." Covering the short distance between them, he took her arm and led her to one of the twin chairs in front of the fire. "Sit down," he ordered. "It's just the two of us, honey. You can drop those fancy airs. Why don't you try being the girl who turned the air blue with her curses a little bit ago."

Handing her the glass of milk she'd ignored on the tray, he hid a smile at her obvious grimace. "I hate milk, Daddy. You know that."

"Drink up. It's good for you now—or so they say."

"Who says? I've lived my life quite well without drinking that awful stuff." When the significance of what he was hinting at reached her fuzzy brain, she nearly dumped the entire glass into her lap. "Why is it good for me now?"

"Don't act daft with me, girl. I didn't spring up out of a cabbage patch and neither did you." Sitting down in the chair adjacent to hers, he stretched out his legs and clasped his hands behind his head. "I've always regretted that you took mostly after my side of the family—hair, eyes, coloring are all Douglas. All I've ever seen of Louise in you is that dimple in your cheek and the small, delicate way your bones are strung together. But this week I've been seeing your mama every time I looked at you. Thought at first it was imagination. Then laid it on the ladylike clothes and these luxury surroundings. But this morning it hit me like a thunderbolt. The circles under your eyes, the . . . the bloom of your figure. I've seen you all but nod off during supper and then shake yourself awake." He stopped and stared into the fire. "A whole lot of little things that seemed different about you. Dev's noticed it, too, but he doesn't have my memories. God, how I worried when Louise started taking naps, sleeping half the day away. Thought she had some awful sickness. Then she'd sit down at the table and eat like a starving lumberjack. Told her she was getting fat and lazy," he choked, and then cleared his throat loudly. "She told me not to complain about what was my fault for putting a baby in her belly."

Jennifer remained silent. She reached for his hand and gave it a squeeze that was painfully tight.

"You weren't going to tell me, were you?" She shook her head, looking at him with tears swimming in her eyes. "Does your husband know?" Again she gave him a silent negative response.

James closed his eyes and leaned back in his chair. "I wish the whole damned world would stop trying to protect me. Not one living soul ever tells me facts I need. Oh, I get lots of advice, but damned little about what's really important. I'm not a babe in napkins, Jennifer Louise. As your father and the grandfather of the child you carry, I have every damn right to worry myself sick or jump for joy. Right now I'm doing a little of both." She watched him take a handkerchief from his pocket and blow his nose.

"Daddy, I know what hell you went through over losing my mother." Jennifer increased her grip. "I'm small, but I'm also strong as an ox."

"I know," he whispered hoarsely. "Watched you work a roundup. Although you must have suffered blisters on your backside, you were too bullheaded stubborn to quit. And too cussed proud to admit the open range wasn't the high-heel kickin' good time you'd expected." With a chuckle, he released her hand to lean forward. Bracing his lower arms against his knees, he stared into the fire for long moments. "You'll get through having this baby in the same fashion. You're not your mama—no matter how hard I've tried to make you like her."

Jennifer was crying now. "I'm sorry, Daddy." She knelt before him, pressing her cheek against his knee.

"What are you apologizing for?" James hauled his daughter onto his lap, cradling her as he'd done when she was a child. "Honey, I couldn't be prouder or love you more if the Lord had given me the entire world of children to pick from. I'd have said, 'I want that feisty little silver-eyed female.'" He tightened his hold, kissing the top of her head. "There's been times I know you've doubted that . . . and sometimes with cause. But everything I've done—right or wrong—has always been because I only wanted the best for you. Still do."

He sat her upright, cupping her chin. "Your happiness is all the world to me, and there's damned little I wouldn't do to insure that the mistakes of foolish, pigheaded men don't hurt you." He drew in a deep breath and let it out slowly. "Dev says we—that's him and me—didn't give you too many choices. Both of us made decisions affecting you without ever bothering to ask or sometimes even consider that you might have to suffer the consequences of our male vanity."

"The taciturn Mr. McShane has been positively verbose lately," she muttered sarcastically, trying to move off her father's lap.

"Indulge me, honey," James asked with a gentle plea. "This may be the last chance I have to baby my baby for quite some time. Besides, I want you to sit quiet and just listen."

When her head was nestled against his chest, he took a deep breath. "Wordy isn't the only thing Devlin's been since that telegram about your marriage arrived. But since Davie put that letter in his hands a few weeks ago, he's been roaring like a wounded cougar. Now I think there are some things you've got to hear—no, things you got a right to know. First of which is that Devlin has not yet accepted my offer of Silver Creek . . ."

Jennifer stood at the window watching the heavy rain, thinking it made a good companion for her gloomy spirits. With the sun completely obscured by dark, heavy clouds, she could only guess at the time. Her hands trembled and her heart beat a staccato tempo against her chest. She rubbed the eyes that burned from another sleepless night and ached for the releasing tears that would not come.

Swallowing heavily, she pulled together the edges of her blue velvet robe, belting it tightly over the nightgown she'd donned after her father's departure. Time was passing. Unpleasant tasks, she had always been taught, should be the first tackled. Again she swallowed, only this time it was the remainder of her pride.

She left her room and quietly crossed the hall. Soundlessly she entered Devlin's room, the soft click of the doorlatch inaudible over her own thundering heartbeat. But the man who was scraping the last of the shaving lather from his face simply looked over his shoulder. With the razor still poised near his chin, he let his dark eyes sweep her head to toe, pausing briefly upon her face before casually completing his task. Devlin reached for a towel and dabbed at the small knick at his jawline, ruefully acknowledging to himself that if the apparition huddling against the door had appeared much earlier, he'd most likely have cut his face to ribbons.

Jennifer was bewildered by his strange behavior. Her hands continued to clutch her robe tightly at the neckline, feeling her pulse leap when the simple movement of reaching for a towel caused the muscles in his back to ripple and bunch.

He was naked to the waist, his soft denim trousers riding low on slender hips, molding his lean, sinewy thighs like a second skin. Her own state of near undress caused alarms to ring loudly inside her head.

In the mirror he watched the emotions flickering upon her face. Expressively they swung from unease to fear, and then the realization of her vulnerable position. Continuing to hug the door, her hand tightly anchored to the doorknob that assured a quick retreat, Jennifer was a woman caught by her own imprudent whim.

Very slowly, so as not to startle her into making that escape, he turned to face her.

"I'm not going to pounce and ravish, Jen. Stop trembling like a trapped hare." He took a step forward and then stopped when it seemed she would meld into the wood at her back.

The beauty and magnificence of him took her breath away: the golden hue of his naked flesh, the ridge of muscle across his stomach covered by the finest, lightest down of silken hair. His flat male nipples were puckered in the morning chill. Irrationally, she wondered if Adrian's body reacted the same way beneath the heavy pelt of chest hair. Her husband's face was so beautiful that it made his slender, white body seem insignificant in comparison. But standing before her was evidence of what God had intended in his creation of the male.

"I . . . I wanted to talk to you." Her words were as staccato as her heartbeat. Her mouth was so dry that speech was almost impossible. "Father told me about Silver Creek. It's yours, Dev. I *want* you to have it. My land to give . . . please take it."

342

"Why?" he said slowly, drawing out the word while one eyebrow quirked.

She shook her head, unable to meet his steady gaze. "It's important to me. My father needs you, Dev. He loves you."

"That's not good enough, Jen. We've played this scene before. Only the last time you were accusing me of trying to steal your land *and* your father's affections." He moved closer. "Now you're giving me permission to take both. Why?"

"Forget it, then," she cried, turning to flee.

"Why?" he repeated with a husky snarl, spinning her around to push her back against the door, pinning her there with both forearms flat against the wood on each side of her head. "Damn you . . . tell me why!"

"Because," she breathed as the clean, earth-warmed scent of him permeated her senses and her eyes moved over the broad expanse of golden skin so near and so forbidden. "Because *I need* you to be there . . . see you there." It was not at all what she had intended to say.

"Dear God, Jen," he groaned, his forehead touching the door above her head, his respirations parting the strands of her hair as he spoke. "You've acted the bitch, but I've never thought you deliberately cruel before. Silver Creek . . . what an exquisite torture you've planned for me. Am I to build my cabin on the thick grass where I held you and kissed the velvet skin of your breasts? Will my thirst be quenched in the crystal water where I watched you bathe in silvered moonlight, your wet undergarments so transparent that I'll never be able to forget how very lovely you are." He pressed closer. "Shall I rest my back against the bark of a tree where we weathered a storm and you sobbed your hatred of me while I was discovering how very much I wanted to turn that hate into something else?"

The deep wretchedness and despair in his voice struck a corresponding chord within her own heart. Her hands came up from her sides to rest lightly against his ribs. Involuntarily her thumbs stroked the silken flesh that stretched taut over muscle and bone.

"Take your hands from me, Jenny girl," he warned on a shuddering breath. "Else I'll return the caress and we'll both go up in smoke."

Jennifer jerked her hands back from the heat of his body as if he truly were the flame and she'd come too close. "Will . . . will you take the land?" Her voice was thin.

He pushed away. "Get out of here—now!"

She was welded to the door, unable to move away from the raw desire in his eyes. Devlin captured one of her hands to place it firmly against the enormity of his need. It pulsed threateningly against her palm with a bold honesty that was no less magnificent than the whole of the man who was reaching for her. It was when his hands slid over her shoulders that she realized the palm touching him so intimately was no longer held prisoner but remained willingly.

Devlin watched her small tongue dart out to wet her lips and knew her mouth must be as dry as his own. Thirsty, so thirsty. Did she even realize what her fingers were doing, driving him mindless, beyond the brink of control.

She saw only his mouth, lips parting, moving closer. Her eyes did not close while her chin lifted, feeling the soft press of his kiss, the tentative touch of his tongue. Blood thundered in her ears, growing louder and louder until it was deafening. And then that jarring voice. "Mr. McShane. I've brought yer coffee, sir."

"Shit," he muttered beneath his breath, flinching as if he'd been slapped. "Leave it by the door, Daisy!" Devlin shouted, his eyes never wavering from Jennifer's stunned expression. "I'm not decent."

"Yes, sir," replied the small voice, and then there was the faint sound of rattling china before silence.

"Well, Jenny girl, now that you've met the beast, are you staying or going?" She hung her head, shaking it slightly. "If you go . . . don't come back again. One of these days I'll run out of scruples and not give you a choice. Then you'll not leave me . . . ever."

She nodded and turned away, her hand gripping the doorknob. "I'll think about Silver Creek," he said quietly, without anger. "You'll have my answer before we leave tomorrow." A gentle hand stroked the length of her hair. "Don't go flailing yourself about what happened . . . might have happened just now. Promise me."

"I promise," she said weakly, slipping into the hallway, running before she lost the courage not to turn back.

Chapter Thirty

When she stepped away from the mirror, Daisy cooed. "Oh, missus, you're the most dazzlin' thing I've seen in me entire life."

Dazzling. Was that the word to describe the collective efforts that had gone into the Armbruster/Lanier original of scarlet silk brocatelle draping in soft folds over the underskirt of black French bobbin lace? Or would *shocking* more appropriately describe the deep vee of the bodice that was tucked and gathered to produce a generous, eyebrow-raising amount of creamy skin above the décolletage?

Daisy fluffed the dyed ostrich plumes sewn into the shoulders of the gown, stepping back to purse her lips. "Ye need some jewelry. Somethin' to take the gentlemen's eyes from yer bust and give the ladies somethin' else to envy."

Jennifer picked up her feathered fan, snapped it open, and fluttered it protectively over the exposed skin. "Let them gawk," she said resolutely. "Besides, from the designs Mrs. Lanier had in her shop, I would imagine bosoms are very fashionable this year."

"Aren't they always?" Daisy giggled. "Especially with the men."

Some of Jennifer's joy in this gown had faded in the misery of her self-contempt. Harlot in scarlet, she observed harshly, unable to keep the promise she'd made to Devlin. Hadn't she already broken a greater vow—forsaking all others—while being drawn like a mindless being into a

346

whirlpool where nothing existed beyond total acquiescence to sensation?

Only a kiss. How many hours had she attempted to dismiss her actions thus? A few brief moments . . . moments when she'd lost herself entirely in a current from which there would have been no return.

"You're wearin' a pained expression. Is it that brutal corset ye've insisted on scrinchin' up yer insides with? Or is it that you're worrying about what I'm going to be sayin' to Mr. Adrian? Rest assured, missus, he'll get nothing from Daisy O'Manion but a piece of her mind and the return of his money."

Jennifer grasped the little maid's shoulders firmly. "You'll say nothing to Mr. Adrian, Daisy. Keep the money *and* out of his way." The maid's eyes snapped with protest. Jennifer gave her a shake. "For me, Daisy . . . do this for me. You say you owe me. All debts are cleared. Now, help me with my gloves."

When the long black lace covered her bare arms and was fastened securely just above her elbow, Jennifer knew she could wait no longer for her tardy husband's arrival. "Husband or no, I'll have to go downstairs."

"Most likely his train was delayed with it startin' to snow and all. No tellin' the weather where he's coming from. Let me go find your father or the master. It wouldn't do not to make a proper entrance on the arm of a handsome gentleman."

"Thank you, Daisy." For far more than I can ever repay—thank you.

While she waited for her escort, she tried to sit, but immediately popped out of the chair when the steel ribbing running from beneath her breasts to the middle of her hips gored her painfully at the bend of her disappearing waist. Two inches since that last fitting. Soon there would be no hiding it. After tonight she'd gladly become the pleasingly plump pregnant lady, eating whatever and whenever she wished. Already her head was beginning to ache, having forced herself to leave untouched the tray of food on the desk. She'd not dared add a single ounce for fear of being unable to fit into her dress at all.

A loud whistle from the doorway spun her around. "If your beauty doesn't blind a man, then the color of that dress surely will, Princess."

"Brazen bold I am, Mr. Douglas," she said with a smile. "But I'm more concerned about you. Look out for the maiden ladies and widows. One glance at the man from Montana with his roguish beard and those smoky gray eyes, and a stampede of females will be following you home. *If* they let you leave." She straightened his slightly crooked tie.

"Good. The territory could use more females—just as long as they leave me be." He looked disparagingly at the back of his evening coat and snorted. "Tails. Only thing they're good for is to swat flies."

"I love you, Daddy," she said fervently. "I don't want tomorrow to come."

He took both her hands and held them. Gray eyes looked deeply into silver flooding with tears. "The door to home will always be open, Jennifer . . . always. And I don't mean just to visit either."

"I know." Taking his arm, she retreated from the sanctuary he offered. "Shall we go?"

Halfway down the curving staircase, father and daughter paused to view the scene below. The entry hall was a bustle of activity. Servants dressed in dark gray uniforms with white starched aprons scrambled to take fur cloaks and silk top hats. The outer clothing was dusted with a fine layer of snow, which would keep other servants busy sweeping the outside walk and stairway clear throughout the evening. The rich and influential would not have slippers or gowns soiled by wet.

"Like to see some of these high-stepping nobs try to get through a Montana blizzard," James chuckled. Looking at his daughter's pinched face, he frowned. "Scared?"

"I'll race you back to my room," Jennifer whispered, her grip upon her father's arm tightening.

"Chin up, girl. We've been spotted now."

They continued their descent of the long curving staircase to mingle with Boston's finest. The gentlemen all wore the customary black evening wear, with only occasional variations of more elaborate waistcoats. The women, however, were a veritable kaleidoscope of colorful gowns, each one more elegant than the next.

Occasionally Jennifer would smile graciously and murmur greetings to familiar faces remembered from Allison's wedding. But as she and her father maneuvered through the crowd and stepped around planters overflowing with red and white poinsettias, she noted the heads twisting, necks craning while various expressions, depending on gender, flashed across the faces of strangers receiving their first glimpse of the woman who had married the black sheep Armbruster. The room seemed to vibrate with their reactions.

"I think you've got their attention," James muttered beneath his breath. Then, noting the nervous darting of her silver eyes and the slight quiver of her chin, he patted the hand resting upon his arm. "Honey, that's envy you see in their faces. I catch you ducking your chin, I'll put your posterior up between your shoulders with a swift kick. Walk proud, Jennifer Louise . . . always."

She flashed him a grateful smile that would melt many a heart throughout the remainder of the evening. The music grew louder and finally they arrived at the entrance of the ballroom.

"Jennifer . . . there you are." Eleanor Armbruster stood with her husband just inside the doorway. "You look stunning. Isn't she breathtaking, Aaron?"

"I expected no less," Aaron Armbruster replied, lifting a gloved hand to brush the knuckles with a courtly kiss. "Ravishing!" he added with a flourish and a wink.

Eleanor looked a queen in a gown of purple velvet embroidered with silver thread. Amethysts surrounded by diamonds circled her throat and wrists. And within the silvery white hair was a tiara that nearly blinded with its brilliance.

"Red is most definitely your color, my dear," Eleanor

assured before she was distracted by the arrival of other guests she had yet to welcome.

Moving into the room shimmering with the golden light of four huge crystal chandeliers, Jennifer tried to take a deep breath, but the vise about her waist made her see stars. The gilt-framed mirrors lining the walls of the room reflected the swirl of dancers as they dipped and turned to the music of a spirited waltz.

Cinderella at her first ball would have felt less awkward if her prince had been by her side. Adrian, with his smooth polished manners, would have made his wife's entry into high society a smooth one, rather than the embarrassing ordeal it was becoming. She would have been given introductions instead of curious stares and critical appraisal.

Servants moved throughout the crowd carrying silver trays laden with crystal goblets that sparkled with champagne. James halted one and lifted two glasses, handing one to Jennifer. "Fortify," he ordered, clinking his glass to hers.

"Where's Devlin?" she asked, trying to mask the agitation his mere name brought.

"Imagine he's found a corner to hug. Hard to hide though when you stand a head taller than the average. And the way he fills out his fancy clothes, he's not hard on the eyes—from a female point of view—if some of the reactions I've noticed are of any account."

"Grrr." The growl near her ear caused Jennifer to whirl, snapping her fan open to cover the deep décolletage revealed above her bodice. Then she closed the fan with a sigh of relief. "Stephen."

"You look . . . you look absolutely . . ." He searched for an appropriate description.

"Outrageous?" Jennifer supplied.

He laughed, producing that endearing lopsided grin. His brown eyes twinkled. "Obviously you haven't seen my wife. Compared to Allison, you look positively demure. For a minute, when we entered the ballroom, I was afraid Mother Eleanor would send her back to our room. There she is," he said, pointing discreetly toward the opposite side of the ballroom. "Still trying to coax your cowboy out onto the floor."

Jennifer had to stretch up on tiptoe, but Allison's flamboyant coloring made her easy to spot. On any other woman the deep-rose satin gown would have clashed with auburn tresses; only on Allison would that particular shade glorify her spectacular beauty. The plunge of the bodice, Jennifer noted with some relief, bordered on the scandalous. Stephen was right; her own gown was, in comparison, quite modest.

"See what I mean," Stephen said with a smug smile.

She didn't hear the pride in a husband's voice. The crowd parted, no longer impeding her vision of the man who continued to smile, shaking his head, until Allison threw up her hands and walked away.

As if by some invisible force, Devlin's eyes were drawn to Jennifer. The music and laughter faded into a distant humming as his long legs quickly closed the distance between them.

Vaguely Jennifer heard her father comment, "Take you back home in those duds, son, and we'll have to beat the women off with a club."

Impossible, she thought. This couldn't be the same man she'd always known. Always ruggedly handsome in dirty, sweat-stained work clothes, magnificent in his natural state, he was extraordinary dressed all in black, except for his shirt and white satin tie. It wasn't possible that his hair be more golden or eyes a more startling cobalt blue in his tanned face. His smile, so rare and beautiful, deepened the squint lines at the corners of his eyes, adding character.

"May I claim you for this waltz, Mrs. Armbruster?" The mellow, lilting voice set her heart singing before the actual question penetrated her mesmerized brain. "What?" she said stupidly, a witless expression on her face as she regarded the gloved palm he extended.

"Dance, Jennifer," he repeated. "I'm asking you to take the floor with me."

"You don't dance," she told him bluntly.

The grooves in his cheek deepened and his eyes glittered with the mocking laughter that made him seem less a stranger. "Trust me." He took the hand she refused to offer and gave it a gentle but firm tug.

Someone gave her a push from behind, and she heard Allison's tinkling laugh. "Get out there, Cowgirl. He's been saving himself only for you."

By the time Devlin's hand rested casually at her waist and he swung her into the circle of dancing couples, her face was nearly as crimson as the dress she wore. "You don't dance," she repeated firmly.

"Then what do you call this—an Irish jig?" He felt the confidence he had pretended slowly become a reality. Lottie had said he had a natural talent. For the last hour he'd watched the movements carefully. His steps were shorter, the turns more frequent, but if it weren't for his partner's graceless movements, he knew few could best him. "Quit your stumblin', Jenny girl. You're making me look bad."

"When . . . how did you ever learn to dance?" she asked incredulously.

"I just got tired of hearing about my extra left feet. Compared to breaking horses, learning a few steps to a waltz was easy."

"You do it very well," she complimented honestly.

"And you are the most beautiful, sensual woman I've ever seen."

Her head snapped back. "Don't," she said, her eyes nervously scanning the couples around them. The hand holding her own tightened.

"When you were just a wee sprout in pigtails and eyes that seemed to dominate your face, you knocked me right off that old nag Sam put me on in Cheyenne."

"You were a skinny, clumsy oaf who didn't know his own . . ." She paused. ". . . from the back of a horse."

"Don't change the subject," he said as he expertly dipped on the next turn, spinning her in a circle before blending once again with the other dancers. "Forgot how lovely you were when you started wearing those big, floppy hats and boy's duds two sizes too big. Then one day I was letting the fire take the chill from my bones. I opened my eyes and there you were with your hair pulled back so tight it looked like it might uproot."

"Oh, no you don't, McShane. I remember *that day* very well. You looked right through me, then brushed me aside without a single word."

"I saw . . . saw a girl turning into a woman. Woman enough to nearly pop the buttons off her dress and beautiful enough to shock a man dumb. If I'd tried to say something that day, my voice would have cracked like it did when all my trousers turned to knee pants in the space of six months." His thumb was gently caressing her palm. "That was my first mistake. I should have jumped on Shannon right then. Should have ridden as far and as fast—"

"First mistake?" she said softly, torturing him as well as herself with these best-forgotten memories. Perhaps if they were voiced they might be purged. "Have you made others?"

"Second was when I didn't claim you beside a pretty little creek in the thick grass." His voice was a husky rasp. He felt her steps falter, heard the music build to a crescendo and then conclude on the gentle notes of violins. She did not look at him when they moved off the floor. "I'm still working on mistake number three. That one should hold me the rest of my life."

"And you said you were awkward," Allison chided Devlin. "You dance beautifully, Dev."

"I have the right partner," he answered. "Excuse me."

He was gone, disappearing into the throng while Jennifer twisted her fan, fighting an ache that knotted her heart.

"Oh, look, Jenny. One of your plumes is coming loose. Let's go upstairs. I'm certain it can be fixed." Allison was dragging her friend out of the room, through the kitchen, and up the back staircase. "For God's sake. You two are going to melt that room downstairs. Stubborn idiot. Told you how it was between two people who were born to be together. But would you listen? No . . . you had to run off with Adrian."

"Stop it!" Jennifer jerked back on Allison's hand. "He

didn't want me. Sent me away like I was just a pest." She found herself pushed into Allison's room. "Forbidden fruit is always the sweetest, don't they say? Now that it's too late—"

"Let it fly, Cowgirl," Allison said, taking command. "You've got it all bottled up inside. You'll explode if you don't let go of all those feelings."

Jennifer shook her head violently. "I won't lose control. He'll leave tomorrow and everything will go back to normal. Dammit, Allie, he's turned my life upside down since the day Daddy brought him home. We're poison for one another. Fight, fight, fight. And when we weren't fighting—"

"You were loving?" Allison said gently, curving her arm around her friend's shoulders.

"I love them both, Allie. Differently, perhaps, but God help me, I love them both." Closing her eyes, Jennifer pressed her lips together to keep those deeper secrets from being spoken. "Adrian is my husband," she reasserted, "and the father of my unborn child."

Allison gasped, her arm tightening about Jennifer's shoulder. She said nothing, there was nothing that she could say. Jennifer would never leave Adrian now. She wouldn't be the person Allison knew her to be if she did. "Shall we rejoin the others?"

"Adrian doesn't know about the baby. Please keep my secret for the time being."

With a nod Allison agreed, and together they returned to the crowded ballroom. They had barely stepped inside the room when they saw Adrian making his way toward them.

"Speak of the devil," Allison said with her customary sarcasm.

He looked resplendent in his evening clothes. Jennifer braced herself against an expected attack, noting the strain around her mouth and eyes, the ashen hue of his face. But as he closed the distance between them, he extended his hands, reaching for and receiving her own, squeezing them tightly before he pressed his lips to her cheek.

"How is it possible," he said silkily, sincerely, "that you could have grown more beautiful in a week?"

There was no hint of anger or jealousy in the glowing amber eyes. His smile declared that he was genuinely happy to see her. With only mild apprehension, she allowed him to draw her away from Allison's protective presence.

"I'm sorry to arrive so late, darling. This snowstorm interfered with the trains, and I had the devil of a time persuading a cabbie to drive me out. Am I all together? I dressed hurriedly at home while the cab waited."

"I should have sent Jenkins for you," she apologized, any remaining tension leaving her body when his arm slid around her waist.

"You couldn't have predicted the weather," he excused magnanimously. "God, how I've missed you. My resolution for the new year is never to get involved in any business with Delaney again. The man is unreasonable."

"Hush, darling," she admonished as he escorted her across the wide room. "He's here, you know, with his wife and"—the name seemed to catch in her throat—"with Erica."

"What?" Adrian fairly shouted with indignation and disbelief. "Delaney here! How can that be?"

"I suppose it was Uncle Aaron's gesture to you. You are business associates, and I imagine he was added to the guest list in deference to that."

"Good God! I'll not acknowledge him if our paths should cross this evening. He's completely unprincipled. But please, my love, don't act the typical wife and say you warned me not to get involved with that man." Adrian attempted a teasing tone, but it was clear he was shaken by the turn of events.

"How could I do that? I never said any such thing. Although I did *think* it rather loudly."

Jennifer was perplexed by Adrian's loving attentiveness. Had Daisy lied? Had the maid cleverly tried to divert Jennifer from discovering her true purpose yesterday afternoon?

When they reached her father and Devlin, the two men were just starting toward the buffet. The warmth in Adrian's greetings further convinced Jennifer that Daisy had, for whatever reason, manufactured the entire tale about her husband's lack of faith. She vowed to give the girl a tongue-lashing she'd not soon forget.

"Mr. Douglas," she heard Adrian say as they moved toward the table laden with delicacies to tempt any palate, "when I was in Buffalo, I happened upon a rather interesting bit of information regarding a paper mill. Because of illness, the owners are being forced to sell out at a most reasonable price. For some reason I thought of you when I heard of this. You have holdings outside the ranch, don't you?"

"According to my attorney, the list is endless," James exaggerated, the champagne already going to his head.

Jennifer watched Adrian skillfully cut James out of the group and away from the buffet.

"Let me give you some of the details," Adrian's voice drifted back.

"Certainly," James was heard to answer. "Any business of that nature is handled by my lawyer. I'll gladly give a listen, though."

"Jen." Devlin's deep voice was harsh, a gut-ripping sound.

She refused to look at him, keeping her eyes fixed on Allison's concerned face. There was no way she could meet his gaze and not reveal the tearing battle going on inside her heart. She felt him move nearer, felt the touch of his fingers on her elbow, and the pressure of those strong fingers was not one-tenth the agony in her chest.

She sent a mute appeal to Allison, but it was Erica Delaney who came to her rescue, slithering up beside Devlin to appraise him with violet eyes turning a lustful purple.

"Jennifer, dear friend," Erica purred huskily. "Introduce me to this handsome gentleman."

With a tight smile, Jennifer performed the courtesy. Part

of her was grateful for Erica's timely intervention; most of her wanted to claw out those covetous violet eyes. Not once did she look at Devlin to gauge his reaction to this brazenly sensual female. She allowed Erica to whisk him away without a whimper of protest.

Allison stepped forward. "The way that woman drools and pants, I don't see how she keeps the saliva from dripping off her chin."

Normally Jennifer would have laughed. But it wasn't funny, not a damn bit.

With the approach of midnight, Jennifer found it increasingly difficult to maintain the smile she forced until her jaws ached. Every pin holding the thick mass of her hair atop her head seemed a spike. The stays of her corset held her their agonized prisoner, making sitting a torture, and when she stood a heavy pressure, lodged at the juncture of her thighs, intensified with each passing moment. She knew nothing about the normal aches of pregnancy, but having experienced a milder form of this discomfort before, she was not unduly concerned.

Loath to cause her father anxiety or bring unwanted attention to herself, Jennifer remained among the guests although the music and noise pounded maliciously inside her head and the heaviness in her groin was close to real pain. Finally, seeing that James's attention was occupied by an attractive widow, Jennifer began her journey across the crowded room. Devlin was nowhere to be seen and she didn't even look for Adrian, who had, much to her relief, chosen not to hover at her side this evening. She doubted her ability to hide her physical and emotional distress beneath his persistent amber gaze.

The mere act of putting one foot in front of the other proved more difficult than she anticipated. Often she was forced to veer around clusters of animated guests; the press of the crowd and the slow progress across the room made her increasingly anxious and desperate. With an alarming suddenness, she felt truly ill.

357

Dizzy from her efforts, she reached the hallway at last. The open door to the library seemed to beckon. Inside she would find dark, quiet, and a long, cushioned sofa.

Inching her way toward sanctuary, she felt tears of relief when she finally stood in the doorway, savoring the cool darkness, the relief from the music that had become merely noise, and the privacy of the room before her. Slowly the tension eased from her body and the unbearable aching seemed to abate as her muscles relaxed one by one.

Jennifer was never quite certain how much time had passed before sounds, muted but distinct, drew her eyes toward the window bay. Her eyes, having adjusted to the dark, saw two figures sharply outlined against the strange illumination that always accompanies snow. Not embracing, they stood apart, a male head often dipping downward toward jutting breasts with hard, elongated nipples.

Unbelieving, Jennifer swallowed hard as she watched, in almost paralyzed fascination, the stroking manipulations upon the aroused male's thrusting organ. Gurgling sounds of pleasure often accompanied each dip or caressing pull.

"Now, lover, now," came the throaty female plea, somehow familiar, recognition on a plane just out of reach.

There was the rustle of cloth as skirts and taffeta petticoats lifted, the slow, unhurried sinking downward until the male was swallowed by darkness and only the curl-clustered head of the female was visible, thrown back, the mouth slack.

"Yes . . . yes . . . deep, so deep. Harder, lover."

It was the almost feral snarl of pleasure that brought voice and face together in Jennifer's mind. Quickly, she turned and fled that room, nausea nearly overcoming her. Staggering, she might have fallen but for the hands that pushed her upright. Lifting her head, she looked into Sean Delaney's murderous gaze.

"Have you seen my daughter?" His voice cut through her like a thousand knives, and she shook her head with a whispered "No." When he would have pushed her aside to continue toward the library, she managed the strength to block him. "No," she said more firmly. "I've just come from there. It's empty." Oh, God, let the world stop spinning so I can prevent murder.

Then Helen Delaney's face was wavering before her own, the voice sounding as if coming toward her through a long tunnel. "Help me find her before my husband does. He'll kill that young man if he finds them together. You don't know her, Jennifer. She's not like other women. She's . . . she's . . . not natural."

Clutching at the small woman, she tried to grasp on to something to keep herself from falling into oblivion. "Sorry, Helen . . . can't think clearly . . . my head . . . awhirl."

"Your father's young man. Erica left the dance floor with him an hour ago. She's not been seen since. Oh, Lord, I'm afraid Sean will kill them both." Too absorbed by her own distress, Helen did not see an already ashen complexion blanch chalk white.

Devlin . . . Erica. He'd found what he had needed, what she would not grant him. "My room," Jennifer whispered, making it sound like a prayer. "Just let me get to my room."

Everything around her seemed unreal. She pushed through the crowd in the hallway, ignoring a servant who paused with her tray of hors d'oeuvres to inquire if she needed assistance.

Reaching the staircase, she took a firm grip on the carved railing and pulled herself up one step, and then another, and another, stopping occasionally when the pain she'd experienced earlier robbed her of breath. Soon both hands were needed to pull, one after the other, knuckles white in a viselike hold. She was near the landing when she felt her strength flag. Looking up to gauge the remaining distance, she saw the figure above her, a shape wavering in the blinding brilliance of a huge chandelier. As her knees gave way, she released one hand to implore.

The figure swooped downward—the hawk, talons gripping, jerking her free of the earth to soar upward toward the sun.

He had died a thousand deaths before reaching the swaying figure upon the stairs, clutching at a fistful of her skirt only breathless seconds before she would have taken that deadly backward plunge. Catching her against him, he'd swept her into his arms in a single motion.

Willing his racing heart to stop pounding, Devlin shifted the near-unconscious form in his arms to open the bedroom door. Kicking it shut behind him, he needed only three steps to place her in the middle of the bed.

"Jen?" His voice was strained with alarm. Her skin was like ice, her lashes fluttered against a face pale as death. The pulse at the base of her throat was rapid, matching the swift rise and fall of her breasts. Twisting, he turned up the wick within the oil lamp beside the bed, cursing continuously until he found matches and the dim figure upon the bed could be viewed in the light.

One touch discovered the ridges of steel running the length of her body from beneath her breasts to her hips. "Goddamn," he spat violently. "Stupid damn woman. Kill yourself for vanity. Dumbest thing you've attempted yet. You better hope there's more wrong with you than that hellish corset, woman . . . I'll beat you black and blue. . . ."

His fear made him irrational. All the while he was cursing the corset, he prayed for her recovery once he got the damned thing off her. When the tiny loops and buttons on her dress impeded his progress, he ripped them from the cloth. There was nothing gentle in the way he jerked the shredded material down over her hips and tossed it carelessly across the room.

His hands, however, were not so sure when they encountered the many ties, laces, hooks, and fasteners of a garment beyond his experience. "Damn it, Jen. Wake up and help me get you out of this contraption."

The strangled gasp from the opposite side of the room brought his head around as he straddled the limp form, pulling and tugging in vain. "Allison!" he shouted, flying off the bed just as the door closed behind the woman in rose satin.

In seconds he was through the door and dragging her back into the room. "Not what it looks . . . she's ill. I'm trying to get that corset off."

"Jenny?" Allison asked softly, one look at her friend's color affirming Devlin's claim. Nimble fingers easily released the constricting garment. "Breathe for me. That's a girl.

"Her color is getting better, but she's still unconscious," Allison observed, rubbing Jennifer's diaphragm with gentle strokes to urge her body to take in the much-needed oxygen. "What happened?"

"I don't know. The noise and the crowds were wearing me down. Came upstairs for some quiet. I was going back down . . ." The vivid memory made him shudder. "If I'd been a second later the fall would have killed her."

"Sit with her a minute," Allison ordered, sliding from the bed. "I'll get Mother's salts."

Devlin lifted Jennifer's shoulders and pulled her across his legs. At this moment he didn't give a dollop of horse dung if the entire assemblage downstairs decided to parade in and out of this room. Checking her throat, he was relieved to find that her pulse had slowed. A hand on her chest told him her breathing had returned to normal.

There was soft rustling nearby, and Devlin looked up into emerald eyes swimming with tears. "You love her," Allison said simply; it was a statement of fact that required neither confirmation nor denial. He reached for the salts. Removing the cork with his teeth, his own head jerked back in reaction to the ammonia.

One pass beneath her nose sent Jennifer rolling. She buried her face against something warm, burrowing and nuzzling until it was Devlin who was choking on an embarrassed gasp. With a quick movement, he shifted her higher so that her cheek rested against his chest. When he would have used the ammonia a second time, he felt her arch away.

"Are you going to snap out of it, Jenny girl? Or do I have to slap you into daylight?"

"You and how many others?" Her words were muffled against his shirt.

"Christ . . ." he grumbled. "Scare the living hell out of me and then you've got the . . . got the . . ." What he wanted to say wasn't appropriate for mixed company nor did it accurately apply. "You've got a lot of cheek," he substituted.

Suddenly her head reared off his chest and she sat up. Her eyes were wide, fingers covered her mouth. "I'm going to be sick."

Faster than he'd thought it possible for any human to move, Allison had dumped dried flowers out of a wide crystal vase and was shoving it beneath Jennifer's chin.

For the next few moments Allison and Devlin worked as a team, but when Jennifer slumped back, trembling and weak, against the man who had been her support while her stomach heaved impotently, Allison moved away. Placing the vase within reach, she said, "I'll wait outside the door. I can't give you much time. Five minutes, maybe ten . . . less if someone should come."

"I understand," Devlin said, his eyes speaking the gratitude he couldn't express.

When the door closed, he inched his way backward until his upper body rested flat against the headboard. Spreading his legs, he settled Jennifer between his thighs, both arms reaching around her waist. His hands rested lightly just above her waist. "Better now?"

Jennifer twisted her shoulders until she was able to look into his face. "It was not you in the library. You were on the stairs, the hawk I imagined. The dream . . . I know it now. At least I can remember most of it. The closed-in, trapped panic. The hawk. You're the hawk, and we're soaring across the sky, flying higher, close to the sun. But it's too bright, and I turn away. Then I'm surrounded by gigantic rocks, and there's no escape. It gets darker and darker and they seem to come closer. . . ."

She trembled and lay back so that her head rested in the groove between his neck and shoulder, giving him a clear view of her heaving breasts. Past the plunging neckline of her thin chemise he could see the periphery of the dusky-rose aureole surrounding her nipple, the bluish veins beneath translucently pale flesh. The memory of her womanly beauty was emblazoned upon his mind, but it was a disturbing memory.

The girl he had caressed had not possessed the ample bounty he now viewed, although her breasts then had been more than adequate to fill a man's hands and his dreams, tipped with the palest, sweetest pink. Slowly, so not to upset or startle, he moved his hands downward until they were spread across the rounded swell of her once-flat stomach. His eyes closed tightly when her small hands rested atop his own. "When?" he rasped in an agonized voice.

"Early summer if my calculations are correct." She didn't pretend not to understand.

"Oh, my Jenny girl. Damn my stupid pride, and the fear you'd think the land meant more than—"

"Shhh." She turned in his arms, pressing her fingers against his lips. "Don't say it. I don't want to hear the echo of it inside my head for all the years to come. Already we've said too much, too late."

"No, I won't accept—" His denial was stopped by her lips. Her arms circled his neck and her fingers threaded into the thick hair at the base of his collar. It was a kiss of finality . . . of good-bye.

Lifting her head, Jennifer lightly fluffed the overlong hair. Her fingers traced the arrow-straight line of his brow, the arrogant nose, the strong-boned cheeks and stubborn line of jaw.

"Take Silver Creek, Devlin Michael McShane. Raise your devil horses. And someday . . . someday take a woman who will give you sons with Irish blue eyes."

A loud rap on the door warned them before Allison stepped back inside. "Devlin," she said. "You have to go now."

Moving to the edge of the bed, Devlin looked back at the woman sitting in the middle of the mattress, her legs folded Indian style while she stared at the hands lying limp upon her thighs.

"I'll not say good-bye to you," he croaked. "Maybe on that someday . . . but not this day or tomorrow. Not yet."

When he was gone, Allison quietly asked, "Do you want company?" Jennifer could only shake her head. "Should I find Adrian? He'll wonder where you've disappeared."

"I doubt that. But if you see him, tell him I was feeling ill and retired early."

"Are you certain, Cowgirl? Are you absolutely certain this is right?"

"A man deserves to be part of his child's life. And the child should know the father," she said firmly with dry, unwavering eyes. This had not been a decision of pride or high-minded sacrifice. Within Jennifer's mind there had never been a choice.

The Boston station was crowded on this New Year's Day. Weary holiday travelers, arriving and departing, surrounded the young woman clinging to the bearded man, fighting sobs and losing the battle despite her valiant but tremulous smile.

"Princess," James soothed, his own voice thick with unshed tears. "Dry those eyes and don't think about anything else except how soon it will be summer. I'm going to hold you to that promise you'll come home." He lowered his voice to a croaked whisper. "Bring my grandson so we can spoil him rotten."

She strangled on a frustrated laugh, thumping his arm with her fist. "Just for spite, I think I'll disappoint you." His certainty that her child would be a boy, despite her argument to the contrary, had become a subject for gentle teasing.

James hugged her fiercely. "You know it would be impossible to disappoint me, don't you?"

She nodded, and he dried the moisture on her cheeks with gentle fingers. Her child, be it boy or girl, would be welcomed with only joy. "Give Maggie and Sam my love," she whispered as he withdrew and turned to Adrian.

The two men shook hands. "It's been a pleasure having you, Mr. Douglas . . . James. Do give some serious thought to that mill, won't you?"

For James the subject of the paper mill had been so talked

to tedium that suspicion overrode any earlier interest. He'd leave it to Grayburn.

"I can be reached at the bank. Have your man telephone if he needs more information." Panic held Adrian in its terrible grip even as reason cautioned him not to overplay his hand. If Douglas didn't bail him out . . .

Jennifer heard the conversation between her husband and father, saw James draw Adrian away until she and Devlin were alone, or as alone as any two people could be amidst the teeming crowd assembling to board the two thirty train for New York. Neither spoke; there was nothing more to be said. The indifferent observer would have assumed them strangers. Both wore expressions of granite, although one face was a little pale, the other so tightly drawn a muscle leaped convulsively in the cheek. Only their eyes were alive, eloquent. Both flinched visibly when the conductor shouted the final call for boarding.

Devlin stepped forward. Taking Jennifer's hand, he pressed a small wadded bundle of tissue paper into her palm. Then, without speaking, he turned and walked directly to the train.

Eternity passed until a husband's arm led her from the station and home to the stony dwelling amidst other stony dwellings that were the essence of her nightmare. But it was when she closed herself in the bedroom, after sending Adrian to seek the more cheerful companionship of his club, that Jennifer knew the enormity and the terrible pain of her rash, youthful mutiny.

From the tissue she lifted a silver chain, gasping as the shamrock amulet caught the afternoon light. She recognized the necklace she'd admired as a child; it had been the cause of the first clash between herself and the boy her father had brought home.

"Keep yer grimy mitts off me mother's chain!" he'd screamed when he caught her admiring the crudely fashioned pendant.

What a brat she'd been, screaming as if she'd been struck until Maggie and her father rushed through the door. But in the end it had been her voice choking out an apology.

With trembling fingers, Jennifer unfolded the paper accompanying Maureen McShane's necklace.

"Silver for Silver Creek," he'd written in an unsteady hand. "A fair exchange to be held in trust until the day when *someday* is an unavoidable certainty. For now, accept this as a token of faith that I will be guardian of what you treasure, as you now hold what is most precious to me."

"Oh, Dev," she whispered on a sob, crumbling across the bed. There were no tears. Someday was now.

Chapter Thirty-One

Adrian ducked his chin, pulling the collar of his topcoat higher to shield his face from the wet spray blowing in off the Atlantic. He pulled a flask from his pocket, drinking deeply. Only the liquor made the waiting bearable.

He shifted, gritting his teeth as the rocky sea wall gouged his buttocks through the layers of his clothing. He tucked his hands beneath his armpits to warm them. Behind him the loud music and bright lights from Todd's casino gave no hint that dawn was near, although the sky did appear less black, the stars less distinct. It was a gauge of his desperation that he stood in the freezing cold at four o'clock in the morning outside Frank Todd's exclusive gambling house because he'd been left with nowhere else to turn.

Arthur Grayburn, that sniveling attorney representing his father-in-law, had been openly contemptuous of Adrian's attempt to involve James Douglas in what he termed a careless and ill-fated business venture.

Even his last resort—an appeal to his uncle—had been snatched from him when some high-minded idealist had informed Aaron Armbruster of his nephew's unprincipled use of privileged information. The old man reacted with shock and disappointment, cutting him off entirely.

Adrian had no doubt of the identity of the man behind Uncle Aaron's informant. He also strongly suspected that Sean Delaney had counted upon Adrian's last-ditch attempt to resolve his difficulties by turning to Todd. Surely he knew that any bargain with the devil would come at a high price when all a man had for collateral was his soul.

He damned himself for a stupid ass. For thirty-three years he'd lived by his wits, surviving on cunning and charm, needing no one, caring about no one. He'd been the user, not the used. He had even beaten Frank Todd at his own game by paying off the debts that would have sucked him into Todd's web. Now the fly was about to crawl to the spider, on his hands and knees if necessary.

Lowell had issued an ultimatum: Adrian could meet his contractual obligations or expect a visit from the Boston police.

It was the deep orange-red sliver of the sun appearing at the edge of the horizon that reminded Adrian of his purpose. He glanced over his shoulder at the converted mansion. How long since the music had been silenced and the lights extinguished?

His body wracked with shudders only partly attributable to the frigid temperature, Adrian dragged his feet through the sand. With joints stiff and aching from the long wait, he climbed the narrow back staircase. When he reached the door where his welcome was uncertain, Adrian fought the impulse to run. Finally he pounded on the thick wood until the entire side of his fist was numb. After what seemed an eternity, the back entrance was jerked open abruptly; Adrian nearly fell across the threshold. He was pushed back, and a cry of fright burst from his throat as he looked upon the apparition towering over him.

"What do you want?" The ugly face illuminated by the lantern held beneath an angry chin appeared inhuman.

"Need . . . need to see Todd," Adrian stuttered. "Tell him Armbruster."

"Mr. Todd don't see nobody this hour. Get gone."

The door was closing, his final hope about to be slammed in his face. "Wait!" he nearly screamed like a hysterical female.

"What is the problem, Harry?" The sultry female voice brought a resurgence of determination.

"Carlotta, it's Adrian. Let me in, for God's sake!"

His head was spinning from a sudden rush of anxiety. His knees were about to buckle when he was rudely jerked upright and hauled inside, then slammed down hard upon a narrow chair.

"Well, well. Look what washed up on our beach tonight," the woman drawled. "Harry, see to the lights on your way out."

"I don't know, Miss Carlotta. What's the boss—"

"I'll explain to Mr. Todd, Harry. Go back to bed."

Light flooded the room, temporarily blinding Adrian. He started visibly when he felt the light touch of a hand on his face. "You look like very hell," the woman called Carlotta observed, moving back as those golden eyes blinked, adjusted to the brightness, and then took a slow and careful inventory of her voluptuous form barely concealed beneath the loosely belted silk wrapper.

Men had been known to give up fortunes, and their self-respect, to spend a single night with this black-haired, black-eyed enchantress. Without question they'd felt no sacrifice was too high. Carlotta was the highest priced, most exclusive whore in this part of the world. But in the end, a whore is a whore, whether she be wife, mother, fiancée, or of the more honest variety. Adrian had no patience with any of them. "I want to see Frank, Carlotta."

"You've lost your mind as well," she said roughly, spinning away to hide the sharp pain in her heart caused by his disinterest. Of all the men she'd had—and they were legion—this was the only one she had ever wanted to keep.

"Will he see me?" Adrian's voice was a harsh rasp.

Carlotta turned slowly, leaning forward, uncaring that her wrapper gaped open to the navel. "For your soul, darling. But you already knew that. Take yourself out of here while you still can, pretty man. You're free." She gripped his shoulders. "Stay free, damn you!"

"Love." A cool, whisper-soft voice capable of turning blood to ice spoke from the doorway. "Don't be so hasty to chase old friends out into a cold dawn."

"Hello, Frank." Adrian pushed Carlotta away, rising slowly to meet Todd's cold, appraising stare.

"Is it business or pleasure that brings you to my door after so long an absence?"

"Business," Adrian replied quickly when Frank's dark eyes rested pointedly on Carlotta. "I—I could use your advice on a problem that's developed."

Todd grinned humorlessly. "Really? How intriguing. Shall we adjourn to my office to discuss this little difficulty?"

He motioned, and Adrian followed on trembling limbs. Why did every instinct in his body tell him that his visit had not surprised Frank Todd in the least?

Full daylight streamed through his bedroom window as Adrian stood staring down at his still-sleeping wife. Even now she was undoubtedly the most beautiful woman he'd known. Once, just looking at her would have brought a scalding flood of desire to his loins. Now there was nothing, and never had anything terrified him more.

With a determined set of his jaw he moved away and stripped down to his trousers. He removed his shoes, letting them drop to the floor with a thud.

Jennifer stirred, her eyes opening just as Adrian's trousers slid to the floor and he walked naked to stand beside their bed. The quick intake of her breath and the closing of her teeth upon her bottom lip was an involuntary response before her will could conquer her aversion to his obvious intent.

"Good morning," she managed. "Have you been out? What time is it?" She struggled to sit up, but was pushed back down onto the pillow by a firm hand. The bed dipped beneath his weight.

His fingers yanked and pulled the ribbons down the front of her high-necked gown. "Adrian, I need to relieve myself." She was full to bursting. "In a minute," he scowled. The neck of the gown parted, and he lowered his head to press his lips to her warm flesh. Immediately he jerked back when his cheek brushed against something cold and metallic hiding just beneath the edges of her gown.

"What's this?" His fingers slid beneath the crudely fashioned chain, lifting it free.

370

"A gift from my father, a family heirloom." She rushed through the lie, unable to meet his gaze. "Adrian, darling, I'm really quite uncomfortable. If you'll just let me rise for a moment . . ."

The plea died in her throat as the links of silver cut into the back of her neck. "Adrian?" He instantly released the necklace at her pained cry.

"Sorry, my love. Did I hurt you?" He was shoving her nightgown off her shoulders, baring her to the waist, feeling a gratifying pulse stir in his groin while he stared at that silver eyesore between her breasts, the shamrock charm that marked his wife an adulteress. Family heirloom indeed. He looked at her then, letting her see his disbelief, watching her eyes widen and then close, the silky black lashes fluttering revealingly upon cheeks pale with a silent admission of guilt.

He ripped the coverlet off her stiff body, shoving her thighs apart, positioning himself. She lay like a sacrificial lamb. He ignored the tears on her cheeks. His mouth swooped down to ravage her breasts while an inner eye saw another mouth feasting, other hands, darkly bronzed workman's hands, gliding over the milk-white pointed globes.

"Please . . . don't . . ." she begged. "Not like this."

He laughed, a mirthless sound, and she looked into eyes empty of humanity. "Adrian, listen to me. There's something you don't know—"

Without mercy he drove himself deep into her resisting body, powerful, enormously strong, huge and potent in his lust for retribution.

Her screams of pain never penetrated his consciousness as he was sucked into a black, spinning whirlpool of lost illusions and hideously grinning faces, all of them waiting to welcome him to hell.

PART V

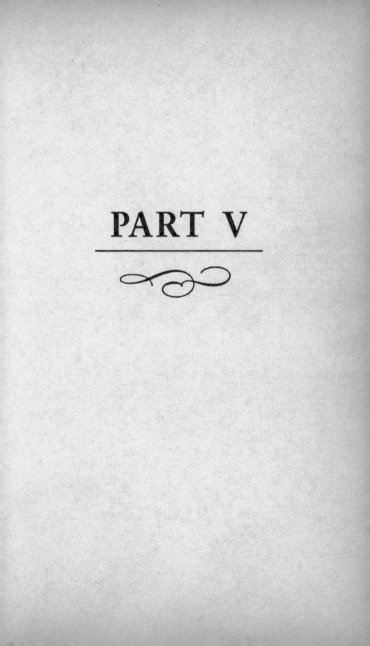

Chapter Thirty-Two

The March winds buffeted the branches of Mr. What's-his-name's pin oaks, forcing the tenacious nut-brown leaves to quit their moorings. They were ripped away to dance upon the wind, for a time buoyant, rising and falling on a cold breath that played with them as a child would keep a feather airborne. Then suddenly old man winter would tire of his game, and with a final ferocious blast, the leaves would be slammed hard against the earth and swept into clusters huddled against the hedge.

Nature was forcing the old to give way so it could begin the process of renewal. And for Jennifer, as she sat in her chair by the window, every subtle change was a glory, a miracle never again to be taken for granted.

She no longer yearned to feel that biting wind upon her face or fill her lungs with its rain-scented sweetness. It was enough for now that she could look out at God's panorama through paned glass while her unborn child did somersaults within her womb.

"You haven't touched your tea, madame," Mrs. Johnson observed, her expression clearly disapproving.

"It's grown quite cold, Mrs. Johnson," Jennifer countered; it was a feeble rebellion in a battle she'd already lost.

"Then I'll have Celia warm it for you."

With a speaking glance, Jennifer downed the tepid chamomile tea, shuddering and pulling a face. "Chamomile to restore me. Asafetida tincture to calm me. No doubt when

Dr. Marshall makes his weekly call this afternoon, the two of you will concoct more tortures for my palate."

"Without doubt, child." Fleshless arms with the strength of a Goliath easily pulled Jennifer from the chair she was always loath to leave. "But then you make such a willing victim for our practice of the black arts."

Cautious steps were taken on legs weakened from weeks of inactivity. Only rigorous daily massage kept her muscles firm and supple enough to make this short journey.

When she had been tucked beneath fresh, lavender-scented linens, Jennifer's eyes automatically closed. "Weak as a cat," she mumbled, sinking deeply into the pillows. Who would believe that the girl who had never willingly walked when she could run would be completely drained of energy from the daily routine of bed-bath and a twenty-minute respite in a chair while the housekeeper made the ivory tower she had always shunned as pleasant and sweet-smelling as possible.

When Agatha Johnson left her sleeping mistress and entered the kitchen, three heads snapped toward her and spoke in unison. "How is she?"

"Brave as Saint Joan. Never a complaint. Oh, I do hope Dr. Marshall will give that child some encouragement."

Jenkins stirred his coffee, looking into its depths for assurances only God could give. "The doctor doesn't want to raise hope. From the beginning he's said it was doubtful she'd carry the child. . . ."

"Well, she's already gone longer than the doctor expected," Celia snipped. "She's got determination—that's what it is—and many a battle it's won, Mr. Know-It-All-Jenkins."

Smiles were smothered at this heated defense. The attitude of the shrewish cook had made a complete turnabout. She painstakingly followed Dr. Marshall's instructions on diet, and were it possible, she would have guarded her mistress's health with her massive girth while wielding a heavy wooden spoon.

And although these people took their pay from and provided service to Master Adrian, they condemned him in their hearts for his neglect of that sweet, brave young woman. Not one would do more than step over his lifeless body if he dropped dead in the middle of the floor.

"Celia," Mrs. Johnson instructed. "Mrs. Shepherd will no doubt be close on Dr. Marshall's heels as is her habit. Please see to it that there are cakes and cookies for tea."

Harold Johnson slipped his arm around his wife's waist as they left the kitchen. Giving her an affectionate squeeze, he allowed her a few moments of quiet tears before they continued their daily activities. Few but the husband would have suspected that beneath Agatha Johnson's black bombazine bodice beat the warm heart of a mother hen. All the love and care she would have lavished on the child they could never have made Agatha Johnson a most devoted and determined nurse.

Soon the house bustled with customary activity. The world continued to revolve at its normal pace. Except for the woman upstairs who waited while every second became an hour and every hour the length of a day.

Oblivious to the curious stares and admiring glances following the sway of her hips, Erica Delaney cut an unwavering path through the crowded lobby of the bank, her heels clicking rapidly on the polished marble floors. A desperate determination overruled pride or propriety. She turned the doorknob, stepped inside Adrian's office, and closed the door softly behind her.

"My, my . . . aren't you the model of the respectable banker." She laughed. When Adrian continued to ignore her, she casually pulled off her gloves and tossed them atop the stack of papers he pretended to study.

"What do you want, Erica?" he said with bored indifference, picking up her gloves as if they were infested with vermin to drop them over the front edge of his desk.

Undaunted, Erica leaned forward, her eyes hard. "I want a few minutes of your precious time, lover."

A cool smile spread across his face. "Would you be offended if I honestly said that any time with you would be a total waste?"

"Listen, you bastard," she snarled. "You'll give me what I need, when I want it, or I'll see your name blackened in every corner of this city and beyond."

"That would be redundant. I believe your father's already seen to that."

Erica changed her tone and tactics. "Give me an hour, Adrian. One hour, and I won't make any trouble for you, I promise." She extended her hands in a supplicating manner. "Please. For old times' sake."

There was a quality in her tone that piqued curiosity. That she would humble herself stroked his ego.

"All right, Erica." He scribbled an address on a scrap of paper. "I'll meet you there in thirty minutes. Wait outside."

"You continue to surprise me, Mrs. Armbruster." Dr. Marshall beamed, patting the protruding stomach. "That baby seems to continue to flourish in defiance of every medical rule I know. Nonetheless . . ."

"I know. Don't get my hopes up too high."

The white-haired physician took his patient's hand and patted it in a fatherly fashion. "As I've told you—each month the child remains in your womb, the chances of its survival outside that protected environment increase. But so also does the risk of premature labor and a life-threatening hemorrhage." Releasing his patient's hand, the gaunt doctor began packing the tools of his trade into the black satchel. He dared a glance and caught the stricken expression flickering on the young woman's face. Rubbing the bridge of his nose, he shut his eyes tightly before once again facing his young patient. "You've always demanded total honesty, Mrs. Armbruster. As I've explained before, the fetal sac has mislocated itself low within the walls of the womb. With every passing month the growth of the infant puts pressure on the neck—" He stopped, and his naturally gruff voice softened. "Never have I guaranteed you could carry this infant to term. All we can do is pray."

Swallowing the useless tears clogged in her throat, Jennifer nodded. "If I . . . if I should lose the child and survive the birth—" She balled her hands into fists. It had taken her three months to work up the courage to ask this question. "Will there be other children?"

He was thoughtful, knowing his silence was not reassuring, yet wanting to be candid within the bounds of his limited knowledge. "At this time, there is no reason to believe that you won't give birth to half a dozen healthy children. But until this child is delivered and I can make a more thorough examination—I wish I could give you the positive response you need."

She managed something resembling a grin. "Pessimistically optimistic, as usual, Dr. Marshall."

Dr. Marshall pulled his watch from his waistcoat pocket and flipped it open. "Already behind schedule, and I've still got to report to Mrs. Shepherd and your housekeeper. One more thing—" He stopped at the door. "It has been reported to me that you've taken to lapsing into long brooding silences recently. Now, I'd be remiss in my duty if I did not consider my patient's mental as well as physical well-being. If, and I do mean if, you are doing equally well next week I will give permission for your transport to the parlor for a few hours several times a week."

Jennifer's entire face lit up, a bright flame in a room long dark. But she sobered instantly at the doctor's pursed lips.

"I'm only granting you a change in location. The restrictions on your movements will remain unaltered. And should there be any complications from what some would consider an ill-advised—"

"Back to the ivory tower to remain for the duration."

His lips twitched. "Good day, Mrs. Armbruster."

A quarter of an hour later Allison popped through the door of Jennifer's room. Her vibrancy animated the somber scene.

"Well, well, Cowgirl. Our good Dr. Marshall seems to think you defy all laws of medical probability." She plopped down on the edge of the bed, dropping the sackcloth bag she always brought with her on the floor near her feet.

"Surely you've known me long enough to realize I rarely

do anything according to accepted formula," Jennifer retorted, scooting backward in the bed, using her elbows to lever herself higher up on the pillow. When Allison would have assisted her, she threw out a hand. "No. I've got to do some things for myself. When the day comes that I can't scoot, roll, or flip and flop in this bed, please do us both a favor and dig me a deep hole. I'll be technically dead anyway."

"Jen," Allison started, but her friend interrupted.

"That wasn't a plea for sympathy, Allie. Just plain simple fact. Now, what have you brought in your bag of goodies today, Mrs. Shepherd?"

With a nervous shrug, Allison began to dig within the bag, finally dropping balls of yarn and knitting needles onto Jennifer's lap. The expression on her friend's face was one of horror. "Well, for heaven's sake," she excused, her voice rising. "I've run out of ideas. Dr. Marshall has forbidden you to do any needlework. Says every drop of your blood is precious and that you can't risk infection with the brutal way you abuse your fingers. I don't play chess. There isn't a book left in my father's library that you haven't read at least twice—unless you've developed a passion for banking as well as law and medicine . . ."

With a glitter of amusement, Jennifer asked, "Do *you* knit, Allison?"

"I've been learning," the auburn-haired woman responded defensively, and then broke up with giggles. "It's awful, Jen. Neither of us is the domesticated type. We'd rather be marching to the drum of social reform or, in your case, riding hell-bent across a meadow on the fastest, meanest horse ever born."

"Have I told you how much your visits mean to me, Allison? I know you give up time when—"

"Give up? My dear friend, I give up nothing. Just watching you and being with you is enriching beyond belief. Your courage and patience through this is admirable."

Jennifer's chin dropped nearly to her chest and her hands picked at the lace-edged sheets with restless agitation. "I'm neither brave nor patient," she said brokenly, lifting her head slightly, her chin quivering. "I lie here days and endless nights wanting to beat my fists on something harder than this damned feather prison I'm trapped in. I'm scared, and I'm not the least bit courageous. The only honest emotion I can summon most of the time is livid, screaming fury." Her face turned into a mask of stony rage. "But if I let go of the shriek that has found a permanent home right here"—she tapped her breastbone—"I wouldn't stop until long after they'd carted me off to Bedlam."

Gathering Jennifer into her arms, Allison patted and rubbed her friend's back, rocking gently. "Shhh—this has been a terrible ordeal for you. You have every right to want to bite something or someone. But, Cowgirl, you *are* the most courageous person I've ever known. You just don't know yet how really strong you are." Allison's voice broke on a sob. In the end it was Jennifer who dried her tears.

"Look at us, blubbering away. You're supposed to cheer *me*, Allison Shepherd. And here I am giving you the hankies."

"See what I mean? I wouldn't last a week if our positions were reversed."

If their positions were reversed. . . . Jennifer pictured Allison surrounded by loving husband, parents, and being teased by her young brother, and for a moment she felt raw jealousy. Then, realizing the self-pitying direction of her thoughts, Jennifer touched her friend's cheek. "Only *you* have gotten me through this, Allie. You and—" She stopped, guarding the secret so close to her heart while her fingers automatically sought the rustic chain she always wore around her neck. "My friends in this house and your mother," she finished.

"You don't mention husband, I notice. Lucky for him he stays completely out of my way. He'd get both sides of my tongue and a kick that would have him singing soprano the rest of his adult life." She rubbed her hands together, licking her lips in anticipation. "What time does dear cousin Adrian usually return home?"

Jennifer mumbled a vague response, not wanting to admit that Adrian rarely returned home. When he did pay one of his brief but dutiful visits, his eyes were always averted, the polite inquiries about her welfare curt, and his restlessness irritating.

Allison knew little about the sequence of events on that now momentous morning. Had she known the truth, she might be tempted to take his life, not merely his manhood. Jennifer shuddered again at the remembered agony she suffered in the service of that manhood. Though Dr. Marshall, kind and wise, would not have believed a wife's accusation of rape against her husband, and the courts of law considered it a husband's right if he so desired to force himself upon an unwilling wife, Jennifer could never forgive or forget that brutal violation. And never would she banish from her mind the memory of his face, twisted in the throes of frenzied ecstasy while she begged, and then cried out at the pain tearing through her abdomen while her blood stained the sheets.

And the words, those echoing words. "How did you manage that amazing feat, my love?" he'd sneered with disgust while cleaning the blood from the instrument of torture that had just ripped her apart inside. "Did you think a second maidenhead might prove you a virtuous wife? Now I wonder if I might not have been duped from the beginning."

"Jennifer!" Allison shook her friend out of that haunted, empty look she seemed to wear more frequently these days.

"I'm sorry. Did you say something?" Her voice was a monotone.

"Nothing important, Cowgirl." Allison's heart was thumping against her breast. This odd behavior frightened her more than anything else. Looking up, she saw Mrs. Johnson enter the room, bottle of tonic and spoon in hand. They exchanged worried looks before Allison began packing away the yarn and needles. "Mother said to tell you she would drop by sometime tomorrow afternoon. And if Dr. Marshall does allow you downstairs next week, I think it would be a good time to start making plans for that redecoration you've always spoken of. I can be your arms and legs; you can be the creative genius. More fun than knitting, I'm certain."

"God bless you, Allison Shepherd. You *do* keep me sane," Jennifer whispered, reaching out for her friend. When Allison had gone she opened her mouth, like a good little bird, for the spoonful of tonic. Before the lethargy of the sedative took her over, she made a final request. "Ask Jenkins if he's free for a game of chess this evening, Agatha."

"I'm certain he'll make every attempt, madame. Unless . . ."

Unless Adrian needed to be driven from pillar to post, Jennifer thought, rolling to her side and tucking the pillow close into the curve of her body.

Each time the asafetida was administered it took longer to take effect; by now it brought scant relaxation—something she kept very much a secret for fear an opiate would be substituted. It was what frightened her most—not being in control.

It was hard enough with all her wits about her to fight the melancholia. She had too many hours with nothing to do but examine too closely her every mistake and failure. She knew them all and forgave herself few.

Her fingers now sought that chain around her neck, pulling it from beneath her gown to rub the little charm between thumb and forefinger in rhythmic motions that soothed more than any tonic. Her talisman, it had brought her through those first critical hours while her body alternately tried to expel and hold fast to the infant within her womb. It was her strength, the links that forged her inexorably to a man and a warm meadow. It kept her sane.

"You are joking, aren't you?" Adrian scoffed while Erica's face flooded with fury. "Oh, I don't doubt in the least you are pregnant. But to name me as father . . ." He laughed outright. "Really, my dear, you'd need a ledger to keep an accurate count of the men who've plowed that fertile soil. I very much doubt our single encounter on New Year's Eve qualifies me for the paternity of your brat."

"How cocky you've become, Adrian, my first love." She moved from the chair to stroll around the apartment. "This is a lovely place, darling." She sat down upon a chaise longue resting in front of the cold fireplace. "How do you afford to maintain this charming hideaway?"

Her lips twisted in a secret smile while her violet eyes inventoried the Aubusson carpet, the brass fixtures, and the richly upholstered furniture. "Very nice, especially for a poor relation."

"Make your point, Erica."

"If I should tell my father this child is yours—"

"Your father is many things, Erica, but a fool isn't one of them. Tell him," he bluffed. "You'll join me in perdition if you do."

"True, very true. Papa does seem to lose all reason when your name is mentioned." Erica shrugged. "Nonetheless, there is the slim possibility you are responsible. In my mind, you owe me something for that, and for my promise to keep your name off my lips."

"What do you want?"

"An abortion. I won't have this—this disaster ruining my life. Arrange it for me, won't you, darling?"

Adrian pushed off the sofa and headed for the door. "Now I'm certain you've gone completely mad!" He grabbed his coat and hat from the brass tree.

"Oh, I don't think so, Adrian. You see, I've had you followed for the past several weeks. This address was already known to me, *and* the detective I hired. Shall I tell you what we discovered?"

When he closed the door, she giggled. "You might be naughty, but you aren't stupid. In my possession is a list of the old birds who squawk and coo several times a week on this very chaise where I'm sitting. Poor dears, it breaks my heart to know how deprived they've been all these years."

"You really are the queen of bitches, Erica." His hands were ice, and a fine sheen of perspiration dotted his brow.

She stalked across the room. "I was an innocent once, reeking with virgin virtue until you so expertly taught me the pleasures I can no longer live without. All I want is for you to arrange a safe, simple, and expedient solution to my dilemma. With your connections it should be easy." Erica smiled sweetly, sensing victory. "I'll even allow you to pay for it, which I'm sure will ease your troubled conscience."

"I'll see what I can do," he said brusquely, turning to leave.

"Don't make me hurt you, Adrian." She had dropped her sickeningly babyish tone, her voice was deadly earnest. "It doesn't take a genius to figure out why you've developed a sudden passion for the wives of half the politicians in this city. You are whoring for Frank Todd, aren't you?" She clucked her tongue. "Blackmail and extortion—nasty business—dangerous too. What would the little wife and family say?"

Adrian's eyes closed. "Meet me here on Friday at this same time."

"Thank you, darling. I knew you wouldn't abandon your responsibility."

He gagged at the wet mouth and searching hand.

Chapter Thirty-Three

Jennifer sorted through the wallpaper samples and fabric swatches Allison had left. Chewing on her lower lip, she arranged the many-colored selections on the large square painter's canvas resting atop her knees. She moved the samples around, studying the varying colors and patterns, and fastened them to the canvas with dressmaker's pins. There was such a thing as having too many choices, she thought with a frustrated shake of her head, unable to decide upon any of the lovely combinations she'd devised.

She propped up the canvas within the window bay and arched back as far as possible on the daybed to help in her decision. Hearing the rustle of bombazine and taffeta, she spoke without turning. "I really do like the green, Agatha. It's soft and cool and reminds me of a spring day. But the only colors that are compatible to that particular shade are the golds and yellows. I've always hated yellow. What do you think of the blue combinations?"

"Blue is depressing, madame," the housekeeper stated honestly. "I rather like that dainty patterned paper with the soft peach flowers. But the choice is yours, of course."

Jennifer laughed. "And I'll have to live with it as well. All I'm really certain of is that I will not tolerate dark or loud colors." She turned to the housekeeper, her hands folded naturally on the mound of her stomach. "It's not time to go back upstairs, is it?" The pleasure of being able to lie before these undraped windows and view the world as it passed by the house was one she didn't relinquish as quietly as she had her smaller confining window upstairs. "I'm not at all weary. Allison's short visit surely could buy me a few more minutes."

Mrs. Johnson smiled. "You may stay downstairs if you promise . . ." The peel of the door chimes interrupted. "Now who could that possibly be?" She left to investigate.

Within minutes Erica Delaney had forced her way into the parlor over the housekeeper's insistence that Jennifer should not be disturbed. At Jennifer's surprised, yet wary greeting, Erica quickly approached the daybed. "I apologize for interrupting your rest period, but I simply *had* to bring you this gift." Erica placed the package she carried on Jennifer's rounded belly, and immediately spun around on her heel. "Happy reading," she tossed cheerfully over her shoulder. Contentment flooded throughout her body, not fading even when she reached the carriage hired to carry her to her appointment. She felt not a whit of guilt for this betrayal of a bad bargain. Her revenge was long overdue. What was it they said about a woman scorned. . . .

Back inside the parlor, Jennifer watched Erica's carriage depart, still somewhat stunned by the woman's abrupt visit. With no small amount of curiosity, she pulled the ribbon on the package and unwrapped the brown paper. When the contents were free of their bindings, she scooted backwards upon the bed, making herself more comfortable before she began to examine the cheaply bound volume. It appeared to be a diary of sorts, but the bold handwriting was difficult to decipher. Large blocked capital letters identified the characters whose daily activities were chronicled. As she turned the pages, three sheets of stationery fell from the diary. She opened the first, noting that the handwriting was obviously feminine. It was a list of names, some quite familiar. The second sheet, really just a small scrap of paper, grabbed her full attention. An address was scrawled on it in Adrian's distinctive script. She looked back at the bound report, carefully comparing the block initials there to the names listed on the first sheet; they matched in every case. Her brows drew together as her interest in what was written grew, along with her suspicions.

But it was the third sheet of paper that connected each thread and clearly confirmed the destructive information Erica, or someone, had maliciously compiled.

She read the childishly written poem aloud in a whispery voice:

> There once was a girl who escaped from the whirl
> to seek a few moments of dark.
> In shadows she stood, stiff as the wood,
> to watch lovers play—what a lark!
> Whose husband, I wonder, so deeply did plunder,
> his staff grinding under a woman's hunger,
> while wifey listened to sweet Erica's bark?

The gratingly explicit verse couldn't have been clearer.

With a snort, followed by a hiccup, Jennifer carefully tucked the packet behind a cushion. There was something about having documentation in bold black and white, of the travesty that was her role that struck Jennifer's sense of humor. She hiccuped again, and again, the involuntary spasms accompanied by short bursts of giggles until she was howling without restraint.

The sounds of uncontrolled laughter brought Agatha Johnson rushing back to the parlor. Her mistress was curled into a tight ball, her entire body shaking, while those awful sounds, somehow not quite human, vibrated throughout the house. "Dear God," she cried, pressing her fingers to her lips before whirling to seek aid.

Within minutes she returned with her husband hard on her heels. In Agatha's hand was the bottle of laudanum kept for emergencies. But what these two found was not the hysterical, frenzied woman of seconds ago, but a perfectly serene and composed Jennifer, who appeared in no distress whatsoever.

"Mrs. Armbruster?" Agatha approached tentatively. "Are you feeling well?"

"Of course, Agatha. I've never felt better." Jennifer

continued to watch the cardinal perched on the tree outside the window.

Johnson backed out of the room, motioning for his wife to follow. In the hallway they whispered together, arguing briefly before coming to an agreement and dispersing.

Johnson returned to the parlor. "Allow me to arrange the pillows to make you comfortable for your rest, madame." As he reached out to plump the cushion behind which Jennifer had concealed the mysterious diary, he was greeted with a mulish expression warning him away.

"I am quite comfortable, thank you, Johnson, but I have no intention of sleeping." She looked him straight in the eye and her voice was steady.

"Now, Mrs. Jennifer, you know the doctor's orders. He'll be in a terrible temper if you miss your nap and afternoon dose of medicine."

There were those not present who would have instantly recognized the futility of argument when that rounded chin jutted just so and those crystal-silver eyes glittered in that manner. Johnson, however, had never seen his young mistress puffed up for full battle.

"When, and *if,* I feel fatigued, Johnson, I will arrange my own pillows and close my eyes, but you may as well forget about the tonic. I wish to be wide awake when my dear husband returns home from his hard day's work at the bank."

The cutting edge to her voice was unmistakable. She was angry, just plain spitting mad. What could Mr. Adrian have done now?

Agatha Johnson entered the room with the familiar rustle of her skirts, carrying a tea service. "Since my heart hasn't started beating normally and I can still feel my hair turning gray, it seemed a good time for a bracing cup of tea to settle the nerves." She placed the tray on a table and poured three cups. "Sit down, husband. I'm sure you are in need of refreshment as well."

With a cup and saucer in one hand and a small plate of cookies in the other, the housekeeper approached the daybed.

"I'm not hungry, Agatha," Jennifer said, attempting to decline, but relenting when the woman glared with beady eyes.

"The brew is a bit strong, Agatha," Johnson observed while handling the fragile cup with ease, "but stimulating."

They lapsed into silence while Jennifer sipped at the beverage and toyed with the cookies lying untouched upon the plate. After a time Mrs. Johnson gathered up the dishes, sharing a conspiratorial look with her husband while their mistress slipped into a deep sleep.

She awakened with great difficulty. There seemed to be a rumbling inside her head, and it took time before she recognized the sound of thunder, faint at first, then becoming more distinct as the storm approached from the west. Her mouth felt dry with the bitter aftertaste of a drug she knew she'd not willingly taken.

One by one muscles responded to mental commands, but her eyelids refused to obey, fluttering like the wings of a hummingbird until her fingers pressed against them tightly, forcing one and then the other open until the spasms ceased.

"Mrs. Johnson," she croaked, knowing that the sound of her voice had been swallowed by a simultaneous crack of thunder. She waited out the next flash of lightning and its accompanying noise and in the lull called for the housekeeper again, this time screaming at the top of her lungs.

By the time Agatha Johnson appeared in the doorway, Jennifer had managed to heave herself into an upright position by using her arms and elbows, abrading her tender skin as if she'd scooted across sand instead of soft linen. "You drugged me," she stated flatly, glaring her accusation with eyes both angry and hurt by the betrayal of those she'd trusted.

"Oh, Mrs. Armbruster . . ." Agatha looked about to cry. "It was wrong, I know. But you were behaving so . . . strange. We were afraid for you and the baby."

The events of the afternoon came back to her with jarring clarity. Somehow, though, they no longer seemed quite the grave revelations that had provoked her loyal friends into a conspiracy. "I understand, Agatha. You did what you thought best. Has my husband arrived home?"

"Not yet. It's past seven o'clock. It could be quite late. Sometimes he doesn't—"

"Sometimes he doesn't come home at all," Jennifer finished. "I've known that for several weeks. Another hour. Give me another hour, and I promise I'll let Jenkins carry me to bed without a fight."

The small smile and the lucidity in her eyes brought a relieved sigh from the housekeeper. "It's Celia's day out, so we're eating simple tonight. Vegetable soup and plain butter sandwiches."

"That will be adequate." She reached for Mrs. Johnson's hand. "Thank you, Agatha. I don't know what I'd do without you."

"Pish," the woman replied, embarrassed by the rush of tears threatening to make her nose drip. "We're happy to do for you." The housekeeper sniffed loudly and left the room.

Staring out at the darkness, Jennifer watched the storm intensify. Large raindrops began to spatter against the glass. Rolling to her side, she traced the path of one drop, following its stream until it spread across the bottom of the sill. Beneath her fingers she could feel the vibrations of thunder while lightning put on a flashy show of power unharnessed, turning darkness to blinding bursts of white.

Jennifer started, jerking her hand back from the window, when the lightning snapped a limb from a nearby tree. "That was close," she said, feeling the house shudder as the sound reverberated at an almost deafening pitch.

Something—sound, instinct—made her look over her shoulder. A scream of terror caught in her throat, and she cowered away from the monstrous figure standing in the middle of her parlor with a face so horrible that it seemed to have stepped from a nightmare.

"Where is he?" Sean Delaney's voice was void of humanity. "Where are you hiding the foul sonofabitch?"

He was soaked to the skin, and water ran in rivulets from

his hair onto his face. His clothes were splattered with what looked—horribly—like blood. She recoiled from the twisted features, inching backward until she was flush with the window. Through her thin wrapper and gown she could feel the driving rain against the glass, telling her this was real, not some drug-induced dream.

Brutal hands nearly crushed the bones of her shoulders as they yanked her forward and upward. *"Where is he?"* Each word was drawn out, the dead tone seeming to rise from the bloodstained chest as if from the bowels of hell. "Where is the bastard that killed my baby?"

Suddenly Jenkins and Johnson appeared and Delaney was being drawn away. Jennifer slumped down onto the daybed, her breath heavy in her chest. She saw Jenkins place himself firmly between her and Delaney's body, now wracked with sobs. "Won't hurt her!" he cried. "Only Armbruster."

The haunted eyes looked almost apologetic as they roamed over the small, pale woman who was clutching her rounded stomach, her eyes pleading a silent entreaty that penetrated his own anguish.

"He's not here. Search the house and the grounds," Jenkins said firmly. "But don't touch Mrs. Jennifer again."

"Only want her husband. Want him in hell with my Erica." Again he looked directly at Jennifer. "I'm sorry if you care for him . . . but I can't let him live."

Wheeling around, Delaney knocked Johnson to the floor as the man tried to block his escape. Jenkins had not moved from his position.

"Find him," Jennifer finally managed in a small voice. "Oh, God, Jenkins, we have to find Adrian. Have to warn him. Delaney's gone mad."

"Mad with grief," Jenkins observed, helping poor Johnson from the floor. The old butler's face was tight with the pain of battered rheumatic joints.

Jennifer began snapping rapid-fire orders, refusing to listen to any dissent, even when rooted in common sense.

"Jenkins—you know all the places. Start at the most likely and proceed from there. If you and Johnson divide them, you'll surely find my husband. Agatha, fetch Mr. and Mrs. Shepherd. Jenkins will drop you there, and then you can return with them. I need Allison, and Adrian just may need a very good attorney before this night is out."

"But you'll be alone." Agatha Johnson squared her jaw and shook her head. "No . . . I'll not leave you. That madman might return."

"You will do as you're ordered, or you will find yourself unemployed within the hour." Jennifer issued the empty threat, hoping Agatha would forgive her later. "Have we a gun, a pistol? If it would make you feel more secure, I assure you I would not hesitate should there be the need to protect myself."

No one doubted her, but if there was any weapon in this house, they'd never seen it. Precious minutes could be lost in search of something that did not exist.

Her loyal crew dispatched, Jennifer found the total solitude more intimidating than she'd anticipated when she had so courageously bullied everyone out of the house.

In her total vulnerability she was aware of every sound, until her nerves were braided as tightly as her hair. Her heart pounding at an alarmingly fast rate at every real or imagined noise, she took deep breaths while reaching deep inside herself to find the girl who had tackled fence posts with bulldog determination. But that girl could run, punch, kick, and fight. Jennifer knew her helpless body could not withstand an attack should the deranged Delaney return. With every flash of lightning she tried to see into the darkness of the turbulent night, her body jerking with fright as every shadow seemed to take on human form.

"Are you the light in the window who awaits her lover's return, sweet wife?"

Adrian's silken voice brought a scream of terror before she slapped her hand over her mouth and closed her eyes with relief. "Adrian . . . thank God" was all she could manage while her heart remained tightly wedged in her throat.

"Isn't it long past your bedtime?" he questioned nonchalantly while shrugging out of his waterlogged coat to drop it negligently upon the floor.

"I've been so frightened. Delaney has gone mad. He's—"

With a wave, he made a lurching step toward the liquor cabinet. "Don't tell me," he slurred, his usual swagger now a cautious negotiation of getting from here to there. "I'm a dead man, right? Sean is so predictable."

His casual attitude toward the very real threat to his life was so outrageous Jennifer knew he must be bolstered by an alcohol-induced bravado. "Why does Sean Delaney want your life?" she said slowly, swinging her legs off the daybed and pulling herself into a sitting position. When Adrian turned back to face her, she felt a cold chill of dread. His beautiful face had aged, the ravages of dissipation and perversity evident. And he was scared, very scared.

Jennifer rephrased the question, fearful of the answer. "How did Erica die?"

He blanched as though the news of her death came as a shock; a dreadful yet anticipated bit of news he'd hoped never to hear. "Dead," he muttered before taking a deep swallow of brandy. "Goddamn stupid female. It was her own damned folly. But no doubt she'll want her pound of flesh, even from the grave." The glass in his hand was emptied and filled again before he began to weave his way across the room. "Not *my* doing. Lied to me, to the doctor. Waited too long, that butcher said when he dumped her back on me. What the hell was I supposed to do with her? Christ, she was screaming with pain." He seemed to fold as he reached her, his entire body going into a slump in front of the daybed. He looked at his wife with eyes that fairly begged for understanding, even forgiveness.

"Wasn't my child, Jennifer. Not my responsibility. I couldn't leave her in some alley to suffer like that, and there wasn't anything I could do to help her. Doctor said it was hopeless, too much damage inside." He made a sick sound that was half laugh, half sob. "Sent her home to Papa in a cab."

Once, Jennifer might have been able to find some pity, if

not some understanding. But his callous attitude toward the near loss of their own child, and the subsequent months of indifference toward her, had consumed all such softer feelings toward her husband.

"You cold-blooded, inhuman bastard," she ground out before she gagged, a spontaneous reaction that vividly expressed her opinion of Adrian's character.

When she could look at him again, his face was colorless. "Wasn't it enough to try and destroy your own wife and child? What revenge were you seeking upon Erica? Not your child . . ." She snorted in disgust. "Are you certain? Shall I read you a pretty little poem I received today?" Reaching behind her, she pulled the sheets of paper from beneath her pillows and began to read in a singsong voice filled with scorn, "There once was a girl . . ."

Halfway through the rhyme, Adrian snatched the paper away. "Sauce for the goose—or gander, in this case. Weren't you having a high time exchanging rides with your cowboy all the while I was gone?"

"No!" she screamed, rising to her feet on the strength of enraged temper. "But I wished to God I had made love with Devlin more times than I could possibly count."

His face contorted into a twisted smile. "Why? So you could freeze his prick off like you've done mine?"

The insult brought a small but amazingly strong fist driving deep into his stomach. Instinctively he lashed back, blinded by pain, backhanding her with a blow that snapped her neck and tumbled her back upon the bed. "Jennifer?" He bent over her, horrified at his own violence.

She touched the swelling of her bottom lip, her fingers coming away from her mouth bloody. "Bastard," she repeated. "You're a disgrace to the name you are so damned arrogantly proud of wearing."

For a moment there was only the sound of ragged breathing and the soughing of the wind in the lull of a storm-swept night. And then nature exploded, releasing ugliness that had shaped a man's destiny.

"Whelp," Adrian sneered, grabbing Jennifer's braid to

yank her upright. His breath was hot, the fumes of alcohol singing her face. "That's what he called me—the whelp. Never said bastard, but it's what he meant. The whore's whelp, Isobel's child. Not an Armbruster, but the seed of some down-on-his-luck actor.

"Dear Papa Charles gave me the full story when I was twelve. The same day, by the way, that I'd caught my sluttish mother sucking on the big, red cock of one of her pretty young boys. Hated her, wanted to hurt her, so I went to the father who had probably said only ten complete sentences to me in my entire life. He laughed . . . he simply laughed until he cried. And then for the first time in my goddamned life my father hugged me and kissed me. For just a minute I wanted to weep with gladness, and then he kept on kissing and started to touch me in ways I knew were not right—but I was so hungry for his love that I hugged him back. When he stuck his tongue into my mouth and stuffed his hand down my trousers, I knew Papa wanted more than affection from his son."

Adrian's eyes were black, his voice bitter while his fingers bit into Jennifer's flesh, and he began to shake her with every word as if for emphasis. "Told me that it wasn't nasty or bad; that it was not incest to touch me that way because I wasn't his son. It was all right to have his way with someone else's whelp. Jesus Christ—the man I had thought was my father wanted to screw me up the ass!"

His voice had reached the high whine of a dangerously wounded animal. She began to slowly pull away. He'd already slapped her, and now she was afraid that his overflowing hatred would match the raging winds outside.

"Adrian?" she said tentatively. "I understand. . . ."

"You bitch! Thought you were different. Slut like all the others. But then every human being on this earth is a whore in one way or the other. You either get it up the ass or shoved down your throat. Can't win . . . never win."

He released her abruptly, tottering in his drunkenness. "Loved you. Why didn't you love me back, Jennifer?" His voice was that of a child who had been scratched or bitten by his favorite pet.

When he would have grabbed for her, she rolled away, finding her feet again, blindly seeking to escape his wrath. He reached again and she wheeled away. Feet tangled with feet, and she felt herself falling, landing hard on her back, the wind driven from her lungs.

She lay stunned and very still. Adrian was kneeling beside her, and she could see his mouth moving, but could hear no sound over the storm. At first she thought, *I'm all right.* Then the look in his eyes and the unmistakable feel of wetness soaking her gown brought a keening wail that had no end.

"Oh, God . . ." Adrian shrank away from the bloody fluid spreading in a widening circle. "I'm sorry," he whispered before lurching to his feet to leave his wife, fleeing the dark continuous horror of his soul.

"Mrs. Shepherd." Dr. Marshall's voice was firmly authoritative. "You must get some rest. We've done all we can. It's up to God now."

Allison refused to budge. "Not entirely. Not while I have anything to say about things." She tightened her grip on her friend's hands. "She is *not* going to die, Dr. Marshall. You've stopped the bleeding. You underestimate her fiber, if you think she'll give up on life now. Right, Cowgirl?"

Dr. Marshall drew Stephen out of the room. "As far as I know your wife is a very healthy, strong young woman. However, what she's been through tonight has been very stressful and unsettling. If you let her continue to hold on to hope . . ." The doctor didn't want to lose Jennifer any more than the woman at her bedside did, but he was also a realist. "It will be all the harder on her if the outcome isn't what we all wish. Your wife's own pregnancy could be in jeopardy."

Stephen was torn between what was best for Allison and what could amount to a slender thread of hope for Jennifer. "Doctor, my wife just helped deliver a stillborn child and had the presence of mind to use compresses to slow the hemorrhage until you arrived. Give her a few more hours. If she shows any signs of difficulty, I promise I'll force her to bed even if I have to drag her out. She's made it this far. Leaving Jenny now could do them both harm."

Dr. Marshall couldn't argue. Sometimes the difference between life and death was determined by sheer force of will.

"Let's go downstairs and report to the family."

Adrian prowled his Boston hotel room like a caged animal, raking his fingers through the tight, damp curls on his head, shaking inside and out. Every so often he would pull his watch from his pocket, check the time, and curse with increasing virulence.

Where was Carlotta? Would she come? Could she slip away from Frank's all-seeing eyes? Had the boy managed to sneak into the casino unnoticed to deliver the note? Maybe Frank or one of his men had caught the youngster. Were they coming for him now? Had the Irish brat pocketed the money without the bother?

He needed a drink to stop this awful, sick trembling that jolted his entire body. Adrian covered his face and moaned as images assailed him once again.

Erica. Her death could be rationalized. He felt no guilt and little regret. Why had she waited so long before insisting on that damned abortion? Christ, she had been nearly five months gone, lying to both the doctor and himself. In essence her death was suicide, and he felt not one whit responsible.

Jennifer. The mere thought of her lying there in a pool of her own blood, losing their baby, made him fear for his sanity. Why couldn't it have been the way he wanted? He'd loved her, really loved her once. The slap he'd delivered hadn't caused her to fall. She'd tripped. It was an accident.

Would he ever stop hearing her horrible scream?

The hours crawled by. Dawn came and went, and still no sign of Carlotta. The sun was bright, hot for early spring, the past night's storm raising the humidity until this airless room was a sweltering prison, musty with damp and mildew. His own body odors were beginning to make him feel ill.

When the long-awaited knock on the door finally came, it did not bring the relief he'd anticipated. His heart stopped and then beat erratically. Who called: friend or foe? freedom or capture?

"Adrian?"

Carlotta. Thank God. He began to breathe again, jerking her inside the room, quickly locking the door behind her. "I'd about given up hope. Did you bring the money?"

"I couldn't get away sooner, and yes, I've brought money. It's not much. One of my customers gave me an advance against some very special services he's had in mind for a time." The wad of bills she pulled from her reticule was immediately snatched and counted. Without a word of thanks, she noted with a frown.

"Adrian, Delaney has the entire city alerted, at least the people who usually know who's coming and going. What are you planning?"

"To go as far as this stake will take me." He waved the money before stuffing it into his pocket.

"Sugar, you won't get six feet from this place without being seen."

"Yes, I will," Adrian stated with more confidence than he felt, producing the knitted woolen cap he'd bought off a drunken sailor. With his head covered, the mud-spattered coat covering his suit, and a day's growth of beard to hide his features, he had a fair chance. This was an Adrian Armbruster this city had never seen. And if his looks weren't enough, his smell should put them off the scent.

From behind the morning newspaper, the Pinkerton detective looked like any other passenger waiting for a train. He kept his eyes on the ticket windows, and it appeared the ass-numbing hours on this hard bench were about to pay off.

The man currently purchasing a ticket might have escaped his notice if it hadn't been for the nervous, almost furtive movements he made, drawing attention to those elegantly manicured hands so incongruous with the general unkempt appearance.

When Armbruster blended into the throng of departing passengers, the detective put his paper aside.

The ticket agent proved very cooperative, even generous, repeating the questions Armbruster had asked. With his own ticket in hand, the detective hurried to join the wool-capped traveler on the first leg of their journey. The destination, it appeared, was St. Louis, Missouri.

Chapter Thirty-Four

The sun in the cloudless sky baked the shingles on the covered platform until not even a whiff of breeze could ease lungs straining to draw a hot breath. The steam engine that had pulled into the Billings station added another furnace to the hell heat of a summer with too little rain. Only June and already the ground was beginning to crack and the grass was turning brown.

But to the man anxiously shifting from one foot to the other as he scanned the passengers disembarking from the train, this drought was a matter of little consequence. Never again would James Douglas consider anything more important than his daughter's health and happiness.

The few passengers leaving the airless compartment quickly gathered their belongings and scurried for dark buildings and cool drinks. Only two seemed less than eager to join their former traveling companions.

The sudden silence was as ponderous as the air, weighing on James's shoulders like an anvil. He watched his daughter's escort urging her to leave the spot to which she appeared to be rooted. He was having difficulty with his own feet as well, and he had to fight the impulse to erupt into a raging roar. The features of the young woman who now approached were painfully familiar, yet he knew if he'd met her on another street, in another place, he would have passed her by without recognition. He'd seen corpses with more color and animation. James shivered in the searing heat.

Jennifer stopped a few feet from her father. She could hear Jenkins's sharp tone, a mixture of frustration and concern, coaxing her to continue. She knew James Douglas expected a greeting filled with gladness, or even grief—some human emotion. She felt nothing. Her eyes registered her father's shock at her appearance and his efforts to hide his reaction behind a false smile. He too would join Dr. Marshall and the others in the campaign to prod her out of her deep melancholy. What no one seemed to realize was that she had lost the ability to feel either pain or pleasure, and was rather content in her unreal world.

When James rushed forward to embrace her fiercely, Jennifer allowed the contact, having found from experience that it caused less difficulty to accept the physical needs of others than to reject them, as she would have done if the choice had been entirely her own. Still, compliance could not mask her aversion to being touched.

"Welcome home, Princess," James managed before standing back to study this stranger with his daughter's features. Her lusterless black hair had been brushed, but the clumsily fashioned bun at the nape of her neck suggested the handiwork of someone more accustomed to horsehair than a woman's toilette. Her dark blue dress was stylish, but stained, hanging limply on a too thin body.

Over her head, James silently questioned the groom with eyes that fairly begged for some sign of reassurance. Jenkins could only shake his head and shrug expressively. For a moment James was tempted to shake Jennifer and order her to stop this ridiculous behavior. Already he could feel the flush of embarrassment at the sidelong looks they were drawing.

It was the numbness creeping into his fingers that made him aware of the brutal hold he maintained on those fragile shoulders. He gentled his touch, lifting his fingers to her cheek. He felt sick when she flinched away. Dear God, he didn't think he could bear this.

"Sorry we couldn't have had better weather for the trip home, Princess."

"Yes, it is very hot," she responded in a low monotone.

This, too, she had learned—compromise. By verbally acknowledging selective appeals and questions, she was saved those uncomfortable scenes caused by her preferred silence.

Her voice made James's flesh creep. "It's time to go home," he said roughly, taking her arm to rush her off the platform, unable to control the cringing inside as friends parted, flashing him looks filled with horror and sympathy while whispering behind their backs. "Half mad," he heard someone say, and his jaw nearly broke from the tension.

Swinging Jennifer up into the surrey he'd borrowed from the Davis family, James directed Jenkins to the back seat and wasted little time in snapping the reins.

By the time James jerked the horse to a halt in front of the house, he'd worked himself into a state. Deep inside he was repelled by the impulse that drove him to snatch Jennifer out of the surrey. He told himself it was for her protection, for the sake of those who anticipated her homecoming with glad expectancy—excuses compiled to justify the compulsion to hide her away.

But too many things happened all at once. The screen door groaned and slapped shut. Sam seemed to appear from nowhere. And a very tight-lipped Jenkins showed a surprising boldness by stepping between James Douglas and the daughter he was hiding with his own body. Then it was too late. Sam was dragging him away, leaving Jennifer in the open, unprotected, vulnerable, and so damned heartbreakingly pitiful he wanted to cry.

It didn't take any great perception to know what James had been about, and the look Maggie blistered him with should have singed the beard right off his face. She slowly descended the porch stairs. Jennifer seemed to withdraw further inside herself. She kept her eyes averted, rounding her shoulders as if to draw some invisible protective cloak about her. Approaching with the same caution she would have used with any wounded creature, Maggie stopped a few feet away, tipping her head to seek, find, and capture those expressionless silver eyes. A gentle smile touched her lips, and her hand slowly lifted from her side, extending in a silent, poignant entreaty that was, at the same time, almost ruthless in its demand for acceptance.

Even through her protective fog, Jennifer was aware of what Maggie was asking of her. She tried to ignore that outstretched hand and its implications. Maggie wouldn't settle for compromise, nor a yielding that was not of her own free will. She was demanding Jennifer give of herself in love and trust. All this Jennifer knew, and it stirred those dead feelings. But before they could rise to hurt her, Jennifer buried them without mercy.

The hot sun was relentless. Shadows moved from here to there with the passage of time. Undulating waves of heat rose from the baked earth.

Why didn't someone stop this? Didn't they know Maggie would stubbornly allow the sun to set, rise, and set again before she'd willingly surrender, if she didn't collapse first. Couldn't they see the older woman's flushed face and swaying body? Would her Maggie have to pitch forward before someone, anyone—

Jennifer shot forward, grabbing those hot fingers, cooling them within her own icy palm. She felt a twinge of guilt that it had taken so long to give so little. Maggie said nothing, and asked for nothing more, turning to lead the way into the house, never relinquishing that fragile bond of hands.

Devlin stood in the doorway. The eyes that touched Jennifer's face were filled with torment as she passed him without acknowledgment or recognition.

Sam's arm tightened across James's shoulders, the anger he'd felt earlier gone. "Come on, Jamie," he said in a raspy croak, "Let's saddle up and go find us something to kill."

Chapter Thirty-Five

It was the end of a very long day. Devlin turned Lucifer over to Jenkins's expert hands with a gruff word of thanks. The past month had been hell in more ways than one, and as the brutal temperatures continued without relief, tempers were on edge.

They had already lost several of the weaker calves, and would lose many more without desperately needed rain. The windmill wouldn't be ready to pump water for several weeks, and the ponds would dry up completely long before then. Hank had come off his horse this afternoon from the blistering sun. Thankfully the young man merely bruised himself, and had revived quickly enough before Devlin had sent him back to the bunkhouse.

Yeah, he was in one hell of a lousy mood, and the setting of the sun was something he dreaded more than having his brains roasted during the day.

He made his way slowly toward the kitchen door, slapping his dusty Stetson against his thigh hard enough to split the sweat-stained felt had the tough fabric been less accustomed to the abuse. He stepped inside a kitchen that hadn't seen a hot meal in weeks. Maggie was pouring him a tall glass of lemonade. Some of the tightness eased at her thoughtfulness.

"This ought to cut some of the dust from your throat," she said, giving him a pat on the shoulder. "I've filled you a tub of bath water, and there's clean clothes hanging on the back of the door."

Devlin swept her into his arms, giving her a bone-breaking embrace. "You're a darlin' girl, Maggie, me love."

"And you smell like an old goat we used to have." She pushed him away, pinching her nostrils together. "Whew! Get out of here before you ruin my appetite for that cold ham we're having *again* tonight."

The door to the room that once was Maggie's and now was his had barely shut behind him before he was stripping off his clothes. The bath felt like ice in the small, stuffy room, but blessedly so, giving him temporary relief from smoldering temperatures and feelings for which there seemed no outlet.

Soft footsteps could be heard in the room directly above, and they hammered into his aching head. His return to the house meant Jennifer would hole up behind her closed bedroom door until someone dragged her out, or until she felt assured he was gone again.

With everyone else, she behaved almost normally now. But with him even an accidental meeting sent her scurrying to retreat, physically and emotionally, with the speed of a jackrabbit taking to the bush. The beast was in the house.

Footsteps, the sound of her voice heard only through walls and behind doors, her face glimpsed too briefly, filled Devlin with an aching torment that was gnawing him to shreds. He lived on the precipice of her life, and was beginning to wish *he* could leap off the edge and join her in that emotional void where love, hurt, and desire no longer existed.

He tortured himself with memories, especially of that morning in Boston when she'd come to him, before the world had intruded once again, when the will-o'-the-wisp of his dreams became warm flesh and blood, her mouth soft and giving, those eyes seeing into his very soul. And there was the sweet, wild touch of her fingers as they explored the straining evidence of his desire . . .

Maggie's knock, telling him his supper was on the table, brought a muffled groan. He grabbed the bucket of rinse water beside the tub and dumped it over his swimming head, flushing the grime from his body, hoping to cool the frustration that burned inside him.

Sam smiled at the young woman who walked beside him. To look at her now, it was hard to believe that ghost-woman she'd been just a few weeks ago. Even in the dusky light her hair glistened once again with blue-black luster. The thick, single braid she'd recently adopted was neatly tied with a dark blue ribbon. Her pale gray skirt was spotless; the lace and cotton blouse hugged her woman's curves to testify the return of vanity and a healthy appetite.

When they reached the corral, he leaned back against the rails to watch this girl he loved as his own, the daughter he and Maggie shared with James. Her face was softly animated while she fed carrots to her aging pinto.

"Careful," Sam warned. "He's so starved for attention, you might find yourself gobbled up whole." Although he referred to the horse, Sam thought the same advice might also apply to the tall man rounding the corner of the house. He saw Devlin stop cold when he spotted Jennifer, change direction, and then go clear back around the house before skulking toward the bunkhouse. Sam shook his head. It was hard to believe a little sprig of a woman could tie a big man like that up in so many knots he was beginning to look cross-eyed.

Raucous shouts and quarrelsome male voices could be heard as some cowhand or the other scrapped for a fight. Sam felt sorry for the man who'd certainly find an obliging opponent in Devlin McShane. He'd never seen a man so close to blowing his top.

"Yep, there's some around here been sorely grieved for a kind word or a gentle touch." Sam heard his own harsh tone and clamped his jaw shut when Jennifer turned those big, misty gray eyes on him. She'd gotten his message, but it brought him no victory to see her smile fade and the haunted look return.

He was torn between his instincts and Maggie's orders to put a padlock on what she called his shotgun mouth. His wife had promised a steady diet of cold shoulder and an icicle for a bed partner if he dared use his blunt methods on her poor, sick girl.

Blunt? What the hell kind of word was that? By Sam's definition it meant something in need of sharpening. If anything needed an edge put to it, Jennifer was a likely candidate. Shit, trying to mollycoddle this girl had always been about as useless as a tit on an old boar hog. In his opinion, she needed a good swift kick, and some straight talk.

Jenkins, who spouted big words and a lot of other hogwash, said her retrogression (Sam called it bullheaded stubbornness) around Devlin was because the young man posed the greatest risk to her fragile heart. She could accept the affections of Maggie, James, and himself, often behaving so like the princess of old it was hard to remember to treat her gently. Then Devlin would appear, and she'd be running scared again. At least she wasn't so far gone she didn't recognize the kind of feelings Devlin was carrying for her. That boy wouldn't be content for long with the distant, careful treatment the rest of them had learned to accept. Nope, he'd want all and then some.

"Adrian sold our Arabians," Jennifer said out of the blue, causing Sam's heart to lurch. Never once before had she mentioned that sonofabitch husband of hers. What made her think of him now? The horses? Was she remembering the bastard had sold the animals to pay for that other woman's abortion? He hoped Armbruster wandered onto Douglas land some day. They'd have a party, one like the Sioux once enjoyed.

A sudden cool breeze swung Sam's gaze away from Jennifer toward the western horizon. "Unless God just slammed the sun to the other side of the world, I'd say that blackness is rain clouds."

A faint flash of light and a distant rumbling were accompanied by another gust of air, definitely cooler and sharply scented. "It even smells like rain." He sniffed, turning full-face into the swelling wind. "Girl, I think we're about to see the end of this drought." Lightning zigzagged across the sky; thunder cracked, rolling across the plains.

Then Devlin was there, standing behind them, his dark blue eyes filled with concern. Jennifer appeared to have turned to stone; she clutched her stomach as if in great pain.

"Jen," he said softly, reaching out for her even as she backed away. "Don't be frightened, Jenny love. You're safe."

For a moment Sam thought she might fly into the arms yearning to hold her close in comfort and love. She swayed toward Devlin like a sapling bending in the wind. Then, with a moaning cry, she whirled and ran for the house.

Devlin's shoulders hunched. He jammed his empty hands into his pockets, looking like someone had poleaxed him between the eyes. "It was storming the night she lost her child."

"Yeah." Sam felt like killing something again. "Well, it could be we're in for one hell of a night then."

Maggie's face was pinched with alarm when she joined the three men gathered on the porch. "That's the first time I've had to dose her with that tonic. She's sleeping peaceful now."

"Should have let her weather it," Sam grumbled.

His wife rounded on him, her eyes spitting with green fury. "You're so smart, so damn quick with your opinions, Mr. Know-it-all! I suppose you think I should have just let her sob and tremble in that bed like some poor cornered creature—"

Sam yanked her into his arms. "Hush, old girl," he soothed, pressing her face into his shoulder. "We'll be dosing you up next. Might not be a bad idea, when I think on it." He patted her rump. "I could carry you off and take advantage of your rare docile state."

She snorted, cuffing him on the chin, then following her light tap with a kiss. "It's bad tonight," she whispered before turning to join Devlin and James.

Maggie linked her elbows with theirs and peered upward

at the black sky. "The clouds seem to be slowing. Maybe we'll get a soaking."

"We could use one," Devlin said tonelessly, trying to wipe out the image Maggie had placed in his mind. He rolled his head upon his shoulders to ease the tension and fatigue coiled there. "I'm beat. Think I'll turn in."

"You'll miss the show," James said in much the same tone of voice Devlin had used. Did a man ever stop paying for his mistakes? And why was it always the innocents who suffered?

Thunder covered Devlin's booted steps on the porch, and the sound of the squeaky hinges on the screen door were drowned out by the gusting wind.

James heard the first heavy drop plop against the roof. He held out his hand to catch the life-giving rain as it began to fall steadily, growing heavier until it beat against his palm and pounded against the earth almost punishingly. They'd wanted rain, and by God they were getting a torrent.

As the full force of the storm unleashed itself, cowhands filed from the bunkhouse, leaping over the corral rails to herd the horses into the barn. They whooped and hollered, hatless, lifting their faces to the driving rain, dancing and stomping, celebrating as only men who know the tragedy of a drought could.

"Damn fools," Sam chuckled, itching to be out there with them, sticking his head out from beneath the porch overhang to drink God's pure liquid.

The commotion masked that first feeble wail. But a full-bodied, bloodcurdling scream sent three people toward the door at the same time.

"Jenny!" James cried in alarm, trying to push Sam out of his way, not understanding why the man was holding him in a grip of iron.

"Dev went up to her, James."

Maggie had also seen Devlin charging up the stairs. She looked uncertain, but then bowed to Sam's insistent glare. "Sam's right. If Devlin needs us, he'll holler."

James looked at his old friends as if they'd suddenly sprouted horns and tails. "My God, can't you hear her?"

"Jamie, you can't give that girl what she needs right now. Ain't it past time you stepped aside and let them work things out without interference?" Sam dragged James back to the porch. "For once, leave things alone."

The room was pitch black until a flash of lightning located the woman on her knees in the middle of the bed. Then it was dark again, and only her harsh, rasping breathing led him to her. She had stopped her screaming the minute he entered the room.

Devlin's hand searched blindly, finding her with the aid of nature's brief illumination. He touched her shoulder. "Jen?"

Her shriek shattered the silence. Sharp nails raked deep furrows into the flesh of his chest, made vulnerable by the gaping shirt he'd been unbuttoning when he'd heard that first awful wail. Another flaming pain scored his breast. Arms and legs were striking blows he couldn't fend off as she evaded his restraining hands with the furious attack.

A cornered wildcat would have been easier to subdue. It had fewer arms and legs than this frantic female who seemed to have grown a dozen more than she should possess. A solid kick in his stomach bent him double with a gasp. When he could breathe again, Devlin lunged, capturing her arms while the force of his body drove her backward until they both sprawled upon the bed.

"Noooo!" she howled, caught in the trap of a nightmare all too terrifyingly real. She fought the hands holding her wrists captive, bucking and trying to kick out with feet spread wide, tied, while merciless monsters waited to destroy her child. She held her breath, refusing to bear down, clenching internal muscles to hold that precious burden while pain tore through her belly and loins. "I won't," she panted, "won't give up my baby!"

A scream of agony rent the air as cruel hands reached between her thighs to tear the baby from her womb. They slapped his blue little bottom, jammed fingers down that tiny throat. "Give him to me! Please, give him to me!"

Her vision was blurred. She thought she saw them wrap

something around his throat before a black-garbed figure stepped up to receive her son and cover his tiny body with a blanket. "No," she moaned, attempting to rise, tearing at the restraints. "Don't take him away. Bring him back. Oh, God, they're taking my baby." When the ghostly figure fled, the light began to grow dim, the room hazy with fog. It was peaceful, so peaceful.

Her sudden limpness sent Devlin scrambling from the bed. Trembling hands found the matches and lantern. When the room glowed with soft light, he turned back. This time it was his bellowing "No!" that competed with the din of thunder. He snapped his fingers in front of those staring, lifeless eyes. Jerking her upright, he gave her a brutal shake before his open palm slapped against her pale cheek. "Damn you, Jennifer! Look at me!" He hit her again, without anger, but with more force than before. This time she blinked and a little sob burst from her throat. When she tried to turn her head aside, he grabbed a handful of hair to hold her firm. "Is this your revenge? Don't you care that you're tearing my heart to shreds?" Her eyes closed, shutting him out. Devlin let her go, but not in defeat. "All right. You want to wall up your heart? We'll stay in this room until we're both loon crazy or dead. But I'm not leaving you, Jenny love. Not ever again."

She rolled to her side, drawing up her knees, bringing her hands to her face. There was blood on her fingers. Her baby's blood? No, the rational part of her mind insisted. Devlin's blood. Her shoulders quaked as she rolled back, flowing into his waiting arms, finding the solid warmth of his chest when he scooped her up, pressing her close, rocking gently while she sobbed. He made no attempt to calm those violent, gut-ripping tears. His own eyes were moist while his cheek pressed against her fevered brow. In time she began to quiet, but her hold on him grew stronger. Then in a raspy whisper she began to talk, and the poisons of a loveless marriage, an ugly list of guilts, and the distortions of those long, agonizing hours in childbirth surged like a flood from her throat.

Devlin listened to an entire catalogue of her sins; he let

her talk, though there were times when he wanted to shout for the unjust judgments she leveled against herself. When her voice finally became an empty croak, his broad hand silenced her with a sharp swat on her fanny.

"Even when you're miserable, you insist on being selfish and pigheaded. You talk as if the evils of the world could be cured but with a wave of your hand. Are we—am I—totally blameless? Did it never occur to you that others might richly deserve a share of your sorrow? Or did you think we'd simply allow you to carry the burden alone?"

He cradled her face, forcing her head up from his chest until their eyes met. "When you talked me out of my hair shirt, Jenny love, it never came to mind that you might be coveting the damned bristly thing for yourself!" The tenderness in his eyes belied the caustic tone.

"You said you wouldn't leave me. Did you mean it?"

With a half-sob he lowered himself to the pillows, pulling her with him until they were side by side, hip to hip, chest to chest. "I wouldn't know how to leave you now, darlin' girl." When she began to cry again, softly this time, he soothed her, whispering a lifetime of accumulated, unspoken endearments into her hair until she slipped into an exhausted slumber.

His own eyes grew heavy. He vaguely wondered why no one else had heard her screams. The thought didn't worry him overlong. He closed his eyes and joined her in sleep.

When something cold and wet burned like hellfire across his chest, Devlin awakened with a jolt.

"The scratches," Jennifer said, pushing him back down. "They need to be washed to prevent infection."

Devlin allowed her gentle ministrations, damning himself for the new fires igniting while she cleaned the stinging wounds, patting them dry, blowing on them to ease the burn of soapy water. "What time is it?" he asked rather unevenly.

She bent forward, her mouth caressing the hollow of his throat. "It's time to love me, Dev."

Chapter Thirty-Six

His arms dropped to his side, and he stared into eyes now glowing with that vital spark that had so long been missing. Jennifer—rash, impulsive, and already wanting to run headlong back into life—had been returned to him.

"You've brushed your hair," he noticed, lifting a strand before his hand curved around her neck to bring her lips closer to the upward surge of his mouth. It was intended to be a kiss of joy, a welcoming; perhaps even a promise for the days and years to come. But at the moment of contact emotions were stirred that had little to do with those nobler feelings. Releasing her quickly, he swung his legs off the bed and pushed himself into a sitting position, cursing himself all the while for the hungry yearnings that were part of his love, a whole of his heart and body.

Jennifer saw him set his jaw firmly. "No," she protested, moving behind him to press her lips to the soft nape of his neck. Her arms encircled his waist. "I need you, Dev. Make love to me."

Her hands spread over the ridged muscle of his stomach. His indrawn breath and a harsh "Don't . . ." only made her more determined. She slid her fingers down over the silken line of hair that grew straight-arrow to disappear beneath his trousers.

Devlin grabbed her wrists and then ducked his head beneath her left arm, twisting to face her. "Jenny, you've ridden an entire range of emotions tonight. You're not ready for more."

She sat back on her heels. Her gaze was direct, although her chin quivered slightly. "I'm asking you to make me feel . . . life. I've been empty inside for so long." Without effort she pulled her hands free. "Life," she repeated emphatically, grasping the hem of her nightgown to draw it over her head in a single motion before tossing it into his lap. "My hair shirt. I'll give it back to you."

He should have risen to his feet, should have left the room. But his body betrayed him. Her hair was ebony satin spreading across her shoulders, a single thick strand curling against the warm cream of her breasts. He swallowed hard at the violent reaction in his groin. Eyes filled with longing moved slowly over her nakedness, resting on the triangle of her womanhood to wonder if she felt as soft there . . .

"No, Jen," he said insistently, turning his face away only to be seared when she pressed against him, coiling her body around his back, over his arms and chest until she lay across his knees. Her fingers plowed through his hair.

"Breathe your strength into me," she pleaded, pulling his head down. "Fill me with it . . . please."

He was only mortal. He covered her mouth with a fierce hunger until their breath did mingle. But it was she who was the aggressor, seeking and searching with her small darting tongue until he moaned deep in his throat.

When the kiss ended they were lying side by side. Neither had any conscious memory of having moved. Devlin's large hand was splayed across her stomach, his thumb tickling the skin between breast and navel. She watched the return of his doubt and hesitation. "For so long I've been afraid I might die without knowing what it means to truly be alive." When he left her, she did not make another plea.

Standing beside the bed, Devlin watched the effort she made not to cry. And he also watched that expression change when he shrugged out of his shirt. Holding it in his hand, he dropped down on one knee and dangled it above her. "No more bristly shirts for either of us." The fabric was trailed across her breasts and down her belly before it was tossed aside. Then his mouth moved down to nip gently at her stomach.

All his movements were unhurried. One button on his trousers would be unloosened, and then he'd find a soft place to caress. With lips, teeth, and tongue every inch of her midsection was explored while he purposefully avoided the uptilted nipples of her breasts, fully aware that his hair brushed and grazed them into pouting eagerness with every pass of his mouth.

Finally he stepped away to strip off that final barrier, leaving common sense and any thought to right or wrong on the floor with his trousers.

Jennifer's stomach contracted at the potent evidence of his surrender. But he gave her little time to fear, or appreciate, his powerful maleness as he floated down to her, touching her mouth with his own briefly. "If you want to change your mind, love . . . do it now." Her response was the parting of her lips.

He explored the honey of her mouth, memorizing the taste and texture that was so uniquely her before moving to her eyes, cheeks, and the sensitive skin beneath her ears. When her hands moved upward along his ribs and she arched to press against him, Devlin had to bite the inside of his mouth to maintain control over passions close to bursting.

"Easy," he whispered into her ear. "I've waited a very long time for this moment. And if you move like that again, it will be just that . . . a moment. I intend to touch and taste every delicious inch of you, my girl."

Returning to her mouth, Devlin's tongue traced the delicate curves, wetting her lips and then sipping them dry. When she seemed inclined to touch him again, he rolled to his side to press her hands firmly against her sides. Although she inwardly rebelled at his restriction, her head fell back when he began to trace a path across her throat and downward. She clutched fistfuls of the linens beneath her hands. Jennifer finally understood what it meant to be adored, the giving of pleasure more important to him now than the taking. When he released her wrists they remained limply at her side.

His fingertips, their roughly callused pads like a cat's tongue, traced circles around the full globes of her breasts, moving ever closer to pluck at her nipples until they ached with a tight throbbing. Then his hot breath was against her skin, his mouth hovering for what seemed an agony of suspense. An inarticulate, so very eloquent plea burst from her throat and she felt him smile against her before the moist warmth of his mouth closed on the tender ache with a gentle suction.

A liquid heat began to flow downward as he suckled. It pulsed deep within her womb, spreading in ripples with each tug of his mouth to center and grow in the nethermost region of her femininity.

A joyful sob released her hands, and she would have touched him. "My fill," he growled, moving downward to rake his teeth across her stomach and discover the secrets of her navel. There seemed no limit to the territory his hands and mouth were determined to explore, roaming to her thighs, kneading the flesh beneath her knees. His lips moved back to her breasts, wetting them and sipping at them as he'd done her mouth forever ago while his fingers moved down over her stomach, parting her thighs. The delicate touch grew more demanding as she began to press against his hand where a hot throbbing seemed to grow and grow until she knew heaven was within her grasp. No delight could be sweeter beyond their final joining.

Quickly he proved her wrong, his mouth following the path of those wonderful hands. Nearly mindless, she shamelessly abandoned scruple to the beauty of discovered sensuality and the melting glory of his mouth.

Devlin brought her to the very brink of fulfillment before moving upward to poise himself between her thighs. Kissing her mouth, he rasped, "Touch me now, Jen. Hold me."

Somehow her leaden arms managed to pull him closer. She drew her breath in sharply as he began to penetrate, uncertain she could contain or control what she had unleashed. His hands lifted her hips. "Bend your knees, love." By cautious degrees he merged himself into her tight, tight warmth until she accepted all of him. Breathing raggedly, his face evidenced the tremendous strain it was costing him to curb the wildfire need racing through his body. He went totally still.

Had she been a virgin, his possession could not have been accomplished with greater tenderness, and her heart ached that it was not so. She could only offer to Devlin what had never belonged to the other—her heart. It was she who moved beneath him, using a woman's knowledge to give him pleasure, finding within seconds that nothing in experience could compare with the perfect synchronization of two souls. The rhythm was older than time; song of the body, cadence of the heart.

Her magnificent free-flying hawk was carrying them both to meet the sun, soaring higher and higher until they were ignited, ablaze, exploding into light and rapture, whirling through space and time.

And she was being filled with the pulsing essence of Devlin's strength. Never again would she turn away or shield herself from this glory.

Only when the sky began to lose its blackness did they separate.

Devlin found James asleep on the sofa in the library. He prodded him awake, stepping back while the man bridged the territory between slumber to full alertness in a blink.

"Is she all right?" James sat up, his eyes searching and finding answers before Devlin opened his mouth.

"You *did* hear her screaming then? I wondered . . ." Devlin leaned back against the desk, stretching out his long legs. "James, we've both, for our own stupid reasons, contributed to the hell Jennifer's been through. Some of it I wouldn't hesitate to reveal, but if I start . . ."

"I understand. She'll tell me if and when she's ready."

Looking squarely at James, Devlin considered all the roles this man had filled in his life. Right now he was only Jenny's father, and there was no telling how he, in that capacity, would react to what needed to be said.

"I love her, James, though I doubt that comes as any great surprise to you now. From the first time I saw her, flat on my backside, greener than the grass, I've loved her. My feelings were impossible then, and as we grew older I got this insane notion that what I felt for your daughter was somehow a betrayal of you. I was wrong."

James remained silent, watchful. Taking a deep breath, Devlin continued. "You're just going to have to trust me not to hurt her more than I already have. But I've no intention of allowing anything or anybody to keep us apart."

Standing, James stretched the kinks from his muscles. "In other words, if I may read between the lines, I'm not to object if you and my daughter wear the carpet thin running back and forth between bedrooms every night?" Devlin winced visibly, as James had intended he should, but there was no denial to the charge. "I guess it would also be a waste of my breath to remind you she's still technically a married woman? Or that your nightly shenanigans might create a child, a child conceived while she carries another man's name. There's no absolute guarantee the Armbrusters will be successful in arranging her divorce, you know. Doesn't any of that bother you just a bit?"

"Those are valid concerns, from a father's point of view. For me, I really can't claim to give a good goddamn," Devlin responded rather tersely, defensively.

James puffed himself up into the stance of the outraged patriarch. "You'd flaunt your affair before me, God, the world, and, in essence, tell us all to go to hell."

"If Jenny were free I'd marry her tomorrow. I'm not pretending to be happy with this situation, but the alternative—living without her—is worse. I can't—won't—give her up. Not again."

Rocking back on his heels, James Douglas thrust his thumbs into the band of his trousers. "Well, it's about damned time you came around to realizing what's important in this life." His sudden turnaround snapped Devlin's head up just as James's hands settled upon his shoulders. "Son, I don't give a rat's ass about moral rights and wrongs. All I care about is my girl . . . and you. Still, I've brought up some hard facts that bear thinking on. The both of you need to understand just what you're going up against. As much as we'd like to forget there's a world outside this ranch, it's not always possible to ignore the rules of that world. There's no way in hell to keep a thing like this private. Now I don't much care what other folks think of me, but she's my daughter, and she'll be branded a whore."

James had Devlin's full attention now, and the dark blue eyes flashed with protective anger. Before Devlin could lash out, James hushed him. "That's the straight of it, Dev, harsh though it may be."

The grim line around the younger man's mouth didn't ease, but he nodded reluctantly. "We'll have to talk—I don't know—Christ, James . . ." Devlin's broad shoulders hunched beneath the weight of reality James had heaped upon them.

The father, who was first a man, admitted, "If Jennifer were my Louise I'd ignore everything, including a father's concern, to love my woman."

Jennifer luxuriated in the warmth of her bath, surrounded by Devlin's things, if not the man himself. He'd ridden out hours ago while she continued to sleep. The rain had broken the heat, washing the earth and her spirit clean. She felt gloriously alive and deliciously languid all at once.

The sound of Maggie's tuneless singing in the adjoining kitchen had her reaching for the towel, drying quickly, blushing at the renewed sensations the fluffy cloth incited as she drew it over every inch of her awakened body.

The plaid shirt and patched trousers felt like old friends against her skin. When her feet were encased in the scuffed, well-worn boots, she wiggled her toes, delighting in the freedom. Releasing the braid she'd pinned atop her head, Jennifer glanced at the face reflected in Devlin's shaving mirror and went completely still, staring hard and long at a total stranger. She touched her cheeks, ran her fingers over the familiar features of her face. It was the eyes, she decided, the eyes of a woman looking out to see a fresh-cheeked girl, her skin glowing. But the change went deeper. Jennifer suddenly perceived that the daughter of James and the wife of Adrian was no more. Then who was this woman? Had she lost herself? Or had she been found?

The day was too bright and her heart too full for introspection. She had the sun and the sky and the man she loved. "Don't muddy it," she chided herself softly. "For once in your life, just feel."

Her feet hardly touched the floor as she entered the kitchen. Maggie poured two steaming mugs of coffee and pointed to a chair. "Put it there," the woman ordered, swatting the trouser-clad fanny when it passed within range.

Jennifer yelped, plopping down to save her backside, her face still radiating a determinedly joyous smile.

"I suppose you expect a lecture," Maggie said with a lift of her eyebrows as she spooned sugar into her coffee. "Well, I ain't got one. And if I did, you'd do what you please anyhow. Besides, seeing those eyes snapping with life makes me blind to everything else."

Jennifer reached across the table to hug the teary-eyed woman. "I feel reborn, filled to overflowing, Maggie. Maybe I should be ashamed or afraid—I'm not."

Maggie patted her girl's back. "Your daddy's out on the porch. Why don't you take him a mug of coffee." The question flashing from silver eyes brought a deep chuckle. "Sugar, he might be a bit thickheaded, but he ain't exactly stupid. No sense in trying to pretend you and Dev didn't do nothing but chew the fat all night either. Only one thing I know can put that kind of glow on a woman's face. So you might as well face the music."

Jennifer found her father perched on the porch railing, watching the birds gorging themselves on worms unearthed by the heavy rains. The pungent smell of wet grass filled her nostrils. "It's a wonderful morning," she said, passing him the coffee, silently begging him to understand.

James slid over and patted the space he'd created, dropping an arm across her shoulders when she joined him.

"I'd say the rain fixed a good many things." He smiled. "In fact I'm feeling so at ease with the world I've decided to take a long-overdue trip to Helena this afternoon."

"Problems?" she asked over the rim of her mug, her gaze loving, tears of gratitude sparkling on her lashes.

"Nary a one," he stated emphatically, giving her a squeeze. "This is strictly a pleasure trip, a little vacation of sorts."

Was there a woman in Helena? Several women? For the first time Jennifer saw her father as a handsome man in his prime. She realized he was too vital, too male, to have lived all these years entirely celibate. "Why did you never remarry?"

He was startled by her question, and took his time in responding. "I'm not really sure. Maybe it's because what your mama and I shared—" He stopped, touching his forehead to hers. "But you understand what that is now, don't you? You and Dev have that kind of loving between you." His voice grew husky before he cleared his throat. "Well, if I'm going to make that afternoon train, I'd best get my butt in gear. I should be back in two, maybe three weeks." He chucked her beneath the chin, giving her that pirate's grin. "Don't do anything I wouldn't do while I'm gone."

"I could give you the same advice," Jennifer said cheekily, although a heated blush stained her cheeks crimson.

Slapping the railing, James rose to his feet. "I love you, daughter."

Jennifer slowed Dusty to a walk when they entered the glade. She felt her pulse begin to race at the sight of the grazing Appaloosa and the man stretched out on the grass beneath one of the oaks, sleeping soundly, his shirt rolled up beneath his head.

Dismounting, she winced slightly at the sweet soreness between her thighs, aggravated by that wild ride across the range to reach this spot. Her fingers felt for the necklace beneath her shirt, and she smiled softly, her footsteps silent in the grass, her legs going liquid with every step until, reaching his side, she dropped to her knees.

Oblivious to her presence, Devlin slept on, unaware of the woman caressing his naked torso with eyes luminescent with love, growing hungry with renewed desire. The sun-darkened skin on his chest and arms glistened like lustrous satin; the light dusting of paler hair was like golden silk. The temptation was too great. Her fingers lightly trailed that line from his breastbone downward to where his trousers hugged a lean waist. With a smile, she remembered Devlin's slow, thorough exploration of the night before. She leaned over him, her lips touching the warm flesh of his belly, her tongue tasting the salty flavor. Her nose inhaled the musky scent of him.

She perceived a subtle change in the pattern of his breathing. Without looking at him, she rested her cheek against his breast to hear the erratic thud of his heart. It accelerated wildly when her palm covered the swelling boldness of his manhood, encouraging its rapid rise until cloth and buttons were strained to bursting. Her own loins responded with a liquid ache. Her breasts tingled beneath the cotton shirt.

Then Jennifer lifted her head to seek that face taut with desire. His eyes were dark with expectancy, bold with a silent challenge. He lay unmoving, his arms spread-eagled as though tied with invisible bonds—a captive to her whim.

When she appeared to quail, the chiseled lips quirked, striking that daring spark within Jennifer that life could not extinguish. With dry mouth and trembling fingers, she began to work free the buckle of his belt, moving then to the buttons concealed beneath the fly-flap of his pants. Her breath grew ragged, matching his, when the denim fabric parted. Still she hesitated, losing courage.

Devlin's hand snaked out to draw her to him, giving reprieve with a long, searing kiss filled with acceptance. When their lips parted the love she read in his velvety blue eyes released her inhibitions.

Every inch of his chest was explored, worshiped while her

hand found and encompassed the velvet steel length of him, her mouth drifting down, stopping when she reached that line separating dark skin from light.

A groan burst from his throat before he could conquer the frustration in the face of her innocent reluctance. Then he saw her smile against his skin, a cat with the cream. His next outcry had nothing to do with disappointment.

Chapter Thirty-Seven

Adrian pulled off his jacket and tossed it over the back of a chair before ridding himself of waistcoat and tie. With a relaxed sigh, he fell across the wide bed. He was at peace with himself, comfortable with his new identity, which fit him as snugly as the white kid gloves that were his trademark in this city by the muddy Mississippi. St. Louis was a gambler's paradise. The elegant old paddle wheelers were now permanently moored to cater to a budding society and its vices. Adrian was now Damien Harrison, a riverboat gambler and rogue. He had lost himself almost completely in that adopted identity and if he occasionally tortured himself with the past, the emergence of Damien's stronger, more flamboyant personality made those times less frequent.

He was respected for his style with the ladies and his skill at the tables. This hotel, the clothing he wore, and the company he was beginning to keep attested to his success. Damien had proved himself smarter than his alter ego, never playing the long shots, always standing on a pat hand, and winning more often than not.

The knock on his door brought a brief resurgence of the terror that had haunted his earlier days in this city. But after four months he stopped jumping at his own shadow. Still he was cautious as he called out, "Who's there?"

A high-pitched giggle brought him springing off the bed with an eager smile. He straightened his shirt and smoothed the beard that lent a rakish air to his perfect features. The women loved it, and it would seem the red-haired wife of that stuffy banker had reconsidered his invitation for a night of pleasure. With a satisfied swagger he went to the door, opening it wide while bending in a low, courtly bow. "Aha, my reluctant beauty."

A nickel-plated, pearl-handled derringer prodded his chest, shoving him backward. "Good evening, Armbruster," Sean Delaney grated with a twisted smile. "Did you think I'd forget you, dear boy?"

Adrian backed away from the weapon. Delaney closed and bolted the door, his smile deadly. "Listen to me, Sean, it wasn't my fault. Erica forced me to find that doctor. She blackmailed—"

The barrel of the small gun was jammed into Adrian's mouth as he was pushed flush against the opposite wall. "I told you, warned you fair what would happen if you fucked with my baby again. We were square, Armbruster. And we'll be square again very soon."

Amber eyes widened, nearly popping out of their sockets at the metallic flash of the razor Delaney pulled from his pocket. Adrian tried to scream, but only choked on the pistol being rammed down his throat. Delaney coolly, proficiently released his trousers. They dropped around his ankles and were followed by his underdrawers. Shrieks of terror rose from the pit of Adrian's stomach at Delaney's maniacal chuckle.

Sean Delaney didn't bother to close the door when he stepped out into the hallway. Wiping his bloody hands with a handkerchief, he sneared at the crowd gathered in the hallway. "Ain't you ever heard a pig squeal when he's castrated?" he asked disdainfully, moving easily through the bodies that shrank back to let him pass.

He marched unhurriedly down the two flights of stairs and entered his own room, immediately pulling the bell rope to summon service. He went to the small writing desk and scribbled out the message. The young man who came to his room was given a generous tip, along with specific instructions regarding the urgency of this telegram.

When the effusively grateful bellhop departed, Delaney returned to the desk and pulled the unused derringer from his pocket. It had been twenty years since he'd felt this good. His broad face lit with a wide grin. He lifted the derringer to his temple and pulled the trigger.

Chapter Thirty-Eight

"Get up, lazybones." The deep voice rumbled in her ear before a ticklish tongue teased her awake. Gooseflesh popped to life on her naked skin. Turning to her back, Jennifer reached for Devlin, but he evaded her searching arms and ignored the soft protest she made when she discovered him fully dressed.

"You'd tempt a saint, Jen. But unless I make an appearance on a horse today, your father will be cutting my pay down to pauper's wages."

Stretching her arms above her head, Jennifer arched her back with a sleepy yawn, knowing full well how provocative the movement was. She smiled with sweet satisfaction when his groan vibrated in the room. "What Daddy doesn't know won't hurt." She tossed back the light covering and rose to her knees, sitting back on her ankles, splendid in her nakedness. "And you are certainly no saint."

He laughed, and it was a full rich sound, one new and pleasant to her ears. Then she was being swept off the bed. Her arms encircled his neck, and her nose stroked the hollow of his throat when he held her high against him. Soft curves yielded to hard muscle. His mouth searched her face and lingered upon her lips until his tongue's lazy exploration of her mouth made the room spin. She used the power of her feminine lure to hold him, but his masculine command of her senses proved again that in love they were equals.

This time, however, Devlin found an untapped reserve of

will and soon she was flying from his arms to sprawl upon the bed, the mattress billowing up around her. "McShane!" she yelled warningly.

"Hold that thought, woman. We'll wrestle it out later." He snatched up his hat and deftly ducked the pillow that flew at his head. A low, rumbling chuckle left its warming echo at his hasty departure.

It was barely dawn. A contented feline smile curved Jennifer's lips as she rolled back to her stomach and reached for the remaining pillow in a single motion, snuggling deep into the feather haven. The compensations of being female were beginning to reveal themselves.

Three hours later Jennifer was still sluggish from oversleeping while she sorted through her wardrobe, scowling at the apparel more suited to elegant drawing rooms than to the postponed chores awaiting her attention. Dust must have accumulated an inch thick in some places. Finally deciding on the old patched trousers, she tossed them onto the bed. When the work was done she could don the frilly garments capable of bringing the glow of admiration to Devlin's eyes.

"Blasphemy," she chided herself for the concessions to femininity that had once been so abhorrent to her.

Had she changed so dramatically? Not really, she admitted with a soft chuckle. True, she no longer equated her personal significance with being able to reset fence posts or handle a roundup with a man's efficiency, but it had long ago been demonstrated that she could hold her own. What shortcomings she had came from inside herself, not because she was female. Inevitably the time had come when only Jennifer herself could be held responsible for her own happiness, and knowing her own self-worth.

The getting of that knowledge, though, she shared with Devlin as they talked long into the nights, holding each other, examining the past, and then loving tenderly to heal the wounds that remained.

Jennifer had just tied the ribbon on her camisole and was reaching for a blouse when a commotion outside drew her to the window. She saw Ben Phillips, the telegraph operator, dismount in front of the barn. Perhaps James had wired his arrival date or a delay in his plans. Grabbing her wrapper, she covered herself and rushed downstairs to meet Ben at the door.

"Good morning, Mr. Phillips," she greeted him warmly, pushing the screen open to receive the envelope he was thrusting at her. "How is your family?"

"May and the kids are well, Miss—Mrs.—" He glanced at the long name on the telegram passing from his hands into hers. "Armbruster," he finished. "I'll tell the wife you asked after her." He seemed uneasy, shuffling his feet. "Well, I'd best get myself back to town. Good day to you. I'm really sorry about . . ."

Ben's behavior put the fear of God into Jennifer's heart. The telegraph operator was as flap-jawed as anyone she'd ever known, and would normally have wheedled a meal and two hours of gossip for the trouble of riding out from town. She stared at the envelope, not at all certain she wanted to know its contents.

Was Allison notifying her that the courts had denied the petition for divorce? Looking up, she saw Ben vault into his saddle just as Maggie approached. The man hardly acknowledged the older woman, leaving her standing in a cloud of his dust.

Knowing that Maggie's curiosity would bring her straight to the house, Jennifer dashed back upstairs, closing and bolting the door behind her. If she had to accept living the remainder of her life legally bound to Adrian while her heart and body belonged to Devlin, she didn't want Maggie to witness the reaction to this unwelcome bit of news. Never, never must Devlin suspect how deeply she was troubled by the possibility of becoming a social outcast and their children bastards under the law.

"Don't let it be," she prayed breathlessly. "Please don't let it be."

The sound of the screen door slapping shut encouraged icy fingers. She heard Maggie call out as she ripped open the envelope. Anxious eyes scanned the message while Maggie climbed the stairs. Then Jennifer heard nothing more as the telegram drifted from her fingers.

Her stomach's violent rebellion sent her flying to the washbasin. She fell to her knees, heaving convulsively, aware of Maggie's frantic pounding, but unable to call out or move while her stomach emptied itself repeatedly. In time, when only the aftershocks jolted through her, Jennifer managed to crawl across the room and pull herself into the rocker.

She was too ill to do more than make a halfhearted attempt to rise and unbolt the door. The closed door was a blessing because she really could not face anyone at this moment. Sean Delaney's telegram had been nauseatingly explicit. Another spasm raced through her, and she pressed her fingers to her mouth to stifle a cry. But there were no tears. There should be tears.

Devlin stood back, his hands upon his hips, a smug smile on his face. The windmill was in operation, efficiently pumping water into the dirt-tank reservoir. "How about that, Davie. You are witnessing the end of water troubles for all time."

"If the well don't dry up," Davie said with skepticism, his faith in these newfangled gadgets reserved. His reward for his cynicism was a hearty slap on the back that nearly knocked him off his feet. "Goddamn, Dev. A blow like that could cripple."

Devlin removed his kerchief and dipped it beneath the icy flow of water to bathe his face and neck. "You're sure cranky for a man with a beautiful wife and a healthy new son. How does Lottie put up with you?" His friend had been a bear the entire morning, volunteering his help, then complaining about every chore.

"Yeah," Davie said. "I've got a rip-snorter of a son who bawls day and night, wearing his ma to a frazzle. There's about two seconds a day when Lottie ain't fussin' with that kid. A drought of a different sort is going on at my place."

The minute the admission flew from his mouth, Davie felt the shame of it. "Oh, hell . . . I don't mean . . . I'm just tired and cranky and—"

"Horny?" Devlin said with a grin. "I'm sure it's a temporary condition, Sprout."

Davie turned away, embarrassed. His mouth fell open when he spied the little man Jennifer had dragged west with her riding toward them. In amazement he watched that old cowpony sail over a fair-sized creek without breaking stride and stretch his legs out like a blooded thoroughbred. "Christ, I ain't *never* seen a stock horse move like that before. Look at the way that old fool can ride."

Devlin was already rushing to where Lucifer was tethered, swinging up into the saddle before Jenkins could slow his lathered animal. "What's wrong?" he asked roughly, not letting Jenkins catch his breath.

"Mrs. Smith sent me to bring you home. She's concerned about Mrs. Jennifer—"

The Appaloosa was already in motion, racing back across the fields.

Davie eyed Jenkins with awe. "Mister," he said with the first smile of his day, "I've seen some fine horsemen in my time. You just plain take the cake."

Jennifer was still dry-eyed and sitting in the rocker when Devlin leapt off Lucifer's back. Craning her neck, she watched him confer with Maggie just below her window. Their worried expressions and movements brought a heated "Damn" as she wobbled her way out of the chair. They probably assumed she'd gone off her head again. Why else would Maggie sound the alarm and send for him? If only Maggie had returned before presuming the worst. Well, there was nothing to be done about it now.

Maybe she was a bit loony: still in her underwear, her stomach caved in to meet her backbone from lack of food, and too wrapped up with herself to make the effort to reassure Maggie's not unjustified concern.

She started for the clothing still lying on her bed, and was shrugging out of her wrapper when her door buckled with a splintering sound. Then there was the loud snap of the bolt being ripped from its brace before the door slammed back against the wall with a plaster-shattering whack.

"You might have knocked," she observed calmly to the giant filling the open doorway.

The hint of sarcasm and the wide silvery eyes, clearly lucid, brought a roar the likes of which had never been heard coming out of Devlin McShane's mouth. Slamming the broken door behind him with enough force to jar the bolt from its remaining fragment of wood, he advanced into the room with the dangerous stride of an enraged stalking tiger.

"Woman, when you are my wife, I'll put up with these fits you're prone to havin', when the mood strikes, just about this long." He measured the length of his patience with a thumb and forefinger. It wasn't much. "Ye've felt the flat of my hand once before, Jenny girl. Would you like your memory refreshed?"

Jennifer's bottom lip quivered. She snatched the telegram off the floor and shoved it at him. "Read!"

His body tightened as he looked down at the telegram. "Shit," he rasped, tossing the message aside to scoop her up into his arms. The rocking chair groaned beneath their combined weight while he pressed her head consolingly against his chest. Delaney must be a lunatic to describe something like that in a telegram and then send it to his victim's wife.

The only sound in the room was the creaking of the chair rolling back, then forward at the dictate of Devlin's long legs. In time anger, relief, and sympathy were replaced by another more basic emotion. The thought that Jennifer might truly be in pain over the death of that bastard brought an irrational jealousy bubbling to the surface.

"Did you love him so dearly you had to lock yourself away to spend your grief while remembering the tender moments of your marriage?"

His icy, accusatory tone sent Jennifer scrambling off his lap, her eyes spitting fire. "The truth, Mr. McShane, is that I've spent the last two hours searching my memory for a single moment, a tiny remembrance of my marriage to Adrian worthy of shedding a tear over."

"Then we won't see you garbed in black for the obligatory year of mourning." He was terrified she might give in to society's dictates out of a misplaced sense of loyalty.

Jennifer took a breath to control her temper. "I may be many things, Dev, but a hypocrite isn't one of them. Do you want to know my first reaction to that telegram—the only real feeling I could muster? Relief. A man is dead, brutally murdered, and I was tempted to shout for joy." She was trembling now, whirling away at the ugliness revealed to him. "What kind of woman would want to celebrate the death of another human being? I was his wife, for God's sake! I shared his bed, carried and nurtured his seed within my body. On our wedding day I pledged him love which he never, never received. Adrian helped me get through a very bad time in my life when you and my father were treating me like so much horse dung—good for fertilizing, but not much use otherwise." Her voice grew small. "And I wasn't able to summon one single, unselfish tear in his behalf."

Devlin came out of the rocker using its downward motion to propel him. He turned her around, and cupped her face. "That you attempted to weep for that bastard is more than he deserved. That you've begun to forgive your father and me for our blindness is more than we deserve."

Of their own volition, her hands curved around his waist, "I might find it more difficult to forget how you crashed through my door with an Irish temper in full sail."

"I was afraid you'd slipped away from me again, Jen. Why didn't you answer Maggie's call?"

"Shock at first. Later I was tossing up the contents of my stomach. I couldn't answer and thought she'd come back." She resisted his attempt to pull her closer.

"Do you want my apology for the door?"

She smiled for the first time. "That would be nice, but I'd rather hear more about being your wife. And not at the top of your lungs this time. It sounded very nice, but with my ears ringing, I wasn't sure I'd heard correctly."

"If it's romantic verses and soft whispers you're

expecting . . ." He tumbled backward across the bed, pulling her with him.

The breathy, erotic suggestion he growled in her ear turned her face crimson while the blood sang hot in her veins. "Devlin McShane! That's . . . that's . . ."

"Interesting? I'm not much with poetry, but we could try a limerick or two." His hands were actively seeking the ribbons and tapes of her underdrawers.

A loud grunt drew their attention to the doorway. "In the library, McShane. Now!" James bellowed.

An hour later Jennifer was summoned to join them in the library by a very stiff and formal parent, making her glad she had taken the trouble to dress in a manner appropriate to his mood in a high-necked shirtwaist, her hair coiled schoolgirl proper.

Taking the chair James indicated, she was careful to keep her eyes turned away from where Devlin slouched on the sofa. Each time she thought of the look on his face when her father had walked in on them, her lips itched to smile.

James took his place behind the desk. "Princess, Dev and I have discussed the current situation regarding your—uh— your relationship. Unfortunately, I'm afraid I've discovered it's impossible to be the broad-minded father I thought myself to be. Now that the impediment of a husband has been removed, I see no reason why the two of you can't be married without delay. Now, that might seem a bit cold-blooded. There will be talk. You might as well expect a good amount of speculation on the haste, with your husband not yet cold in the ground."

"James, you are doing it again." Devlin rose to move behind Jennifer's chair, his hands closing over those stiffening shoulders to knead the tight muscles to pliancy. "What your father is saying, in his typically roundabout manner, is that I've asked for his daughter's hand in marriage and he's given his blessings."

She looked back over her shoulder at him. "You're not much of an improvement."

His increasingly easy laugh flooded the room. James

cleared his throat. "I'll leave the two of you to discuss the particulars." His exit was hasty.

Devlin looked acutely uncomfortable when he bent down on one knee before her. She made an impatient sound deep in her throat. "Get up, you oaf!"

"Now, you won't be tossin' my lack of pretty words back in my face twenty years from now, will you? Of course, I'm assuming you'll agree to be my wife so it will be legal to give me both sides of your tongue."

"I wouldn't miss the opportunity for all the world," she said, making her double meaning quite clear. Yes, she wanted the romantic avowals of love, but not if they were dragged out of him because it was expected. But she would take Devlin McShane any way she could get him, with, or without, a memorable proposal.

He eased her disappointment when he captured her mouth in a long, exquisitely moving kiss with its own eloquent message. She was weak from it when he twisted away to pull several sheets of paper off the desk. "And now to the final business. In Ireland it's customary for the intended bride and groom to come to a prenuptial agreement regarding ownership of properties." He saw her stiffen and smiled. "Since the groom is bringing little more than the shirt on his back into the marriage, this document is uncomplicated. Basically it states that I, your future husband, cannot, for the space of my lifetime, make any claim to your rightful property or wealth. Nor can I buy, sell, or barter without your approval, acting in the capacity of your representative. Of course, there is a provision that names me guardian of our children until they reach their majority. They, naturally, will have full rights to this property and inheritance from birth. Any questions?"

"One," she said tightly. "Have you gone insane? This is a joke. You can't be serious, can you?"

"Sign the agreement, Jen." His expression was deadly earnest when he passed her the pen.

She pulled back as if he'd handed her a snake. "No! I'll not sign any such thing. My father couldn't have agreed to this nonsense."

"I didn't give him a choice."

That he wasn't giving her one either hung unspoken between them. "This is so unnecessary," she protested before remembering that instinctive flinch when he'd first broached the subject. Now she wanted to kick herself, knowing that she could argue, plead, and yell herself blue and he'd not believe any of her denials. Experience had taught him otherwise, and the justification for this was on his side. "Dev, I refuse to sign this agreement."

"And I refuse to allow this ranch ever to come between us in our marriage bed." The tears springing into her eyes were like a knife in his belly. "Jenny, do this for me, for us, please." He took her hand and pressed his lips against the palm before closing her fingers around the pen. "Sign . . . please."

"Don't you call me pigheaded or stubborn or prideful again, Devlin." The pen scratched across the surface of the paper. With her signature affixed, she handed him the document, which he refused. "Keep it, love. It's our insurance against arguments."

This time it was her laughter exploding within the room.

Chapter Thirty-Nine

The marriage between Jennifer Louise Douglas Armbruster and Devlin Michael McShane took place six days later, an unseemly short time that set tongues wagging from one end of Yellowstone County to the other, and beyond. And to defy the disapproving gossip, James Douglas was throwing the biggest wedding party Montana had ever seen. Half the state legislature had made the trip along with the governor. Had the President of the United States been available, he would have toasted the happy couple as well. Nothing had been overlooked to guarantee the public acceptance of this marriage and to curb the spite of only a few old biddies.

Currently James and Sam were holding up the north wall of the parlor, well away from the crush of bodies surrounding the new bride. It had been the proudest day of James's life, and he had thought he might burst when he'd escorted Jennifer down those stairs in her mother's lace and ivory-satin wedding dress. She was wearing Maureen McShane's shamrock pendant as well, and had carried a blue handkerchief Maggie had held during her own wedding. Entwined in her lustrous black hair were the wild flowers of the prairie, gathered by Sam, who had scoured every square inch of the ranch property to find the sturdy grassland blooms. James knew his old friend equated his princess with these enduring flowers, brought back to life by the recent rains.

Feeling another lump of pride rise in his throat, James turned to Sam. "Isn't this something? Have you ever attended a circus?"

"Nope. But I went to a travelin' freak show once. How many do you reckon have come to eat and gawk?"

"Sticks and stones, Sam. This is the day I've been praying for almost from the first day I dragged that boy home with me. Our friends—and most of them are here—don't give a damn." James downed his champagne in a single gulp. "Have you seen Dev recently?"

Sam grunted. "I think he got pushed right out into the kitchen soon as the cake was served by that wall of females who went after the princess like hounds chasin' a fox. Thank the Lord for Lottie Garrett's quick thinking. Pushing that squawling kid into the girl's arms was a smart maneuver. Now they're a'fussin' over the baby instead of firing out questions."

Little Luke David Garrett was indeed the center of attention with his beet-red face and ear-splitting wails. "Shush," Jennifer was crooning, rocking him in her arms, patting his small bottom, and loving every minute.

"Sugar and water is the best thing for colic," Ada Rodgers advised his somewhat chagrined mother. On the heels of that came more sage advice than Lottie could have wished for, or needed, in a lifetime. She accepted all suggestions with good humor, but wondered if anyone had noticed her two other sons, which she assumed made her as much an authority on motherhood as any woman present. Jennifer being the exception, of course. "He's hungry. Is there somewhere I can feed him in private?"

Jennifer looked up with a dreamy smile. "Devlin's room is right off the kitchen. Follow me." Still cradling the baby in her arms, she backed out of the dining area. When they entered the kitchen, she saw Devlin standing near the door, talking to Davie. The look they exchanged had the heat and longing belonging to people separated for eons rather than the few days it had been since James's return from Helena. Neither knew exactly who had enforced this chaste existence.

When Lottie and Jennifer disappeared into the bedroom, Davie chortled. "Now who's suffering droughts?"

"It will be midnight or after before people start clearing

out of here. With that full moon to guide them home, they'll stay until they can't find a crumb of cake or a drop of champagne."

"There's always the barn."

Devlin grinned as an idea occurred to him. "Sprout, go and find Sam. Tell him there's going to be a switch of quarters tonight. And if you'll keep these good folks from getting ideas about a shivaree, Jenny and I will watch the boys—all three of them—for a few hours later in the week."

"Irish, you've got yourself a deal." They shook on it before Davie went in search of Sam. He returned a few minutes later with a triumphant grin. "It's all set."

With a soft knock on the bedroom door, Devlin called Jennifer out. "Let's go for a walk in the moonlight," he suggested, taking her hand and pulling her behind him.

"We really shouldn't. Our guests—"

"Won't miss us in the least, wife." He turned at the bottom of the steps. "Wife. I like the sound of that, Mrs. McShane."

"And I love hearing you say it, Mr. McShane." She slid into his arms, not protesting the arm beneath her knees as he swung her out of the doorway. "You look magnificent in your wedding suit," she said, smoothing the dark lapel, running her fingers beneath the black broadcloth.

"You're so beautiful I ache." His voice vibrated with need and love. Suddenly getting inside the cabin was a matter of urgency.

A few of the cowhands loitered outside the bunkhouse, uncomfortable with the fancy setting and hullabaloo going on inside the house. They saw the direction the groom was headed and hooted words of encouragement, careful though not to say anything they might later regret.

"Where do you think you're taking me?" Jennifer said, lifting an eyebrow.

"Someplace where we can be alone. Sam and Maggie will sleep at the house tonight. Maggie will probably be up all hours cleaning up anyway. And I've no intention of being without you another damned minute." He pushed open the cabin door with his foot and shut it the same way. "I guess I should ask if you mind leaving your own party."

"You noticed how I've kicked and screamed every step," she said against his mouth, her tongue flicking out to trace the shape of his lips until they opened. She kissed him boldly, the aggressor for a time until he joined the battle, their tongues mating, their mouths possessing until they were both breathless and trembling.

"God, you taste good," he said, releasing her legs to let her slowly slide down his length until her feet touched the floor. The blooms were plucked from her hair one by one before he searched through the thick mass for the long pins. The silken length slid down her back, touching the swell of her hips. She held her hair aside while he deftly unfastened the satin-covered buttons that ran down the back of her wedding dress. They shared another kiss, and then another, before he moved away and began removing his own clothing, carelessly tossing jacket, shirt, and trousers helter-skelter until he was standing unashamedly male before her.

Her breath caught. His potent desire would have frightened a virgin bride. Jennifer knew only the anticipation of a pleasure beyond imagining. Her knees trembled.

Devlin walked to the double bed. He sat down upon the edge, outwardly patient, but the burning hunger in his dark blue eyes was ravenous. When she had slid her dress over her hips and neatly draped it over the back of a chair, he said, "Come here." The gruff timber of his voice betrayed the enormity of his arousal.

Still in her petticoats and camisole, Jennifer approached him, tormenting with the gentle, seductive sway of her hips until she stood in the place he'd created for her with the spread of his knees. Her fingers threaded through the thick, sun-shot golden hair while his mouth moved above the swell of her breasts and below, his breath scorching through the thin cotton. He mouthed her nipples, coaxing them to jutting firmness. Heat flooded and throbbed through her belly, settling in the very core of her being. She cried out softly when he jerked at the fabric concealing the silken flesh of her body, pulling it downward until it rode beneath the quivering globes, pressing them upward for the feast of his lips and tongue.

Her own hands moved over his shoulders, exploring the play of muscle and the smooth texture of taut skin. "Dev," she said against his hair. "What you whispered . . . suggested . . . before my father . . ."

"Yes," he breathed. "Oh, God, yes." Impatiently Devlin began to strip off petticoats and bloomers, needing her help to draw the camisole over her head. When she was naked some of his eagerness stilled at the incomparable beauty before him. "Wife," he said softly as if it were a benediction, his touch worshipful while he stroked hip and thigh, breast and belly, slowly inching back upon the mattress until the back of his knees were curled around the edge of the bed. His fingers discovered the warm, moist evidence of her answering need. Then he was guiding her astride his lap, molding her hips until his tumescent desire could caress the sensitive bud hidden in the folds of her womanhood.

Their mouths met with an incendiary touch, stoking the flames of passion high until Jennifer was teetering on the edge of ecstasy.

"Rise up on your knees, love."

Only her fierce need made the movement of fluid muscle possible. She was wild, demanding, but still he denied the joining that would end her torment, driving her to heightened frenzy as he laved the throbbing nipples of her breasts with his tongue, taking them deep into his mouth, drawing out her very soul with the gentle suckling of first one, and then the other. She was sobbing, her fingers digging into his shoulders, when finally she felt that searching touch. With a deft twist she spread her thighs, ending this sweet torture by impaling him with her downward thrust, convulsing immediately in shattering fulfillment.

Caught up in the violence of those powerful internal paroxysms, Devlin exploded with a hoarse cry while those natural caresses went on and on until he was wrung dry.

He fell back, and she followed, her hair clinging wetly to his damp chest, both of them boneless, trembling together.

Eventually he managed to roll so that she lay beneath him while he stroked her hair and kissed her tear-streaked face ever so gently, smiling down upon her with a tender reverence.

"Husband," she whispered, awed by their experience. "I love you with all my being."

Devlin looked deeply into the moonlit silver of her eyes. "Longer than the moon and the stars have been in the heavens, I have loved you, my sweet Jennifer."

Her arms lifted to curl around his neck, and her smile alone could have turned night into day. "Beast. You've made me wait more than half my life to hear those words. Say them again." He did. "And again . . ."

It was the heat that awakened him, and he reared up to search for the woman no longer at his side. "Jen?"

He found her kneeling down in front of hearth, her face bathed in the light of a blazing fire. Devlin rolled off the bed. "It's August, the middle of the hottest summer in living memory, and you've decided on a fire." He shook his head. "Don't you think that is a bit strange?"

"Not at all," she said, favoring him with a pleased smile that made him pause. How many times had he seen just such a superior grin on her face? Then he noted she had dressed. "Have you been somewhere, Jenny girl? Or are you goin'?"

"Please stop looking at me as if I've lost my mind. I promise you I've never been saner." Looking back to the fire, Jennifer fed the last sheet of paper into the hungry flames and watched its edges curl and turn black; then it too was ash like the others. When she turned her gaze back on Devlin, she found him crouched down beside her, his expression partly angry, but mostly filled with wonder.

"You burned the agreement. Why? That was your guarantee that nothing, no one, could take what is rightfully yours."

"I need no guarantees, Dev. We have a marriage, and that means a partnership. You are me, and I am you." She touched his cheek, laying her palm against his strong jaw.

"Besides, a wise man once said, 'We can't possess the land, because it belongs only to itself. All we do is borrow it for our time upon this earth.' Won't you borrow it with me? For our time together, for all the years of our lives, will you share with me this glorious land?"

He pressed her hand, not bothering to hide the wealth of emotions that made him rich in love. "You always have to have the last word, don't you, Jenny girl?"